Miss Purdy's Class

Annie Murray

Miss Purdy's Class

MACMILLAN

First published 2005 by Macmillan
an imprint of Pan Macmillan Ltd
Pan Macmillan, 20 New Wharf Road, London N1 9RR
Basingstoke and Oxford
Associated companies throughout the world
www.panmacmillan.com

ISBN 1 4050 4789 5

1 3 5 7 9 8 6 4 2

A CIP catalogue record for this book is available from
the British Library.

Typeset by SetSystems Ltd, Saffron Walden, Essex
Printed and bound in Great Britain by
Mackays of Chatham plc, Chatham, Kent

For Rose

Acknowledgements

Thanks are due to the South Wales Miners' Library, Swansea, the Labour History Archive and the Peoples' Museum, both in Manchester, to the Big Pit at Blaenafon, to Tonypandy Library, Birmingham Central Library and Castle Vale Readers' Group, Birmingham.

To written resources – most especially Lewis Jones (d. 1939, RIP), to Hywel Francis, and to Peter D. Drake for his thesis on the Birmingham Labour Movement and the Spanish Civil War (1977).

To people – especially Alannah Darcy at Castle Vale Library, Sheila Ward, Jane and Lewis Jones for impromptu lessons in Birmingham's social history and to Susan Langford-Johnson for her hospitality in Wales.

Boxing Day, 1935

The bottle smashed through the window and shattered on the blue bricks of the yard.

'You filthy stinking whore!'

His father flung the door open so that the children's screams echoed round the yard. He lurched outside. Joey stood dry-eyed, paralysed in the one downstairs room.

There had been plenty of fights. He knew it was different this time.

'I'm not stopping 'ere one bleeding minute more!' Wally Phillips stood out in the yard, yelling back at the house. He was a thin, stooped man. 'I've had all a man can take. Four bleedin' whelps to feed and clothe, and that brat in your belly ain't even mine! I've put up with your boozing and your carrying on ... I ain't slaving myself to the bone for you no more ...' He stumbled backwards and cursed, just managing to regain his balance. 'You're in here with your legs spread for any tomcat who calls at the door ... You're filth, Dora – there's no helping you.'

The children's crying did not abate. Joey froze somewhere deep inside. His father was circling the yard.

'That's right!' Wally yelled. 'You all listening, all of you? Call yourselves neighbours? What've you ever done for us, eh? Couldn't stop my wife being a fuckin'

1

whore, could you? Lying here pouring my wages down her throat ... What did I do, eh? Loved 'er, I did. In the beginning ...' He lowered his voice. 'Christ, I did.'

For a moment he stood swaying, then he raised his fist and punched at the air so hard he almost fell over. He turned to go.

'Dad!' Joey fought to unlock his muscles. He ran outside, seeing his father striding towards the entry bare-headed, shoulders sagging in his threadbare coat. The boy tore after him.

'Dad – don't!' A great sob forced up inside him, as though his chest was ripping apart.

Wally pushed him off with the force of a drowning man. 'Don't, son. I can't. Just can't. Look after your mother, Joey. You'll have to be a man now. I can't live with it no more.'

Joey reeled back, clutching at the sill, his boots crunching on the broken glass. 'Dad!' It was a weak, childish cry now, of despair.

Through the broken window came the screaming of his brother and sisters, and his mother's coughing, on and on, from where she crouched on the bed they'd moved downstairs for her. She was in her twenties, her pale hair unkempt and straggling round her face. She coughed into scraps of rag which came away streaked with blood. Joey didn't turn to look at her or his howling brother and sisters. He had eyes only for the dark figure hurrying away from them down the entry. A moment later, his father turned the corner and was gone.

'You'll never make a wife if you carry on like this before you've even reached the altar!'

2

Her mother's bitter words propelled Gwen upstairs to the landing, where she stood in the darkness, hands clutching at fistfuls of her festive red skirt, her eyes squeezed shut. She could hardly believe herself! She had done the one thing the Purdy family never, ever did: she had made a scene. How had her inner feelings suddenly popped out like that in front of everyone? Their faces – how awful! Yet she could feel laughter threatening to erupt too. She'd *enjoyed* shocking them!

'However am I going to tell Edwin's parents? You're abandoning him on the eve of your wedding – heaven knows what the shock might do to an invalid like his mother!'

This was too much for Gwen. She stormed back to the top of the stairs.

'What are you *talking* about, Mummy? You're being completely ridiculous – I'm not getting married for eight months! I've taken the job for two terms, that's all. Until the end of the summer and then I'm coming home to marry Edwin. If it's too ghastly I can always throw in the towel. Whatever is the matter with that?'

'But *Birmingham*, darling!' Gwen's mother stood beneath the streamers criss-crossing the hall. Though colourful, they sagged joylessly. 'Gwen, what has come over you? You've taken this job without a by your leave and the school sounds . . .' Ruth Purdy gave a shudder, '. . . well, an absolute *disgrace*. There's no telling what kind of rough people you'll be dealing with! And there'll be no time to plan the wedding properly. You're being very selfish. You are my only daughter . . .' Her mother's voice was wheedling now. 'Your father thinks it's quite appalling.'

'Does he? Since when has Daddy ever cared what I do?' When she had made her announcement, carefully leaving it until after Christmas Day, her father had sat in the corner with his newspaper, opting out of family life as usual. His was the only unscandalized face apart from the baby's.

'Of course he cares.' Her mother lowered her voice to hiss up at Gwen. 'Don't be so ridiculous.'

Gwen clenched her fists so that her nails dug into her palms. 'Mummy, Daddy wouldn't notice if I did the dance of the seven veils in the middle of the parlour.'

'Don't be vulgar . . .'

But Gwen could not contain herself. She could not keep the bitterness from her voice. 'He's only ever wanted the boys! In fact, let's face it, he wanted Johnny to hand the pharmacy on to. Poor old Crispin hardly gets a look in either! All Daddy requires from me is that I keep out of his way and toe the line. Mummy – I am going to do this job in Birmingham. It's not for long, and whether Edwin likes it or not is not the point. I'm not a vicar's wife yet. I shall have the rest of my life to fall in with Edwin's plans. And we *shall* sort out the wedding, but it doesn't take eight months' continuous labour. I'm sorry, I've made up my mind. You're not going to change it.'

Ruth Purdy pushed her hands down into the pockets of her long cardigan in extreme agitation. She was a thin, faded version of her curvaceous daughter and was always terrified of what other people would think. And until now her daughter had been the sweet, biddable teacher at the local school of whom everyone thought so highly.

'You're a complete fool, is all I can say. You've caught a good man with a respectable profession, you're teaching at one of the best schools in Worcester and now you want to go and live in a slum!' She seemed ready to explode with anger.

'Well, maybe I'm just what they need,' Gwen retorted. 'I don't expect they get many good teachers there. I'll be able to teach them all a thing or two!'

'Oh really, there's no talking to you.' Ruth began to walk away. 'You'll live to regret it – and don't be surprised if Edwin doesn't think again about who he's marrying. He's not going to want a wife who just takes off without any warning. He's quite a catch, don't forget. There are plenty of others who'd jump at him, and it'd serve you right!' She stalked back to the sitting room, closing the door hard.

Gwen put her hands over her face, opened her mouth and let out a silent scream which came out as a prolonged hiss of breath. She sank down on the top step.

Whatever happens, she vowed, *I'm going. She's not going to stop me.*

They'd all be there by the fire – her mother, two brothers and Johnny's wife, Isabel. They had little James, and already another on the way. And now she'd broken her news they'd all be discussing her in that sober, let's not really say what we're thinking, oh-dear-what-a-shame sort of way, pretending that her mother's cry of horror and her outburst at Gwen had not really happened, like a bad smell in the room which everyone would ignore out of politeness. Especially her sister-in-law, 'dutiful, beautiful Isabel', as Gwen secretly called her. She was dark-haired and endlessly serene like the Mona Lisa and she was another reason Gwen wanted to scream.

Gwen crept into her room and sat on the bed looking out at the apple tree. On the bedside table was a small picture in a frame. She picked it up, smiling ruefully. She really ought to have a picture of Edwin by her bed, with his thick blond hair combed back and his ever-optimistic smile. Edwin looked almost permanently like someone who'd just enjoyed a good cricket match. Instead she was looking at a picture of Amy Johnson, her heroine. She thought Amelia Earhart was wonderful too, though her being American made her seem more distant. Amy was her favourite. Gwen had clippings about all her famous flights: to Australia in her Gypsy Moth in 1930, then later to Japan, Cape Town, the USA. This was her favourite picture. It showed Amy in her flying helmet, goggles perched on her forehead, wearing a leather flying jacket, the high astrakhan collar turned up round her chin. Her strong face looked out from the picture, up towards the sky, as if she was seeing all the places she would soar away to. Gwen stared longingly. How must it feel to fly a plane by yourself? To climb into the cockpit and take off, away from everyone, knowing your life was in your hands alone?

She put the picture down and sighed. Lately she had felt so odd, thoughts and impulses bubbling up in her that she'd never known before. And the way she'd spoken to Mummy! Gwen wasn't used to disapproval. She'd always tried to be good. She thought of Edwin: tall, good-looking Edwin, who was always so sure he knew right from wrong.

My fiancé, she thought. Dear old Edwin, so good and solid. Her rescuer. She just needed to get this great restlessness out of her system, then she could settle down and marry him.

She sat staring out of the window as the winter sky darkened smokily outside.

SPRING TERM
1936

One

'Miss Purdy!'

Knuckles rapped hard on the door. 'I don't seem to see you downstairs. I did say breakfast would be at seven forty-five sharp!'

Gwen sat up, heart pounding. Where on earth was she? She took in the dressing table next to her bed, the colourless light filtering in between the curtains. Heavens, the new job! Birmingham! And that voice was her chain-smoking landlady's. She was out of bed and peeling off her nightdress all in one move.

'Coming! I'm coming, really I am!'

'Mr Purvis and I are waiting,' the voice complained. 'And your kipper's spoiling.'

Mrs Black's tread departed mincingly – Gwen knew it was mincingly because it was the only way she could walk in those heels.

Gwen pulled her clothes on: brassière, camisole – a squeeze to pull it over her generous breasts – stockings, cursing as a splinter from the bare boards snagged into the ball of her foot. Normally she liked dressing: she enjoyed bright colours, hair ribbons, scarves, but there was no time now. Washing herself would have to wait too.

'Oh, damn you, you wretched things!' She pulled savagely at her suspenders with trembling fingers. How could she have overslept when she'd spent the night

9

wide-eyed as an owl, staring at those limp curtains which didn't quite meet in the middle? The last thing she could remember was hearing a tram rumble past outside and dimly, as she faded into sleep, a rising groan of sound which Mrs Black had told her she'd have to get used to when several went off at once the afternoon before. They were the factory 'bulls', the sirens indicating the beginning or end of a shift. She must have fallen into a deep sleep only minutes before it was time to get up. What a dreadful start to her first day!

She pushed her feet into her shoes without unfastening the straps, hastily coiled her thick hair up at the back, skewering it into place with a hairslide and tore out of her room along the brown lino of the landing and down the sludge-coloured runner of stair carpet. Dear God, this house was awful! But it was an adventure, she told herself, and adventure was what she needed.

'Do I hear you coming, Miss Purdy?' Mrs Black's plaintive voice came to her. 'Your kipper's almost on its last legs.'

Meals, Mrs Black had informed her the evening before, were to be taken in the back room, a fussy place crammed full of pictures and ornaments. A row of dolls with china heads and big sad eyes sat along the dresser. They had sat together, a most meagre fire struggling for life in the grate, for a meal of Welsh rarebit edged with crinkly slices of pickled beetroot, topped off with cherry Madeira cake and a cup of tea. Gwen's fellow lodger, a Mr Harold Purvis, had only arrived two days earlier himself, to take up work in the accounts department of a local machine-tool firm.

'So nice,' their landlady had said fawningly as she introduced them, 'to begin the new year with new faces

10

in the house.' She gave a sigh. 'I'm reduced to lodgers since I lost my George.'

Mr Purvis blushed and murmured a greeting. He was well into his thirties, with a doleful face and a bald pate, around which clung a ring of black, neatly trimmed and rather oily hair.

The Welsh rarebit had had a strangely lumpy consistency which made Gwen grateful for the sharp vinegar in the beetroot.

'It's hard to go wrong with pickles, isn't it?' Mr Purvis remarked gloomily. He was evidently cursed with adenoids.

Gwen smiled and agreed, thinking: *Oh my goodness, are we going to have to sit here making polite conversation every night?* They had asked one another a few questions – yes, he was new to the area, had moved across from Oldbury. Oh, she was a teacher, was she? That was nice. From Worcester? Gracious. Bit different here, eh?

Mrs Black's voice sounded as if she gargled with tin tacks. All the time they were eating, she raided her packet of Player's for one cigarette after another and the air had a blue tinge. She kept calling Mr Purvis 'Harold'.

'Harold is a musical man, he tells me,' she informed Gwen. 'He plays the trumpet. I hope you don't mind me calling you Harold?' She told them her own name was Ariadne.

'I like people to know.' She held a little piece of cherry Madeira between her stubby finger and thumb, little finger crooked. 'The name Black is so very ordinary, isn't it? I like to feel my Christian name is something rather *out of the way.*'

'It's certainly that,' Gwen agreed.

'Latin, isn't it?' Mr Purvis ventured, wiping his chin. 'Wasn't she the er ... lady with the hair made of snakes?'

'Oh, aren't you *clever*?' Mrs Black cried, leaning towards him.

Gwen, from reading books of myths to school-children, knew perfectly well that Ariadne was the one who helped Theseus escape from the Minotaur in the Cretan labyrinth using a ball of string, but this didn't seem the moment to mention the fact. She eyed Ariadne Black, trying to decide how old she was. Anywhere, she decided, between forty-five and sixty. Mrs Black favoured floaty, diaphanous clothes and wore her hair shingled and shaded a gingery blonde that could only come out of a bottle. She looked, Gwen decided, as if she'd just stepped off the stage of a variety performance. And her affected Brummy accent made Gwen want to giggle.

This morning, as Gwen dashed in, mouthing apologies, she found Mrs Black standing behind Mr Purvis's chair, slightly to the side of it, one hand resting on the back almost as if she was expecting someone to come and paint a portrait of the pair of them. Her eyebrows were brown lines pencilled in at an enquiring angle and even this early in the morning she had applied a fulsome coating of scarlet lipstick.

'Oh!' she cried. 'At last! Mr Purvis has been *ever* so patient, haven't you?' She leaned down and patted his arm before taking her seat.

Harold Purvis said, 'Good morning,' and stared so hard at Gwen's chest that she felt compelled to glance down and check whether the buttons of her dress had come undone. She hurried to her seat, bracing herself for the food.

They sat in morning light strained through net curtains. The one window faced over the side alley, but Mrs Black still kept it well shrouded. There was no fire in the grate and the room was cold. On plates in front of them, the kippers lay like a pair of moccasins left too long in the sun. Ariadne Black seemed to be breakfasting on cigarettes and tea. Beside her plate lay a copy of the *Birmingham Gazette*.

'I hope you won't mind.' She pursed her lips coyly at them both. 'Mr Purvis already knows I like to have my little read of the paper at breakfast time.'

'Not at all,' Gwen said, picking up her knife and fork.

'You do *like* kipper?' Ariadne Black leaned towards her and Gwen saw swirls of powder across her cheeks.

'Oh yes, thank you,' she lied, wondering how, this morning of all mornings, she was ever going to swallow it down.

In the homes around Canal Street School, the children were getting ready for the first day of term after the Christmas holidays.

Two boys burst out from the front door of a shop, setting the bell clanging madly. Parks's Sweet Shop was situated almost under the railway bridge, so on sunny mornings the colourful array of goodies in the windows blazed in the light, but by the afternoon it was so dark and shaded it was, as Mrs Parks often remarked, 'like living buried in a plot in the bleeding cemetery'. This morning, as it was the first day back at school, she followed her two youngest offspring to the door, pulling her cardi round her in the freezing morning. The two lads were off along the street, hands going

13

to their mouths pretending they were smoking and puffing out warm breath to condense in white clouds in front of them.

''Ere, Ron, Billy!' she called after them. 'You come back 'ere dinner time. I don't want you going down the cut!'

'Awright, Mom!' Ron, the younger of the two, shouted back.

'And go straight to school – it looks like rain!'

They waved in a token fashion.

Not listening to a flaming word as usual. Mrs Parks sighed, watching them with fierce pride. Her lads, bless 'em! Those jerseys she'd knitted them for Christmas had come out a treat. Just right for this weather. She lit a Woodbine and stood, half in, half out of the door, enjoying the warm smoke in her lungs. Cold enough to freeze your entrails out there. She blew a mouthful of smoke out of the door and turned to her husband.

'Reckon I'll have some of them down today, Bert. Give 'em a bit of a spring clean.' She felt wide awake and suddenly enthusiastic about washing the jars of bonbons and cough candy, the bowl of warm, soapy water.

One child, a girl of eight with long blonde plaits, came along from her house in Franklin Street with a slow, dreamy-looking gait. Clasped tightly in her hand was the halfpenny her mother had scrimped to give her for her milk. She was terrified she would drop it and it would roll off down the drain. Mummy would know somehow if she did, she was sure!

'We can't afford it,' her mother had said, the tears coming again. 'God knows – a halfpenny a day! But I'm not having anyone knowing. Don't you go losing it, Alice. And don't say a word to anyone . . .'

With her other hand Alice teased and rubbed at her hair, trying to make it look more untidy. She pushed one of her socks down a bit and tried to walk with a slouch. That was the trouble at the last school. Mummy just didn't understand. It was all right looking neat as a pin when they lived in Solihull. In that other life when they weren't poor. Everything was different now.

'Alice, Alice, lives in a palace!' The girls at Foundry Road School had circled round in the playground, chanting. A palace! If only they knew!

She'd begged to leave and start again at a new school. If it could only be different this time! Would she be able to fit in? Just to be invisible – that was her dream. She left home early so as not to meet too many other children in the street. As she drew nearer the gates of Canal Street School, the butterflies in her stomach got worse. She swallowed hard. She mustn't be sick – she just mustn't! In front of her she could make out the blurry mass of the school building. Squinting, she found her way to the gate. Alice didn't know that not everyone saw the world in this soft-focused way, with people looming up close to her alarmingly, as if she was underwater. All she knew was that it was frightening.

'Please,' she prayed, even more nervous when she could see the blur of other children moving in the distance. 'Please let it be all right this time.'

'You're going to school, Joey, so shut your gob.'

His mother was almost too breathless to speak, but there was no mistaking the iron in her tone. Joey swelled inside. If he felt anything these days, it was always anger, blasting up inside him.

15

'I ain't – I ain't going! You can't make me!'

'I said shurrup! You're going – d'you hear me?' Her voice rasped at him. 'And for fuck's sake do summat to shut *'im* up an' all or I swear to God I'll finish 'im!' The sentence ended with a long bout of coughing.

The babby, two-year-old Kenny, was crying, nose plugged with green snot. Joey looked at him in disgust, then pushed a scrap of stale bread at him.

'Shurrup, Kenny, will you?' he roared. Then seeing the futility of this, softened his voice. 'Come on – eat the bread, Kenny. Oh, pwor! Mom – he's shat on the chair!'

'Well, clean it up then! No good blarting to me about it.'

Joey carried the chair to the tap in the yard. He turned the tap on, waiting for the icy trickle to sweep the excrement off the seat. It wouldn't budge. He picked up a soggy cigarette packet and poked at it, scowling furiously.

His sisters Lena, six, and Polly, four, chewed their scraps of bread like frightened rabbits. What use were they? Joey looked at them in fury as he put the chair down with a crash which made his mother curse. He'd have to wipe Kenny's arse now. It was he who had to do everything, take it all on. He was the man of the house. Inside it was so cold they could see their breath on the air and there was no food – yet here she was trying to push him off to school like a fucking babby!

'Send Lena to school. I ain't going.'

'Joseph – I've told you, today you're going to that effing school if I have to carry you myself.' The look on his mother's face then frightened him. She frightened him when she yelled and carried on, but even more he hated her crying and now there were tears in her eyes.

16

Joey felt like crying himself, but he forced the feeling down inside him and crammed his piece of bread into his mouth. It had blue spots on it and was hard work to chew. He tried not to look at his mother, struggling for breath by the dead ashes of the fire. The sight of her gaunt, sick face frightened him too much for him to let himself think about it. Two red patches burned on her cheeks. Her belly stuck out like a growth from her stick body. She stayed most of her day on the bed now. Since his Dad left everything was getting worse, all hope running out of him like water down a drain. He had to fight to stop it with every ounce of his strength.

'The bread's all mouldy, Mom,' Lena whined.

'Shurrup, will you!' Joey yelled at her. 'Just get it down you!'

'Sssh, Joey,' their mother protested faintly. A sob came from her, which made her cough until she retched.

'You gunna be better soon, Mom?' Polly said, frightened.

Still coughing, she tried to nod her head. The tears she had been trying to hold back began to pour out. She sat on the bed, rocking in anguish.

Joey stood up, bracing himself, and frowning fiercely.

'It's all right, Mom. I'll get us our tea. Don't you worry.'

'Joseph,' she snarled. 'Take Lena to school. Go on, clear off!'

Joey jerked his head at his sister. 'C'mon.'

The door rattled on its hinges as it slammed shut behind Joey and Lena, letting in a blast of even colder air.

Dora sank her head into her hands.

The day had come – the first day of school. It was what she had willed herself to reach. What choice did she have? Her cheeks burned against her cold, bony hands. Christ, if only she had a few bob for a drop of summat to knock herself out! She couldn't let herself feel. Not now. It was too late for that. As soon as her eldest left, she'd have to call Mrs Simmons in. She was the only one of the so-called neighbours who'd have anything to do with them now.

Her two young children sat lifelessly. Dora stared between her fingers at the filthy brick floor. A drop of sweat trickled down her back, though her hands were frozen. All she wanted now was to lie down and sleep and not have to wake. God, she and Wally had had dreams. And it had come to this, a slum house up an alley, backing onto the wharf with its dank, stinking air. She thought of her elder son's pinched face and the pain she tried to keep pushed away in her twisted inside her. The lad was already like an old man. Man of the house, protecting her, going out raking in coppers by selling orange crates as firewood or buckets of horse shite. Christ Almighty. She had thought when Wally took her away from her father's gross clutches everything would be a dream. And now . . .

Desperately Dora looked at her younger children.

'Polly, Kenny – come 'ere.'

Warily, they came to her and she pressed their heads to her bony chest, sobbing. She couldn't stop the pain now, had no way of numbing it. It felt as if her heart was cracking apart.

*

18

Joey and Lena went along the entry and out into Canal Street. Both children wore thick, scratchy socks and heavy boots from the *Daily Mail* charity. Joey's were too big and his feet slopped about in them.

'Why's our Mom always crying?' Lena's long brown hair was a mass of tangles. The last teeth had fallen out of the old comb days ago. She tried combing it with her fingers, but it didn't work.

Joey walked with the tough swagger of a much older boy, hands shoved defiantly into his trouser pockets. 'She's poorly, stupid. You know that by now.' They passed the Golden Crown on the corner. Joey was trying not to look at it: his Dad's watering hole. Many's the time he'd waited outside for him, been handed a packet of crisps odd times when Wally was in a good humour.

'I wish she'd stop crying,' Lena said miserably. 'Why can't she get better? My feet hurt.' She was hobbling. Her boots were too tight, her toes a mass of chilblains.

'Oh, shurrup moaning,' Joey said savagely.

The school was halfway along on the right, a red-brick, soot-encrusted building which announced, in figures carved into a stone plaque that it had been built in 1888. The middle of the building was topped by a low spire. Children of infant and junior age were moving towards it in gaggles of three or four, some family groups, some friends, and all from the neighbouring streets, separating into the entrances marked 'Boys' and 'Girls'.

Gwen's morning had not got any better.

'Come on, come on . . .' She found her lips moving.

She was going to be late on her first day! The tram seemed to be forever stopping. The pungent smell of sweat was overpowering, with everyone crushed in there together, and she was all in a lather herself despite the cold. Her neat navy coat and hat felt too hot in here. And she was a bag of nerves. There hadn't even been time to get the splinter out of her foot and she was conscious of its nagging little pain as she stood on the swaying tram.

As they lurched along, bell tinging, the glimpses she saw out of the window did nothing to cheer her up. Birmingham looked even more drab and cheerless than everyone had assured her it would be. All those factories and chimneys smoking – no wonder the buildings looked so grimy and the houses so mean and depressing. Everything seemed to be coated in black!

What am *I doing here?* she thought glumly. *Mummy was right – this is horrible!*

Edwin, however, had been rather in favour.

'I must say, I think you're jolly brave,' he'd said. Edwin was nearly always enthusiastic. He seemed conditioned to be. 'It's splendid. You'll be a great asset to me in the parish – used to mixing with anyone and everyone.'

'That's true,' Gwen agreed. It was not a thought that had occurred to her, but she was glad he was pleased. It made everything easier.

The tram moved along the high wall of the prison and stopped near to the end of Canal Street.

'Anyone for the nick?' the driver shouted.

As she crossed over the road and hurried towards the school it began to rain. For a moment she felt a powerful desire to be back in her old school in Worcester. She could sleep in her own bed instead of Ariadne's, and not have her clothes stinking of smoke or Harold Purvis staring at her chest over the kippers. For a moment she thought of getting back on a train and admitting to them all that she'd been a fool. All she'd have to do then was carry on as before and wait for her wedding. Simple. Predictable. But no. She didn't really know why she was here, doing something her family kept saying wasn't 'her', but she burned with the conviction that she just had to be. And she'd show them she was right. She pushed her chin out and looked ahead of her along the street, freezing rain stinging her cheeks.

Two

The child had an iron caliper on her leg.

She was among a group blocking the gate into the school. There were four of them, dark haired, dark eyed and Gwen guessed they were all from one family. In the middle of the knot they made, the little girl was crying miserably.

'You'll be all right,' the tallest boy was saying as Gwen reached them. He had a sing-song accent that Gwen couldn't place. The older girl took the hand of the crying one and started to pull her into the school playground. She seemed in a panic.

'Come on, Lucy, you've got to go in. We're gonna be late, else. You're all right, you're near our mam now. See you later!'

The clock in the school tower said five to nine. *Oh Lord*, I'm *horribly late!* Gwen realized. But hearing the girl's cries, her distress tore at Gwen. Poor little mite.

'I don't want to go in here,' she was sobbing. 'Don't make me, Rosa. Let me come with you!'

Two other children pushed past them to get through the gate. Gwen hesitated. She couldn't just walk by, so she went up to the children.

'What's the matter?'

'She doesn't want to go in, Miss,' the older girl said. She must have been eleven or twelve and had a strikingly pretty face. The four of them drew back, fearful

22

at being challenged by a teacher. 'She can't go with us no more – she's got to go to this school. Only she won't go in.'

'You all go to a different school?'

'St Joseph's, Miss,' the girl said.

'Well, you get along. I'll see to her.'

They obeyed, glancing back at their distraught sister. Rosa called, 'See you later, Luce!' and they departed briskly along Canal Street. The remaining sister was sobbing more quietly now.

'What's your name, dear?'

The girl looked fearfully up at her, and seemed slightly reassured by seeing a pretty, smiling face.

'Lucy Fernandez,' she whispered.

'Well, Lucy, I'm Miss Purdy, and this is my first day too. Shall we find out where you are supposed to go?'

The girl nodded, still wary. She sniffed and reached up to smear the tears across her face. Head down, she limped along beside Gwen dragging her calipered leg. In the playground a number of mothers were standing talking. One of them was a huge prizefighter of a woman with a red, beefy face. Gwen quailed. They all looked terrifying and very rough. And how dark and drab their clothes were! Her spirits sank even further.

As they reached the girls' entrance, a teacher came out and rang a big brass bell, shouting, 'Into your classes!'

'Ah, there you are at last,' a voice said as soon as Gwen set foot inside. She realized this must be Mr Lowry, the headmaster. He seemed to have been waiting for her and stood peering through his spectacles at a brass pocket watch, evidently most displeased. He was tall, thin and balding. Lucy Fernandez immediately

23

slipped away from her side and disappeared from view round a corner.

'I hope this isn't going to set the standard, Miss . . . er . . . Purdy.' He snapped the watch shut and slipped it into his tweedy pocket. 'The very least I expect is that you will be punctual; you should have been here at least fifteen minutes ago. We've a couple of minutes before assembly. Let's proceed to your classroom now. Meeting the other staff will have to wait.'

'I'm ever so sorry, Mr Lowry,' Gwen babbled as they moved along a corridor at high speed. 'Only I wasn't sure how long it would take, and I missed the tram . . .'

'Nothing like a practice run if you're not sure,' Mr Lowry corrected her. Gwen felt flustered and unprepared to meet a new class. In the distance she could hear someone thumping out a marching tune.

The pianist, a middle-aged lady, was playing at the far end of the school hall beside the stage. A dark red cloth covered the back of the piano. There were high windows to the left and the floorboards were waxed and shiny. To the right were three classrooms, partitioned off from the hall by a wall which was solid up to waist height, but with glass windows above. A low rumble of footsteps approached and the classes began filing in one by one, filling up the hall in rows along the floor. Gwen saw a young teacher with red hair tied back leading a class in and showing them where to sit. She turned and gave Gwen a friendly smile.

'You'll take Form Four,' Mr Lowry said. 'Ah – and here come your charges.'

Gwen turned to watch her class file in. All between eight and nine years old, they moved in a restless, fidgeting caterpillar, staring and muttering, some of the

24

more cheeky-faced boys chattering and poking each other. The line seemed to go on and on, a pale, skinny-legged, motley group of children in an assortment of ragged, ill-fitting clothes. Last in the line came the hobbling figure of the little girl with the caliper on her leg, her face still blotchy from crying. Somehow, Gwen felt pleased to see her.

Once all the school was gathered, they sang 'Praise my soul the King of Heaven' to the tinny piano. Mr Lowry was on the stage. He looked austere in his tweed trousers and jacket, peering at the children through his little spectacles. Gwen saw that now he had something in his hand which looked like an old riding crop. He only put it down when he picked up a book to read some prayers, after which the whole school parroted 'Amen'.

'Today finds us at the beginning of another new term,' Mr Lowry said, picking up the crop again and fingering it. 'And I want to begin by saying a few words about discipline in this school . . .'

Seated on a chair beside her class, Gwen felt her heart sink. There was no welcoming smile for the children from this headmaster, unlike at her old school. She had disliked Mr Lowry instantly and had already put him down as petty and probably a bully. She stopped listening to him and stared round her, trying to acclimatize herself. In front of her was the woman with red hair, who couldn't have been much older than her. The other teachers looked as much of a hotchpotch collection of humanity as the children. Opposite her, across the hall, was a soft, rounded-looking lady with grey hair in a bun and a pink milkmaid's complexion. She wore a full grey skirt and a blouse covered in striking blue and green swirls. Gwen thought she

25

looked rather comforting. She wished assembly could go on for ever as she felt nervous and ill-prepared for what was to come.

When the children filed into their classrooms, Mr Lowry accompanied her. They stood at the door as the children came in, staring curiously at her and eventually organizing themselves behind the rows of desks.

'Quiet!' Mr Lowry bawled, although it already was quiet. The children seemed overawed by him. He glowered at them. 'What is this pandemonium? That's better – I should think so. This is your new class teacher, Miss Purdy. You will behave yourselves properly and you will work *hard* and be *polite*. Any trouble from any of you, and you'll be in my office, and you know what that means, don't you?'

There was silence. A few heads nodded.

'What does it mean?'

'The cane, sir,' a boy said.

'Quite right. So bear that in mind.' And he turned on his heel, looked as if he might salute, then left the room.

Gwen was confronted by a sea of young faces all peering curiously at her. She felt suddenly overwhelmed and full of panic. She had never felt this nervous about teaching before. There were so many of them! Mr Lowry had said fifty-two – twice the size of her form in Worcester. She realized she had not even taken off her coat yet and summoning all her dignity she removed it and laid it on the tall teacher's chair. She could feel the children's eyes on her. Her crimson paisley dress had a full skirt which hugged her hips and she had fastened her hair with a matching crimson ribbon. Some advice came back to her that she had been given during her teacher-training course. *Start off tough with them ... Then they'll know where they stand with you.*

'Right,' she said, stepping forward commandingly and wiping any trace of a smile from her lips. 'We're going to start off in this class as we mean to go on. Like Mr Lowry said, I expect you to be polite and hardworking. Now –' she reached under the desk lid. To her relief, what she needed came to hand – 'I'm going to take the register.'

A little girl at the front leaned towards her. 'Miss?' she lisped. 'We've got no monitors yet. For the milk and biscuits, and the dinner tickets.'

'Of course,' Gwen snapped, as if she'd known this all the time. How was she to choose monitors when she didn't know the children?

'Who were your monitors last term?'

A boy and girl raised their hands.

'You'd better come and help me today as well. I shall select new monitors later in the week.'

The two children went round the room collecting halfpennies from those who paid for milk. Gwen stood watching. Some children shook their heads or lowered them as the monitors passed. Gwen was opening the register in preparation when she heard a low voice say, 'I don't need no milk.' The words were almost snarled. She looked up to see the milk monitor standing beside a boy with a gaunt, frowning face and large, deepset eyes. She was struck by the intensity of his expression.

'All right, I only asked,' the monitor replied.

Gwen picked up the register.

'Donald Andrews?'

'Yes, Miss.'

'Joan Billings?'

27

'Yes, Miss.'

As she went down the long register, Gwen gradually became aware of the smell in the classroom. It was cold in there, but with all those little bodies breathing and giving off warmth there was already a frowsty, unwashed aroma which made her want to wrinkle her nose. In her last school most of the children had come from comfortable homes, and there had only been one child who smelt regularly: Eric Hutchings, the son of poor farmers on the edge of the town. He was out milking cows before school and there was no telling what he might come in smelling of. Here, though, the smell seemed to get stronger by the moment, as if emanating from every corner of the room. And one of the boys to her left couldn't seem to stop scratching himself. His skin was dotted with spots of gentian violet.

The names went on. Suddenly, there was one she recognized.

'Lucy Fernandez?'

'Yes, Miss,' came the miserable reply. Gwen followed the direction of the voice to see a head bent over the desk, hidden behind a curtain of dark hair.

'Ron Parks?'

'Yes, Miss.' She caught Ron in mid-grin towards one of his pals. His teeth – surely she'd been mistaken? They looked black – the whole lot of them! It must be the light, she decided.

'Joseph Phillips?'

A sullen, tight voice. 'Yes, Miss.' She looked up to see the boy with the pinched features who looked angry with the whole world.

Towards the end, when she read out 'Alice Wilson' and received a timid 'Yes, Miss,' the reply came from a

28

girl on the far right, under the window, staring across at her in a slightly vacant manner. She had long blonde plaits and looked startlingly clean and well dressed compared with many of the others, almost like little Heidi off the alp. Taking in the sight of her charges, Gwen saw what a pale-faced, poorly dressed group of children they were. She was just starting to feel tender towards them when a ragged sound burst into the room and most of the children erupted into laughter, all watching their new teacher to see how she would react.

'Jack's farted, Miss!' one of them informed her.

'Where e'er you be, let wind go free!' Ron cried, beaming. Startled, Gwen realized she hadn't been mistaken. The boy had the blackest, most rotten set of teeth she had ever seen.

She stood composed, not a hint of amusement on her face, waiting for the laughter to run its course.

'Have you quite finished?' They stared back at her, some nodding. The boy in the back row was scratching himself frantically. 'Good. I should think so. Now let's get on with our lesson.'

She handed out exercise books and got the children to write their names on them, appointed someone to recharge the inkwells and got every child to check the nib on the cheap wooden pens which were lodged in the groove at the front of the double desks. These desks, each attached by an iron runner to a hard-backed bench, were crammed into the room in tight rows. There were a couple of framed pictures on the walls, one of a road with trees on either side, and one of the king.

We'll need to get this brightened up a bit, Gwen thought, remembering the church schoolroom she had taught in before with her children's paintings stuck up all round the room. 'Her children' was how she had thought of them. And there had only been half as many!

All morning she was taut with nerves, on the verge of thinking she couldn't manage, would never be able to teach these children anything. She couldn't even understand what half of them were *saying*, when the Birmingham accent was combined with lisps or missing teeth or adenoidal pronunciation. By the time the dinner hour came and the green and white tickets were handed out, she had struggled through arithmetic, a spelling test and getting them to write a letter. She wanted to get the measure of them, who was able and who not. But her head was throbbing and she wondered how she was going to make it through the rest of the day.

'So – you're the new girl are you?'

Gwen saw the smiling face of the ginger-haired teacher waiting for her as she followed the last of the children out of the class at midday, some to run home, others to stay for the school dinners.

'I'm Miss Dawson,' she said in a soft Birmingham accent. 'Millie. Nice to see someone else who doesn't look as if they've come out of the ark!' She giggled, and Gwen could only join in, feeling cheered already. 'I gather you were late in. Did Glowery-Lowery whip you by any chance? He rather enjoys whipping people, I'm afraid. D'you want to come to the staffroom for dinner? You can meet the gargoyles in there.'

'Yes...' Gwen hesitated. She already liked Millie,

with her friendly, freckly face. 'Only I didn't think to bring any food.'

'Oh, never mind. My mother sends me off with enough for six every day. Come and have some of mine. So – how were the little demons this morning?'

'It's not what I'm used to,' Gwen said. She was feeling overwhelmed by the newness of the experience, the state of some of the children. 'I suppose they weren't too bad – I just feel rather at sea. How I'll even remember their names I don't know.'

'Oh, it'll come to you. They're not bad children, most of them. And when you consider what some of them are coming from ... It's been an eye-opener to me, I can tell you. If you live in a different part of Birmingham it's like another world. I grew up in Edgbaston. The way some people live – it beggars belief.'

'There's one boy who's forever scratching and he seems to have scabs all over his skin ... Is that impetigo?'

'Umm – I should think so. Nasty. Sounds as if he's over the worst, though.' Millie rolled her eyes. 'If you want infestations you've come to the right place!'

She pushed the staffroom door open and Gwen saw a dingy space with a few old chairs scattered round and a table to one side with cups and saucers on it. No one else was in there yet.

'You'll want to wash your hands, and then you sit down and I'll get us a cup of tea before you meet everyone properly.' Millie disappeared into the little scullery at the back. Gwen felt tears of gratitude come to her eyes. The children had been testing her all morning to see what they could get away with and she had had to work hard to maintain authority over them. It was nice to feel taken care of now.

As she was waiting, the door swung open and a woman marched in. Her hair was a lifeless brown, pinned up in a bun, and her expression severe. Her lips were moving as she came through the door as if she was completing an angry outburst at some absent culprit. She caught sight of Gwen sitting near the table, so Gwen smiled and stood up, holding out her hand. The woman stopped. Close up, she was younger than she at first appeared. She could barely have been forty, but she was dressed in shapeless brown clothes and flat shoes which made her look much older.

'Oh! My, my . . .' She laid her hand over her heart as if Gwen's presence had endangered its welfare. Her voice was high and whining. 'Who are you? The new one?'

'Yes – I'm Gwen Purdy.' Gwen's smile faltered. *How very rude*, she thought.

The woman stared at her. 'I'm Miss Monk. How old are you?'

'Actually, I'm twenty-one.'

The woman gave her an unwaveringly hostile stare. '*Twenty-one?* God in heaven.' She tutted, apparently in outraged disapproval and went to the scullery. 'Oh, for goodness sake, let me light it,' Gwen heard her say impatiently to Millie.

Gradually the other staff trickled in from their classes. Millie brought tea over, shared her sandwiches with Gwen and whispered, 'Don't worry about old Monk-face. She's like that with everyone. Goodness knows why she's a teacher. She loathes children.' Millie rolled her eyes and moved even closer to Gwen. 'I think she's really the limit, to tell you the truth – but no one dares gainsay her. Not even Mr Lowry. Actually, Lowry's the root of the problem.'

Gwen frowned.

'She's mad for him,' Millie hissed, with delicious glee. 'And he never takes the blindest bit of notice of her.'

Millie was the most cheerful part of Gwen's day so far. She added her own comments to the introductions after the other teachers had said hello and sat back to drink their cups of tea. Gwen's headache started to ease.

She met Mr Gaffney, the teacher who had rung the bell outside as she first arrived. He was a gentle, middle-aged man with receding hair and trembling hands. 'Something happened to him in the war. He's very nervous. And he is one of the ones who's never actually trained as a teacher,' Millie said. And Mr Lowry was all right as long as you did everything to the letter. He was a Scout leader in his spare time. Very 'pip-pip'. The dumpy-looking lady, Miss Pringle, who wore square-toed shoes, had been the one playing the piano during assembly.

'She makes the children count whenever she gets lost,' Millie whispered. 'They only ever give her Form One and they spend half the day counting out loud. She writes where they've got to on the board and when she loses her thread they start again from there.'

'Well, at least when they go into Form Two they'll be able to count!' Gwen grinned.

A little later the rounded lady in the blue and green blouse whom Gwen had noticed during assembly came in and shook Gwen's hand warmly.

'Welcome to the school.' Gwen felt the plump hand in hers. She couldn't help noticing that the woman's

33

nails were green underneath. She must have been doing painting with the children, Gwen thought. She looked up into a round, rather plain face, which was full of life.

'I'm Lily Drysdale.' The woman's eyes shone. 'I hope you'll be happy here, dear.'

'She looks a bit dotty,' Millie said, when the woman had moved on, 'but she's completely on the ball. And she's a real poppet. Nothing she wouldn't do for the children – especially the ones most in need.' Millie leaned closer and whispered behind her hand. 'And things aren't quite what you might think. I've heard she lives with a man – a *lover*!'

'What – you mean they're not married?' Gwen giggled. The woman was so *old* and so odd looking!

'*Miss* Drysdale!' Millie whispered. 'Hard to believe, isn't it? I think she's one of these arty types. I admire her really – the way she is with the children. I could never be like that. I wish I could. I always wanted to be a teacher, from when I was little.' She looked curiously at Gwen. 'Did you?'

'Not really,' Gwen admitted. 'I thought I'd better do *something*. Couldn't stomach nursing and I thought secretarial work sounded so dull. Oh dear –' she laughed – 'that doesn't make me sound very dedicated, does it?'

'Oh, I don't know,' Millie said. 'By the way, I do like your frock. What a lovely colour! It won't stay clean for long here!'

Millie told Gwen that her 'friend' Lance was a teacher as well. 'I met him at the Martineau Club – on the Bristol Road. Oh, you must come some time. It's the teacher's club – Lance teaches at a secondary school. He's a dream. Oh!' Millie caught sight of the ring on Gwen's finger. 'You're *engaged*?'

'We're marrying in August.' Gwen smiled at her enthusiasm. 'Edwin's a clergyman.'

'Oh.' Millie sounded less enthusiastic. Gwen wondered whether to her a man of the cloth would seem the height of dullness.

'But he's very ... well –' she searched for a word to sum up Edwin – '*jolly* really.'

When Gwen went in to take the afternoon register, she was struck afresh by the pallid, undernourished look of many of her charges. The class that looked back at her in Worcester had been mostly bright-eyed, rosy-cheeked children, who after dinner would have come in fresh from playing in the field behind the school. She felt a pang of pity for these urban juniors, cooped up between grimy rows of houses. Already, in the afternoon register, she noticed one absence.

'Lucy Fernandez?'

Silence.

'The cripple's got lost on the way,' Jack Ellis jeered.

There were sniggers round the class.

'Enough!' Gwen reprimanded sharply. 'Has anyone seen her?'

'No, Miss,' the class droned.

The afternoon seemed to go on and on. There was no hint of brightness in the day; cloud and smoke lay in a pall over the city. They sat in dreary greyness until Gwen was forced to turn the lights on. She stood in front of the rows of desks and tried to hold the class's attention by reading them a book about the Romans in Britain. Often, when she looked up, Ron Parks was picking at his thumbs or grinning at the boy next door. Joseph Phillips, who was right in the middle, stared down at his desk top, his eyebrows pulled into a stormy frown.

'Ron, Joseph, are you listening?'

Ron, chastened, stared innocently at her. Joey Phillips glanced up for a second as if she was summoning him from another world, then looked down again. There was something about him that disquieted her.

She struggled on, and when the bell rang at four o'clock she almost cheered with relief.

Walking back in the freezing afternoon to the tram stop opposite Winson Green prison, she felt as if her whole body was full of an urgent, heavy ache. It was some time, sitting on the tram, before she knew it for what it was: homesickness. The day hadn't been so very terrible, she reasoned with herself. She'd managed the children, just about, and Millie Dawson looked as if she'd be a good friend. And she didn't want to go home, did she? But it *felt* terrible, and the thought of going back to Ariadne Black's house did nothing to cheer her. It was the first time she'd been properly away from home. Birmingham felt big and cheerless and she longed to see a familiar face. If only good old Edwin was here with his buoyant approach to life to put his arms round her!

She let the tears roll down her cheeks. Her mother was right. She had been mad to come away and do this. She could have just stayed where she was, where she was comfortable, the children loved her and it would have been easy to work out the last months before she married Edwin and they settled down together to a life of village parishes, church fetes and a family of their own.

But this thought made the feeling of panic which she could never fully explain rise up in her. Why did it all feel so inevitable, so stifling, when it was so obviously the right thing to do? No – she had been right to come here! She had to get out. Spread her wings. Then she'd be able to settle down and be the kind of wife Edwin needed and expected.

Three

'Come *on*, will you?'

Joey Phillips strode out of the school gates, hands pushed fiercely into the pockets of his shorts.

Lena trotted behind him.

'Wait for me!' she wailed.

'Can't,' Joey snapped in his gruff voice. 'Things to do.'

He elbowed past a knot of boys from the form above who were peering at cigarette cards in the gloom.

'Oi!' one of them shouted after him. 'Stop shoving! Who d'you think you are?'

'Well, get your bleedin' arses out the road then.' Joey squared his shoulders as if waiting for them to come for him, striding along with his eight-year-old swagger. Insults followed him along the road.

'Got more important things to do.' He put his head down, clamping his jaws tightly so they didn't chatter in the cold. This was money-making weather all right. Fetching coal from the wharf for the people in the bigger houses up the street was one trick. Sometimes he hired a barrow for a penny to carry it. And selling firewood. He could beg a few boxes from a greengrocer he knew among the shops along the Flat and sell them broken up for a penny a bundle. However long it took, he was going to get enough to buy a bowl of hot faggots and peas for Mom tonight. That'd help make her better.

'Good food – that's what you need, Dora,' Mrs Simmons was always saying. And she did her best helping out, bringing round broth or leftover pease pudding when she could. 'You want to get some flesh on those bones.'

Joey wrenched his mind away from the rumbling of his own stomach. The watery scrag end he'd had for dinner seemed a long time ago, but it was more than Mom would have eaten all day.

'You gorra penny, Joey?' Lena said longingly, slowing as they passed the huckster's shop on the corner of Mary Street. There was nothing Lena loved more than the boxes of cheapest sweeties at the back of the shop behind the shelves of matches, gas mantles, needles and string: sweets two for a halfpenny, liquorice laces and imps and gobstoppers.

'*No*,' Joey roared. 'Where would I've get a penny from? And if I had I wouldn't give it *you*, would I?'

It felt as if night had arrived in the entry, between the black walls of houses. In the yard the drain was blocked and a scummy puddle of water lay round it. Lena tiptoed along the edge, watching the water lap at her boots. Impatient with her, Joey strode across to the house.

'Mom?' He thrust open the door, full of his plan to go straight out, earn the coppers to get them their tea.

He recoiled, hurling himself out into the yard, slamming the door with all his strength.

'Fuck! Fuck it!' Frantically scanning the blue bricks at his feet he reached down and found a lump of something and hurled it at the door. It turned out to be a soggy cabbage stump and the impotent thud it made only enraged him further. Lena was coming

39

across the yard and he went over to her and yanked her hand.

'Ow, Joey – that hurts, you pig! Stop it!'

'You're not going in the house! Go to Mrs Simmons's and stay there till I get back.'

'But Joey!' Lena's eyes widened under her scruffy thatch of hair. His tone made her obey. Mouth trembling, she went along to number five.

Joey tore along the yard, his body taut with an electric energy, so highly wired that it was almost out of his control. He wanted to run and run for ever, spend himself, do anything to wipe out the sight in his mind of the bed, the dark bulk of a man jerking up and down on top of his mother.

Gwen sank down on her bed after tea with a long, miserable sigh. What a day! She lay back for a moment across the rough sheen of the eiderdown and closed her eyes under the light with its tasselled shade. Her head throbbed. Faces swirled behind her eyelids: the rows of new children she had met today, the teachers ... Her mind was a mass of names which she could barely attach to faces. The one face that stood out was that of Lily Drysdale. There was something so alive about her eyes.

She groaned and sat up. Don't think about school! Kicking her shoes off, she rolled her stockings down, wriggling her toes. She peered at her legs. She was filthy! The Birmingham air was impregnated with soot. What she would have liked more than anything was a good hot bath, but Ariadne ('the spider' as Gwen had begun to nickname her since she always seemed to be lurking about in the hall) was very strict about all that.

'I really favour the male lodger,' she had said when Gwen first arrived. 'They don't indulge in so much electricity.' Baths were strictly rationed to two a week, and there was a piece of wood in the bathroom with a line marked on it to measure how much water they were allowed.

That evening there had been a fire burning in the back room as they ate. Ariadne had a woman come in to do a bit of cleaning. It was all she could afford, she said, now she'd 'lost George'. George observed them eating from his frame on the mantelpiece. He had a military bearing and a grand moustache. With the blue velvet curtains closed and the fire burning, the room should have felt cosy. Instead, Gwen felt trapped, like a bluebottle stuck in a jar. The food didn't help: chops tonight, with lumpy gravy and tired-looking cabbage.

Ariadne Black positioned her chair close to Mr Purvis's. The night before Gwen had thought this was by chance. Ariadne was wearing rouge and a black lacy shawl over her dress. Her heels were so thin that she wobbled as she walked.

'Did you have a satisfactory day, Harold?' She tipped the gravy jug over his plate as if dispensing nectar from the gods. The dark liquid bulged forward under its skin, then broke through and glooped out in a rush. Mr Purvis murmured that yes, his day had gone very nicely, thank you.

'I'm sure we're both looking forward to hearing you play you music.' Ariadne glanced at Gwen, as if grudgingly including her. As they got up at the end of the meal, Gwen saw her stroke Mr Purvis's arm.

Oh Lord! Gwen thought. *What have I got myself into here?*

It was a relief to be away upstairs, although now she

41

was on her own she felt restless and lonely. She had tried to make the drab white room as pretty as she could. Her picture of Amy Johnson was arranged on the dressing table. She had draped a scarf over the mirror and arranged a colourful crocheted blanket on the chair, but the room still seemed bleak.

She took her writing case from the chest of drawers and sat under the eiderdown with her legs folded beneath her to keep her toes warm.

I must drop a line to mother, she thought. *And Edwin, of course.* Unzipping the worn leather, she took out two plain postcards and wrote the addresses on each of them: to Mr and Mrs Purdy and the Rev. Edwin Shackleton.

She sat chewing on the end of her fountain pen and twiddling the ends of her hair. It all seemed such a bother. She felt gloomy tonight but she certainly wasn't going to tell them that. She sighed. Amy seemed to be watching her.

'Not terribly brave or glamorous coming here, is it?' she said to her. 'Hardly in the same league.'

Her stomach turned with dread at the thought of going back to Canal Street School in the morning, to those drab, alien streets and to the smell of unwashed clothes, to those pale, scratching children who looked as if they came from some of the poorest human stock. But that's what she'd said she was going to do and she was going to have to stick it out.

She was about to begin writing when a melancholy tune drifted along the passage. Of course – Mr Purvis's trumpet! He was playing a twiddly melody that she half recognized, but could not place. He played it, haltingly, several times through, then stopped.

She picked up one of the cards and turned it over. In her shapely copperplate handwriting she began.

Dear Edwin,
    First day in my city school – finding my feet, but a simply marvellous experience so far. You would find it very interesting. And you should meet my landlady . . .! Will write properly soon.
    Love to all, Gwen x

Night had fallen by the time Joey got back to the yard in Canal Street. The house was dark. His pockets full of coal and a dish of hot food in his hands, he pushed the door open.

'Mom?' Though he didn't know it, his voice was high, little boyish.

There was no reply. The room was deadly cold. Joey put the bowl down on the table and groped to find matches and a candle. He saw his mother lying curled on her side in the bed. He frowned. He often saw her sleeping – she seldom had the energy for anything but lying down these days – but she looked different. In the dim light he could see the blanket pulled up, almost covering her, only the top of her head with its lank hair visible above, and she was curled round, her knees pulled right up as if she was in pain.

'Mom?' His breath condensed in the air. He moved closer with the candle. Slowly, reluctantly, Dora unfolded herself and pulled the cover away from her face. Her expression was terrible, her eyes blotchy from hours of weeping. The sight of her son set her off again. At the sound of her weak, defeated sobbing, Joey's face darkened. His fists clenched in his pockets.

'What's up?' He meant to speak gently but couldn't.

Dora Phillips sobbed all the more, setting off her cough, which racked through her, stealing her breath. She clamped a rag over her mouth, then drew it away carefully, folding it to conceal the bloodstained phlegm. He could hear the crackle of her lungs. With a struggle she pushed herself up in the bed.

'Come here, bab – sit down. Mrs Simmons brought our Lena back. 'Er's asleep.'

Joey perched on the side of the bed, folding his arms, elbows jutting out as if to protect himself.

Dora's face was sunken. Although not yet thirty, the sickness and suffering of her life had worn her and she appeared twenty years older. In the gloom her eyes looked huge and dark in her face and, hard as she tried, she couldn't stop them filling with tears.

'I'm poorly, you know that don't you, Son?'

Joey gave a fierce nod, his face a scowl. 'I'll look after you. I can help you get better. Look.' He showed her his bulging pockets. 'I've got coal. And there's faggots and peas for you . . .'

'Whose bowl is that?'

'Someone borrowed it me.' He wasn't going to tell her the truth, that he'd whipped it from the pawn shop when the man's back was turned.

Dora was overwhelmed with emotion, hearing the intense determination in his voice, pride covering up the fear and grief of a small boy. She reached out her hand to try and pull him nearer to her, but he didn't budge. Slowly she shook her head.

'Joey.' She spoke softly. 'Your mom might not be able to get better. It's the consumption. You know that's bad, don't you, bab? I can't hide it from you any

44

longer. My boy's too grown up for me to hide things from him.'

Joey's frown deepened and he stared down at his boots, his jaw clenched.

Dora was taken by another fit of coughing. Once she had recovered, she went on. 'I'm not much of a mom to you in this state.' Her face puckered. 'Never have been.' She fought to control herself. 'Mrs Simmons'll help us all she can, but she's got so much on her plate already. I can't even manage to get a fire lit for you, let alone feed you right . . .' Her voice cracked again.

'I can feed us, Mom!' Joey burst out. 'You know I can! If I daint have to go to school, I could feed us easy. I don't do nothing at school!'

'You've got to go to school.' Dora raised her hand to stop him. 'Learn to read and write and do your sums, or you won't get nowhere.' She took his hand in hers. 'Listen to me, Joey. Listen carefully. You know that's why your dad left us, don't you? Because I was poorly and he said he couldn't stand to see me getting worse by the day . . .' She had to believe that. Wanted Joey to believe it, in spite of all he'd seen. The truth was too cruel. How could she say it to her son? *I ruined a good man because I can't help myself. I'm carrying another man's child, spawned for the comfort of it . . . And now I've done the worst thing a mother can do . . .*

'Now he's gone I've got no one in the world to help me except for Mrs Simmons and God knows why she bothers with me when the rest don't. So –' she choked over the words – 'I've had to let Polly and Kenny go to be looked after for a bit.' Tears running down her cheeks, she looked into her son's uncomprehending face. 'The lady came for them today to take them to the home. She'll be a sort of ... auntie to them. Just until things get better. Only I couldn't manage – not with all of you ...'

Her head sank to her chest, her whole body shuddering.

'She ain't coming for me!' Joey leapt to his feet.

Dora looked up quickly. '*No*, not you. Course not. Nor Lena. Not unless ...' She shook her head, her face creasing with pain. 'No – you're staying with me. And she said we can see them, sometimes.' She was weeping again. 'Now and then.'

Joey scarcely seemed to hear her. Staring at the flickering candle, he made no movement. On the table the faggots and peas went cold.

Four

'Well, I never!'

Ariadne Black peered long-sightedly at her newspaper, moving a finger along the line of print as she read.

'The ferrets and dogs of Henley-in-Arden Rat Club killed 435 rats this week – on one farm! What a *thing*!'

Gwen, distracted from wondering how Ariadne could make such an incredible burnt offering out of a rasher of bacon, looked up, unsure how to react to this latest piece of information. Ariadne often regaled them with snippets from the newspaper. Gwen exchanged a glance with Harold Purvis, who gazed back at her so soulfully from above his tightly buttoned collar that she wished she hadn't.

'Don't you think, Harold' – Ariadne leant towards him and laid a hand on his arm – 'that rats are, well . . . *vermin*?'

'Er, yes, I suppose they are,' Mr Purvis agreed, his plump face colouring. He edged his arm away and picked up a slice of limp toast.

Gwen sighed and downed the last of her tea. Meals at the table with Ariadne made her sympathize with how a fly must feel caught in a cobweb, though in fact Ariadne more or less ignored her: it was Mr Purvis she was spinning her thread round and round. But Gwen felt more uncomfortable than ever after what happened last night. Or at least, what she *thought* happened.

Ariadne served tea at six-thirty sharp. Gwen left her room and started off down the murkily lit stairs, assaulted by the depressing smell of boiled swede. Mr Purvis appeared at the bottom and started up the stairs with surprising energy. She saw his bald pate moving towards her through the gloom. He looked up, suddenly noticing her, murmured, 'Oh! Sorry!' and flattened himself to one side to let her go by, but as she passed him he began to turn again, too quickly, to continue up the stairs. They all but collided and as they did his hand closed over her left breast, just for a second, so that afterwards she was left wondering if she had imagined it. Yet she knew she hadn't. She kept her eyes on her plate and ate up her singed bacon as fast as possible. Ariadne wiped her full lips with her hanky and complained about the cold.

Gwen prepared herself hurriedly for school – a deep blue ribbon in her hair today – and rushed out, screwing up her eyes against the sudden bright sunlight. She knew now exactly the right time to catch the tram and could get to Canal Street on time in order not to incur Mr Lowry's fury.

Two weeks had passed in a blur. Each night she came home to the house in Soho Road exhausted, washing herself in a basin of water and sinking into bed early, not even kept awake by the sound of Mr Purvis's trumpet. After a time it had become clear that Mr Purvis's repertoire consisted only of one tune, which he told her was 'I Dreamt I Dwelt in Marble Halls', a piece of information which just about helped her to recognize the trumpet's wandering vagaries. At least it didn't stop her sleeping. It was a struggle even to stay

48

awake long enough to write to Edwin, though she did manage it twice a week, sending him cheerful letters full of the doings of school, and receiving equally jolly ones from him about his life in the parish. He always signed off his letters, 'Look after yourself, old girl. Much love, E.'

She was getting used to Canal Street School's routines, and the sheer size of it compared with the tiny church school in Worcester – the high ceilings and windows, the ominous groans of the plumbing, the smell of disinfectant and the ragged, grubby state of the children. As the days passed the mass of faces began to settle into individuals, and she learned their names and, gradually, their characters: the naughty ones; the ones like Joey Phillips and Ernie Toms, who always had the elbows of their jumpers out and holes in the seat of their pants; the little boy who scratched and scratched all day, his skin encrusted with the last stages of impetigo; the tooth-decayed grin of Ron Parks; and the vague, slow-witted look of the blonde girl, Alice Wilson.

And there was Lucy Fernandez. Lucy stood out, with her long, dark-eyed face and thick hair, and her lurching gait, hampered by the caliper on her leg. She was a timid child in class, and during Gwen's turns on dinner duty, she watched Lucy hugging the edges of the playground, obviously trying not to attract attention to herself, keeping out of the way of the able-bodied girls as they flung themselves about with their hoops and skipping ropes. The others called her the 'cripple girl'. This was not usually meant unkindly, just as a statement of fact. The only one who started to hang about at Lucy's side was Alice Wilson. Gwen found this strange to begin with as

Lucy was clearly a very intelligent child who picked up everything straight away, whereas Alice, though having neat handwriting, hardly seemed to be able to follow the work or complete anything properly in her exercise book.

That morning, though, the class were all to discover something else which made Lucy Fernanadez different. Gwen was standing by the blackboard, writing up long multiplication sums. 643, she wrote, adding x 46 underneath it. Light poured in through the long windows, sunbeams dancing with dust. The class fidgeted, longing to be out playing.

'Now.' Gwen pointed at the chalky numbers with a ruler. 'Who can tell me the first thing we have to do?' She moved the ruler between the six and the three. 'Alice?'

Alice Wilson squinted at the blackboard. A desperate expression came over her face and she blushed in confusion. Some of the others had their hands up and a couple sniggered at Alice's discomfort, but Gwen persevered.

'Quiet, the rest of you! Come on now, Alice – six times three? Surely you know that by now?'

A light dawned in her face. 'Eighteen, Miss,' the child whispered.

'Yes. Good. Now – what do we do next?'

Before anyone could answer there came a little clattering noise from the middle of the room. The children all craned round to see what was going on, then started giggling, staring at the floor. In the last fortnight Gwen had established her authority over them, but they knew she was not so fearsome that they couldn't afford the occasional laugh in class.

'What's the matter?' Gwen asked sharply.

'It's Ron, Miss,' one of the girls volunteered. 'His pocket's got an 'ole in and his sweets 've fallen out.'

Ron Parks's face was split in a black-toothed grin.

'Ron, come up here.'

The boy got up. As usual he was wearing a thick wool jumper, which covered his shorts reaching almost to his knees, and was trying to clutch at the hole in his pocket, but as he came up to the front a trail of several more sugar-coated pellets dropped to the floor, red, yellow and green, rolling away under the benches.

'What are those?' Gwen asked.

'Liquorice comfits, Miss.'

'And what are they doing in your pocket?'

'I was going to eat 'em after school, like.'

Gwen stared at Ron, trying to suppress at smile at the artless cheekiness of his face.

'No wonder your teeth are the colour they are, Ron,' she said severely. 'Do you want to spend the rest of your life sucking soup off a spoon because you've got no teeth?'

'Dunno, Miss Purdy.'

'Why do you eat so many sweets?'

Ron looked bemused. 'That's what there is. I live in a sweet shop, like.'

'Oh, I see.' At this, Gwen could no longer prevent herself smiling. An image came into her mind of Ron's entire family settling down in the evening with their knives and forks poised over platefuls of liquorice comfits, dolly mixtures and coloured marzipan. 'You do know sugar rots your teeth, don't you?'

'No, Miss.'

'Well, it does . . .' She was about to enlarge on this when there came another crash to her left. Lucy Fernandez had toppled off her chair and into the space

51

between the desks. Gwen rushed over to find the child lying rigid on her side, hands clawlike, her body convulsing.

'Oh my goodness!' Gwen cried. The child's face was tinged with blue. Her eyes were half closed. She saw immediately that Lucy was suffering from some kind of fit, but she had no idea what to do.

'Stay in your places!' she cried, and ran next door. She was about to hiss 'Miss Dawson' to get Millie's help, when to her horror, instead of Millie's friendly face, she saw the severe features of Miss Monk. The woman's head whipped round.

'Yes?' It was almost a snarl.

Gwen went up close. 'Could you please come and help me a moment? One of my girls seems to be having a fit.'

Miss Monk turned to the class. 'If any of you move or speak it'll be straight to the headmaster's office.'

'Looking for attention, I expect,' she said to Gwen. 'Soon sort her out.'

To Gwen's relief most of her class were still seated at their desks. One or two were in a huddle round Lucy Fernandez, but the others all looked frightened.

'Out of the way! Sit down! How dare you block the aisle?' Miss Monk roared at them. She cuffed one of the boys round the ear as he moved away, then stood looking down at Lucy. Peering over her shoulder, Gwen saw that the child's face had returned to a more normal colour, but she was still convulsed, her body in spasm.

'Hmm. Seems genuine,' Miss Monk acknowledged grudgingly. 'Need to get something in their mouths, stop them swallowing their tongues. Give me that rule.'

Taking the ruler which Gwen used to point at the

blackboard, Miss Monk squatted down, flustered, a lock of hair working itself loose from her bun and hanging over one ear. She rammed the edge of the ruler between Lucy Fernandez's lips, forcing it back as if she was taming a horse to accept a bit. Gwen winced.

'Is that really necessary?'

Miss Monk's brawny complexion turned even redder. 'Are you questioning my judgement, Miss Purdy?'

'No, but . . .'

'Did you, or did you not, ask for my help?'

'Yes,' Gwen agreed. She clenched her hands to stop herself pulling Miss Monk away. To her relief she saw that Lucy Fernandez was beginning to lie still, her muscles more relaxed, but then she saw a pool of liquid spreading out from under her. Miss Monk noticed it a few seconds after and recoiled in disgust, backing away from Lucy's prone body.

'She's wee'd herself,' Gwen heard one of the children whisper.

'Oh, *really*,' Miss Monk exclaimed. 'Filthy little beggar!' She stood up, and to Gwen's horror swung her leg, and with her flat, brown shoe delivered a hard kick into the small of Lucy Fernandez's back. The child let out a grunt, as if air had been expelled from her lungs. Gwen gasped.

'What on earth do you think you're *doing*?' she burst out. 'I don't think that was necessary, was it?'

Miss Monk looked as if she was going to explode. She seized Gwen's wrist.

'Come with me, Miss Purdy.'

She forced Gwen out into the hall.

'I'll thank you not to question my judgement, *Miss Purdy*. Especially in front of a class of children. What do you know? Coming in here all dressed up like a fourpenny rabbit! You've only been a teacher for five minutes and don't you forget it. It was no more than she deserved.' Her face twisted with disgust. 'Trying it on like that. Messing on the floor.' She went to go back into the class, but turned for a second. 'You needn't go running to Mr Lowry. He'd never believe you.'

She marched back into the room.

'Go and fetch a mop,' she ordered a plump boy, Kenny Campbell. 'And hurry up about it! Miss Purdy, make that girl get up now and stop malingering. That's quite enough!'

Gwen was trembling with shock and rage, though she tried not to let the class see. Once Miss Monk had swept out of the room, she took a deep, emotional breath. She was appalled by what she had just witnessed. She had never before seen a teacher treat a child with uncontrolled viciousness. For a second she felt violently homesick for her old school, with its homely ways, and Edwin popping in from the church to help with assemblies. But she became aware of her class watching all this in cowed silence and tried to compose herself.

'We must look after Lucy,' she said, and was surprised she could sound so calm. Avoiding the pool of urine, she went to kneel beside the girl, laying a hand on her head. Lucy's hair felt thick and wiry. She was lying still and appeared to be asleep, her pale face composed. She was not as strikingly pretty as Rosa, the sister who had brought her to school, but the slender line of her cheeks, her almost translucent skin and, when they were open, large dark eyes, combined to give her face an overall sweetness, and Gwen felt tender towards her, especially in the light of all the physical burdens she had to bear. She looked up at her silent

54

class, sensing that in some way they had drawn closer together through sympathy with what had happened.

'Jack – go and find Mr Gaffney for me, please.' She knew the gentle assistant headmaster would help arrange to get Lucy home.

She would have liked to pour out all that had happened to Millie Dawson, but Millie had apparently been taken ill, which was why Miss Monk had taken her place. The staffroom felt lonely without Millie to chat to. Gwen went in at dinner time, dreading having to see Miss Monk again. The woman's cruelty and bitterness horrified her. *She must be unhinged*, Gwen thought. Of course the children were aggravating and a trial at times, but there was no need for that!

Miss Monk was in the staffroom, but had settled herself in the corner with her back to the world and was reading a book in a manner that forbade anyone to come near her. For a moment Gwen felt like doing something childish to release her feelings – sticking her tongue out or thumbing her nose at the woman's forbidding shape.

'Would you like to give me a hand, dear?'

Lily Drysdale was in the corner near the scullery, kneeling in front of what looked like a pile of old rags, sorting through them. Seeing Gwen, her face lit up under its frame of soft, white hair. Looking at her, though, Gwen realized that despite her white hair and spectacles, Miss Drysdale was not as old as she had supposed. She was wearing an unusual dress with a large-buckled belt at the front, in a fabric of a thick, loose weave in a rich green, a colour she seemed to favour. She shifted back on her knees a little with a grimace, then gave a rueful smile.

55

'Legs aren't what they used to be!'

Drawn in by her, Gwen knelt down. 'What are you doing?'

Lily spoke quietly. 'I do what I can to give a bit of extra to some of the little ones. You'll have seen the state of their clothes. Some of these families are living under such terrible strain. I ask around for contributions, you see. People have got to know – my neighbours and so on.'

'How kind,' Gwen said, touched. 'There are certainly a few in my class whose clothes are in shreds.' She thought of Joey Phillips. His filthy, ragged state was not the only thing that had struck her. She found her gaze often drawn back to Joey's intense, frowning features. Just occasionally, when he was playing with Ron, or when his face relaxed, she saw that his pinched, wide-eyed face had a real beauty.

'Well, that's what they're for, dear. Have a fudge through and see if you can find anything that fits, and take it to them. I'm just trying to sort them into different piles for size.'

Dinner time flew past. Gwen had found a bakery near the tram stop, from where she bought her lunch every day. She munched on one of her cheese and onion cobs, and when Lily Drysdale said she had forgotten about bringing in food, Gwen gave her the second one.

'That's so kind,' the other teacher said, holding the bread with one hand and continuing to sort through clothes with the other. 'I'm really so disorganized about food . . .'

Gwen stored Lily Drysdale up as another thing to tell Edwin. To her Lily seemed more alive than most people she met, but then she wondered if Edwin would really appreciate Lily. He could be quite dismissive about some of the older ladies of the parish, as if in the nervous fussiness of widowhood or spinsterhood they didn't quite count as people. She decided to keep Lily to herself.

Some of the clothes were threadbare, but among them she found a pair of short trousers and a slate grey jersey with patched elbows which she thought might fit Joey Phillips. She wouldn't humiliate him in front of the class. She'd call him aside to wait until after the others had gone. She imagined the austere face of the withdrawn little boy lighting up at the sight of some new warm clothes.

Folding them into a small bundle, she put them away in the teacher's high desk as the children came in chattering from their dinner break.

'Quiet now!' she commanded. 'Time for register.'

Down the list of names she went again, to the mumbles and whispers of 'Here, Miss.'

'Speak up a bit, do,' she urged them. 'Joseph Phillips?'

There was silence. His place was empty.

'Does anyone know where Joey is?'

She saw a couple of the boys exchange glances.

'Jack? Eric?'

'No, Miss. Dunno where he is.'

Gwen frowned and continued calling out the names. It wasn't the first time Joey Phillips had gone missing from afternoon school. In fact it was happening with increasing frequency. She found herself feeling disappointed at not being able to give him the clothes. But where was he? Why had he not returned to school?

*

57

His hands were warm and sticky from the gravy seeping through the rag. Joey had tipped his school dinner into it in his lap, and the moment he was free to go outside he tore home along the street, cradling it in his hands.

Dora was hunched up close to the dying coals of the fire Joey had built that morning, hugging the blanket round her with her thin arms. Joey had replaced the soggy cardboard over the broken window with a piece of orange box, propped up inside.

'Here y'are, Mom. Brought you some dinner!'

He tipped the cooling stew and potatoes onto a plate. His mother struggled for breath. Her cheeks were red and she was obviously feverish.

'What've you got there?' she whispered once she could speak. 'Oh, Joey – that's not your dinner, is it?'

'Eat it, Mom,' he ordered, feverish himself in his feelings. He handed her the plate and a fork. 'It'll make you better.'

Dora's features twisted. 'No, Joey. It's for you.' *It won't make me better*, she could have said. *Nothing will now.* The sickness and the baby inside her were taking every last ounce of her energy. How would she ever find the strength to bring the child into the world? She had nothing left, no courage, no feeling, only instinct seemed to keep her alive. A force which drove her to survive for this unborn child, no matter how hopeless it was. She'd given up her two babies to the home. Loss and shame were eating away at her from the inside. Shame had been her life's companion, but now it was worse than ever. Joey and Lena would have to go to Barnardo's too when her time came, and it couldn't be long now. When she was alone, she slipped down into complete despair, lying for hours with her

58

eyes closed or rocking back and forth in distress. But now Joey stood mute before her, holding out the plate. She sighed, ashamed, and took it, picking at the tepid stew.

'That fire needs seeing to,' he said gruffly.

No, don't go, she wanted to beg him. *Don't leave me.*

But he'd gone, ignoring the harsh comments of the women he passed in the yard, along towards the coal wharf to stuff his pockets. Once he'd built the fire, he was off again to beg some orange boxes. He walked tall, swaggering. School be damned. That was for babies. He was a man. And he had work to do.

Five

The School Board man turned down the entry off Canal Street. There were two women in the yard, busy with a maiding tub full of washing and a mangle. They looked up and stopped work, arms self-righteously akimbo, and as he went to number three and knocked, they rolled their eyes at each other.

'Huh. Might've known it'd be that whore's lad.'

'You don't want to go near 'er,' the other one called to him raucously. 'You never know what you might catch!'

The man waited, tapping his pencil on his notebook, taking in the state of the house. The door looked about to fall off its hinges, the window frames were all rotten and half the downstairs window was smashed and blocked off with a flimsy bit of wood. *What a bloody awful state to live in*, he thought. And why was no one answering? He peered through the top part of the filthy pane and saw a shadowy movement inside. A second later the door squeaked open a few inches. The man felt the shock of what he saw register on his face. Flaming hell, the woman was no more than a living skeleton!

She was stooped, as if very old, though he could see that in truth she could not be more than a young woman. Between matted strands of hair her face was a yellowish colour except for two burning spots high on her cheekbones. Her eyes, which bulged unnaturally in her gaunt face, held complete hopelessness. She stared at him without speaking.

'I've come about your lad. He's not been to school when he should. Keeps running off of an afternoon.'

There was no reaction, as if she couldn't hear or make sense of his words. A sickening stench came from the house.

'Joseph Phillips? He is your lad?'

She nodded, opening the door a little further. The man's sense of horror increased. The woman was wearing an off-white, soiled garment which looked as if it had been stitched out of an old sheet, and made her look as if she was already clad in a shroud. She was obviously heavily pregnant and the bulge of the child looked grotesque against her wasted body. For a second he caught a glimpse in her features of someone who might once have been pretty, but then her face took on a sly, aggressive look.

'My Joey goes to school. I seen him go off every morning, like.' Talking made her cough alarmingly and she pressed a rag to her lips. The man looked at the ground until the fit passed. The cough looked as if it might split her body apart. In his revulsion he found some pity.

'You might think so, but the school says he hasn't. Goes some days, half the day. Some days he stays away all day. You need to make sure he attends. It's the law.' For some reason he found himself adding, 'I'm only doing my job, Missis.'

He felt the eyes of the two neighbours boring into him as he left.

'You won't get nowt out of her!' one of them called to him. 'Too busy whoring for the rent money to care about her kids.'

'She hands 'em over to Barnardo's when she can't be bothered with 'em no more! Bloody disgrace, that woman.'

The man didn't turn his head. Christ, he'd seen everything now. This job was the limit at times – the way some folk lived! It was a relief to hurry past the slimy bricks of the entry and out into the street again.

Joey's name was read out in assembly. The first time, Mr Lowry stood on the little stage at the far end of the hall, looming over them all, tall and forbidding in his tweeds, and read out a short list of names, among them Joseph Phillips. Heads turned. Form Four whispered to each other. Joey wasn't there. But the next day he was.

Mr Lowry's office was a small, austere room upstairs with a desk and chair and a bookshelf behind them. On the desk lay his two canes. The small, thin boy kept his eyes on them as he stood before the head-master. They were all he was aware of, mixed with the smell of Mr Lowry's shoe polish. You could almost see your face in his black shoes every day.

'Joseph?' Mr Lowry stood up and came round the desk. Joey didn't look up at him, but he knew that, as usual, the headmaster was holding the riding crop, fingering it. He could see the bottom edge of the man's jacket, his legs. 'You haven't been attending school.'

Joey didn't answer. He was numbed by exhaustion. His mind floated off elsewhere. School, Mr Lowry, all of it, was as nothing.

'Have you gone deaf, boy?' Mr Lowry spoke in his commanding, Scoutmaster tone. 'If I ask a question, I expect the courtesy of a reply.' He bent lower and looked into Joey's face. Joey felt forced to look back into Mr Lowry's large, pebbly eyes. They were cold and frightening. He had hairy nostrils and his breath smelt of stale tea.

'No.'

'*No?*' He was working himself up now.

'No, Mr Lowry.'

Stung by the boy's sullen tone, the headmaster straightened up, laid the riding crop very deliberately on the desk and took up the cane.

'You must be punished.' There was exaltation in his voice. 'Give me your hand, boy. You're a disgrace!'

Mr Lowry took a deep breath through his nose with each hard swipe of the cane on Joey's hand. Six times he raised it and whacked it down. The boy flinched physically each time but his expression didn't alter. There were no tears. Joey stood picturing that man he'd seen on top of his mother. One man, a stranger, who could have been any of the others whom she'd let use her. Pain went through him. He stuck his chin out and clenched his teeth. Mr Lowry stopped for a moment and Joey looked up at him. At the sight of Joey's hard eyes something seemed to snap in Mr Lowry. He seized the boy by the shoulder and spun him round.

'Bend over. You will be affected by me, boy. You *will* be.'

Joey heard the cane as it came through the air. He screwed his eyes shut. Mr Lowry thrashed him again and again. Joey couldn't count. He was lost in the pain. It cut through his buttocks, travelled in shock waves down the backs of his legs, but he didn't cry out. Mr Lowry was grunting. At last he stopped and there was silence for a moment in which all Joey could hear

63

was Mr Lowry's panting breaths. The boy clenched his jaw and forced himself to stand straight, steeling himself against the pain, forcing it away in his mind as he had done with his feelings so many times in his life.

Mr Lowry's face was flushed. He ran a hand over his sparse salt and pepper hair.

'Now.' He laid the cane methodically back on his desk and adjusted the shoulders of his jacket. 'I shall be checking with Miss Purdy, and I want to see an end to this truancy, Joseph. You will be in school every day from now on. If your record deteriorates again I may have to think about expelling you. Do you understand me?'

'Yes, Mr Lowry.'

Joey left the room, his face blank of expression.

'Joey – stay behind at the end of the morning, please.'

Gwen knew Joey Phillips had had a caning that morning. But he had come in after his punishment, not wearing the defiant grin boys usually put on to show how little they minded. Nor were there any tears. He just looked as he always did: closed and indifferent.

He stood beside her desk once the others had filed out.

'You have school dinner, don't you, Joey?'

He nodded, glancing at her, then away. Gwen sensed that he was somehow overwhelmed by the sight of her. She was wearing her pretty crimson dress again with a matching ribbon, which made her more colourful than anyone else around, except for Lily Drysdale. Gwen was darned if she was going to give in to the grime and just wear black and grey! She climbed down from her chair so as not to tower above the boy. He was still

64

wearing the clothes she had given him a couple of weeks ago. They had not reached the rotten state of his last set of garments, but she wondered if they had parted company with his body at any time since she had handed them to him. Their state was of general, all-over grime. He had no shirt on, but seemed to have some sort of vest under the grey jersey and his neck and face were uniformly grubby. He was such a poor little thing! Up close this was even more obvious. His limbs were very thin, his pallor evident despite the grime. He stank of poverty. Yet, in his expression, beneath the puckered brows, was something that both puzzled and affected Gwen. In this pathetic, dirty child's eyes was a mysterious strength. Over the past month, after she had offered him the clothes and he had accepted them with silent dignity – if not a word of gratitude – she had found herself paying more attention to him, watching him sometimes when he was bent over his sums or geography. His work was poor. His mind never seemed to be on his lessons. He didn't make many friends. The only boy she saw him have anything much to do with was Ron Parks, who gave him sweets and asked him to play sometimes. He appeared indifferent to the other children, though sometimes he got into fights and usually came off best in them. She had once seen him leave the school with his little sister Lena trotting behind him, striding off like a man with a mission, and the sight had moved her. There was something about him, small and pathetic as he appeared, that was intimidating. In looking into Joseph Phillips's eyes, Gwen felt she had struck up against rock.

'Mr Lowry is very concerned and angry about you playing truant, Joey. You know that, don't you?'

'Yes, Miss.' He spoke woodenly, looking at her only at waist level.

She sat down on one of the little desks. 'Can you not look me in the eye, Joey?'

He looked up, just for a second, then dropped his gaze again, taking a step backwards and Gwen realized her mistake. Teachers were distant, foreign people to him, who often exercised control by fear and violence. Faced by her friendly, smiling eyes he didn't know how to react.

But she had begun so she persevered. 'Where do you go to – when you skip school?'

A shadow seemed to fall across the boy's face. 'Nowhere, Miss.'

'Nowhere?' she spoke teasingly. 'Well, that can't be a very interesting place to be.' She wanted him to laugh, to show some sign of being a child. 'Where's nowhere?'

'Just . . . about, like.' He looked up, but not at her. He stared at the blackboard. That morning she had drawn the parts of a flower on it, with a bee drinking the nectar. *Proboscis* she had written, with an arrow pointing to the bee's long tongue.

'I see.' She stood up. There was no getting to the bottom of it, that was clear. 'Well, don't do it again, that's all. You don't enjoy getting caned, do you?'

'No, Miss.' She couldn't help noticing the utter indifference in his voice.

'Let me see your hands.'

He held out his wizened hands, in a way which reminded her of an organ grinder's monkey. They were grubby, of course, and the left palm was red and sore.

'Bathe it in some salty water when you get home,' she advised him. 'All right, Joey. You'd better go and get your dinner.'

She watched him go to the door with an awkward, stiff gait. Gwen frowned.

'Joey, are you in pain?'

Over his shoulder he replied, 'No, Miss.'

Six

'Cripple, cripple!'

Gwen heard the shouts across the girls' playground. A group of them, including Dora Evan, the class bully, had surrounded Lucy Fernandez. They had a long skipping rope and were swinging it, faster and faster.

'Go on, cripple – get in and jump!'

Gwen hurried over, saw Lucy standing, arms by her sides, her head down. Close to her was Alice Wilson, her eyes screwed up tight as usual, looking frightened and upset. The rope was a blur of movement.

'What d'you think you're doing?' Gwen demanded. They stopped abruptly and the rope hung still in the air for a second then sagged to the ground. No one answered. She saw Dora Evans sniggering behind her hand.

'You think it's funny, do you, you wretched girl!'

She was infuriated by the ignorant look Dora gave her through her slitty eyes and had to hold tightly onto herself not to lose her temper. 'You think it's amusing to bully someone who can't do the things you can! How would you like to wear a caliper on your leg? Go on – away with you. Leave the poor girl alone!'

She chased them away and they went up the other end with the rope.

'Just try and keep out of their way, Lucy,' she said. The two little girls linked hands and slunk off to stand by the blackened wall away from the bullies. Gwen watched them for a moment. What was it about Alice Wilson? The girl was obviously not as stupid as she appeared. Sometimes when Gwen asked her a question she was very quick off the mark. At other times she looked completely vacant.

Late that afternoon it began to rain hard. The sky turned deep smoky grey, and rain drummed on the roof and ran in streams down the long classroom windows. The last lesson was arithmetic. Gwen set the children to measure various objects in the room with the spans of their hands, so they were busy sizing up the desks and benches, the size of their friends from knees to the floor and writing the results in their exercise books. Joey Phillips had once again gone missing from school. Gwen was uneasy. He had been there for the afternoon register. During the first period he had asked to be excused to go to the toilets out across the playground. He never came back. Well, the boy would have to be taken in hand. But if only she could deal with it without Mr Lowry having to know.

Gwen looked out at the rain and wondered if it was raining at home. Edwin might be out on his bicycle. She thought of him with a sudden pang. He was so safe, so kind. She'd be able to see him again as soon as the half-term holiday came. *And I'm going to spend the rest of my life with him.* The idea came to her as strange and unreal. Her mind wandered back to Joey Phillips. Was he out in this? He'd be drenched. She felt very uneasy. Why did she feel so worried about this particular child?

'Have you recorded all your results?' She collected herself and spoke to the class. 'All right, finish up now!'

There was a scurry of activity as final figures were written down. They were all finding their way back to their desks when Lucy Fernandez went down again.

'Miss Purdy – Lucy's having a fit!'

Gwen rushed between the desks to the child's side, panic rising in her. Miss Monk had said something should be put in her mouth to stop her biting her tongue. Was that right? It had looked so harsh and cruel the way the other teacher did it. Gwen knelt by Lucy and held her hand under the girl's head as she began to go into spasm, surprised by the wiry force of her body.

'Our Mom says you have to put a spoon in their mouth,' a voice said. 'D'you want me to go and ask for one in the staffroom?'

Gwen tried to sound calm. 'I don't think that will be necessary. Just sit down all of you.'

The bell rang out across the assembly hall then, signalling the end of school.

'Go along all of you,' Gwen said. 'Go home. I'll see to Lucy.'

The children all hurried out, except little Alice Wilson, who hung behind. She peered down at Lucy.

'Will she be all right, Miss?'

The worst of the fit was passing and Lucy was growing still again and sleepy.

'Yes, she will, Alice, don't you worry,' Gwen said, intensely relieved. Thank heavens, she didn't seem to have swallowed her tongue! Once again, though, the pool of urine was seeping from under her on the floor. Alice didn't seem to notice this.

'How's Lucy going to get home, Miss Purdy?'

'D'you know where she lives?'

'Number fifteen, Alma Street.'

'Thank you, Alice. That's not far. You run along home now. I'll look after Lucy.'

'Yes, Miss,' Alice said, though with apparent reluctance. Once she had gone there was silence, except for the wind and spattering rain outside, the classroom clock's ticking and the quiet breathing of the skinny, dark-haired child. Then Mr Lowry put his head round the door.

'What *are* you doing, Miss Purdy?'

When Gwen explained, Mr Lowry came closer and frowned at the child, prone on the floor. He tutted impatiently. 'Oh goodness, what a nuisance. There's not a child left in the building we can send for the mother.'

Gwen felt her hackles rise. Anyone would think the child had fits on purpose! 'Don't worry, Mr Lowry. She lives very close by. And she's only a little scrap of a thing. I'll take her home myself.'

Mr Lowry raised his eyebrows. He seemed to disapprove of any act of kindness. He and Miss Monk deserved each other, Gwen thought sourly. They'd be a perfect match, those two. After a moment's thought he said grudgingly, 'Well, I suppose that might be a solution.'

'Yes,' she muttered in the direction of his departing back, 'and thank you for taking the trouble, Miss Purdy.'

She put her coat on and scooped up the child into her arms. Lucy's back and legs were wet with urine. Gwen wondered if she had a coat, but guessed that she probably didn't. Hardly any of the children had top coats to wear, but ran along to school in the same clothes, rain or shine.

It was pouring again. She hesitated by the door, but

realized she could wait for ages and it didn't seem about to let up. She stepped out, cursing that she hadn't brought a hat, the rain seeping through her hair, cold on her scalp. It was raining so hard that when she turned out of the school gate she could hardly see her way along the road. A cyclist loomed out of the murk, head down, battling against the wind.

Gwen's hair was soon drenched, the cold water running down her face, dripping from her nose. A few people passed her, hurrying home. The splash of water from roofs and gutters was all around. Gwen leant forwards as far as she could, holding Lucy close to her, trying to protect her, and staggered along. Lucy slept on, undisturbed by the wet. Although she was a skinny child, her weight was still enough to be an effort and Gwen's arms soon began to ache. She was glad to see the turning into Alma Street and the Alma Arms looking like a warm haven on the corner.

The houses at that end of the street were small terraced ones. Some of them appeared quite cosy, though in others the windows were dark and desolate looking. She passed a few, then crossed a side street, realizing that number fifteen must be the shop on the opposite corner. The windows were lit up but with advertisements stuck all over them and so full of shelves of tins and packets that she could not see in. She also couldn't manage the handle without putting Lucy down, though she managed to hoist Lucy up in such a way that she could knock.

There was a pause, then she saw someone coming and the door opened with a 'ting!' To her surprise, a man opened the door. For some reason she had automatically assumed the shop would be run by a woman.

In the dim light, the two things she took in about the man were his head of dark, curling hair and the fact that he was walking with a crutch and had a plaster cast on his left leg, the trouser leg rolled to the top of it. She also had the impression of someone solid and immensely strong. Gwen assumed this must be Lucy's father. She could hear other children in the background and became aware of faces watching from the back of the shop. What a sodden spectacle she must look standing there!

'How d'you do. I'm Miss Purdy – Lucy's class teacher. I'm afraid she's just had another fit.'

'Mam!' one of the boys shouted in the background. 'It's Lucy – she's bad again!'

'I see,' the man said, and she heard that he was not local. He spoke differently from Lucy. 'You'd better come in, then.'

Gwen manoeuvred Lucy carefully inside, along a narrow way between two rows of shelves. Lucy's feet caught the handle of a broom and knocked it over. They passed into the back room, which seemed crammed full of people, boys mainly. Rosa, the pretty elder sister, easily stood out among them. The man indicated that Gwen should lay Lucy in the chair by the fire, and as she put the child down, Lucy began to come round. Dazed, she looked round the room as if she couldn't think where she was, especially when she saw her teacher standing there.

'You all right now, Lucy *fach*?' the man asked, bending over her, and she nodded. She seemed happy to see him. In the light, Gwen saw that he was much younger than she had imagined. His hair was black, wavy, the face strong, dark-eyed and weathered look-

73

ing and she saw a kind warmth towards the child. His voice was deep but soft. She was still trying to place the accent.

'Miss Purdy?' Lucy whispered.

'Yes, dear?'

'Was it you brought me home?'

Gwen nodded and saw the girl smile sleepily and her face was suddenly pretty. She could sense the man appraising her. Though he was standing slightly behind her, his presence was very powerful. She felt something coming from him that was abrasive, close to hostility, but it was not blatant enough for her to be sure and was belied by the teasing light in his eyes.

'So you're Miss Purdy,' he said. 'We've heard a fair bit about you.'

'All good, I hope? Gwen Purdy.' She turned and held out her hand, though she immediately felt somehow foolish for doing so.

The man hesitated, then a strong, rough hand took hers and shook it. 'I'm Daniel, Lucy's brother.'

'I see.' Gwen smiled, surprised. 'I took you for the man of the house.'

Daniel Fernandez did not return the smile. 'That I am when I'm here. There's no one else.'

Gwen felt very awkward because of the serious, unwavering way he was looking at her. The crutch somehow added to his dignity rather than undermining it.

'Thank you for bringing our Lucy home.'

'Not at all.' To herself she sounded posh now and prim, and she was conscious of her bedraggled appearance. All this seemed to put her at a disadvantage. She felt like a foreigner in what was obviously a house of limited means. This room was evidently the family's

74

only living room behind the shop, so that although it was sparsely furnished – other than the armchair by the fireplace there was a table and three chairs, and a dilapidated dresser stacked with crocks – it also contained the gas cooker and shelves, with a small scullery beyond, and everyone seemed to be squeezed inside. The room was lit by gaslight and the mantles 'pop-popped' in the background. The Fernandez children stood round, silenced by the momentous, unheard-of event of a teacher calling at their house. Once more, the man did not smile. He sank down, balancing on the arm of Lucy's chair.

'So – you've come to see how the other half live then, is it? See how the world's workers get by?' His tone was jaunty, but somehow provocative as well. 'You don't sound as if you come from round here.'

'My family live in Worcester.'

'Nice town, Worcester. Been through there myself. Comfortable place, I'd say.'

There was nothing in his words that was actually rude, but they were spoken as a challenge. Gwen saw he had decided to tease her. Despite the laughter in his eyes, it got under her skin.

'You don't sound local yourself.' She met his stare defiantly. His eyes looked black in the poor light and to her bewilderment, as they faced each other, she felt the most peculiar sensation, as if all the hairs on her body were suddenly standing on end. She gave a shiver, then blushed, confused, feeling somehow that the man would sense the odd, electric sensation that had come over her. She was distracted by the sound of someone coming down the stairs, and then the door opened.

'Daniel? What's going on?'

'It's all right, Ma – it's our Lucy, had another fit at

school. This is her teacher, brought her home. Miss Purdy.'

Mrs Fernandez was small in stature but wide and large breasted. She seemed like a larger person than she was. She had round, rosy cheeks and striking blue eyes, which Rosa had evidently inherited. She nodded at Gwen, looked across at Lucy and saw she was all right, then turned back to Gwen.

'Miss Purdy?' Her accent was as strong as her son's and it only then dawned on Gwen that they were Welsh. Lucy, however, spoke with a Birmingham accent like nearly all the other children in the class. 'Brought our Lucy back, is it? Very good of you. Very good. And you're soaked to the skin. *Duw*, Daniel, what're you thinking, not offering Miss Purdy a cup of tea for her trouble? Kettle's nearly boiled – come on now. Where your manners? Rosa, bring Miss Purdy a chair.'

Mrs Fernandez moved with a stately gait across the room to the scullery. She was dark haired, though not swarthy like Daniel. Her hair was taken back softly in a bun and she wore a deep blue dress and black crocheted shawl. She seemed friendly and down to earth, more welcoming than her son, and Gwen warmed to her immediately. Perched on a chair by the fire, Gwen felt more at ease now she was not in conversation with Daniel alone and able to take in more of the room. The walls were painted a rich blue, which made the place dark and cosy in the firelight. Looking up at the mantelpiece, which was draped with a deep rust-coloured strip of material, she noticed a photograph of a dark-haired man, though it was faded and she could not make out much except that he looked too old to be Daniel. Was he Daniel's absent father?

Beside it, flanked by brass candlesticks, stood a small, blue-robed statue of the Virgin Mary. She heard Mrs Fernandez lighting the gas and the kettle hissing and realized she was being watched closely by all the children.

'So I don't suppose you're living round here are you?' Mrs Fernandez asked. Steam curled into the air as she poured water into a huge brown teapot.

Gwen turned to her. 'No – I come in from Handsworth. Soho Road.'

'Oh yes.' The lid clinked into the teapot. 'Vincent *bach* – fetch me the milk. And Paul – go and get the chair from upstairs.'

Both the boys, a good deal older than Lucy, jumped to do as they were bidden. The younger one disappeared into the scullery and came back with a bottle of sterilized milk. Their instant response made Gwen realize that Mrs Fernandez was more steely than her soft appearance indicated. Gwen watched her, trying to guess her age, and thought she must be in her mid-forties. Mrs Fernandez brought the pot and willow-pattern cups and saucers to the table, then poured the strong, orange tea. Gwen moved her chair over to sit nearer. Vincent, who told Gwen he was fourteen and would soon start work, sat across from her. Paul sat on the chair he had brought down and another boy and Rosa sat by the hearth. Gwen could feel Daniel observing her from his perch on the arm of Lucy's chair.

'You don't sound local either,' Gwen said shyly. She couldn't work this family out at all – Welsh accents, Birmingham accents, Spanish name. 'Are you Welsh?'

'Me?' Mrs Fernandez sat down and handed Gwen a cup of tea. She stirred three spoonfuls of sugar into her own cup. 'Not originally, no. I'm Irish, I am – from County Wexford. My mother and father brought us over the water for a better life when I was seven years of age. Met my husband Arturo there – course they'd all come over from Spain to the steel works down in Dowlais – that was before he left to go down the pit.' She stopped and sipped her tea. She seemed quite happy to keep talking. What she was describing though was an unknown world to Gwen, who nodded, hoping her ignorance was not too obvious.

'Arturo died eight years ago, God rest him – after the strikes and that. We didn't want to leave the valleys, but there was no work, see, not down there. My sister Annie's in Birmingham, and her husband Pat, and they wrote and said there's jobs to be had here ... Well, none of us wanted to go, and Daniel here wouldn't come, not straight away. His home was the valley, was all he wanted. He stayed on with my brother in Aberglyn...'

'Ma, d'you think Miss Purdy wants to hear all our family history? I expect she'd find it very dull, an educated young lady like her.' Again, the tone was ironic, a challenge.

'But I do,' Gwen said sharply, wondering why Daniel Fernandez seemed determined to despise her on sight. She resented this – after all, she'd brought his sister home, hadn't she? 'It's very interesting.' She could barely imagine what Mrs Fernandez's experiences could have been. In fact she realized she knew nothing about anything. The inside of this house was very different from and much poorer than any other she had ever been in. She'd barely ever met a Roman Catholic before. Her mother talked about them as if they were sinister. Even drinking tea with sterilized milk was new

78

to her. She was having to get used to the taste of it. She sensed that this family had come through enormous hardship, while her own life had been so sheltered, so comfortable! It made her feel almost ashamed. She sat forward, elbows on the table.

'I'm so sorry about your husband. What a terrible thing. And you were left with so many children.'

'Eight to bring up. Oh yes. Lucy was born after he died.' She shook her head, took another sip of tea in the silence. 'Course, Daniel stayed in the valley, and our Ann was the only one out at work. But at least there was work to be had over here . . .' She gave a long sigh. 'Oh yes, hard times.' Suddenly Mrs Fernandez seemed to brush the memories aside. 'Would you like a hot drop in there before you go?'

'Yes please.' Gwen held out her cup. 'It's thawing me out nicely!' She was feeling wet and uncomfortable but she was too interested in the family to want to rush away. She turned to Daniel.

'Birmingham isn't your home then?'

His mother replied before he could. 'Our Daniel's a valley boy. Down the pit at Aberglyn when he was fourteen. Now he's up to his eyes in politics and books – a proper red, he is, just like his da – there's no talking to him sometimes.'

There was a bitter note in her voice. Daniel made no reply but she saw that the twinkling, teasing light had gone from his eyes and his face was moving as if he was clamping his jaw in the effort not to retort. Gwen saw there was tension between mother and son that she had no understanding of. She had never taken any interest in politics, never heard much about it except when Edwin talked about pacifism and the League of Nations. Her family were quietly conservative. Politics had always seemed a dull, provincial affair. Its importance had never touched her, and she certainly knew nothing about Wales. She could tell the other children had heard all this before and weren't interested, two of the boys poking each other and giggling. Only Lucy was really listening.

Mrs Fernandez changed the subject. 'You being a schoolteacher – marvellous, that is. I'd like to have done that if I'd had a better education.'

'Yes,' Gwen said. 'It is quite nice.'

'It's the seedbed of revolution, that's what it is.' Daniel's voice cut through from behind her. Though he was talking quietly, his voice carried round the room. 'Give people an education and you give them power to change their lives.'

'Yes.' Gwen turned to him. Once again, something about Daniel Fernandez seemed overwhelming; she had that odd sensation of electricity sweeping over her, though she spoke coolly. 'I suppose you're right. I've never thought about it before.'

He looked steadily back. 'Perhaps it's time you did.'

There was a knocking at the front and a voice called cheerfully, 'Theresa? It's only me!'

'That's my sister. Come in, Annie!' she called. 'There's tea in the pot!'

'I must go.' Gwen got up as the woman came in, a thinner Theresa Fernandez, older and a little more faded, but with the same candid blue eyes. 'I've disturbed you long enough.'

'You're no disturbance. Annie, this is Miss Purdy, Lucy's class teacher. Lucy had a turn today and she brought her home. Wasn't that kind now?'

The woman smiled warily. 'You're from St Patrick's?'

'No – I told you, we've put her in the Protestant school to have her nearer by. It's just along the way.'

Daniel stood up as Gwen thanked Mrs Fernandez for the tea. 'I'd offer to walk you home, but I think I'd hold you up.'

For the first time there was a touch of warmth in his tone.

'There's no need. The tram stop's just at the end of the road.' She glanced down at his leg. 'What have you done?'

Daniel's mouth went up at one side. 'Let's just say I had a little disagreement with a policeman.'

'Oh.' Gwen smiled. 'I see. Well, I don't, but I hope it gets better quickly. Bye-bye, Lucy. I'll see you in the morning.'

A delighted smile met her from the chair.

'Bye-bye, Miss Purdy.'

Seven

The nit nurse was in school.

About once a month she turned up to check the children's heads and this time she arrived the week before the half-term holiday. They lined up in the hall, class by class. Form Four waited for Form Three to finish.

Alice Wilson was sick with nerves.

'Line up now!' Miss Purdy called to them. 'Ron, put those away. I don't want to see those out in school again. Why is it that you always seem to *rattle*, one way or another?'

Ron Parks sheepishly pushed a handful of marbles back into his pocket.

Alice followed the others as they lined up. Squinting anxiously, she managed to get behind Lucy Fernandez.

'I hope I haven't got nits!' she whispered to Lucy.

Lucy turned and peered at her, puzzled by the desperation in her voice. 'You won't have. Your hair's lovely and clean.'

'I know, but my head's itching something terrible.' Alice started scratching at the very thought. Several of the others were doing the same and giggling nervously.

'Ooh – nits're horrible!' Lucy said, quivering, but trying to make a joke of it. But there was no answering smile on Alice's face.

'My Mom'll go mad if I've got nits.'

They filed into the hall and stood on the scuffed floor, which had lost its beginning-of-term sheen. Form Three were going back into their classroom with Miss Dawson. Alice could see their blurry shapes moving through the bright oblong of the classroom door, but she couldn't make out who any of them were without screwing up her eyes so tightly that her face ached. She already had toothache, a nagging pain at the top left of her mouth. She hadn't told her mother. Mummy kept saying she couldn't stand any more bad news and toothache seemed like bad news to Alice. What was she going to do if she had nits? She knew what it would be like.

'Those dirty, dirty children!' Her mother would be shouting, crying. 'How can we go on in this place? I can't stand it, can't stand living any more . . .' It was frightening when she talked like that.

Up near the stage Alice could make out the stout figure of the nurse. She was wearing a white overall and the tops of her arms seemed squeezed into it because they were so plump. She started to move along the back of the line from child to child. It was the same nurse who always came and she was brisk but kind. Miss Purdy walked along in front of them all, in her soft green dress and neat shoes.

Alice felt a pressure inside her as the ordeal moved closer. She needed the lavatory, urgently. *I should've asked to go before.* Panic was rising in her. *It's too late now. Miss Purdy'll be cross with me if I ask now.* She liked Miss Purdy, with her sweet, pretty face and the the way her hair hung in little waves round her cheeks. And she spoke softly and had lovely curly handwriting. She was the nicest teacher Alice had ever had, but she could still be quite strict and Alice was frightened of being told off by anyone. Everything was frightening, the way it seemed to be for her mother since her daddy had disappeared and they'd become poor. Mummy didn't like being poor. She sat in the house and cried and wouldn't go out because everyone was rough and she was afraid. She hadn't wanted to send Alice to school, but she knew she had to, she said it was the law.

From Miss Dawson's classroom came the sound of voices reciting the three times table. 'Three nines are twenty-seven,' they droned.

The nurse worked her way along. Jack Ellis had nits.

'There's one here,' the nurse told Miss Purdy, who wrote down his name. When you had nits the teachers sent a note home to your parents.

Alice felt a surge of pressure in her bladder and she crossed her legs, looking down at her scuffed brown shoes. Daddy used to make her polish her shoes every evening but now they didn't even have money for polish. She couldn't keep still because she needed to wee so badly. Only nasty, dirty people had nits, that was what Mummy said.

The nurse reached Lucy. She brought with her a smell of disinfectant. Alice thought her heart was going to break out of her chest. Her palms were wet with sweat and she fought a desperate need to scratch her head. If she didn't move, maybe they wouldn't notice!

Miss Purdy moved in front of her and she could sense the nurse behind her.

'Nice head of hair, you've got, dear,' Alice heard the nurse say. She felt the nurse's fingers on her scalp, separating the hairs. The nurse lifted her plaits and Alice could feel her staring, first at one side, then the other. Her cheeks burned and she held her breath. She looked up at Miss Purdy, who did not see the desperation crying out from her eyes. A second later the worst thing of all happened. She couldn't hold her urine any more and she felt it start to trickle down her legs, then come in a rush. She let out a whimper of distress. Miss Purdy's eyes met those of the nurse for a second.

'It's all right, Alice.' She spoke gently. 'Let's take you out to the toilet, shall we?'

But the damage was already done. There was a puddle on the hall floor. Weeping with humiliation and fright, Alice followed Miss Purdy out and across the playground to the toilets. The wind blew freezing cold on her wet skin and she could feel the soaked elastic chafing her legs.

'You go and take your knickers off,' Miss Purdy said kindly. 'I'll be back to you in a moment.'

Alice sat sobbing in the toilet cubicle. She had to blow her nose on a sheet of the hard toilet paper. She felt so ashamed, but how she loved her teacher for being so kind! A few minutes later Miss Purdy came back.

'Alice, I've got something you can put on for the time being.' An old pair of knickers was passed under the door. They were going to holes, but anything was better than the humiliation of staying in wet ones all day.

'Thank you,' she whispered.

Miss Purdy was waiting for her by the roller towel when she came out, feeling a little more comfortable.

'I've rinsed your others through and I'll put them on the radiator in the staffroom. Don't you worry – they'll be dry by home time.' Miss Purdy leaned closer to her and Alice could smell the sweet scent of rose-water. 'Now look, Alice. I could see you were very worried about something in there. Was it about having nits?'

Alice nodded.

'You know you've got some nits in your hair, don't you? I'll have to send a note home to your mother so she can help you get rid of them. But the rest of the class don't need to know. All right?'

Alice's heart sank. It didn't matter about the other children. Whatever would Mummy say!

'You know, Alice – you can check your own hair for nits. Either get your mother to look, or you can sometimes see in the mirror if you look carefully.'

Alice shook her head dejectedly. 'No – I can't.'

Miss Purdy smiled into her face.

'Why can't you?'

Desperately she looked into her teacher's eyes.

'I can't see. I can't see anything, hardly.'

'Would you believe it?'

Gwen threw herself down in a chair beside Millie at dinner time. 'Some of these poor children. I've just discovered that Alice Wilson in my class is practically blind and nobody seems to have noticed – including me, come to think of it! I thought she was just slow, but no wonder the poor girl can never answer any of the arithmetic sums when she can't see the blackboard.' She pulled a ham cob out of a paper bag. 'I'm *ravenous*. Heavens, what a morning. It feels as if the day ought to be over by now. Is there any tea in the pot?'

'Think so,' Millie said quietly.

Gwen got up and fetched them each a cup. She and

Millie had become good, comfortable friends during these weeks of teaching. They always spent their dinner times together sharing groans and jokes about the day. Millie had invited Gwen to her home a few times, where her mother and younger sister Joanna had made Gwen welcome.

'Here you go.' Gwen handed Millie her tea and sat down. 'Have you had your dinner already?'

Millie shook her head and it was only then that Gwen saw what a state she was in. She sat with her hands clenched in her lap, fighting tears.

Gwen put the cup down on the floor. 'Millie? Whatever's wrong?'

Millie shook her head. 'I can't tell you. Not here,' she whispered. The tears began to run down her pale cheeks.

'Come on – finish your tea and we'll go out,' Gwen suggested. She fetched both their coats.

'Off for a walk, dear?' Lily Drysdale said to her. 'Good idea – it's a lovely day.'

They walked through the watery February sunshine, all along Canal Street past the end of the prison wall, to the bridge which crossed the canal, and stood looking down into the long line of murky water. A pair of boats slid away from them in the distance, their bright colours cheerful against the sombre banks and trees.

Millie could hold back no longer. She burst into tears.

'Oh dear – do tell me what's the matter,' Gwen said, worried. Millie was usually such a jolly soul.

'Oh, what am I going to do?' Millie cried desperately. 'I'm so ashamed.'

It took her some time even to begin.

87

'I feel so ill. I keep being sick.'

Gwen frowned. She was ignorant enough not to put two and two together.

'Perhaps you'd better go and see a doctor.'

'I've *been* to the doctor,' Millie sobbed. 'And he said . . . I'm . . .' It came out in a great rush of emotion. 'I'm going to have a baby!'

Gwen struggled to know what to say. She had only the haziest idea of how babies came about. 'Well, *how*? Whose is it?'

'Lance's of course! What d'you take me for?' Millie turned to her passionately. Her freckly face was blotchy from crying.

'Does he know about it?'

'No – I only found out yesterday. Oh, what *am* I going to do?'

Gwen was almost speechless. Once again she realized what a sheltered life she had led. 'Well . . . surely he'll marry you, won't he?'

'He's going to have to, isn't he?' Millie sounded angry now. 'I never meant for it to happen, Gwen. I didn't even know what he was doing until it was too late. It was one afternoon when Mummy and Joanna were out. Lance came round and we were talking and having a cuddle and gradually . . . well, we got carried away. Or at least he did. I mean it was . . . it was quite peculiar to begin with. I never knew it would be quite like that. Lance got so excited and I couldn't really stop him . . .' She spoke haltingly. 'I felt . . . afterwards I felt almost, sort of *dirty* . . . And now this.'

Gwen tried to digest this information. She thought of Edwin's embraces.

'Don't you want to marry him, Millie? I thought you were mad about him.'

'I thought I was.' Millie stared along the cut with a desolate expression. 'I don't suppose I really have a choice now, do I? That's if he'll do the right thing. It's just . . . oh, Gwen!' Her tears began to flow again. 'I'm such a silly fool. I've been in love with the idea of love but I don't really want to marry Lance – not yet anyway. I've always wanted to be a teacher so much, and I shan't be able to now. Lance can carry on being a teacher for his whole life if he wants to, but I can't, can I? My life'll be all babies and housework. Oh, I wish I'd never let him come anywhere near me!'

Eight

'Gwen, darling!'

Edwin was waiting on the platform as the train chugged slowly into Worcester Foregate Street. Even in the gloom, under the dim lights, she easily spotted his pale hair. Seeing her through the window, he strode alongside her carriage beaming with delight. Gwen felt as if she had returned suddenly to another, childhood existence.

She stepped down into his arms, his cold cheek pressing against her warm one.

He drew back and looked down at her, full of merriment.

'At last! How's my brave little woman? It feels as if you've been away for months!'

'It does to me too,' Gwen said. 'It's another world.'

'Well, I think it's *marvellous*. Well – except that I have to do without you, of course. Come along, let's get you home.' Edwin picked up her case with his left hand and kept his other arm round her as they moved through the crowds on the platform. She could feel his hand between her shoulder blades, steering her. Gwen looked round. It did feel good to be home! Birmingham had already receded like a dream and now here she was back in her real life again, or at least for the half-term holiday.

'Your father let me bring the Austin,' Edwin told her.

'Thank goodness,' Gwen said, surveying the rainy dark outside the station.

'You wait here – I'll bring her up.' Edwin ran zestfully out into the rain. Gwen smiled at the sight of his eager form, wrapped in his huge black coat, a trilby perched on his thick hair. There was something about Edwin that was somehow inevitable.

They drove from the middle of Worcester to her parents' house, right on the edge. It felt cosy in the car, spots of rain on her coat, Edwin's large, capable hands steering them along as they chatted. She gave him a fond sideways glance. She waited for her heart to leap in some way, to feel excited. It didn't happen, but she felt safe, and at least affectionate. Surely even those two things were more than most people had in marriage?

'How's your mother?'

Edwin's mother was in a wheelchair. Year by year her state degenerated and Mr Shackleton, a retired clergyman himself, battled on, looking after her as his own health faded. Edwin's one sister, Judy, lived nearby with her family, and Edwin tried to visit as often as he could since they lived in a village a few miles away. Gwen knew they would visit sometime over the next few days. Edwin was a very dutiful son.

'Well . . .' He sounded gloomy and she felt for him. They paused at a junction, then pulled out, turning right. She could see the rain falling slantingly in the light from the headlamps. 'I managed to get up there in the week. Dad's arthritis is getting worse and his chest is bad. The nurse comes in, but of course he's lifting Mum far more than he should be.' He paused again. 'It's hard to watch. I feel pretty helpless.'

Gwen reached over and squeezed his arm. 'They

know you do all you can. And they're so proud of you.'

'I know. Almost makes it worse.'

In a moment he was cheerful again – Edwin was never cast down for long – and he was asking her more about things she'd told him in her letters, laughing at her description of Ariadne.

' "Come into my parlour," said the spider to the fly!'

'Yes – just like that! And creepy Mr Purvis looks as if he's going to explode with nerves every time she goes near him!'

'What a pair!'

'He scoots off to his room and plays the trumpet – same tune, over and over again.' She was giggling now. 'I think if I hear it again I'll go mad. And he never gets any better at it!'

They both laughed. Gwen had decided not to tell Edwin much more about Harold Purvis. She tried to avoid any encounter now which could involve being alone with him. One evening, when Ariadne had left the room to fetch something from the kitchen, Mr Purvis had leaned over and placed his plump white hand over hers, gazing soulfully into her eyes.

'Please,' Gwen reprimanded him sharply, 'don't do that. I don't like it and, as a matter of fact, I'm sure I've mentioned that I'm engaged to be married.'

She almost had to laugh at herself, at how prim she had sounded. But she knew she hadn't imagined him fondling her on the stairs, and what with Ariadne drooling over him and the endless renditions of 'I Dreamt I Dwelt in Marble Halls', she was finding the household a trial. This was not, however, something she needed Edwin to know.

Gwen's mother was listening for the car, and had

the door open, waiting as they ran in through the rain in her usual tense stance.

'Come on in, dears! That's it. Thanks so much, Edwin.'

Gwen's mother was always terrifically nice to Edwin. She stood back to let them in, holding her thick cardigan round her. Mrs Purdy was a slim, neat woman in her late forties. Mr Purdy, a few years older than his wife and with a permanent air of anxiety, was also hovering in the hall.

'Hello, Gwen dear,' he said.

'Hello, Mummy, Daddy.' Gwen kissed each of them briefly, struck by the fact that even after an absence of a few weeks they seemed different. Didn't the remaining hair round her father's bald head look greyer? And her mother seemed smaller, somehow, and more compact.

'Come along.' Ruth Purdy hurried down the hall. 'The kettle's boiled. I'm sure you must need a good cup of tea. Morris – take Gwen's case up will you, dear? It's cluttering up the hall.' Her tone managed to imply that he was cluttering up the hall as well.

They sat by the fire in the back room with tea and biscuits. The table at the far end had a huge jigsaw puzzle on it, partially complete, and on the mantelpiece were pictures of the three children: Gwen's two brothers in a rowing boat off the Welsh coast as children, and one of Gwen when she was nine, a rounded, healthy-looking child with a wide smile, standing by the apple tree they had planted in the garden.

Though they didn't say so, Gwen sensed, rather to her surprise, that her parents were pleased to have her home. As the youngest, she had left them with an empty nest, as Johnny was married and Crispin off in the RAF. Poor old Crispin, Gwen thought, looking at the younger of the boys in the rowing-boat picture. Never could do anything right compared with Johnny. No wonder he left home as fast as possible.

They exchanged news about the past few weeks. A neighbour had died a few days ago, a school friend of Gwen's was moving away. Gwen asked her father whether everything was all right at the pharmacy.

'Oh, yes.' He nodded. 'Everything's going along nicely. Yes – ticking along.' She could see him struggling to think of something else to tell her. 'I, er—'

'So,' Ruth Purdy cut him short, staring appraisingly at Gwen, who thanked heaven that Edwin was there – he acted as an excellent buffer against her mother. 'Your manners don't seem to have deteriorated too much.'

She made a great joke out of this, eyeing Edwin to encourage him to join in and Edwin laughed with her, oblivious as ever to the undercurrents in the room.

'Oh, I think I can still remember how to eat with a knife and fork,' Gwen said. She suppressed a smile at the thought of meals in the smoky Soho Road house.

'Well –' Ruth Purdy gave another light laugh – 'I'd think by now you'd have had enough of this silly little experiment of yours. You've proved your point, and Mr Jenkins said they're missing you.' Mr Jenkins was the head of the parish school where Gwen had met Edwin. 'He's very keen for you to come back. I don't know if you realize how disappointed they were when you left.'

Despite her mother's antagonism, Gwen felt temptation tug at her. In a way it was nice to be home, and it would be so easy to stay, to slip into the old routine, comfortably surrounded by the familiar, then slip easily into marriage. She thought of Millie Dawson, who wasn't coming back to school any more. But already Gwen could feel the old claustrophobia coming over her. There was something about this house, about her parents' marriage, that was so static, so *dead*.

'Actually, I'm rather enjoying it where I am,' Gwen replied evenly. She felt very tired suddenly. Her mother was keeping her criticism mild while Edwin was present, but was she going to carry on like this for four days? 'Can we drop the subject now – *please*?'

'It's only that we're missing you,' her mother said tetchily. 'That's all. And Birmingham sounds so *grim*.'

Gwen watched her parents as her mother asked after Edwin's family. Her father sat silent as ever, in his slippers. He leaned forward to poke the remains of the fire. She could sense him longing to be able to settle down with the newspaper. Her mother had evidently had a cold, which had left her nose pink and sore, and she looked tired. She was such a *good* woman, Gwen thought guiltily. At least as far as everyone else was concerned. She had a strict sense of propriety, and always did the right thing for her children with little thought for herself. That was how a virtuous woman was supposed to be, wasn't it? Mummy must love her and Crispin because of all she did for them. So why didn't it *feel* as if she did? And why did this kind of virtue feel so tyrannical?

They chatted about local events and Edwin's work. Edwin had a go at fitting in some of the jigsaw pieces. Later, they all had cups of cocoa and everyone was yawning. Edwin got up.

'Best be getting back.' Gwen saw the warmth and approval in her parents' eyes as they looked up at their son-in-law to be. Edwin, she thought, was the one thing she had ever really done right. She felt very low suddenly. The only way she ever seemed able to get along with her parents was to act as a version of herself that they had decided upon – pretty, biddable and conventional.

Mr and Mrs Purdy stayed tactfully in the back room as she went to see Edwin out. He put his coat on, and as soon as the sitting-room door was closed and they were alone he took Gwen in his arms.

'Oh, I've been waiting for this!' His good-natured face beamed down at her. It was a thoroughly English sporty face with a pink complexion and kindly blue eyes. 'I miss you dreadfully, you know that, don't you?'

'I miss you too,' she said, smiling up at him. 'But it's fun being able to write. And it's not for long.'

Edwin pulled her close and held his face against hers with a sound of pleasure. 'It's still far *too* long! It feels pretty bleak around here without you. I'm counting the days.'

She drew back and looked up at him. 'Me too.'

He put his mouth close to her ear. 'How about coming out into the porch for a moment?'

Sheltered from the rain, they kissed, holding each other close. 'That's my girl,' Edwin murmured, his hands stroking her sides. 'Those lovely curves!' Then, very self-controlled, he drew back. 'Must go.' He kissed her cheek. 'But we've got tomorrow. I'll see you in the morning, darling.'

He stooped to put on his bicycle clips, then went round to retrieve his bike. She waved as he swerved off along the road, then stood for a moment thoughtfully, looking at the empty path. Was she counting the days?

she asked herself. She turned back into her parents' warm, orderly house, preferring not to answer that question.

They walked out to the hills the next day. The rain had stopped, the air was damp and mild and ragged clouds moved swiftly across the sky. As soon as they set out, Edwin took Gwen's hand, smiling down at her. They were both well wrapped up, Edwin in plus fours and thick socks, Gwen in slacks and both in layers of winter woollies under their coats. Edwin wore a little knapsack with a Thermos and their sandwiches in it.

'Got you to myself at last!' he said.

Gwen laughed. She felt rested and more optimistic this morning, setting out with Edwin's big hand wrapped round hers. They squelched uphill through the mud, dark trees to one side of them. Edwin told her news about his work, the latest on some of his parishioners. There were people he was worried about: he had misgivings about his preaching. Was it relevant to anything? Once Edwin got talking there was no stopping him. She had always been his audience.

'Tell you what I have done.' He reached for his wallet. 'I've been doing a lot of thinking. About war and so on. There was a little meeting here last week – look – I'm going to send this off.'

He held out a little buff-coloured card. Printed along the top were the words, 'I renounce war and will never support or sanction another.'

Gwen frowned. 'Is this the white poppy people?'

'It's Dick Sheppard's Peace Movement. Now there's a priest setting a real example. He's quite right,' Edwin was becoming emphatic. 'The whole thing *is* lunacy.

The way things are going we'll be into another war soon. And it's utterly un-Christian! How can we ever justify such violence against other human beings? It says very clearly in Micah that we must beat our swords into ploughshares. Look at the Great War – do we want that again?'

'No, of course not.'

Edwin put the card away. 'Sorry, darling.' He smiled ruefully. 'Am I keeping on?'

'No – it's quite all right. I entirely agree with you. But you can step out of the pulpit now.'

He laughed, helping her over a stile. They climbed, chatting, to the top of the hill, where they rested, looking over towards the dark peaks of the Malverns. Edwin hugged her from behind, arms wrapped round her shoulders.

'Beautiful, isn't it?' His mouth was close to her ear.

'Umm,' Gwen agreed. For some reason, she found herself thinking about Lily Drysdale, wondering what she did at the weekend. She imagined her moving briskly from house to house, asking for clothes for her charges. At the thought of returning to Birmingham on Tuesday evening she felt a pang of dread and excitement mixed.

'We'll be able to come up here every week, if we want to,' Edwin was saying. He turned her round, looking deeply into her eyes and she could see the longing in his. 'When we're Mr and Mrs Shackleton.'

'Reverend and Mrs,' she corrected him, teasingly.

'I'm so lucky, my love.' He looked down at her and she could see he was moved. She smiled back, touched by the look in his eyes. Edwin was so good, so true and lovely to her. She loved him, she was sure . . . wasn't she? How was anyone supposed to be sure about love? In church they sometimes said love was more about actions than just emotions. About caring for people: doing the right thing. But wasn't it possible to feel more than this? Edwin took her smile as encouragement and leaned down, gently fastening his lips on hers. His tongue searched her mouth longingly and Gwen kissed him back, feeling excitement rising in her, and a great surge of relief that she could feel this way. Edwin's desire, the constant conflict between it and his sense of duty to restrain himself until they were married, could move her more than anything. His hands pressed her close and she shut her eyes and ran her hands up Edwin's strong back. *It's all right*, she thought, with a sense of peace. *It's going to be all right.* Then, abruptly, he pulled away, shamefaced.

'Oh God, darling. I'm sorry. I mustn't.' He was blushing. 'I don't want you to feel that I'm – well, I don't know. Taking advantage – or anything like that.'

'It's all right. I don't. I know you wouldn't dream of it.' Released from his embrace, she felt suddenly cold.

Nine

They were kissing. She had never, ever felt like this before. Even as she saw his lips moving closer, her body seemed to shiver into life as if all her skin had been scraped raw. She was trembling, the touch of his hands throbbing through her, leaving her helpless, only able to surrender to sensation, the hard press of his lips and body against hers as their touching became more intimate. What had come over Edwin? was all she could think. Over herself, for that matter! The feelings became mingled gradually with a sound, a siren, and as sleep slid away and she surfaced into the day, she realized it was the 'bull' from a nearby factory. Desolate, she tried to hold on to the images, the pleasure of it. But it was fading and he withdrew from her, leaving her bereft. As she glimpsed the face receding away in the dream, her heartbeat quickened even further with shock.

She sat up in bed hugging her knees, a burning blush spreading all over her.

'What on earth is the matter with me?' Imagine if anyone else could see inside her head!

As he withdrew, she had seen a tough, dark-eyed face, black curls. Not Edwin at all! She had been making love with Daniel Fernandez.

The dream was so vivid it was hard to shake off. Glimpses of it kept coming back to her through the day, disturbingly real. It happened in the middle of a

100

spelling test. The children were bent over their books, Ron Parks with his tongue stuck out in concentration as usual. Gwen looked at Lucy Fernandez, her neat, intelligent demeanour. Her spellings were almost always all right.

'The next word is "ashamed",' she instructed them. 'That can be a tricky one.'

Lucy's dark hair made her think immediately of her brother and again a hot flush went through her. *For heaven's sake*! her thoughts protested. *This is awful!* There must be something wrong with her, having these depraved thoughts about a man she had only met once in her life.

Dinner time was dismal now, without Millie. She had left because she felt so unwell, and she also knew that it would not be long before her pregnancy began to show and she didn't want to have to face the disgrace. But with no Millie to grumble to and share her lunch with, the staffroom felt a lonely place. Mr Gaffney was always kind and would stop for a little chat, and some of the others were reasonably friendly. But today it was Lily Drysdale who came and sat beside her, a worried expression on her face.

'Hello, dear . . .' Lily paused, frowning, stirring her tea. What was she wearing? Gwen thought, trying not to smile. She looked quite unlike everyone else, who seemed to wear the drabbest possible clothes to school. Lily had on a neat frock which gently swathed her rounded body, but it had unusually wide sleeves, and it was a rich blood red with purple binding round the neck and sleeves and a purple belt at the waist. Gwen was about to mention that she liked the colour but Lily plunged straight in.

'I'm very worried – about one of your boys.'

101

'My form?'

Lily nodded, swallowing a mouthful of tea. One of the particular things about Lily Drysdale was that, although she was in charge of Form Two, she seemed to know every child in the school and take an interest in them. She also seemed to find out things about them that Gwen had no idea of.

'Joseph Phillips,' Lily said. 'Has he come to school today? I haven't seen him.'

'Yes – he was here when I took the morning register. It's the afternoons when he often seems to disappear. The School Board man has been round but . . .'

Lily was shaking her head. As she held her cup Gwen saw that her fingernails were all blue underneath today. 'There's something wrong there. Have you seen the state of the child? And his sister – Lena. She's in my form, of course. The girl doesn't look as if her hair's been touched for weeks. She's filthy and I don't like the sound of that cough. She's in a bad state. And the boy – they look half starved.'

'Oh dear,' Gwen said helplessly. She felt put to shame by Lily's vigilance. Now she mentioned it, Lena Phillips did look ill, poor little waif. And Joey's attendance had been patchy. There had been several days before the half-term break when he had not come in at all. He always looked thin and pale. 'I feel a bit unsure how to judge what's normal,' she said.

'A child who looks as if they're wasting away is something to be looked into in my book.' Lily spoke robustly and Gwen felt even more foolish.

'See if Joseph comes in this afternoon. If not, tell me. I think I'll pay the Phillipses a visit.'

*

102

Joey was absent when Gwen took the second register.

She felt uneasy as she took the afternoon classes, and when they broke for a cup of tea at three o'clock she told Lily Drysdale that Joey had disappeared again.

'Lena's still here,' Lily said. 'I'll take her home at the end of the day and see if I can find out what the situation is. They live on one of the yards at the far end of the street.' She looked very directly at Gwen. 'My dear, you may not appreciate quite what a struggle life is for some people in this area. Perhaps you should come with me.'

Gwen thought of Daniel Fernandez's challenging eyes. *Perhaps it's time you did ...* he had said. *You don't know anything about life*, the words implied. And it was true. What did she know about the way people really lived around here? She felt put on her mettle.

'I'd be glad to,' she told Lily.

An hour later Form Four put away their drawings of Roman soldiers and hurried out of the classroom. Only two children remained: Lucy Fernandez always waited until last so as not to get pushed over in the rush, and with her was Alice Wilson. Lily had told Gwen she would meet her by the gate. Gwen was nervous. She put her coat on, glad of the two girls' presence to distract her. They all walked out at Lucy's slow dot-and-carry-one pace.

'Are you feeling all right today, Lucy?'

'Yes, Miss.' Lucy glanced up at her with a shy smile.

Outside it was bitterly cold, the sky an iron grey. Gwen saw that there was no sign of Lily at the gate and she stopped the children just outside the door. 'Alice? You did give my note to your mother, didn't you?'

'Yes, Miss Purdy,' she whispered.

As well as informing Mrs Wilson that Alice had nits, Gwen's note told her that her daughter was evidently very short-sighted and needed to have her eyes tested.

'And what did she say?' Gwen asked gently.

Alice's face seemed to close over. 'She did my hair. I don't think I've got nits any more.'

'Well, that's very good.' Gwen smiled. 'And what about your eyes?'

Alice's gaze dropped to the ground again.

Gwen was puzzled. Alice was a clean, well-dressed child. She looked as if she came from the sort of home where she was being well looked after.

'Alice?' she prompted.

'I don't know, Miss.'

'Well, you ask your mother to go to the doctor and get your eyes tested. Once you've got some specs you'll be able to see the blackboard – you'll be amazed how different life will be!'

Though Alice tried to hide it, her eyes filled with tears.

'Has no one suggested you see about your eyes before?'

'No, Miss.'

Lucy Fernandez stood beside Alice, watching with sympathetic eyes. Gwen felt perturbed and wondered if Lucy knew what was behind the sense of melancholy that seemed to come from Alice. *It's not my job to get involved, I'm only their teacher!* she told herself. But somehow she couldn't help feeling for them.

They had walked across the playground to the gate and were saying a shy goodbye.

'Miss Purdy! Good afternoon.'

The voice was unmistakable: Daniel Fernandez.

He came to the school gate, limping on his crutch, his leg still in plaster. Once again his expression was amiable but with the smile she could sense challenge, something close to mockery. Was it because she was fair-haired and blue-eyed, Gwen thought irritably to herself. Everyone seemed to assume she had no sense and couldn't think seriously about anything!

'Oh! Good afternoon.' Gwen hoped her voice sounded calmer than she was feeling. Her heart was beating ridiculously hard. This was awful! How could someone she had had such a dream about just appear like this, as if she had summoned him?

'I see your leg isn't better yet.'

'Oh, I wouldn't say that.' His tone was calm, relaxed. 'I'm not quite so lame. It'll be back to normal soon.' Lucy stood looking adoringly up at him, very proud that her big brother had come to walk her home. 'All set, Lucy *fach*?'

She nodded and smiled, and once again Gwen saw how pretty she looked when she was happy. But Gwen's eyes were drawn quickly back to Daniel Fernandez. In the daylight he looked younger. He was bareheaded, dark curls falling over his forehead, and dressed in working clothes, old black trousers and waistcoat, the sleeves of his shirt rolled to the elbow to show his swarthy arms. How could he go out in this cold dressed like that?

'Are you getting on all right here then? Hammering some learning into them, are you?'

'Yes, I'm doing my best, thank you.'

Again, to her own ears she sounded prim. And she was amazed that she sounded so calm when she felt such confusion. She tried to detect the mocking tone that he had used to her before. There was a twinkle in his eye and she struggled to work out if he was teasing her or whether he was simply being friendly. It was hard to tell and this was discomforting.

'How are your family?' she asked.

'Well enough,' Daniel said. 'Yes, they're all right. Best get you home, Lucy, eh?'

As he spoke, Lily Drysdale appeared, moving across the playground with Lena Phillips at her side, and Gwen saw Daniel glance at them. It would have been hard not to notice Lily. Over the dress and flat brown shoes she had put on a worn-looking pigeon-grey cape with a ring of white fur round the hem. She was scurrying along with a basket over one arm.

'Are you ready, Miss Purdy?' she called.

Gwen said she was, then saw Daniel's look of enquiry.

'Miss Drysdale is worried about one of the children,' she told him. 'We're going to see the family – to find out if everything is all right.'

'Very good of you,' Daniel said. Both his tone and look were steady, but she felt very aware of being appraised, that he was still trying to form an opinion about her. Her skin prickled. Why should she care what he thought? Yet she did – she desperately wanted him to think well of her.

Lena Phillips's hair was a matted mess. She was coughing and looked feverish. Gwen saw Daniel watching the girl. Something flickered in his eyes, an emotion she could not read. Then he looked back at Gwen.

'Well, we'll be going. Come on, Lucy. Bye, now.'

'Goodbye,' Gwen said.

For a moment she watched the three of them go off along Canal Street, Alice Wilson walking alongside the brother and sister, both of whom were limping.

Ten

'Not far,' Lily Drysdale said, turning off to the left. 'Just along here.'

Gwen pulled up her coat collar against the wind, which suddenly felt very cold. She realized that she had not even been aware of it while she was talking to Daniel Fernandez.

The little girl, Lena, looked very intimidated at having to walk along her street between two teachers.

'It's all right, dear,' Miss Drysdale told her. 'We're just coming to see your mother. You're not in trouble. Is your mother poorly?'

Lena nodded, wide-eyed. She coughed. Gwen thought the child looked most unwell. She noticed that Lily Drysdale did not bring up the subject of Joey Phillips's absence.

Outside the grimy frontage of the Golden Crown, Lily tutted. Her shoelace had come undone. 'Hold this a moment will you, please?'

She handed Gwen the basket. There was a cloth over it so Gwen could not see what was inside, but it was surprisingly heavy. Lily had been carrying it apparently as effortlessly as if it contained feathers.

'Let me take it,' she offered, when Lily straightened up. 'It's quite a weight.'

'Just a few groceries,' Lily said. 'But thank you. Now, Lena – court five did you say?'

Ahead of them they could see the dark, high prison wall, and the bridge over the canal at the bend in the road. But Lena was leading them into an entry at one end of a row of houses. Gwen had passed the rundown back-to-back houses every day on her way to the tram stop and barely given them a glance. Now she found herself in a dark alley, which looked as if it never saw sunlight. The walls were black and slimy looking. Following Lena and Lily Drysdale, she saw that the alley opened up into a long yard, with houses along the right-hand side. Never had she seen a more dismal place. The yard was dark, filthy underfoot and the only things to be seen were a lamp, unlit as yet, in the middle and two lines of washing strung across from wall to wall. Some boys were in the gloom at the far end, kicking something between them which looked like a soggy ball of newspaper. Seeing strangers, they stopped and stared.

Lena led the two teachers along to her house and went inside. Lily Drysdale paused on the threshold, listening, then she knocked. Even a gentle knock made the door look as if it might collapse inwards off its hinges. Gwen was full of misgivings. Fancy having to live in this horrifying place! This house was the worst one of the lot. At least the others had curtains, but the windows of this one were bare and it was in a terrible state of repair, with one window broken and the other filthy, its walls caked in soot. And how small the rooms must be. She looked along the yard and realized that someone in the next-door house was watching. A round moon-face was looking out at them.

'Hello – is there anyone there?' Lily called. There was no reply.

Lena came back to the door and beckoned them in. Her eyes were wide and troubled.

It was dark inside. Daylight could get in only through the top part of the window and there was no other light. Otherwise, the first thing Gwen noticed was the smell. She did not know enough about life to recognize the stench of human sickness and of imminent death, but the room made her feel instinctively full of dread. As her eyes grew used to the gloom, she took in the spartan poverty, the empty grate, the broken floorboards. For a moment Gwen thought the bed, to their left, was unoccupied, that the pathetic shape lying there was simply a twist of bedding. It took seconds for her to realize that it was the figure of a woman.

'Oh, my dear!' Lily immediately moved closer and leant over the silent form. As Gwen followed and took in what was before her, her heart began to pound with shock and pity. The woman on the bed – and she was identifiable as a woman only because of her long hair – was a living skeleton. Her features were pinched and hollow and, even in this light, could be seen to have a sickly yellow tinge. But where the thin blanket covered her body, her stomach was a disturbing mound. Gwen put her hand to her heart. She was beginning to feel sick and faint. Surely the woman could not still be alive!

But the next shock was the sound of her quick, shallow breathing. Lily Drysdale searched under the cover for the woman's hand. Gwen had never seen such emaciation. Lily felt for a pulse and there were seconds as they all stood, waiting. The woman did not move or open her eyes. Lily shook her head.

'Lord above,' she whispered, 'the poor young thing. She's not long for this world.'

Only then did it occur to Gwen that the woman wasn't old. 'Shouldn't she be in hospital?' she said, trying to compose herself, not to show how deeply she was affected by the sight.

'Too late for that,' Lily said. Carefully she laid Mrs Phillips's hand back at her side and turned to the little girl, who sat shivering behind them.

'Lena – where's your brother?'

'He'll've gone to get coal,' she said. Her cheeks were flushed with fever. 'From down the wharf. Before he goes out to get us some dinner.'

Gwen and Lily Drysdale exchanged glances.

'Where does he go for your dinner?' Lily asked.

Lena looked vague. 'I dunno. He goes out to get firewood and that. Tells me to stay here with our mom. And then he comes back with summat to eat. Most nights he does.'

'Is that what Joey does in the afternoons?' Gwen asked. Her heart was wrung with pity. The solemn nod Lena gave brought tears to Gwen's eyes.

'Mom can't get us our dinner no more,' the young girl said.

There was a tap on the door then and a voice said, 'Dora? Can I come in?'

A very fat woman appeared, dressed all in black, with loose tresses of greasy brown hair. Gwen was sure hers had been the face peering at them through the window from next door. Just walking a few steps here seemed to have exhausted her and she was wheezing and struggling for breath.

'I know she can't answer me, like,' she panted, 'but

I don't like to come in without asking. Are you from the Welfare?'

'No.' Lily spoke with a gentle courtesy which impressed Gwen. 'Miss Purdy and I are from the school. We've been concerned about Joseph and Lena.'

'Well, it's terrible. I'm Mrs Simmons and I live next door. I do what I can but no one else on the yard'll raise a finger and I can only do so much. She's sinking fast.'

'Has she seen a doctor?' Gwen asked.

'Oh ar – the doctor. Oh yes. But it's the consumption . . . Galloping, it is. Ain't got nothing they can do for her . . . and she daint want no one taking her away. She weren't even this bad yesterday. Still got the two here, of course . . . I mean the orphanage had the others.' Mrs Simmons sank down on another of the decrepit chairs. Gwen watched, expecting it to give way under the weight. The woman was forced to pause between each phrase of her speech. 'I said to her . . . don't do it, Dora, not to your own flesh and blood . . . but what can you do? . . . I've seven of my own, so I bring her a bowl of summat . . . when I can, but my old man's been laid off, and now . . . by the look of her she's past it, bless her . . . And a babby coming . . . Six month gone 'er is.'

'What about Mr Phillips?' Lily asked.

'Oh, he upped and left – Christmastime . . . Never seen a hair of him since. Couldn't cope with her no more, he said . . . Had a basinful with her . . . She weren't much of a wife to him, it's true. Not much of a man though, neither, Wally weren't, in my opinion.'

As she was speaking, there came the sound of boots hurrying along the yard. They all became aware that a

111

small figure was standing listening at the door, holding a newspaper pressed to his chest.

'Joey.' Gwen moved closer, moved by the sight of his tense little figure. Joey's face was furrowed by a deep scowl at Mrs Simmons's words, but he didn't say anything. He looked unnerved at seeing two teachers in the house, and stood poised to run away again. 'It's all right. We were worried about you – Miss Drysdale and myself. We've come to help you and your mother.'

'Let me know if I can do anything,' Mrs Simmons said, getting up and lumbering to the door. She was evidently relieved that someone else had come to take over.

Joey came in warily. Gwen saw that his pockets were bulging and he went to the hearth and turned them out, depositing coal in a pile and getting ready to light the fire.

'Joseph, could you please show me where the gas meter is?' Lily asked. 'I can get the gas on again and make you all something to eat.'

He did as he was bidden, and when Lily had fed the meter she said to Gwen, 'Come along – I've some soup in the basket, and bacon. Let's get these children fed.'

As Gwen carried the basket to the tiny scullery, Lena looked up at her with feverish eyes.

'Will you give our mom some soup? Joey says if she has some hot food she'll get better.'

A lump came up in Gwen's throat. The poor woman on the bed was a death's head with barely any breath left in her body. Soon she wouldn't be anyone's mother any more.

'We'll see if she wants any,' she said to Lena. 'And

112

we'll get you lying down. You look a very poorly little girl to me.'

'And you've been a really good boy,' Lily said to Joey. 'You've done everything you could for your mother.'

Gwen watched him for some kind of reaction, of softness even, but Lily Drysdale might as well have been speaking to a block of wood. With his head bent over the grate, he was working desperately to kindle some smoky life into the fire.

Chicken soup bubbled gently in a pan. Gwen stood stirring it by the light of a candle and the kettle was heating up gently over the other flame on the stove. She couldn't get over the bleakness of the house. Half the ceiling in this grim little scullery was bulging with damp and within the small space were the little gas stove, an old stone sink with a pail underneath to catch the slops and a rickety shelf on which stood Dora Phillips's few humble cooking implements. Apart from the remains of a packet of tea, there seemed to be no food in the house.

Lily had packed into her basket two tins of soup, a loaf of bread and pat of butter, bacon, tea and a tin of condensed milk, a packet of porridge oats and half a dozen eggs. She had also included two gas mantles, a box of matches and a bar of coal-tar soap.

'I popped out during the dinner hour,' she told Gwen. 'I had a feeling they'd come in handy.' Gwen didn't have to ask whether she had spent her own money on the food.

Every so often Gwen heard Lena coughing. She looked out into the room. One of the gas lights was

113

going and Joey had built a fire. He and Lena were sitting close to it, staring at the flames. Lena was slumped against her brother, hugging herself, and Gwen was surprised to see that Joey let her lean against him like that. Every so often he looked longingly at the stove towards the smells coming from it. Gwen could see he was ravenous. He reminded her of a hungry little wolf cub. In all those absences from school he had been struggling to be grown up and look after his mother, yet now he didn't seem to want to look at her or sit near her. He seemed unaware that he would shortly lose her for ever.

'Won't be a minute now.' She smiled at him, but Joey merely gave her a blank, almost hostile look and turned back to stare into the fire.

There was only one bowl in the scullery. Gwen poured some of the soup into it and the rest she shared between two cups and a jam jar. She cut good thick slices of bread and set the children to eat at the table. Lily was sitting on the edge of Dora Phillips's bed, trying with a cup and a teaspoon to encourage the woman to drink. She tilted the spoon to Dora's thin lips, saying, 'Come on now, dear, just a sip.' But they saw the water trickle from her insensible mouth. Lily turned and shook her head sadly.

'She won't last the night, I don't think,' she whispered, eyeing the children.

'What shall we do? Lena's not right either.'

'I know. We can't leave them. I'll stay here the night. I don't think the end can be far off, looking at her now. But if you need to go, dear, I'm sure I can manage.'

Gwen thought about Ariadne and Harold Purvis sitting over the latest sample of Ariadne's cooking and speculating about why she was missing. She had no

114

way of letting them know, but how could she leave? She felt somehow bound to Joey Phillips, awed and moved by what he had already endured.

'I'll stay,' she told Lily Drysdale. 'Of course I will.'

'That's very good of you, dear.'

'Not at all. Shall I cook up some of that bacon?'

'Oh yes – that's why I brought it,' Lily said and moved over to sit at the table with the children, sipping carefully at her soup. The bacon was soon ready and Gwen cut more bread and butter to go with it. Joey ate ravenously, though Lena only managed a little of the soup.

'Now,' Lily said, 'when we've eaten our tea, how would you two like a nice scrub in the bath?'

Lena's eyelids looked heavy, as if she was ready to fade out, but she beamed with delight. Joey nodded grudgingly.

'And Miss Purdy and I will give your clothes a wash and put them by the fire to dry. Miss Purdy, let's get some water on the boil now, so it's ready.'

Gwen went out to the tap in the yard and filled the kettle and a pan. The lamp was lit now and she could hear voices from the other houses along the yard. It was a cold night and all the doors were closed. Inside, she settled the pans on the gas and wondered how the fire was doing for drying clothes. When she went to look, she saw that Joey had accumulated quite a little pile of coal.

'Where d'you get all that from?' she asked, joining them at the table again.

He gave a backward jerk of his head. 'Over the wharf.'

'There's a coal wharf just behind here,' Lily said. 'Lumps of it lying about for anyone who'll take the

115

trouble to fetch it – and get away with it. This young man is obviously an expert.'

Once the food was finished Lily went out into the yard and came back dragging a tin bath. She set it by the fire and they poured hot and cold water into it, refilling the kettle to heat up again. Gwen found tears in her eyes at the sight of the children's bony little bodies. Their skin had an unhealthy greyish tinge and they were dotted with bites. Joey's head looked too big for his body and the bones stuck out down his back, pathetically incongruous when set against his tough, manly way of carrying himself. He was a beautiful child, Gwen observed, as Lily set about him with the coal-tar soap, with those big eyes, strong brows and prominent cheekbones. But what sadness he had in him! She wanted to wrap him in something soft and warm, take him to her and cuddle him, but she knew he wouldn't let her. They dried the children on the cloth with which Lily had covered the food, then Gwen put all their clothes in the bath water and scrubbed and pounded at them.

By this time Lena was almost unable to keep her eyes open.

'She's running a high temperature I'd say.' Lily laid her hand on the child's forehead. 'Poor little lamb. We must get her into bed.'

Gwen had her first sight of the upstairs floor. Lily went ahead with a candle, led by Joey, who was wrapped in her coat, and Gwen carried Lena, swathed in hers.

'Watch it,' Joey said when they neared the top of the twisting staircase. To her horror Gwen saw that the third tread down was missing altogether. How easy it would be for a small child to fall right through, she thought.

116

There were two rooms upstairs and Joey led them into the back one, a small space in which there were two single iron bedsteads each pushed to a wall. There was nothing else. The candle threw their shadows huge on the bare walls. Joey climbed onto one bed and pulled the cover over him. Gwen went to lay Lena down on the other.

'No!' Joey's head shot up. He was all scowls again. 'That ent her bed, it's Polly and Kev's! Lena sleeps here with me.'

Gwen put the little girl down at the other end from her brother. This was what they were used to, of course, and they would help keep each other warm. She and Lily left their coats on the bed for extra warmth.

'Goodnight, dears,' Lily said, face shadowy in the candlelight.

'Goodnight, Joey,' Gwen said tenderly. She knew Lena couldn't hear her. She was already asleep.

Joey didn't reply.

Eleven

Downstairs, Gwen and Lily cleared away the bath, bailing out panfuls of water until it was light enough to carry outside to the drain. The exertion kept them warm, but freezing air poured into the house as they went in and out and they were thankful to come in finally and close the door. Steam rose from the children's clothes. Gwen put the last of Joey's coal on the fire. As soon as it died the room was going to be very cold.

They moved quietly, respectfully tidying the room, always conscious of the sick woman on the bed close by. Every so often they went to check on her, holding their breath until they were certain that hers was still fluttering in and out of her lungs. She was very quiet, as if she had already surrendered.

'It's terrible,' Gwen said, as the two of them stood looking down at her shrunken face. The woman's swollen stomach looked terrible against her body. Gwen was deeply shocked by all she had seen. She had had no idea that people had to live like this! The evening had opened up a world of poverty and suffering that she had never known to exist.

'What a terrible, terrible life. And those poor children!'

'I only wish I'd cottoned on sooner,' Lily Drysdale said. Her pale eyes were full of pity as she stared down at the dying woman. 'Poor thing. All we can do now is try and keep her comfortable until her end comes.'

'It's so cold.' Gwen shivered. Their coats were upstairs keeping the children warm.

'Yes.' Lily looked round the room. 'It's no good. We've got to keep the fire going somehow. Look – this is fit for nothing. We'll burn it.' She was sizing up the most decrepit of the wooden chairs. The back was already coming loose from the seat. 'They won't be needing it for much longer. Poor little mites'll be off to the orphanage by the sound of it. There's no family around them.'

Between them they dismantled the chair and fed the fire. The dry, worm-ridden wood burned well. They sat and drank a cup of tea and after a time, Gwen, rather embarrassed, had to ask, 'Er, Miss Drysdale – where do we go to spend a penny here?'

'Oh, you have to go along the yard.' Lily got up stiffly. 'There'll be a key.' Sure enough, on the mantelpiece there was a key attached to a cotton reel. 'You'll have to take a candle, dear.'

Gwen stepped outside, a stub of candle burning on a saucer. It was bitter. The wind had dropped and the night felt still and deadly cold. The dim light from the lamp barely reached the end of the yard, where there were a couple of dustbins and then the toilets. The stench from each mingled together. There were three cubicles and from the middle one, she could hear someone urinating vigorously and a man humming to himself. She was unlocking the one next to it when the middle toilet door opened and he lurched out and started at the sight of her.

'Christ alive – you made me jump!' he said cheerfully and made off whistling along the yard.

Gwen stepped cautiously inside. Her shadow squirmed ominously on the rough brick walls. A few squares of newspaper hung from a nail. Closing the door, the full impact of the smell hit her. She grimaced and breathed as shallowly as she could, trying to keep the stench at bay. She put the candle down on the floor and, as she straightened up, saw something horrifying moving along the wall above her head. A gigantic spider! She gasped, feeling her skin all come up in goose pimples, before realizing it was really quite a small spider, its shadow stretched monstrously by the candlelight. Giggles of tension rose in her. Standing over the toilet she realized it wasn't a flush toilet at all, but a dry pan, everything dropping down into a hole beneath. She shuddered at the thought of it. What would her mother say? This thought tickled her even more, her nervousness came close to hysteria and she burst into unstoppable fits of giggles. She was in such a hurry to get out of there, fumbling at her clothes and almost knocking over the candle as she tried to push the door open. Fresh air at last!

A hard-faced woman was standing outside, an oil lamp in her hand.

'Something amusing is there?' she asked snootily.

Gwen sobered up as she went back across the yard. What was the matter with her? Joey and Lena's mother was dying and here she was tittering like a nine-year-old. Her spirits sank and she felt almost tearful. It was only then she realized how tired and overwrought she was.

'Let's have a cup of tea,' Lily said. 'We'll need to keep going somehow. I think we could take it in turns to have a doze, though. After all, we've both got to stand in front of our classes tomorrow.'

120

'All right,' Gwen agreed, though the thought depressed her even more. She didn't want to sit up alone in the small hours of the night with a dying woman. The thought frightened her, and she craved company and conversation, had hoped to spend more time getting to know her fellow teacher. Lily had volunteered a few pieces of information about herself. She had never trained as a teacher but just 'picked it up', starting, aged fifteen, in the school she had attended in Minworth.

Gwen went out to the icy yard again to fill the kettle, and when the tea was ready they both sat close to the fire.

'Goodness me, what a cold house,' Lily Drysdale said.

'No wonder the poor woman's so ill,' Gwen agreed. 'I don't know how they've survived at all.'

Lily put her head on one side. 'Are you all right, dear? A shock, all this, isn't it?'

'It is rather.' Gwen sipped her tea, glad it was sweet and warm. 'Those poor children. There's something about Joey, isn't there?'

'Pathetic. And rather striking somehow, I agree.'

Lily asked Gwen a few questions about herself, and her family, things they hadn't had time to talk about in the staffroom. Gwen wasn't sure whether to ask questions back. It seemed nosy. But Lily was happy to talk. She told Gwen that she spent all her spare time painting.

'I've a little studio in the attic, you see. We go on trips every summer – somewhere glorious like Assisi or the south of France and I paint there and store up all the images in my mind for the winter. Not the most accurate method of reproduction, but it's my way.'

121

'How lovely,' Gwen said. It explained why Lily's nails were so often stained with colour. She wondered if the 'we' who went on these journeys was the lover Millie had talked about. Or had Millie been spinning fantasies and Lily really lived with a spinster sister?

'Do you have any artistic interests?' Lily was asking.

'Er – no, not really.' She wondered what her interests were, apart from daydreaming about aeroplanes and other means of escape. As hobbies went, this felt a little inadequate.

'Never mind – there's time yet,' Lily was saying. 'I suddenly discovered painting when I was nearly thirty. It's been a great pleasure.'

Later, once they had finished their tea, Lily told Gwen to sleep first, in the old horsehair chair by the fire.

'I'll keep an eye on Mrs Phillips for now.'

Gwen watched as Lily settled herself on one of the remaining two wooden chairs by the bed. Her rounded presence was comforting. Gwen was quite keyed up and she thought she would not sleep, but after a time staring into the red glow, she felt drowsy and dozed off, head resting on the arm of the chair. It felt quite a while later when a hand shook her shoulder.

'Miss Purdy? I think I should like a rest now.'

Gwen was immediately wide awake, heart pounding. 'How is she?'

'No change I think, dear. It could just go on like that, but if anything happens come and wake me.'

Gwen sat on the chair by the bed with her arms folded, shivering. What time was it? There was no clock in the room. The still watches of the night, she thought, glad of the one gas mantle still alight. It was so cold. She eyed up the other chair. That would have to be turned into firewood soon.

Dora Phillips's face seemed to Gwen to be even more sunken than when they had first arrived, as if she was being pulled down towards the earth. Gwen tried to imagine her looking young and well, or to make out some resemblance between her features and those of her children, but found it impossible. The woman's face was too ravaged. She wondered what her life had been, but only knew that it had been so different from her own as to make it impossible to guess.

In the stillness, and the dim light, it was hard not to imagine things. For a second she thought she saw the woman's eyes flicker open and she jumped violently, her heart racing. But there was nothing. How would Dora look if she opened her eyes? What would she say if she could speak? She seemed scarcely human now and Gwen found her frightening. She felt ashamed. What was there to be afraid of in this pitiful wreck of a person? She leaned towards her, wanting to make some contact with her.

'I hope you rest in peace,' she found herself whispering. 'After all you've suffered.' She almost hoped there would be a reply, but there was nothing and she sat back again.

The night seemed endless. After a time Gwen's eyelids grew heavy and she was fighting sleep. She could not tell whether a minute or half an hour had gone by. Lily Drysdale was breathing heavily across the room. Gwen clenched her hands in her lap, feeling the soft wool of her skirt. She was really beginning to shiver. It was too cold to fall asleep: she ought to get up, make tea and see to the fire.

Some sounds broke the quiet. Gwen jumped and held her breath. A wheeze followed by a tiny grating noise which it took her a couple of seconds to understand was coming from Dora Phillips's throat. Her body lifted slightly from the bed, went rigid for a moment, then fell back. The sound stopped. The silence grew deeper, became an absence. Gwen leapt up and pulled the cover back, reaching for Dora's hand. It was ice cold. She could not find a pulse. Leaning down she listened to hear her breathe, felt for her heartbeat.

'Miss Drysdale!' She ran to her fellow teacher, but didn't like to shake her awake. 'You'd better come! I think she's ... I think she's gone.'

Lily got to her feet immediately, seeing Gwen's stricken face. Going to Dora Phillips, she repeated Gwen's search for a pulse, then looked round, shaking her head. 'Bless her. She's not with us any more.'

She was pulling the blanket up to cover Dora's face, when they became aware of soft footsteps padding down the dark stairs. Joey, his face heavy with sleep, stopped halfway down. Wrapped in Lily's grey cloak, he looked like something out of a pantomime. He stood staring at them and for a moment Gwen wondered if he was sleepwalking. But then, she made out his alert dark eyes. He knew, Gwen saw immediately. What instinct had roused the little boy from his bed at that moment?

His eyes met hers. 'Come down here, Joey,' she said softly.

Slowly, he climbed down, placing one foot then the other on each step before he moved onto the next in a way that twisted Gwen's emotions. It was the first truly childlike characteristic she had ever seen in him. He climbed down until he was standing in front of her,

124

his eyes fixed on the bed across the room, where Lily was still standing over Dora.

'Mom?'

'Joey dear.' Gwen knelt down in front of him. 'Your mummy's not here any more. She's gone to heaven.'

He didn't move, barely blinked, but nor did he resist as she reached out and gently took his thin body in her arms. For just a second, as she held him, she felt him rest his head on her shoulder.

The children sat by the hearth, mute, staring into the fire. They were dressed in their dry clothes, but Gwen had had to dress Lena, who was barely well enough to move. She sat propped against the wall, seemingly unaware of what was going on around her. They had told her gently that her mother was dead, but it seemed unlikely that she could take it in. There was a busyness in the house of people coming and going.

Once dawn had broken, Lily went next door to fetch Mrs Simmons. Gwen had not formed a very good impression of the next-door neighbour, who seemed to her of low intelligence and anxious to pass responsibility for Dora Phillips on to anyone else who appeared. But she had to rethink her opinion. For a start it became clear that none of the other neighbours was prepared to lift a finger, even though the news spread fast and a cluster of women stood in the yard staring at the house. Among them, Gwen recognized the hard-faced woman whom she'd met outside the toilets. But Mrs Simmons waddled round with a pail of coal for the fire and sent one of her daughters to summon the doctor and the midwife, a woman who also laid out the dead for a small fee.

'The poor thing. She looks peaceful now, don't she?'

Standing behind her, as she looked down at Dora Phillips's waxen face, Gwen could hear the heave of Mrs Simmons's lungs. She stank of grease and sweat. 'She weren't no saint, that's for sure – but she were all right if you took your time and got to know 'er . . . She had a good heart – always stood by her kids. She'd've done anything for 'em . . . There's always them that'll judge.'

Gwen wondered what Dora had done to make the neighbours hostile, but she didn't like to ask.

'Would you like a cup of tea?' she offered.

'Yes, ta.' Mrs Simmons nodded and sank onto the one remaining upright chair, which squeaked in protest.

Lily looked quite fresh and composed, considering the night they'd had. Gwen felt exhausted and overwrought.

'The children,' Lily Drysdale said gently. It seemed awful to discuss them with them sitting there, but what choice did they have? 'What's going to happen to them?'

Mrs Simmons considered for a moment. 'Well, there's no family. *He* –' she gave a jerk of her head – 'hopped it a few months back. No sign of him since. They'll have to go with the others – no two ways about it.' She lowered her voice for a moment to a whisper. '*Barnardo's* – they came and took the two little 'uns, couple of months ago. But for the moment –' she shifted on her seat, her huge belly shuddering as if with a life of its own under her voluminous black skirt – 'they'll have to come and stop with us.'

'Well, isn't that kind – how good of you!' Lily cried. 'You've been a good neighbour to her, I can see that.'

'Someone had to be,' Mrs Simmons said. 'Anyroad – it'll likely only be for a day or two.'

Gwen, standing beside Mrs Simmons, looked across at Joey and Lena. They sat by the fire, not moving, as if they had been turned to stone.

Twelve

'Get your books out, children – this morning we're going to learn something about the roads the Romans built here in Britain.'

Gwen forced herself to concentrate. Everything felt wrong today. She had had one night's sleep to recover since the night up with Dora Phillips, but she was still tired. And Millie had gone and Joey Phillips wasn't here either. The sight of his empty place in the classroom whenever she looked up made her feel desolate. Of course it had often been empty before, but having seen the heroic struggle which explained his school absences, the little boy had touched her heart. The thought of him and his little sister being sent off to an orphanage was terrible. But what else could be done?

The day before, once the doctor had issued a death certificate, Mrs Simmons waited while the midwife laid out Dora's body, then took Joey and Lena home with her. Gwen and Lily Drysdale hurried back to school to begin another day's work.

'I could do with a nice hot bath,' Gwen had groaned as they went out into Canal Street and the cold morning. She was so bleary from lack of sleep that she almost walked into the path of a dray from Davenport's brewery.

Lily seemed quite unperturbed. 'We just need to get

ourselves going and keep busy,' she said cheerfully. 'The day'll soon go by.'

Gwen never understood how, since she never said a word about it, but by the end of the day the entire school seemed to know that Miss Purdy and Miss Drysdale had spent the night with Joey and Lena Phillips and their dying mother. She heard some of her class talking about it in the playground, looking at her and murmuring to each other. Ron Parks came up to her at dinner time.

'Is Joey coming back to school, Miss Purdy?'

'I don't know, Ron.' Gwen felt glad he'd asked. 'He doesn't have a mother or a father now, you see. So I'm not sure who's going to look after him.'

'Only, he was a pal. He was all right, Joey was.'

Gwen looked at Ron's simple, cheerful face. 'Yes, he was. He *is*. It's just that I don't know where he'll be living, so he may not be able to come to this school.'

The whole day she had been affected by melancholy, and a strange feeling that life could now never be the same. When she had arrived back at Ariadne Black's house she had been so weary and downcast that she had forgotten completely that Ariadne did not know where she had been for the past twenty-four hours. Ariadne, clad in a shimmering, pale green dress, opened the door and, seeing Gwen, gasped theatrically.

'Oh! Miss *Purdy*! How could you do this to me? I've been on the point of going to the police. All night! All day! Waiting here in uncertainty! I've been through everything in my mind – right down to the white slave trade. I said to Mr Purvis – will we ever see her again, d'you think? Oh, we passed a terrible evening. And did I sleep a wink? I can assure you I didn't! Where have you *been*?'

To Gwen's surprise, mixed in with the dramatics, she detected genuine pleasure to see her back.

'I'm so sorry, Mrs Black . . .'

'Ariadne, *please* . . . I must put the kettle on . . . Oh, I'm ever so relieved, you've no idea . . . I don't like my lodgers to go missing . . .'

She listened, one hand clasped over her heart as Gwen explained.

'The poor little mites. To an *orphanage*. What a wicked world we live in! Of course, George and I were never fortunate enough to produce children so I can't speak with the feelings of a mother. But to see a child deserted in the world with nowhere to call home – it's wicked, that's what it is. I'm sure Mr Purvis would think it was terrible. He's a very sensitive man, Harold is.'

'May I have a bath tonight do you think?' Gwen asked while the going was good.

'Oh, *yes*. I'm sure we could move you forward a day, dear. I'll strike you off for Friday.'

Over the evening meal, for which Ariadne had done something unique with a fillet of hake, she insisted that Gwen tell them all about the adventures of the night. Harold Purvis ate his meal in silence, listening. He gave off an odd, metallic smell. Every so often Gwen felt him giving her a sideways look. She tried these days to keep out of his way, but later, when she went out of her room to have a bath, she found him standing on the landing, blocking her way. She moved towards the bathroom, expecting him to stand back, but instead he waited. He was standing in the darkest place, away from the light.

'Could you let me through to the bathroom, please?' she said sharply.

Mr Purvis took a step towards her. He was in his shirtsleeves now and he smelled more strongly than ever.

'Who were you really with last night, eh?' She could see his face now, smiling strangely at her.

'What *are* you talking about?' She gripped her towel with a sense of panic. Something about Mr Purvis's manner made her feel deeply uneasy.

'You don't think I was taken in, do you? A young lady like you playing Florence Nightingale in some slum yard. Who were you really with?' He was standing even closer to her now. Gwen felt herself begin to tremble, but at the same time she became furiously angry.

'Get away from me!' she commanded. 'I don't know what you think you're doing, but you come any closer and I'll shout for Mrs Black.'

'Go on then – call her,' Harold Purvis mocked, but he did take a step back.

'Just keep away from me,' Gwen said, trying to maintain her dignity. She passed him to get to the bathroom and, as she did so, felt his hand squeeze her left buttock.

'How dare you!' she cried, but he was walking away, laughing. Gwen locked the bathroom door, shaking. What on earth was she going to do about him? Suppose he was waiting out there when she came out?

After all this, it was a struggle to keep her mind on Form Four and the Romans the next morning. She told them about the Fosse Way and Watling Street.

'The roads were built a little bit higher than the land around them so the water could drain off,' she said. 'And they built them in layers with materials they could get hold of nearby.' She drew a little diagram on the blackboard.

Mr Purvis had not been outside the bathroom. While she was soaking in the bath she could hear him playing his blasted trumpet. Marble halls again. The incident had really unsettled her, though she told herself not to be so stupid. In her bedroom she had sat looking at her picture of Amy for courage. Would Amy Johnson let a creep like Harold Purvis get under her skin? Of course not! If anything else happened she would tell Ariadne what was going on.

As the children copied her diagram of a Roman road, Gwen's eyes were drawn back to the the empty space left by Joey Phillips. Seeing where Joey lived, what he and his family had to endure, had come as a profound shock to her. She had had no idea that such extreme poverty existed and the fact shamed her. How comfortable and easy her life had been. What other children in her form might be suffering terrible things as well? There was Alice, still squinting, half blind with no glasses to help her. But the thought of Joey tore at her especially. She'd go back and see him, she decided. At the end of school.

I'll get some groceries on the way, she thought, putting her coat on, once the last lesson was over. And a few sweets for the children. She thought of Miss Drysdale's generosity the day before. She had told her that she was going to see the Phillips children.

'Well, that's very kind of you,' Lily said. 'I've got a couple of garments I can send along with you if you'd be so good. I suppose the two of them will be gone in a couple of days.'

It was a little milder outside today, threatening rain. The playground was full of children streaming towards the gate. Suddenly nervous, Gwen walked among them, trying to decide what to buy. There were only a couple of small shops in this street – she'd just have to see what they had.

'Afternoon, Miss Purdy.'

Daniel Fernandez was standing just outside the gate.

'Oh!' She had been completely preoccupied and she was startled by the way the sight of him set her heart thudding. Once more he was only in shirtsleeves, white cuffs rolled. Against them his forearms looked very dark. 'Good afternoon. Have you come to meet Lucy?'

'Yes – thought I'd come down as it's not so cold.'

She smiled, and for the first time saw him smile back. A genuine warmth lit his eyes. For a few seconds she held her breath, then remembered to release it again, aware that gaggles of children were coming out of the playground, all staring at them.

'Looks as if spring's on its way today.'

'Takes a while to feel it here.' Daniel shifted his weight, manoeuvring the crutch. 'In the Welsh valleys you can see the work of the seasons more directly.'

'Yes,' Gwen agreed. She felt suddenly more relaxed, that he was not testing her as he had been before. 'That's true where I grew up as well. There's so much smoke in the air here it's hard to pick up anything else.'

There was silence for a moment. Gwen realized she ought to move on, but found she didn't want to.

'Takes our Lucy a bit longer than the others,' Daniel said, looking into the playground.

'Yes, but she does very well. She's settled in now.'

'She likes you.'

This directness threw her off guard.

'Well.' She laughed. 'That's good – I suppose! She's a good girl.'

Daniel was looking at her searchingly, as if trying to work her out.

'I hear you stayed all night with that boy's mother. The one who died.'

'Gracious!' Gwen said. 'News travels fast around here, doesn't it? Who told you that?'

'Lucy. It was good of you.'

'Not really. I went with Miss Drysdale and there was really no choice. Those poor children had been struggling on for I hate to think how long, trying to look after her. It was consumption. And the house . . . honestly, I've never seen anything like it.' Her indignation grew as she spoke. 'The place is practically falling down with damp and neglect and there was no fire, no food. I don't know how she survived for as long as she did. She was expecting a child as well. It's awful – just *terrible*.'

She had not noticed the passion in her voice until she saw it register in Daniel's eyes and she blushed, feeling as if she had somehow given herself away.

Just then, though, Miss Monk stepped out through the gate and, seeing Gwen standing there with Daniel, gave her a poisonous, disapproving look as she passed.

'Looks as if you're in trouble with her!' Daniel said. 'Goodness, that was a killing look.'

'Yes,' Gwen stared after her. 'She's not the sweetest of women. I'm not sure what I've done to deserve that though.'

Daniel laughed then, deep and wholeheartedly, and she found herself laughing with him.

'Ah, here comes Lucy!' He leaned slightly to see through the gate and almost overbalanced.

'Careful!' Gwen reached out and caught his hand,

helping him to keep his balance. As he pulled against her she felt his immense strength.

'Thanks!' Daniel laughed at himself. 'I'll get this blasted thing off in a week or two.'

'Daniel!' Lucy hurried to him as fast as she could. She looked pleased to see them out there talking together.

'Hello, Lucy.' Gwen smiled at her. 'You've done some good work today.'

There was a pause while no one was sure whether to move away. Then, to her surprise, Daniel said, 'If you're not in a rush, would you like to come back with us – have a cup of tea?'

Everything else left her mind then. She was surprised to hear an almost bashful note in his voice, and she found that there was nothing she wanted more at that moment than to go with Daniel Fernandez and spend time in his company.

Joey sat in the very corner of the hearth.

Mrs Simmons's house was full of people. Four of her seven children were home from school, and on and off all day there had been a stream of people in and out, all keen to learn from the horse's mouth about Dora Phillips's death and who those women were who had been in the house for the night. The room was full of steam as the kettle boiled again and again. Mrs Simmons lorded it over the proceedings, dispensing titbits of information. Joey and Lena, the subjects under discussion, were gradually being dismissed as minor characters in a story in which Mrs Simmons had somehow become the main part.

Lena was upstairs on one of the beds. She had grown more and more unwell and her fever was running high. This morning, when she had got up to go out to the toilet she fainted, collapsing on the floor.

'We'll make her a cup of Bovril,' Mrs Simmonds had said. 'That'll help her along.'

Lena had sipped a few mouthfuls of the dark broth, then been sick over the bed. After that, she lapsed into delirium. Mrs Simmons was far too fat to keep going up and downstairs so Lena was left alone.

Joey sat on the hard floor near the fire, skinny knees pulled up close to his chest. He stared at the flames as the people swirled round him, talking about his mother and all that had happened. He tried not to listen. He couldn't feel anything. Although he was quite warm, he was cold and numb inside, as if someone had filled him up with ice. He barely knew where he was, was unaware of time passing. He spent the day sitting in a dream. At dinner time Mrs Simmons had given him a plate of mashed potato awash with thin gravy and he must have eaten it, although he could not remember anything until he handed the plate back empty.

Sounds roused him: the tearing noise of paper – Mrs Simmons's kids were playing at something – then another knock at the door. More voices.

'I've told them.' It was a man's voice. 'I've just been to Barnardo's and the other place – they said they were full. Too many already. Barnardo's said they couldn't be sure they'd all be kept together. But there'll be someone round in the morning, sharp.'

Barnardo's. The word reached Joey, hammered into his stunned mind. The people who took Polly and Kenny were coming for him and Lena! The ice in him melted to be replaced by a tight sensation, as if he was going to explode. He strained his ears, listening to every word.

'It's for the best,' Mrs Simmons said. She coughed convulsively, her whole body quivering. Joey thought he would burst, waiting for her to recover, to hear what she had to say next. 'Still – what else can I do? Sooner the better – get it over with. They'll be best off in a home. Poor little buggers.'

Thirteen

There were two women in the shop when they reached 15 Alma Street and they stood back to let Gwen and Daniel through with Lucy. Theresa Fernandez was behind the counter. Gwen saw she was wearing a navy blue blouse buttoned to her throat and her dark hair was taken back more tightly than last time they met. The overall effect was to make her look neater and younger.

'Afternoon, Miss Purdy,' she said, sounding a little startled. Her eyes were anxious. 'Everything all right with Lucy?'

Gwen could feel the two ladies' eyes examining her coat, hair, shoes.

'Oh yes, she's perfectly all right,' Daniel said, nodding at the customers. 'I just asked Miss Purdy back for a cup of tea.'

'Hello.' Gwen smiled. 'I hope you don't mind.'

'Oh, no!' Theresa lifted the hatch in the counter to let them through. 'It was just, seeing you, I thought the worst for a minute.'

As they went out, she heard one of the women in the shop say, 'Pretty little thing, ent she? She really a teacher? She don't look old enough!'

Daniel led her into the blue back room, then seemed at a loss.

'Won't you sit down?' he said awkwardly, nodding

138

towards the table. Resting on it was a block of salt, obviously newly delivered. The end where it had been cut was a gleaming white. The chairs were all tucked neatly under the table. Gwen pulled one out and sat down. She felt nervous too.

Next to the salt was a newspaper. The *Daily Worker*, Gwen read. She felt Daniel watching her as she looked at it. She was acutely conscious again of being in a household utterly foreign to her: people who were Catholic, spoke differently, read newspapers she had never heard of before. The thought was both unsettling and exciting.

In the sudden silence she became aware of Lucy making faces at her brother and looking meaningfully at the stove. When he still didn't get the message, she hissed, 'Daniel, aren't you going to make Miss Purdy some tea?'

'Oh yes – sorry!' Daniel looked enquiringly at Gwen.

'Tea would be very nice,' Gwen said, smiling at their awkwardness. But she too felt flustered and self-conscious.

'Right then.' Daniel hobbled over to the stove and stared at it as if he'd never seen it before. He leaned down to turn on the gas.

'Is there any water in the kettle?' Lucy prompted.

'Ah well – no, probably not...' He turned suddenly, gave a disarming grin and went to lean his crutch against the wall.

'Let me do it.' Gwen got up and swiftly took the kettle to the stone sink in the scullery in a fraction of the time it would have taken either Daniel or Lucy with their bad legs. It was a big kettle and she had to lift it with both hands once it was full.

'There – you must need a big one like this with a family this size,' she said, putting it down over the lit flame. Lucy was smiling, appearing thrilled at having her beloved teacher making tea in her house.

There was a clamour at the door and Rosa came in, followed by Vincent and Dominic.

'I'm hungry!' Dominic cried. He was eleven or so, Gwen calculated – older than Rosa and younger than Vincent, who was soon to leave school, and a handsome, dark-eyed boy with an intense expression, more like Daniel than any of the others.

'You're forever hungry, Dom,' Daniel said, cutting slices from a loaf for them all. 'I think you've got a worm inside you.'

'Sister Bridget took my dinner away when I'd hardly started it – she said I had bad manners,' Dominic said resentfully.

'Why – what were you doing?' Daniel teased.

Gwen watched his face. *He's lovely*, she found herself thinking. For a moment she remembered her dream and a blush flooded across her cheeks. She hoped none of the children had noticed.

'He put his knife in his mouth,' Rosa sounded disparaging. She seemed old for her eleven years. 'You're stupid, Dom – you know Sister Bridget's mad on manners and all that sort of thing.'

'Just mad, more like,' Dominic said sulkily.

'Now, now,' Daniel said. 'We have a teacher here, remember.'

'It's all right.' Gwen laughed and stood up to slip off her coat.

'Take the salt, Dom, will you?' Daniel nodded towards the scullery and Dominic came and lifted the block off the table.

140

The Fernandez children each wolfed down a slice of bread and margarine, all talking at once, then the room went quiet as they disappeared out through the shop again, Rosa taking charge of Lucy.

'She's very beautiful,' Gwen said, watching the older girl lead her sister out of the front door.

'Rosa? Yes, I s'pose she is,' Daniel said. Clearly he'd never thought about it before. 'She's a good girl. Helps our ma a lot.'

'It sounds as if you all do.' She had been struck by how close the family were.

Daniel nodded, limping to the table with the brown teapot. For a moment his expression was serious. 'Needs must.'

He sat opposite her, the tea brewing between them. There was an oilcloth on the table today, and Daniel had brought over three thick white cups. She looked shyly across at him.

'So – do you have a job? Yourself, I mean, apart from the shop?'

Daniel nodded, jiggling the handle of the teapot. 'Off and on. What I can get. I do a bit of house painting, repairs and that. Can't do any of that with this though –' He looked down ruefully at his leg with the plaster cast on it. 'And I'm not always here, see.'

Gwen was confused. 'How can you keep a job if you keep moving about?'

'I work when I can. But my real work is with the movement and the party.'

She could hear the passion in his voice, but she had no idea what he was talking about and just stared at him, feeling foolish.

'The NUWM – National Unemployed Workers' Movement,' Daniel explained. He leaned forward, elbows on the table. His tone was patient but she could sense his disbelief at her ignorance. 'The valleys are full of unemployed men who've been locked out of the mines or forced out by scab labour. They're expected to let their families starve while the bosses rake in the profits. The princes of capitalism have all the power to decide the fate of the working man. They can cast him aside when he can't or won't produce the profits they want to wring out of him by the sweat of his labour. And even when he's unemployed they beat him down with the means test, take away the last of his dignity and make him live like a beggar, a pauper on the parish. The movement is getting unemployed men together as a body to say – enough!'

All this came pouring out fluently. The intensity of his words thrilled through her. He spoke without looking away from her, eyes ablaze under the thick black curls. In those moments, Gwen knew for certain that she was with someone quite unlike anyone she had ever met before.

'Only when we're together can we be strong, can we stand up to them. We will not be the slaves of capitalist dictators!'

Daniel seemed about to thump his fist on the table, but instead he poured the tea. He got up to take a cup to his mother in the shop and was talking on the way back before he had even sat down.

'Look what happened at Mardy – 1931, when the means test was biting into mining families who'd had no work in months or years. That's what they do, see?' He sat down, leaning forward to impress the words on her, knowing she came from another world, did not understand. She could feel the force of his need to

142

make her understand, and she wanted to know, but already she was floundering. Where was Mardy?

'They steal their jobs, then steal their homes. The movement stood with a household where they'd come to take away the furniture before they'd pay them a penny to feed their bellies. Well, they got them for unlawful assembly, didn't they? Called them "conspirators – little Moscow". When they went to the assizes in Cardiff, twenty-nine of them were sent to prison – seven years' hard labour for the lot of them.' Daniel sat back, his lip curling. 'Police courts – that's what they are, lock, stock and barrel. No one else's word counts.'

He took a gulp of tea and there was silence for a moment. Gwen could just hear the distant sounds of children playing out at the front.

She didn't know what to say, where to begin. There had been marches in protest against the means test, that she remembered. Grainy newspaper pictures of groups with banners. But the test had been something far away, had not come near to touching her. Had it touched any of her pupils in Worcester? She didn't know, hadn't thought. One or two, perhaps. She felt ashamed that she didn't know. Everything Daniel was saying seemed so new, so different from the life she had known.

'And the party? You said you worked for the party?'

Daniel reached to take something out of his back pocket.

'My party card,' he said, showing it to her proudly, before replacing it. 'Communist Party of Great Britain.' His voice contained a swell of pride. He was watching for her reaction, but she didn't understand what sort of reaction he expected. Russia, she thought. The Soviet Union. Revolution. Lenin. What else should she know about Communists? She just thought of them as foreign and even more distant from her life than the means test. And she'd never been interested in politics. Edwin talked about it sometimes – about Hitler and Mussolini, how they had to be stopped. But it never felt real and Edwin did tend to go on a bit. Usually she just waited until he'd finished. Her parents never said who they voted for, but she knew they voted Conservative. She wasn't sure how she knew: it seemed to be taken for granted in the circles they moved in.

Blushing, she said, 'I'm dreadfully ignorant, I'm afraid.'

Daniel watched her in silence for a moment, as if trying to decide something. Then he got up. 'Just a moment. Let me show you.'

Taking his crutch, he went to the tiny cupboard under the stairs. Gwen heard a sound like a tin box opening. A moment later he came limping back with a big leatherbound book. She was startled. Of course Catholics had statues of Mary and Jesus, but somehow she hadn't imagined Daniel to be religious. Religion was another thing her family didn't talk about at home. They simply went to church on Sundays and that was that. Even Edwin, in a funny way, didn't actually say much about what he believed. It was taken for granted that it went with his calling, with the dog collar.

'Are we going to do a bible study?' she asked, flippant in her uncertainty.

Daniel stared at her, then burst out laughing as he put the heavy book down on the table. The sound of his laughter passed right through her.

'Well, it's my Bible,' he said, moving his chair closer

to hers. 'And I dare say Jesus Christ would find a lot in here to agree about. Though Mam might have a go at me for saying that!'

Gwen leaned down to read the gold lettering on the spine. 'CAPITAL. KARL MARX.'

'This,' Daniel said solemnly, his hand stroking the worn maroon leather, 'is the message of justice and liberation for mankind.'

She was struck by his certainty, felt in herself immediately a hunger to understand what gave him such passionate conviction. Daniel sat down next to her and in those moments she became aware of an over-whelming combination of feelings, as if her whole being, mind and body, was subject to an electric current stimulated by his physical proximity, by his words, the fact that he was about to tell her his thoughts. Once again all the hairs on her body were standing on end, as if raised by a magnet. She gave a small shudder, as if something had stroked her all over.

'You cold?'

'No! I'm perfectly all right,' she said, smiling.

Daniel opened the book. Its flyleaf was covered in tiny writing in a neat, copperplate hand. Gwen saw a note. 'Read page 786. This chapter is one of the classics of Socialism.' As Daniel turned the pages, she saw that there were footnotes and annotations in the margins, and sheets of paper inserted between pages, again all closely written over. She read various chapter headings, 'Commodities and Money', 'The Labour Process', 'Division of Labour and Manufacture'. Her eyes met Daniel's.

'All that writing – did you do that?'

'Oh yes. I've studied every line of it.'

'But it looks so . . . *dense*.'

'It's not easy. But there were lectures, see. I went to the Labour College down London for a time. Now I study on my own, keep it going like.'

'I've heard of it. But I don't know *anything*,' she said wretchedly.

And Daniel began to talk. He talked about the working classes, about how the only way they would achieve justice for themselves was by uniting together against the enemy, which was the capitalist system. He talked and talked about Marx and his writings, some of which she understood and some she didn't. How, in the course of history, capital had become the basis of commodity production. The workers made something from materials that cost almost nothing, and through giving their labour turned it into something that could be sold for profit.

'Profit is theft from the workers of what is rightfully theirs,' he said.

Gwen nodded, trying to keep up with him.

'The capitalist owners have the power to keep the workers in their place. Capitalism survives on their exploitation. And while we're all divided, our energy sapped, nothing is going to change. Our task in the Communist Party is to unite the workers, that's when we're powerful. I've seen it – I've caught glimpses of it, Miss Purdy, in the valleys, in the coalfields, when the workers unite and speak with one voice.' His voice was low and passionate. 'And it's a vision. A force and a vision of what could be. So yes –' once again he laid his hand on the book. It was a strong, fine hand and she found herself longing to lay her own over it – 'it's my Bible. My vision of the heavenly city if you like. Against oppression and the scourge of fascism.'

She watched him, entranced. For moments, as he

talked, he reminded her of Edwin, talking without pause, eager to voice his ideas. But with Edwin she tended to find her mind wandering, whereas with Daniel she was caught by the earnest force of his words. She felt as if her mind, her life, was expanding as she listened to him, as if a wide window was being flung open onto a way of thinking and seeing that she had never experienced before.

'But . . .' she stammered, 'how?'

'By making them wake up! By education, by speaking and showing people that they don't have to lie down under oppression! By showing them that unity is our strength. That's what I do, you see. That's my life's work.'

This last statement resulted in a pause, during which Paul Fernandez came in from work. Gwen felt as if she had been woken from a dream.

'Afternoon, Miss Purdy,' he said shyly. He was the fairest of the Fernandez children and very like his mother. Gwen guessed him to be about sixteen.

She roused herself. It was time to get home! She was going to be late for tea, and there was no telling what Harold Purvis might accuse her of getting up to.

'Goodness,' she said, 'time's getting on – and I had marvellous intentions of going to see that boy, Joey Phillips – the one whose mother died. I'll have to go tomorrow now.'

'I waylaid you,' Daniel said.

'No, I was willingly waylaid. It's been very interesting – thank you.' Her words sounded feeble compared to the way she felt.

They stood up and for a moment were unnervingly close to one another. Gwen stepped back.

'I'll be here a while longer,' Daniel said. 'Will you come and see us again?'

'Lena. Lena!'

Joey whispered urgently to her in the darkness. There was no reply. He could only hear her rasping breaths beside him.

'Wake up – you've got to get up!' He shook her, desperate now. Lena's only response was a little cat-like whimper.

All day Joey had waited, trying not to show the neighbours anything of what was going on inside him. *Barnardo's.* They passed the word around the room with each new visitor, whispered or spoken aloud as if he was deaf or didn't exist. *Tomorrow morning.* Someone would be coming to take them away. In his mind it was always a man, so tall that his head was out of sight up in the sky, and he would have huge hands, gripping chains which he'd wrap round them like the strong man in the Bull Ring then drag them away to the orphanage. *Orphanage.* The word clanged in his mind over and over, like an iron door slamming shut.

All day he said not a word, but the fear twisted and tightened in him. At last the Simmons family had made their rowdy way up to bed and Joey and Lena were put downstairs to sleep on a straw mattress. Lena had hardly opened her eyes all day. In the evening she woke for a short time and sipped some milk, but then she sicked it up again and went back to sleep.

'Poor mite.' Mrs Simmons gave a quivering sigh. 'Let's hope she feels better in the morning.'

The room was very dark. Joey lay back for a moment. He could hear the fire shifting, the tap dripping in the yard. There was a smell of bleach. He could not sleep. His heart was thudding. The thoughts hammered at him again. The man from the orphanage was coming in the morning! He had to get away, out of here. Whatever he had to do, they were not taking him away. But what was he going to do about his little sister?

'Lena!' He tried again. For the first time since his mother died, tears came into his eyes. He thought of Miss Purdy. Maybe she'd help, but she wasn't here. He tried not to let himself think of her because it gave him an ache inside. No one was here – not even Lena. Who did he have in the world? Dad – where was he? That was another thought he tried never to have.

The memory of his father's back disappearing down the entry that day made him cry in earnest. He lay curled tightly on his side. The night pressed round him. He thought of the dark roofs outside, the streets, endless streets beyond them, and he sobbed. Afterwards, without meaning to, he slept.

He woke with a jolt, heart banging hard. He could see the dim shape of the window, the table across the room. Dawn! And they were coming to get him!

'Lena!' Frantically, he made a last attempt to rouse her. She did not move.

'Lena – come on!' He shoved her. There was no reaction. He'd have to leave her! They'd have to take Lena, but they were never taking him. He'd rather die.

He was seized with the urgent need to relieve himself and he went into the scullery and peed in the bucket under the sink. Then he helped himself to half a loaf of bread. Without a backward glance he went to the door. As he was feeling for the latch, his hand met a garment hanging from the hook on the back. Mr

149

Simmons's coat. He hesitated. It felt threadbare and soft. It would be far too big, but it would keep him warm. He had nothing of his own. With a jump he managed to get it off the hook and wrap it round him. He tore the loaf in halves and put a piece in each pocket. Then he let himself out into the silent yard.

Fourteen

After the last bell the next afternoon, Gwen walked to the gate among the crowds of children, trying to convince herself that she was not excited, not hoping that Daniel Fernandez would be waiting outside. When she made her way out to the street, Lucy was standing there and smiling shyly up at her.

'Walking home on your own today?' Gwen asked.

'I think so.' Lucy nodded.

There was no Daniel, but instead, waiting a little way along the road, was Millie Dawson. Some of the younger children were gathered round her and a few others called, 'Hello, Miss Dawson!' to her in daring voices.

Gwen waited, smiling, until the children had moved on. 'Hello! 'What're you doing here? It's lovely to see you!'

Millie smiled wanly from under the brim of her hat. 'I'm on my way into town.' She looked towards the school. 'Everything much as usual, is it? How's old Monk-face?'

Gwen rolled her eyes. 'Crabby as ever. I bet you're not missing her!'

'No.' Millie's eyes filled. 'I don't half miss the rest of it, though. Look, Gwen, will you come and see us at the weekend? It'd be good to have a chinwag.'

'Oh, Millie!' Gwen saw the tears roll down her

friend's face. 'Of course I'll come – I'd love to! I'm sorry you're feeling so miserable.'

'I'll get by.' Millie tried to smile, wiping her eyes determinedly. 'I seem to be forever crying these days. I think I'll go mad if I can't have a proper talk to someone! Look, I'll have to go. See you Saturday – about three?'

Poor Millie! Gwen walked along Canal Street towards Joey's yard with a heavy heart. She was going to Mrs Simmons and felt nervous about what was to come. In her hand was a big bag of sweets. She'd gone out in the lunch hour to find Parks's Sweet Shop, which was tucked in the lee of the railway bridge where it passed over the junction of Canal Street and Wellington Street. During the school day they heard trains go by, steaming over the bridge. The windows were crammed with jars and bars of chocolate and toffee. Gwen thought of Ron's terrible teeth and smiled to herself.

'Yes, bab?' the woman behind the counter had said. She was very plump, with thick brown hair, and wore spectacles and a big brown cardigan.

'Hello,' Gwen said. 'Are you Ron's mother?'

'Yes.' The woman immediately looked guarded and folded her arms beneath her large breasts. 'Why?'

'Oh, nothing to worry about.' Gwen smiled. 'I'm his teacher, that's all.'

'Oh ar . . .' Mrs Parks still looked wary. 'Miss er . . .?'

'Purdy,' Gwen said brightly.

'Oh yes – he's mentioned you.'

'Nothing bad, I hope?'

Mrs Parks just looked at her.

'He's a good boy, your Ron.'

At this, the woman's eyes lit up behind her spectacles and she nodded enthusiastically. 'Oh, he *is*. They're good 'uns, my boys. Golden, they are.'

Gwen had been taken aback and rather moved by this declaration. Imagine her mother saying that about her!

Now, as she came in through the entry to the yard in Canal Street, Gwen thought the back-to-back houses looked even more mean and dreary than she remembered. Immediately, though, her attention was taken by the two men standing outside Mrs Simmons's house. They wore long, dark coats and one of them had, tucked under his arm, a child-sized white coffin.

She hovered at a respectful distance until Mrs Simmons came to the door and showed the men in. She spotted Gwen behind them.

'Oh dear, what a carry on! You're too late, I'm afraid, if it's about the children.'

'Whatever's happened?' Gwen was appalled. 'What d'you mean, too late? Is Joey – has one of them passed away?'

'The girl. When we got up this morning she was laid down there, stiff as a plank . . .' Mrs Simmons's voice thickened. She groped in her extensive cleavage and pulled out a rag to wipe her nose. 'And no sign of the boy. The people from the orphanage came this morning and I had to tell 'em the bird had flown! What they must've thought . . . He must've scarpered in the night . . .' She stood back to let the men out again, thanking them. 'I don't know if he saw his sister'd passed on and it frightened him, or what. And my husband's coat's gone . . .'

Gwen stood, nonplussed, the bags of sweets in her hand.

'Come in a minute – oh, my word – they've put her in . . .'

The coffin was on the table and Gwen looked in at the terrible sight of Lena's little figure laid in it in her ragged dress, eyes closed, hands laid to rest on her stomach. Dora Phillips had been the first dead person she had ever seen. It was awful for this to be so quickly followed by another, especially a child. She could hardly take it in.

'Oh God, how awful!' she breathed. 'Poor little thing. How could she have died?'

'Well, she was bad last night,' Mrs Simmons said. 'You know, feverish, but I daint think she was that poorly. Ooh – I feel quite peculiar myself.' She sank down on a chair and mopped her face with her apron. 'There's been that much upset . . . My Dolly was beside herself . . . And with the boy going off like that. It's not good for me, all this – that it isn't.'

Gwen could see that Mrs Simmons was genuinely in a state.

'I'm ever so sorry.' She felt tearful herself. 'You've been a good neighbour and ever so kind to these children. You couldn't have done any more than you have.'

'I've done my best.' Mrs Simmons mopped her eyes. 'Only I never expected this.'

'Do you have any idea where Joseph might have gone?'

The woman shook her head. 'No. Not unless he's gone off to look for Wally, that good-for-nothing father of his. He's not been about here for months now. Be like looking for a needle in a haystack.'

Gwen took her leave and walked back slowly down the entry, full of misgiving at the thought of Joey Phillips roaming the streets. He was so small, so ill-fed and fragile. Whatever would become of him? Should she try to look for him? But Mrs Simmons said he had gone very early in the morning. He could be anywhere by now.

She found herself standing out in Canal Street, lost in thought, holding the bags of jelly babies, sherbet lemons and toffees. *What am I going to do with these?* she wondered. *I don't want to eat them all.* She thought about taking them in to school to treat her class. Then another idea came to her. Where was the one place she really wanted to go, to be able to sit in a homely room and where she would find a large collection of children?

Hardly knowing she had decided to go there, almost daring herself, she found her feet straying past the school and pub and into Alma Street. She didn't give herself time to think about whether she would feel embarrassed turning up at the Fernandezs' house again so soon. The desire simply to go there was too over-whelming.

'Afternoon, Miss Purdy,' Theresa Fernandez greeted her as soon as she walked into the shop. She had a good view of the door, between the two rows of shelves and Gwen could see her, surrounded by tins and packets. At one end of the counter were all the cigar-ettes. 'I don't know if you've come to find Daniel, but he's not in, I'm afraid.'

Gwen felt a pang of disappointment, but then she was almost relieved. She would have felt a bit foolish at him seeing her arrive here again. She could explain about the sweets and just leave them without embar-rassing herself.

'Will you have a cup of tea?' Theresa asked. 'Shop's quiet, and I can hear if anyone comes in.'

'Well, that would be lovely,' Gwen said. She enjoyed the woman's Welsh accent and her homely presence. She was wearing her black shawl today over a white blouse. There was something about Theresa Fernandez that felt solid, rock-like, as if you could rely on her for anything. And there was a great warmth about her. To her surprise, Gwen found herself saying, 'To tell you the truth, I could do with someone to talk to.'

'Could you, lovey?'

Once they were through in the back room, Gwen explained, 'I really came to give you these sweets for the children.' She put the bags on the table and explained about Joey and Lena Phillips.

Theresa was distracted from pouring the tea by Gwen's story. She stood at the stove, her hand on the handle of the kettle as it warmed.

'*Duw, duw* – there's terrible, isn't it? The little girl passing on like that! And you think that young lad's out roaming the streets on his own?'

'Well, I suppose he must be – unless he's found somewhere else to go.'

'P'raps it's an auntie or uncle somewhere he's gone to?'

Gwen sighed. 'I hope so. He's such a poor little thing. I hate to think of him out – it's still cold, especially at night.'

Theresa sat down. Gwen wanted to ask where Daniel had gone, but it seemed so forward and she felt self-conscious. But his mother immediately said, 'Daniel's out at one of his meetings – least, getting ready for one.' Gwen was taken aback by the impatience in her voice. 'Just like his father was, only Daniel's even redder than red. 'Twas politics killed my husband. Ate

156

away at him till his heart gave up the struggle and now my Daniel *bach*'s going the same way.'

Gwen wasn't quite sure what to say. 'Don't you agree with his work in the Communist Party?'

Theresa put her cup down and gave out a great sigh. 'I have to struggle with myself, Miss Purdy. The priests say Communism's an ungodly creed which we should never put in place of our faith and the Church. Our Daniel tries to keep the two side by side. He says you can be a Catholic and Communist. I don't know.' Another sigh. She got up and spooned tea into the pot while she continued chatting. She seemed glad to talk.

'I'm a selfish woman, I suppose. All my life it's been going on, all my marriage, lockouts and strikes at the mines, never any work ... I lived through it, like we all did. They were bitter times, Miss Purdy – still are for a lot of them. There was no choice. Then the means test. All the meetings, the protests. Arturo was in the thick of it, you see – never a moment's rest, what with the miners' lodges, the party, the unemployed. Meetings, leaflets, making speeches. Hardly ate or slept sometimes – and I told him, "You won't do yourself any good, Arturo – you'll kill yourself with overwork." And that's how it was.' She paused, steam rising round her as she poured from the kettle.

'One of the meetings, the first protest in Aberglyn, they were marching to the Public Assistance people, police all round, of course. Arturo was one of the ones speaking. He got up and gave it to them – oh, he had a voice on him! So loud and strong. He could have spoken to the whole valley and they'd have heard him!' For a moment she smiled, and Gwen saw the love in her eyes. 'Got to the end, just, and he collapsed. His

157

heart. Never came back home alive.' She carried the last things to the table and sat down.

'That's what's made me selfish now. I suppose it knocked the fight out of me. Once we came up here I just wanted an end to it. There's work here – something you can do, not just the colliery. I want my children fed and schooled, not picking cinders off the heaps in the winter just to survive. I want to forget it all ... go to Mass Sundays ...' She shook her head. 'But not Daniel. He can't forget what he's seen. He's ablaze with it. Whatever I say to him falls on deaf ears. It was a police horse broke his leg – doesn't stop him. Back for more! It's no good me saying anything, any more than it was to Arturo. "I'm doing it for you, Ma," he says. "For all of us – for the revolution."' Gwen could hear the mingled pride and anxiety in her voice. 'And I say to him, "All I've learned about revolutions is that they end up with people losing their heads." But will he take heed of me?' She poured the tea. 'I've seen politics tearing families apart and I don't want it breaking up mine. So I hold my peace most of the time.'

'Thank you,' Gwen said, taking her cup. 'I learned a lot from listening to Daniel yesterday.' She felt like defending him. All his passion for people, for the workers of the valleys. Surely his mother shouldn't be trying to dampen that down!

'Oh, I dare say. He's a one for book learning all right. And a proper firebrand with it.' Theresa smiled ruefully, stirring her tea. 'I suppose I'm just getting old. And there's no stopping him, that I do know. Let's put it away, love. Talk about something else. Tell me about yourself, now.'

*

158

'Late again, Miss Purdy?' Ariadne Black purred reproachfully as Gwen tore in, barely in time for tea.

One of Ariadne's quirks was that although she insisted on being called by her own first name she never called Gwen anything except Miss Purdy. Gwen thought perhaps it was because she was a teacher. When it came to Mr Purvis, though, he was very definitely 'Harold'. Tonight Ariadne was wearing a floaty dress in a pale coffee colour edged with chocolate brown, and smelled strongly of perfume.

Gwen stared at the plate Ariadne plonked down before her. Shrivelled chops with potatoes and cabbage, boiled to death as ever, and the house stank of it.

'Thank you,' she said with an effort. Thank goodness it was almost the holidays and she could get out of here for a bit! When she looked up, Harold Purvis was watching her with quiet insolence. Gwen put her head down and ate as fast as she could to get away from the pair of them.

That night, she was just falling asleep, when she heard the boards on the landing creak, then a soft, furtive knocking on a door at the back of the house.

'Harold? Harold, darling?'

Gwen sat up, hugging her knees, barely able to believe what she was hearing.

'It's all right, darling. You can let me in,' Ariadne pleaded in a purring voice.

Gwen put her hand over her mouth. She wasn't sure if she felt more appalled or amused. Explosive giggles rose in her chest.

There was a pause, then the knocking again.

'Harold, my beautiful great big panther ... Come on, let your little pussycat in ...'

Snorting, Gwen stuffed the end of the sheet in her

mouth. What kind of household was she living in? Once more she thought of what her mother would say and the laughter began to erupt from her. She lay down, shaking with giggles so much that she didn't hear the door along the landing open to admit Ariadne, then close again.

EASTER HOLIDAYS

Fifteen

'Here we are – eat it while it's hot.'

Gwen's mother dropped a boiled egg into the egg-cup in front of her and sat down, opening out her table napkin.

Gwen obediently removed the top from her egg and dipped in a finger of toast. The yolk overflowed, rich yellow, down the side.

'Really,' Ruth Purdy commented. 'You're no more tidy an eater than when you were four years old.'

Gwen said nothing. She tipped a helping of salt onto the edge of her pretty floral plate. Ruth Purdy liked everything to be dainty: bone-china plates and little tea knives. Gwen thought of the thick white cups in the Fernandez household and wished she was there instead. The clock ticked on the mantelpiece and her father coughed and tried to pretend he wasn't eyeing the newspaper because his wife said it was rude to read at the table. Had her parents ever liked one another? Gwen wondered. It was her third day at home and already she was fit to scream.

'So,' her mother said, 'today's the ideal day for us to go to Mrs Twining and then Russell & Dorrell. We'll start early and that'll give us plenty of time . . .'

Ruth Purdy had been mentioning Russell & Dorrell, the large draper's at the end of the High Street ever since Gwen arrived home.

'It's going to be hard enough for Mrs Twining making your dress with you away so much. We'll have to squeeze in fittings. So we mustn't leave it too late. It would be most unfair on her. And there are so many other things to think about!'

'Edwin and I want to keep the wedding as simple as possible,' Gwen reminded her. She pushed her teaspoon into the bottom of the egg with such force it smashed through the shell.

'I know – but even so. Everything must be done properly. It's *so* important to get it right!'

Important to whom? Gwen wondered.

'And your father has his business to think of – haven't you, Morris?'

'Umm?' Mr Purdy dragged his gaze away from the front page of the *Telegraph*. 'Er . . . of course. Yes.' He obviously hadn't heard the question.

'So you mean the purpose of our wedding is to enhance Daddy's business reputation?'

'No of course not – don't be so silly, dear. I just mean there are standards. People in the town would expect us to put on a good show. That's all.'

Gwen hurriedly drank down her tea and left the table before she said something she'd regret. Up in her room she stood at the window. There were tiny buds on the apple tree just waiting to burst into flower. The grass was sodden underneath, the sky a pale arc above.

How did I stand living here all this time? she asked herself. She tried to imagine Daniel sitting at the breakfast table with her parents. She found herself setting the idea of him, his dancing eyes, that restless muscular body, his burning ideals, against the nervous respectability of her family. It was as if they were

164

asleep, she saw. And until now she'd been asleep also. She ached to see Daniel. She had to be away from Birmingham for two weeks and how unbearable that felt!

She tried to force her emotions back to where they should be. Daniel was from another world. He wasn't a true part of her life! Perhaps these feelings were just a reaction to the idea of marriage – to the closing down of the possibility that she should ever feel anything for anyone else. She shook her head. What did she really know about Daniel Fernandez? She had known Edwin for three years now and he was kind and true and had never let her down. How could she be so disloyal to him?

'Well, you *have* grown up into a lovely girl, I must say!'

Mrs Twining was a small, plump lady with a tight little voice, several chins and bright red lipstick. For years she had run her tailoring business in a cramped upstairs room and had made a little dance dress for Gwen when she was only six years old. She ran her busy hands up and down Gwen's body as if she was sizing up a cow for auction.

'Lovely curves. Oh yes.' She eyed Gwen's breasts so intently that Gwen found herself blushing. 'You're very *full*, aren't you? Oh I can make a lovely job – something pretty you'll be after? Satin and tulle perhaps?'

'Something quite simple,' Gwen said.

At exactly the same moment, her mother said, 'Silk, perhaps?'

Mrs Twining approached with her tape measure. Gwen quickly felt any control she might have over the situation slipping away.

'Now,' Mrs Twining said, when she'd taken the measurements, 'come here a minute.' She took Gwen's arm and pulled her over to a long mirror on a stand near the window. 'You take a look in there. You're a lovely shape, dear – a real hourglass. I can do something really pretty with a full skirt and perhaps some lace across here.' She ran a finger across Gwen's chest. 'Can't display cleavage on our wedding day, can we?'

Gwen looked at herself, trying to concentrate on the matter of a wedding dress. Her oval, blue-eyed face looked back at her, her full lips, wavy hair tied back from her face, the same green tartan skirt and cream sweater, everything just as ever, and yet suddenly she was a stranger to herself, as if the outer Gwen, who looked the same as she had always been, suddenly did not match the person she felt herself to be inside in the least. Panic rose in her.

Her mother was saying something about seed pearls. Gwen dragged her attention away from the stranger in the mirror. She felt distant from it all suddenly. What did any of this matter really? How selfish she was being, she told herself. Her mother, Edwin, everyone was excited about the wedding. It was every bit as much their occasion. She must stop all these silly thoughts she was having and try to get into the spirit of it.

'That sounds a lovely idea,' she said to Mrs Twining, though she had scarcely any idea what the woman had said.

In the mirror she saw her mother's tense face light up with relief.

'Do you really think so? Oh, I am pleased, dear. And I thought you were going to be so difficult about it all!'

Gwen did not see very much of Edwin. It was Holy Week, one of his busiest times of the year. She spent most of the time with her mother, surrounded by scraps of silk and lace, discussing sleeves and bodices and what colour dress her cousin Jane's little daughter Patricia should wear as a bridesmaid. She tried to be as agreeable as she could to her mother. After all, it was her wedding, she must be enthusiastic, and her mother was doing her best!

On Easter Sunday they all went to the morning Communion service. Gwen stood between her parents. Her father hummed the hymns in a vague sort of way, her mother wore a green hat with a colourful peacock feather tucked in the band and held the book a long way from her to read the print.

'*Christ the Lord is risen today, alleluia!*' they sang as Edwin processed in behind the vicar, Bernard Thompson, looking very upright and solemn, his hands clasped. Gwen watched Edwin's long back in his white surplice move along the aisle. And once again, just for a moment, the strangest feeling came over her. A sense of distance, of tiredness with everything, with the idea of watching Edwin parade about for the rest of her life.

As the service went on, her mind wandered. Sunlight slanted in through the windows and she found herself wondering about Joey Phillips. No one knew where he had gone and there was really no one to ask. Where did a small child just disappear to on the streets?

Just a couple of days before the end of term she had

thought she had seen him when she was outside on playground duty. Standing in the spring sunshine, she she looked along towards the boys' end of the school-yard and caught sight of a small figure outside, pressed against the railings near the gate. Her heart beat faster. Putting her hand up to shade her face she stared, screwing her eyes up to see better. Was that Joey? Something about the size of the child, his slightness, made her think it might be. By the time she had hurried to the end to see, there was no one there. She had opened the gate and looked along the road. Nothing. She was taken aback by how bereft she felt, staring along the empty street.

'Did you see anyone looking through the railings?' she asked the children who were playing nearer that end.

'No, Miss,' they chorused. They were all caught up in their games.

She still wondered now, unsure whether it had been him. Keeping her eyes turned towards the pulpit where Bernard Thompson was preaching, she pictured all sorts of terrible misfortune coming over Joey. Perhaps someone had already picked him up and he was in a home somewhere. That thought didn't cheer her at all. The little she had heard about orphanages was grim and she couldn't imagine Joey in an institution. But to be eight years old, a little scrap like that, and alone on the streets. Her eyes filled at the thought, and she lowered her head, pulling her hanky out from up her sleeve. She felt her mother eyeing her. Why had this one child got so much under her skin?

After the service they were all greeted by the Reverend Thompson.

'Happy Easter to you!' He shook Gwen's hand outside the church door and added with smile, 'I shall let Edwin off the lead a little after today!'

Edwin was waiting outside. He didn't kiss her in greeting – it didn't seem right to him when he was 'on duty' – but came up to her immediately.

'Hello, darling,' he said fervently. 'I'm longing to see you properly. *Sorry* about this week. It's been non-stop.'

'Not to worry,' she said brightly. 'I can hardly complain when I'm hardly ever here anyway. And Mummy's had me on wedding duty all week. I think I'm the one who needs letting off the lead, not you!'

Edwin appeared slightly wounded. 'I thought you'd enjoy all that.'

'Oh, I do!' She smiled. 'Look, I'll see you for lunch. You'd better go and meet and greet a bit more.'

They were able to spend some of Easter week together, going for walks, visiting each other. On the Monday they went to see Mr and Mrs Shackleton out in Callow Hill. Gwen's father once again lent Edwin the motorcar.

'Mummy's in bed pretty much all the time now,' Edwin said as they drove between spring-green fields. 'She's happiest there really. It's such an effort to move her, and her speech is going as well.'

Knowing that they were expecting visitors, the Shackletons were well prepared, or rather James, Edwin's father, was.

'Well, hello-o, both!' he greeted them, beaming. Rufus, their old red setter limped at his side.

Despite his brave cheerfulness, Gwen was shocked by the sight of him. He was a slightly smaller man than

169

Edwin, but now in his mid-seventies he had become very stooped and his kindly face seemed more wrinkled and worn than when Gwen had seen him at Christmas.

'Joan has been worth her weight in gold today,' Mr Shackleton said, leading them through the hall. Joan was the woman who gave them extra domestic help. 'There's a leg of pork in the oven – and I'm sure I saw signs of an apple pie. Now, how about a spot of sherry before lunch?'

'Is Mummy up to having one?' Edwin asked.

'Oh, I think so, with a bit of help,' Mr Shackleton said, pouring amber sherry into a row of little glasses. He handed one to Gwen with a smile. 'There – and how is life in old Brum treating you?'

'Very well, thank you. Full of interest – just as you said it would be.' Mr Shackleton had been an ally in her decision to work in Birmingham.

'One of my early parishes was up there,' he had told her when she announced her decision. 'Yes – in King's Heath. I had a marvellous time – splendid place, Birmingham. Jolly good idea.'

Now he picked up two glasses. 'Come on through. We'll go and have a drink with Edwina. She'd like that. Best thing is if I help her with her lunch and then we three can come through and eat here. Easiest that way.' He lowered his voice. 'She's not keen on having an audience – not with eating.'

Gwen felt a plunge of dread as he spoke, despite his considerateness in trying to smooth over the distress of what was happening. Edwina Shackleton's decline over the past three years had been terrible to witness.

Edwina's bed was downstairs now, in a back room overlooking the garden. When Gwen first met Edwin's mother she had been in the very early stages of her illness and was still a tall, hearty woman with a thick head of gingerish blonde hair, frizzy, cut to shoulder length, and a healthy, freckled face. She strode about in slacks, working hard in the garden, and in the summer she put on big, loose sandals. She had a loud, ringing laugh and she had laughed often.

They all filed into the room.

'Darling? Edwin and Gwen are here,' James Shackleton announced. 'And I've brought you your little tipple.' His tone was very loving. Gwen felt a pang go through her. Everything here was good and kind, had been settled for her until now. It *had* to be right. And yet, and yet . . .

Edwina's bed was arranged to face the sunny garden, where she had spent so many hours. There was a paddock at the far end, owned by the neighbours, with a piebald pony grazing in it. Edwina was propped up on pillows, her head inclined to one side. She tried to move and say hello, but her neck went into spasm and her words of greeting came out as an indistinct groan. She did manage a smile. Rufus came and laid himself in a patch of sunlight close to her.

'Hello, Mummy.' Edwin leaned over and kissed her. They were strikingly alike and Gwen had often smiled at the sight of them together.

'Hello, Edwina.' She had always insisted, in her hearty way, on Gwen calling her by her Christian name. Gwen kissed her pale cheek and took her hand for a moment. She smelled sourly of sickness, mingled with rose-scented talcum powder. Gwen felt her hand give an answering squeeze.

'Here we are – take a pew,' James said. 'You can both tell us all about everything.'

With loving carefulness, he helped his wife to tiny

sips from her sherry glass. She no longer had reliable use of her arms, so he had to tilt the glass delicately to her lips. At the same time both of them listened as Gwen tried to think of things they would be interested in: Ariadne's dreadful cooking and about the school and her class. She told them about Joey Phillips. She could see that Edwina was listening intently although she could make little comment, and she made sure she spoke to her as much as to anyone. She had always been very fond of Edwina, who was the free spirit of the family. Edwin was much more proper by comparison.

James Shackleton shook his head sadly. 'Yes – what a terrible thing. Life is so very harsh for so many people.'

'Gwen's certainly seeing how the other half live,' Edwin said. She wondered if she imagined the terse note of disapproval – or was it envy? – in his voice. Hadn't he thought that that was the value in her going to Birmingham? She had always talked about school and her pupils before. Now Edwin seemed put out by it. She stopped talking and asked after affairs in the parish instead.

'Well.' James Shackleton stood up finally. 'Our lunch is all ready for us.'

While he gave Edwina her food, Gwen and Edwin walked to the end of the garden. The air felt clean and fresh and a brisk breeze riffled the daffodils. The pony strolled over to join them at the fence and Gwen stroked its soft nose.

'How lovely to see animals again!' She smiled at Edwin, but he was preoccupied.

'She's not looking too good is she?'

'No,' Gwen agreed sadly. There was no point in

172

pretending otherwise. His mother's decline was painfully obvious.

There was a long pause while she patted the pony's smooth coat, then Edwin said in a tight voice, 'Not getting too involved up there are you?'

Gwen turned, her hand still on the animal's neck. 'What – in Birmingham?'

'You seem very steeped in it all of a sudden.'

'Well.' She laughed. 'I suppose I'm living there all the time at the moment. I get involved in the things I'm doing, you know that. I always have.'

'It's not for much longer, though. You've got duties and obligations here, don't forget.' He wasn't looking at her. He spoke staring across the paddock, which made his pomposity worse. His hands were pushed into his jacket pockets. She wondered if he was still hurt that she had shown less than his expected enthusiasm for the wedding arrangements.

'I know,' she said, baffled. 'But that's where I am at the moment. And I'm learning so much! Understanding things for the first time.' Her enthusiasm spilled out. 'I mean about the way things work. You know – about capitalism, and the way the workers, who are kept poor, are exploited by the capitalist bosses. There's no justice for the poor in the way things are organized – I've seen it, the way people have to struggle to survive. The way some of the people live round our school – you'd hardly believe it!' Her uneducated impressions tumbled out clumsily. She could have told Edwin about who she had begun to learn from, about Daniel Fernandez, but she didn't want to. Daniel felt like her precious secret.

Edwin looked startled. 'Where on earth did you get all these ideas from?'

173

Gwen brushed her skirt. 'Karl Marx,' she said rather haughtily. She didn't like Edwin's implication that she should not have any ideas.

'Oh, I *see* . . .' Edwin turned back towards the house, laughing in a dismissive way which enraged her. She found herself clenching her teeth. 'I hope you realize that Communism is an atheist philosophy?'

'It may be.' She folded her arms, not automatically following him. If only she knew more, could express what she wanted to say better, the way Daniel could! 'But what if it's *right*?'

'Darling Gwen –' Edwin beamed indulgently, coming towards her with his arms open – 'you've always had your heart in the right place. But you don't want to tangle with big political ideas and such like. Best leave those to the politicians. And they don't have much bearing on our life here, do they? It may be all very well in the Soviet Union.'

She didn't return his embrace. 'What about the poor?' she demanded. 'And the miners in Wales? It has some bearing on *them*. Surely there's more to things than our life here – the parish?' She could hear the sarcasm in her voice.

Edwin chuckled and insisted on embracing her anyway, although she was stiff in his arms.

'Yes, yes – of course. And you know what I think about the fascists. But we can all only do so much, darling. We belong *here*. And your job is going to be to work at my side. Communists or no Communists.' He looked down into her eyes. 'Isn't it?'

Until now she'd always thought of him as knowing best. Kind, stolid old Edwin, her husband to be. She was destined to marry him and be here, in the place she knew. Why was she even thinking otherwise? She felt completely deflated. Everything would be all right as long as she toed the line. She looked back at him and said neutrally, 'Yes. I suppose so.'

On the Friday Gwen went for a fitting with Mrs Twining, who had hurried to stitch together the beginnings of her wedding dress. As usual she had done an excellent job and the white silk hugged Gwen's curves like a second skin. Gwen stood in her stockings, suspenders and brassière as Mrs Twining prodded and pinned and tucked fabric round her abdomen.

'Very nice,' she mumbled, pins nipped between her lips. 'Oh yes – we'll need to bring that in a shade . . .'

To Gwen the whole idea that she would process along the aisle in this silk creation seemed more and more unreal. But her cooperation and attempts at enthusiasm had done a good deal to appease her mother. They had chosen a pretty fabric for the bridesmaid and agreed on how they would wear their hair, so Ruth Purdy had relaxed and become quite excited. Gwen was glad she had managed to keep her happy.

With Edwin, she kept off the subject of politics. It was a mistake to let Daniel and his thoughts anywhere near life here. Daniel was part of somewhere else, a temporary kind of dream life, and the two should not be brought into contact. She did her best to make it up to Edwin and he was easily appeased, as soon as she settled back into being her old biddable self. She had spent an afternoon putting together the parish magazine with him and he had been very pleased and grateful.

She said her goodbyes to him on the Saturday night

before she was due to return to Birmingham for the summer term, although she would see him at church the next morning. Edwin, ever proper, embraced her outside her parents' house.

'It's the downhill run now!' Edwin looked very pleased with himself. 'Another four months and we'll be married!'

'I can't really take it in,' Gwen said. An odd, physical sensation accompanied the thought, a kind of twist inside her.

Edwin stroked her hair. Longingly, he said, 'Heavens, I wish it was tomorrow.'

Gwen smiled.

'Darling,' he went on miserably, 'I know it was what you wanted, but I do wish you were here. It's miserable without you. It's seemed such a long time.'

'I know, but it'll soon pass. It's only a term, after all.' Teasingly she tapped his nose. 'The best things come to those who wait.'

He kissed her then, in his ardent yet restrained way, hands pressing on her back while managing not to let her body come any closer to his.

'Oh.' He pulled back regretfully. 'Look, I'd better go, darling.' He was wide-eyed, suddenly boyish, hoping that she would try to prevent him.

Gwen stood on tiptoe and kissed his cheek.

'See you *soon*,' she said. 'It'll be the half-term holiday in no time.'

'Yes.' Edwin sighed. 'I suppose you're right. That's if your landlady doesn't finish you off with her cooking first!' He went to fetch his bicycle.

'I love you!' he called, weaving off along the road.

She opened her mouth to reply, but he was already a good distance away.

The next afternoon she caught her train back to Birmingham. It was raining and water ran down the windows, which were steamed up inside. She sat with her coat still on and rubbed the wet window, trying to see out, excitement rising inside her.

Joey's hand slid along the bottom edge of the large windowpane above the frame, which was covered in flaking sky-blue paint. He liked the smooth feel of the glass, as if it was water and he might sink into it, cool and soothing on his body. He pressed his forehead against it. On the other side of the pane were shelves arranged with jars and packets: bottles of HP Sauce, packets of Tetley Tea and Bournville Cocoa and Bird's custard powder. He pressed his burning cheek against the glass. For a moment all the colours blurred. Then his eyes focused. Pan Yan Pickle, he read on the label of a bottle.

''Ere – you still hanging about? I thought I told you to clear off!' A plump woman stood on the doorstep. Her voice seemed to boom out from somewhere very high up. 'Look what you've done! I only polished that window this morning and you're making it all smeary. Go on with you! You should be at school!'

'Oh, Mom,' another voice said. 'The poor little thing. He don't look very well to me.' Through his hazy senses, Joey felt her come closer, battering him with questions. 'Are you poorly? What's your name? Where d'you live? Does your mother know you're here?'

He didn't know what else to do except nod his head, which felt too big for his body. But it hurt his neck when he did and he screwed his face up in pain.

177

A cool hand touched his forehead. 'He's burning! You been sent home from school have you?'

He nodded.

'You hungry?'

Another nod.

'What's that round your neck?' No answer. 'What's that, Mom? Looks like an old sheet. 'Ere, I'll find you summat to eat. Then you'd best get home to your Mom.'

'You're a soft 'a'p'orth, you are,' the older woman scolded, disappearing into the shop. 'He'll be off round the corner right as rain once you've given 'im summat.'

Joey propped himself against the window frame. Time passed. Then he opened his eyes to see a greasy brown paper bag being dangled in front of his nose.

'Go on, then – take them and away with you,' she said, though not harshly. 'Mom don't like you hanging about.'

Round the corner, in a quiet street, he came upon a pair of big green doors. He sank down on the step and looked in the bag. She'd given him a handful of broken biscuits. He shoved one in his mouth. It was soft and stale and, as he chewed, it turned into a thick lump in his mouth which he only managed to swallow with an effort. He closed the bag. The cold of the step crept up into him, making him shiver violently. He hugged his arms across his chest. Something had happened to his head. It was so heavy he had to lean it against the door, and his eyes wouldn't stay open. Darkness sank over him.

Most of the time now, he didn't know where he was. The first days, after he ran away from Mrs Simmons's

178

house, he'd stayed round Winson Green. Mr Simmons's old trenchcoat was long and heavy and he draped it round his neck, the top half of it hanging down the left side of his chest, the tails on the right side. If it wasn't for the night-time he would have ditched the thing. It stank of snuff and Mr Simmons's stale sweat, and it weighed him down. He felt stupid carting it about. But there was also something comforting about the feel of it, the way it hugged warmly around his neck, and when the light began to fade he was glad he'd carried it all day.

The bread had lasted him until the next day. He had no idea what to do with himself, and he walked the streets, up and down, watching out carefully for anyone who might know him. He was frightened they'd be looking for him – the Barnardo's man with his long chains or a van to push him into and lock him in. He walked along the wall of the prison as fast as he could, looking over his shoulder. There was nowhere to duck into here and hide! What if the orphanage man came now and tried to get him?

He went down to the cut, where he and Lena used to go and play. He didn't want to think about Lena, or Polly or Kenny. He wandered back and forth along the towpath. There were warehouses opposite and he kept hearing the trains going by on the railway behind. At the back of one factory a pipe let out hissing clouds of steam just above the murky water. Joey stood and watched. The canal was busy with boats, the motors put-putting by, the narrowboats passing each other on the thin channel. He liked it down there. There were people about but they didn't bother him. He spent a long while throwing things into the water, stones, twigs and cinders. The coat annoyed him, swinging in his face every time he bent down. Stones were the best, the 'plop' they made, then the little rings of ripples. He had to stand back to let a man go by who was leading a big black and white horse, hauling a boat, its hold heaped high with gleaming coal. The man winked at him as he went past.

Soon after he felt gripes in his stomach and suddenly, urgently needed to relieve himself. He just made it up behind a bush and yanked his short trousers down, grunting at the pain in his stomach. Afterwards he had to wipe himself with leaves and his hand stank. He went and leaned over the bank to wash and found tears running down his face. Those he wiped away on the coat.

He kept away from Canal Street, from the house. In his mind they were all still there for him, those giants from the orphanage outside the house, prepared to wait for ever.

In the afternoon he stole a bottle of sterilized milk from a crate at the back of a shop. If he ran off down the road with it, he knew, someone would be suspicious. He was already quite skilled at pilfering. He held the bottle inside the folds of the coat and slipped quietly out of the entry to the street, walking as if he had every right to be there. In Blackpatch Park he ate some of the hard bread and drank all the milk he could.

As evening came, it grew bitter. The air stung his bare legs and he was too cold to stay still. Joey walked the streets, draping the coat round him, along the Flat, the shops all closed now, past the Railway Inn, the baths in Bacchus Road. Smells filled the air: beer from the pubs, the hot whiff of chips and vinegar and smoke from chimneys. He walked along streets, seeing the lights through the windows, hearing voices as doors opened and slammed shut. He carried with him the remainder of the bottle of stera. His feet were tired and sore, but he didn't think about anything. That night he slept in Blackpatch Park rolled up in the coat, pulling it right over his head. He found a spot under some bushes. He heard little rustling noises in the leaves around him, but he kept his head down, exhausted. The next morning he was woken by a magpie's croaking call on the grass nearby.

Over the next few days he walked further out of town. He found other ways of getting food. In Handsworth, he discovered, there were people in the big houses who were rich enough to throw away food. There were the pig bins – usually full of a reeking mulch of leftovers – but in the misken at one house he found a cooked lamb chop and a lump of stale cake. He gnawed for ages at the chop bone. Later, over the side wall of another house, he saw that someone had left a basin of something to cool on the step by the back door. He couldn't see what it was, only the steam rising. He had been walking the streets for three days now and the temptation of warm food possessed him so much he was trembling. Gritting his teeth, he climbed the wall, seized hold of the basin and tried to get back over with it, but it slipped from under his arm and as he leapt to the ground he heard it smash on the path behind. Heart hammering, he ducked down behind the wall. But no one came.

Slowly, still driven by desperation, he inched himself up, pulled up on his arms and looked down over the wall. Amid the smashed shell of the bowl lay soft lumps of egg custard. Saliva poured into his mouth. He *had* to have some! At that moment he didn't care about anything else, would have risked everything for the comfort of that warm, sweet pudding sliding down his throat. In a second he had scrambled over and was scooping the stuff into him in handfuls, separating it from the bits of broken crock. He crammed in as much as his mouth would take, cheeks ballooning, swallowing convulsively.

He heard footsteps in the house and was on the wall in a second, hands smeared with custard.

'Oi – get back 'ere, you little bugger! Look what you've gone and done!'

But he was over, running and running, the coat weighing him down. He ran until he was well away, gasping with exhaustion. He felt terrible. His innards heaved, splatting custard along the Hamstead Road.

That night he slept in Handsworth Park and it rained. He thought about sleeping on the bandstand, but it felt too exposed. Instead, he burrowed himself as far under some bushes as he could, near the churchyard at the side of the park, wrapping himself right up in the coat. In the night he was woken by something tugging at him. Then he was being dragged and he tried to put out his hands, but he was tangled in the coat. Suddenly he felt himself flipped over, banging his back on something sharp and the coat was yanked away from him.

'Oi!' He leapt up. 'That's mine!'

'Not any more it ain't,' a gruff voice said. He barely even got a glimpse of the man as he ran off across the park.

'Give it back!' Joey wailed. 'It's mine! It's my dad's!' In his mind it felt as if it was his father's. He pushed back into his spot under the bushes and hugged his cold legs. Without the coat, he felt naked. It had been like a companion.

Hungering for the sight of something familiar, he

wandered back towards Winson Green the next morning. The day brightened, but it took his damp clothes a long time to dry out. He went to Canal Street under the railway bridge, all his senses alert for meeting anyone he recognized. Near the school he could hear the shouts and screams of children playing. He couldn't help it: he was drawn closer, just wanting to be near, to see. The school playground was lit up with sunshine at the far end. He stood at the corner in the shade, pressed against the railings, peering through. There was a group playing hopscotch. He saw Lucy Fernandez with her long dark hair, limping in the heavy caliper. And Ron – wasn't that Ron? But then his attention was snatched away. Miss Purdy was on dinner duty! At the sight of her in her neat blue coat, with her pretty hair and pink ribbon, something seemed to expand inside him, right up to the back of his throat, an ache that made him swallow to try and make it go away. But then he saw her shade her eyes and he thought she was looking at him. She began to move towards him. He tore himself away, running fast along the street and round the corner.

The nights were the worst now. All he had to wear were his short trousers, his ragged vest, the grey jersey that Miss Purdy had given him and his boots and socks. In the daytime all he thought about was finding food and keeping out of trouble. He wandered from neighbourhood to neighbourhood, begging and stealing food from shops and houses, drinking stolen milk and water from water butts and taps. He went for several days without speaking to anyone, or them speaking to him. Sometimes he felt as if he was invisible.

183

At night he always found a park to sleep in. Once he slept in a shed at the bottom of a big garden, and was very glad he had as it rained hard that night. In the shed he found a soft old sheet, which was full of dust and made him sneeze. He rolled it up to take with him in the morning and found it was a dirty cream colour and encrusted with stains of deep green paint. It was not much against the night-time cold but he found it a comfort. In the daytime he slung it round his neck, as he had the coat.

By the time darkness fell he was usually exhausted from moving round all day and fending for himself. He wrapped himself round in the sheet and pushed himself under a bush where no one could see him. He had grown used to the rustlings of the night. One night, as he lay curled up in the sheet, he heard miaowing close by. He could sense the cat looking at him and he uncovered his head.

'Here, puss,' he whispered, reaching out his hand. His own voice felt strange to him. The cat allowed him to touch it and began to purr.

'Come on – come in here with me.'

Curled up beside the warm, purring body he slept, comforted. Sometime before dawn the cat woke with a commotion and scrabbled about, frantic to be released from the sheet.

'Don't go!' he heard himself say, but as he lifted his head the cat shot past him. He lay down, feeling how sore his throat was. His head ached and his neck felt stiff. He didn't feel well all day and he didn't move far. That night he slept in the same spot, hoping the cat would come back, but there was no sign of it. He lay on the hard ground, cheeks burning, yet his body was shaking and the cold seemed to bite right into him. He barely slept and when he did his dreams were frightening. When he woke in the morning he could hardly tell who he was, and it was later that day that he found himself waking on a doorstep, propped up next to two big green doors, with a greasy bag of broken biscuits in his hand.

He leaned his head against the rough bricks. His breathing was too quick, his body pulsing like a chick he once saw hatch from an egg in the brewhouse when his father kept hens. Everything about the baby bird had seemed too fast, as if it must burn itself out with living within minutes of being born. Joey's vision blurred, then corrected itself. He could hear his pulse banging in his ears. It was a quiet street and only a couple of people passed, who gave him no more than a glance. Joey didn't move. He sat still, his eyes half open.

A figure was approaching briskly along the street. Joey watched dully, then his eyes snapped open. That uniform! It was the School Board man, whistling as he came along the road! He'd come to get him, to take him away and lock him up behind the walls of the orphanage! Joey wanted to get up and run away, but his body wouldn't obey. He managed to turn himself sideways and cringe back into the darkest corner of the doorway, pulling his knees up tightly to his chest and turning his face away. The whistling came closer. Joey pushed his head down against his knees, eyes squeezed shut. His kneecaps felt huge and hard. He held his breath. The whistling passed without a pause and he uncurled, trembling.

He couldn't bear the thought of sleeping out again that night. He would have liked to go and find the shed from where he'd taken his sheet, but he didn't have any

185

idea where it was, or where he was now. By the time darkness was falling he found himself in a street of high houses with roofs like triangles and front gardens and gates. There were curtains and lights on inside – electric lights like the ones in school. He had eaten nothing all day except that one mouthful of biscuit and his legs were shaky. A road intersected with the one along which he was walking, and at the end the last two houses were dark with no curtains in the windows.

Hardly knowing what he was doing, Joey pushed open the gate of the end house. The path was over-grown and plants brushed against his legs, scratching him. Joey wondered if anyone lived there. He went round to the back. There might be a shed down the garden. He was desperate to lie down anywhere under cover and rest his pounding head and shivering bones. Even the weight of the sheet he was carrying felt almost too much to bear.

The path took him round to the back door. To his surprise, when he went up close, he saw it was slightly ajar and he pushed his way in. It was dark and he noticed that the floor felt uneven underfoot. There was a sound like running water somewhere near him. If he could just lie down anywhere – he didn't care now if someone lived there, if he got caught. He had to lie down, to sleep . . .

In the hall he felt his way along the wall and came to a doorway on his left. He fumbled for the handle and stumbled inside. Here – he'd sleep here. It was the last thing he would remember for some time after that: taking his sheet from round his neck and sinking onto it on the hard floor, as he pulled it round him. Later he remembered that, as he drifted quickly into uncon-sciousness, he heard the sound of someone snoring.

SUMMER TERM

1936

Sixteen

'Donald Andrews? Joan Billings?'
  'Yes, Miss.'
  'Here, Miss!'
  'Ernie Davis?'
  'Yes, Miss.'
  Gwen smiled at her class as she took the register. It was a bright spring morning and she felt full of energy and enthusiasm. The classroom looked colourful now, with all the Easter pictures they'd painted pinned up round the walls, and the sun was pouring in through the long windows. It occurred to Gwen just how much she liked being a teacher.
  'Lucy Fernandez?'
  'Yes, Miss.'
  She glanced up to see Lucy's intense dark eyes fixed on her face.
  'Ron Parks?'
  As usual, there was some sort of kerfuffle going on round Ron. His hands were stuffed into his pockets and the boys round him were grinning from ear to ear.
  'Oh – yes, Miss!' he said distractedly.
  'Ron –' Gwen looked sternly at him – 'if you're going to be our milk monitor this term, you're going to have to behave much better and learn to be sensible.' She moved closer to Ron's place in the third row. 'Aren't you?'

'Yes, Miss.' Ron clamped his mouth shut, looking as if he was going to burst with the need to laugh.

'Well, take your hands out of your pockets and sit up straight. What *is* the matter with you today?'

Ron carefully extracted his hands from his pockets. Puzzled, Gwen could see the other children watching intently. Freddie Peters's mouth gaped open. Doreen Smith had a hand clasped over hers. Gwen was just about to ask whether the sight of Ron Parks taking his hands out of his pockets was really so fascinating when she saw Ron give a great squirm and his expression turn to one of horror. Suddenly everyone was staring at the floor by his chair. Sitting in a confused heap, after its escape into the light, was a sizeable toad. The children erupted with equal delight and revulsion, the boys roaring, some of the girls squealing.

Then everything went quiet for just a second. They all looked at Miss Purdy, waiting for her reaction. Ron had gone very red.

'Sorry, Miss,' he said.

'Sit still, all of you!' Gwen dashed across to the corner, seized the empty wastepaper basket and stalked along the aisle towards the toad. Even in the midst of everything, her capacity to view the situation from the outside and see its funny side was bringing her dangerously close to giggles herself. The terrible thought that Mr Lowry might be patrolling in the hall outside and peering in through the windows somehow made it even funnier. He'd probably give her the sack!

The toad saw her coming and began to hop frantically towards the back of the classroom.

'Don't let it get under the desks or we'll never catch it!' Gwen cried. 'Hold your hands out – fend it off!'

The toad reached the skirting board at the back of

190

the room. On each side children's hands were flapping at it and a strange creature was homing in on it with a waste bin. Caught in this impasse, the toad looked understandably gloomy. Gwen dropped the bin over the top of it and held it down with her foot. The children all started to clap. Gwen couldn't help a grin spreading over her own face.

'There!' she laughed. 'Got him!' She attempted to look more sober. 'Well, Ron has given us an interesting natural history lesson this morning – before I've even finished taking the register. Unfortunately, though, we're supposed to be having a geography lesson. Ron, come and remove this toad, please, and take it outside. Preferably without running into Mr Lowry.'

She finished the register.

'Alice Wilson?'

'Here, Miss.'

Gwen was reassured. Alice had been absent the day before.

'Were you poorly yesterday, Alice?'

'Yes, Miss.' The child barely spoke above a whisper.

Gwen frowned. She was growing increasingly concerned about Alice. Even though she had suggested such a time ago now that Alice should be provided with some spectacles, she still had none and sat through the classes squinting hopelessly, unable to see the blackboard, even though Gwen had seated her at the front. And, having begun the year neat as a pin, she was looking more and more down at heel.

'Now – books out, children. We're going to learn some more about Australia. But first of all – can anyone tell me the name of a famous lady pilot who flew to Australia all on her own?'

Alice Wilson's hand flew up.

'Alice?'

'Amy Johnson,' the girl said enthusiastically. 'And her aeroplane was called Gypsy Moth.'

'Very good.' Gwen smiled. 'Amy Johnson landed in Darwin on May 24th, 1930. That's *eleven thousand* miles away. Now, I'm going to show you where Darwin is.'

At the end of the morning, she told Ron Parks to stay behind. He came to her as she sat at her desk.

'What I should do by rights is send you to Mr Lowry.'

'Yes, Miss.' Ron lowered his head.

She paused, thinking with distaste of Mr Lowry and his collection of canes. 'I don't think it will be necessary this time. But, Ron, do you think you could try to come to school with *nothing* in your pockets – just for once? No gobstoppers, marbles, toads . . . Nothing except a handkerchief, perhaps?'

The corners of Ron's mouth twitched.

'Yes, Miss Purdy.'

Fondly she looked at his round face, the rumpled brown hair. Ron seemed to her to be a boy without a streak of malice in him.

'Ron, have you seen anything of Joey Phillips since he left?'

Ron's face creased in a worried sort of way. 'No, I ain't seen him. Don't know where he can've gone to. I s'pose they took him to the home. That's what they said.'

'Who said?'

Ron shrugged. 'I dunno. Just, you know, our Mom. I ain't seen him.'

'All right. Well, if you do, will you tell me?'

Ron nodded.

'All right – go and get your dinner or your mother'll be cross. And . . .'

'Yes, Miss?' he said, from the doorway.

'Where exactly did you put the toad?'

'I put him down over by the wall of the pub, like, so he daint have to cross the road by himself. I thought he might be able to get back down to the cut.'

'Well, let's hope so,' Gwen smiled. 'Go on. Off you go.'

They'd been back at school for a couple of weeks. Millie Dawson had been replaced by a young woman called Miss Rowley, who was now teaching in the room next to Gwen, and she was civil enough, though Gwen didn't find the immediate warmth of friendship that she had with Millie. Charlotte Rowley was a tiny, doll-like person with brown eyes, a sallow complexion and black hair cut short and very neatly round her collar. She was always immaculately dressed and, despite her shrill, childlike voice, seemed to wield absolute control over her class. At the same time, the fact that she was young and had a slightly sultry air about her provoked the immediate and bitter suspicion of Miss Monk, who couldn't find a polite word to say to her.

'What is the matter with *her*?' Miss Rowley asked Gwen on her second day, when Miss Monk had been blatantly rude to her. 'Have I done something to upset her?'

'Only being young and pretty,' Gwen said. 'She thinks anyone younger than her is a threat to her chances with old Lowry.'

'Lowry?' Charlotte Rowley's brow wrinkled.

'She keeps waiting for him to notice her. It'd be sad if she wasn't so incredibly unpleasant to everyone else.'

Miss Rowley said nothing in reply. She just stared back at Gwen, who decided she was rather strange.

The first weeks of term had been a period of calm. Gwen returned to school full of common-sense resolve. She had been measured for her wedding dress, she had managed to get on amicably enough with her mother and she was going back to marry Edwin in August. Edwin was right: that was where she belonged, not trying to concern herself with the woes of the poor of Birmingham or anywhere else. Something about her marriage to Edwin felt inevitable. Anything else would be unthinkable now. And this was not just because of herself and Edwin – it involved her parents, and James and Edwina Shackleton. She was almost like one of their family already. There was something reassuring and safe about this, but at the same time it was frightening, as if she had no say in deciding her own fate.

All brides are nervous and worried, she'd told herself as her train chugged its way closer to Birmingham at the end of the holidays. *This is just normal.* And on the first day of school, as soon as she reached the prison and got off to walk along Canal Street, her whole being seemed to tingle with anticipation and she worked hard to persuade herself that this was not because she was in the neighbourhood where *he* lived, that she was not hoping with every fibre of her body that round every corner might appear Daniel Fernandez.

The first afternoon, as the children left at the end of school, Lucy was the last one out as usual.

'Lucy.' Gwen called her to her desk. Surely it would not be out of place to ask after the family now?

'How are you all?' She tried to sound casual, fiddling

with the top of her fountain pen. 'Everyone well at home?'

Lucy nodded with a shy smile. 'Daniel's not here.'

Gwen felt the blood rise in her cheeks. It was as if the child could read her mind! Was it written all over her face that this was the one thing she was really longing to know? But she soon realized this was not the reason.

'He's gone to Cardiff,' Lucy announced proudly. 'He's going to speak to people outside the assizes and tell them not to send all the miners to prison.'

'Is he?' Gwen replied, startled. She hadn't the least notion of what the child was talking about. 'Why should the miners be sent to prison?'

'Because of the strikes. They stayed down the mine at Taff Merthyr.' As Lucy spoke, Gwen could see in her the same fire that she saw in her brother. 'Daniel says they were on strike against the company's union – last year. They stayed down the pit for days and wouldn't come out. And now the bosses want to send them to prison.'

'And Daniel?'

'Daniel goes all over the place, speaking and that.'

Ashamed of her own ignorance once again, Gwen bought a newspaper on the way home. Why was she so unaware of everything going on in the world? It was as if she had been living in a dream all these years. Waiting for her tram, she scanned through the paper. In a column inside she read that the trial at Cardiff Assizes was to be the biggest mass trial of industrial workers ever held in Britain and she sat on the tram burning with pride that Daniel was there, would be speaking out against injustice. She wasn't even sure why it was unjust, but Daniel would know. She imagined him standing in front of a crowd, shouting out with the passion she had seen when he talked to her.

She had found the courage to ask Lucy whether he was coming back to Birmingham. 'He'll be back,' Lucy said assuredly. 'He always comes home to our mam – we just never know when, that's all.'

But the days had gone past and there was no sign of Daniel's return. She read that the court had sentenced fifty-three men and three women to terms of hard labour, ranging from three to fifteen months. How could this be? she wondered. If all they were trying to do was to defend their livelihood? Surely they must have done something terrible to be sent to prison to do hard labour. For a time she doubted Daniel. What was he really involved with? After all, she barely knew him. She wasn't used to being associated with people who went to prison.

When he didn't return she calmed down a little and tried to persuade herself that it couldn't possibly matter if she ever saw him again. After all, he was just the brother of one of her pupils: he was nothing to her, nor she to him. It was true that she found his company a novelty. It was exciting. But Daniel must see her as an ignorant little miss, with her comfortable middle-class home. He probably despised her. And she was engaged to be married, for goodness sake! Even if she hadn't been, Daniel was certainly not the class or type of person her parents could ever conceivably approve of. The very thought was absurd! So she kept herself in a calm, sensible mood and wrote jolly letters to Edwin, telling him the details of her daily life that she thought he would want to hear. And they certainly did not include Daniel. Nor, for that matter, did she describe just what it was like living, these days, in the Soho Road house.

196

Seventeen

Ariadne shuffled into the breakfast room, bearing a rack of toast which left a trail of blue smoke in the air behind it.

'I've overdone it again just a little bit, haven't I?' she said with a playful glance at Harold Purvis. She deposited on the table the charred remnants of what had been a reasonable loaf of bread, shedding a miniature cascade of black crumbs onto the embroidered cloth. Harold Purvis stared gloomily at it. Gwen tackled her egg with the vigour it demanded after fifteen minutes fast boiling and managed to prise the top off to reveal a pale yoke, ruffled and dry as old velvet. She tried not to think about who had slept in whose bedroom last night, or feel Harold's little sideways glances at her. Every morning was like this now. It might have been amusing to begin with but it certainly wasn't any more.

While she had been away, things had developed. Almost every night now Ariadne crept along the landing and begged to be let in at Harold's door. Or Gwen might hear her saying, through the door, 'You come to me, Harold, darling. Why don't you come along to me? I'll be waiting for you.' And once or twice she had heard him go. She lay in bed picturing Harold plodding along the landing in his striped pyjamas, his white hands hanging below the sleeves. Every time he passed her door she tensed, her heart pounding. He had never tried to come in, but she still had the feeling that he might. She had started pushing her chair up against the door just in case. What with that and Harold's trumpet dreaming of marble halls every evening, living in Soho Road was becoming a horrible strain.

Ariadne had lately got into the habit of coming down to breakfast in her dressing gown. It was pale green cotton, reaching almost to her ankles and she fastened it very tightly at the waist. Her bright pink slippers had ribbons at the front and made little slip-slap noises as she walked. Her hair was bagged up in a brown net, under which were rollers, and pins securing kiss curls round her forehead. She invariably had lipstick on and had pencilled in her eyebrows.

'I put my face on after,' she once confided to Gwen. 'But I can't come down completely *naked*, can I?'

Ariadne breakfasted on her usual diet of tea, cigarettes and whichever newspaper came to hand, which this morning was the *Birmingham Gazette*.

Gwen smeared margarine over the raven-coloured toast.

'Oh, my word,' Ariadne said, 'look at this – "Man Chased to His Death by a Dog..."' She took a long drag on her cigarette and blew smoke across the table.

Gwen frowned. 'So how did he die?'

There was a pause as Ariadne ran her finger along the lines of print.

'Says here he drowned – jumped off a pier ... And oh, look – that Nurse Waddingham's going to be hanged – day after tomorrow.'

Nurse Waddingham had been sentenced in February, but now the hanging was about to happen, on 16 April,

198

and it was the talk of Birmingham. Ariadne was full of it and the teachers at Canal Street School debated the pros and cons in the dinner hour, sitting round on the battered old chairs with their sandwiches.

'There's no smoke without fire,' Miss Monk declared, crossing one hefty brown stockinged leg over the other. 'She's benefited from the woman's will – seems obvious she had a hand in hurrying the old girl's end. Good riddance to her, the scheming shrew.' She cast a bitter glance at Charlotte Rowley, as if bracketing her in the insult as well.

Gwen had learned from Ariadne that Nurse Waddingham was a thirty-four-year-old mother of five children, who had been nursing eighty-nine-year-old Louisa Baguley in a home in Nottingham. Both Louisa Baguley and her daughter Ada, who was fifty-five, had died in mysterious circumstances, having willed money to 'Nurse' Waddingham.

'I think it's a scandal,' Miss Drysdale declared, with an emphatic gesture which caused tea to spill from her cup onto the brown linoleum. 'Imagine, that we're still hanging people in this country. Taking a life for a life – it's most un-Christian!'

'Huh – calling *yourself* a Christian!' Miss Monk scoffed half to herself, and Gwen wondered what on earth she meant. How vile the woman was! Otherwise, though, there was a general murmur of agreement. Mr Gaffney was nodding.

'You're right,' he kept repeating. 'It's a terrible thing. Terrible.' Gwen saw that he was quivering, as he did from time to time, seemingly overcome by his nerves. He had wispy remnants of hair round his bald pate and kind, watery eyes. She wondered what had happened to him in the war.

'Well, I agree with Mr Lowry,' Miss Monk pronounced.

'Of course you do,' Gwen said, managing to keep her tone so neutral that Agnes Monk wasn't sure whether she was being insulted or not. Gwen looked back innocently at her, and pulled a cheese and onion cob out of a paper bag. From the corner of her eye she saw the corner of Charlotte Rowley's mouth twitch with amusement.

Miss Monk glowered suspiciously at Gwen. 'You may be aware, Miss Purdy, that Mr Lowry is a strong believer in discipline and I have respect for his views.'

'There's discipline, and there's barbarity,' Lily Drysdale said. 'The woman has five children – the baby's only a few months old! Who's going to bring them up? I shall protest with the others who'll stand against this, in the strongest terms.'

'Huh,' Miss Monk said contemptuously. 'A lot of good that'll do you. They're set to hang her, whatever you say, or that red, Violet Van der Elst, and all her campaigning. Good riddance to her.'

Gwen listened to the arguments, feeling immediately opposed to the hanging because Agnes Monk was for it. Her whole being rebelled against the idea – she thought of the woman waiting in her cell, imagining the rope tightening round her neck, her last gasp of life followed by everlasting darkness. Frightful even if she was guilty. But what if she wasn't?

'It *is* barbaric, isn't it?' she said to Miss Rowley.

'Oh, I don't know,' Miss Rowley said. She sat very straight and neatly, her feet lined up side by side in little blue shoes with straps. 'She took someone else's life, after all. She showed no pity.'

200

There was a coldness in the way she spoke that made Gwen like her even less.

The day before the hanging Mr Lowry announced in assembly that school would be starting late the next morning. The streets would be cordoned off round the prison to keep the crowds away until the hanging was over.

Gwen did not sleep at all well that Wednesday night. First of all, when she came back from the bathroom before bed, she found Harold Purvis on the landing, blocking the way to her room. Gwen felt her pulse begin to speed up with alarm. She told herself not to be so silly. What could Harold Purvis do to her, with Ariadne just along the corridor? But he loomed over her, standing there in his suit, shiny with wear and his big black shoes. And she was already in her nightdress, dressing gown over the top with no underwear on and felt naked and very much at a disadvantage.

She folded her arms tightly, and in a sharp tone said, 'Excuse me – could you please let me get to my room?'

Harold leaned against the wall, facing her, a half smile on his face. Gwen realized instinctively that he wasn't actually going to do anything, but that he enjoyed the feeling of power he gained from tormenting her.

'You look very nice,' he said, in a snaky, repellent voice. 'Very nice indeed.'

'I'm waiting to get to bed,' she said, more annoyed now than alarmed. 'And I don't like personal comments, thank you.'

'Not even nice ones?' He smiled suggestively.

Not from you, she wanted to say, but sensed that getting into that kind of banter with him would be to play his game. Instead, she stood her ground, staring back at him.

'A man can't resist the sight of a beautiful woman,' he said softly.

'No. Well, that's obvious,' she snapped, then lurched inwardly with alarm as Harold moved suddenly closer.

'D'you think *she's* really what I want?' His breath stank of onions. 'An old thing like her, when I can see you in front of me, day after day?'

Gwen froze. To her horror, she felt Harold Purvis's hand slide round her left buttock, over the silky, peach-coloured dressing gown.

'You're *much* more my type,' he whispered, dealing her another blast of onions.

'Get *off!*'

She gave him a hard push, and Harold staggered backwards against the opposite wall.

'Stuck-up little cow!' she heard as she fled into her room and pushed the chair up against the door.

'I've got to get out of here,' she thought, sitting up shakily in bed. She didn't want to turn off the light. She knew she wouldn't be able to sleep. All her senses were alert to what was going on outside her door. Once she was sure things had quietened down outside, she lay in the dark and tried to settle. But she felt humiliated and one nasty thought followed another. Once she'd managed to get her mind off Harold Purvis, the thought of Nurse Waddingham came to her, living through her last night. However must she feel? She imagined her with long, dark hair, sitting with her head lowered, tortured by the thought of her children, soon to be motherless, and of her own remaining hours before her thirty-six-year-old life was snuffed out.

The next morning Gwen picked at her breakfast, which was Ariadne's porridge – not burnt for once, but still a strangely unpleasant consistency – and avoided looking at Harold Purvis. Ariadne smoked and avidly read bits of yesterday's paper.

'"Fiancé's Suicide on Wedding Eve" – oh, what a *shame*. Found with his head in the gas oven ... That'll be money, won't it?' She lit another cigarette and turned the page.

'Here we are ... Protests outside the prison. That Mrs Van der Elst says she wants aeroplanes flying over, dropping leaflets protesting against capital punishment ... First woman this century to be executed at Winson Green Prison.'

Gwen swallowed her last mouthful of porridge and fled. It was a relief to be out of the house. She got off the tram a stop early, making her way through the grey morning. There were a lot of people about, milling through the streets as she got closer to the prison, and an atmosphere of anticlimax. The hanging was already over. Following the crowds, she walked to the end of Villiers Street, where the main entrance to the prison loomed forbiddingly, like a dark castle. A row of policemen stood across the entrance and a large number of people were gathered round the gates. Gwen found herself being herded towards them, carried along by the press of people.

'Why's everyone going over there?' she asked a woman whose face was alight with an eager expression.

'We want to read the death notice!' the woman said avidly. Gwen found her excitement repugnant. The crowd was under control, but the force of it was still alarming. Gwen was knocked from behind so that her hat was pushed right down over her eyes.

Oh, I've had enough of this, she thought, shoving it back so she could see and trying to push her way towards the edge. There was a lamp post out to the right of the entrance and she headed for that.

'Here you go.' A policeman stood aside to let her through as she forced her way out, and stood beside the lamp post to get her breath back, looking back at the prison.

'Come to join the baying crowd, have you?'

She turned, thinking for a split second that she had mistaken that voice, or dreamt it, but found herself staring up into Daniel's challenging smile. He looked exactly as he always did: shirtsleeves, no collar and bareheaded today, a cigarette at the corner of his mouth. He was holding in front of him several copies of the *Daily Worker*. Immediately she was aware of a new sense of life, as if a light had gone on.

'You're back!'

She felt foolish then, as if she had let him know she had been waiting, and it was only in that moment she realized how much she had been doing just that and the realization made her blush.

'I'm back,' Daniel agreed. He took a last drag on his cigarette and threw it down. She wasn't aware of having seen him smoke before. Edwin didn't approve of tobacco, she thought, seeing Daniel crush the stub on the cobbles with his heel. 'Who told you I was away? You been round to find me?'

'No!' she said quickly, resenting his assumption that she would come trotting round to find him. But then she saw from his eyes that he was teasing. 'Lucy told me. She said you were at the trial in Cardiff.'

Daniel's face darkened. 'Trial's not the word,' he said contemptuously. 'But yes – I was there.' He glanced round. 'Let's get away from here. Too late now. The woman's dead. We can't bring her back. And no one's buying these.' He rolled up the *Daily Workers* and put them in the bag, slung over his shoulder. 'All too keen on baying for blood.'

She felt him take her arm and let him steer her through the edge of the crowd, which was thinning and dispersing now, along the surrounding streets. She was filled with a prickly awareness of his closeness.

'Were you part of the protest?' she asked.

Daniel nodded curtly. 'Fat lot of notice anyone takes. Even that Labour woman, Van der Elst . . .'

'Who *is* Mrs Van der Elst?' Gwen asked. They reached a quieter part of the street and Daniel let go of her arm. The warmth of his grip faded from her skin.

'Oh, she's a toff who's got ideas about standing for the Labour Party – round here first thing, she was, with her car and her furs on. Giving out leaflets.'

'Against the hanging?'

'Against *all* hanging. Barbarism, that's what it is. They wouldn't listen. If they won't listen to someone like that, what chance does the ordinary working man have to be heard?'

'Well, yes,' Gwen agreed. 'I suppose that's how things are.'

'Things are as they are because we let them stay like it!' he exploded. Apparently she had just said the one thing that was a red rag to Daniel. 'We make the world – every one of us – by choosing to act or not act on what we see. It doesn't just happen. We're not puppets!'

'I wasn't saying I thought things *should* be like that,' Gwen flared, annoyed at being misunderstood, at always being seen as someone who didn't know anything. 'I just meant that's how they *are*. Exactly like you just said – with no justice for the right people. I don't believe they should have hanged that nurse. It was wrong and terrible.'

Daniel was walking fast, hands thrust into his pockets. It suddenly occurred to Gwen that she had never seen him without the plaster cast on before. He moved so fast she had to trot sometimes to keep up.

'Your leg's better,' she remarked.

'Oh yes,' he said carelessly. 'Sound as a bell. I can get a bit of work now here and there.'

'I still don't understand what it is you do,' she said, as they turned into the end of Canal Street. 'Are you some sort of roving speaker?'

'I work for the party and the movement, like I told you. I work as much as I can, in between, but I go wherever I'm needed. They say I'm a good speaker. I rally people, see – not just in the valleys – here, and wherever the work takes me. But I don't like to stay away from Mam for too long. Her life's been hard.'

Gwen was puzzled. Theresa Fernandez had sounded hard, bitter even about Daniel's activities. Yet here was he speaking about her with such care, tenderness even.

'Has it?' she said.

Daniel stopped. They were only yards from the school gates and he looked down into her eyes.

'You've no idea, have you? What it's like?'

'No,' she agreed quietly, 'but I want to learn.'

The look on his face dizzied her. His brown eyes stared hard into hers, not teasing now, but examining, challenging. She held his gaze, feeling it go right through her. Then he looked away. There were children coming in groups along the road. Gwen caught a glimpse of Alice Wilson moving along in her dreamy way. Why did she feel responsible now for these people? Really they were nothing to do with her.

'Sunday,' Daniel said abruptly. 'We could go up to the hills. If you want to, that is.'

'Yes,' she said. 'Yes, I do.'

Eighteen

'How old are you, then?' Daniel asked as they sat squeezed close together on the tram. Daniel was seated to Gwen's right.

She laughed, taken aback by his directness. He was in a jaunty mood. She had already seen that when he wasn't talking about politics he could be full of cheek and banter.

'Twenty-one last October. And you?'

'I'm twenty-six.' He grinned and lit a cigarette, eyes full of laughter. 'An old man compared to you.'

'Oh, ancient!' Gwen agreed.

They were squeezed onto the tram seat. Gwen had been excited and nervous all at once about spending the day with him. She thought it might be very awkward, conscious as she was of the contrast in their backgrounds, how different her life had been from his. But now they were together she found they talked more easily than she had expected. And to be going anywhere with Daniel felt like embarking on an adventure, as if his very presence made life exciting.

They met at the tram stop where she usually got off for school. She arrived at the stop first, and saw him walking up the road towards her with his muscular stride, his jacket over his shoulder in the sunshine, looking quite leisurely and different from how she had ever seen him before.

'Morning, Miss Purdy!' He smiled mischievously.

She tutted, but returned the smile. 'I'm never called Miss Purdy on Sundays. It's the rule.'

'Ah well – I like breaking rules, see. Gwen though, isn't it?'

Of course Lucy would always call her Miss Purdy, she realized, so Daniel barely even knew her name!

'I think I can let you call me Gwen,' she said, with a mock primness that seemed to amuse him.

They had a brief discussion about where to go. Sutton Park would have been nearer, but Daniel was determined to find hills.

'Let's get up high somewhere – have a good walk. You can't breathe, sometimes, walled up in this place.'

'You'd like it where I come from,' she told him as they waited for the tram. 'It's at the edge of town and then you get out and there are beautiful hills and views. And the Malverns not far away – it's lovely.'

'Nothing like it.' Standing beside him, she could sense once again the power which seemed to emanate from him. He looked at the sky. 'Don't think this is going to last, though.'

It was sunny, but clouds were piling up ahead of them. Gwen was glad she had put on practical clothes – slacks and flat walking shoes. By the time they were halfway down the Bristol Road, rain was spattering against the tram windows.

'Soon be over,' Daniel said, twisting round to wipe the steamy window. 'It's bright over there.'

Gwen didn't care two hoots whether it rained or not. They'd make the best of it, whatever. It was being here that mattered. Being with him. A wave of panic went through her when she realized how strong this feeling was, but she pushed it away. Now was what

209

was important. These moments and the day ahead of them. She would not think of anything else.

Each of them had a coat lying on their lap – Gwen's blue macintosh and Daniel's old jacket. She looked down at them, at Daniel's right hand resting on the faded black serge. His fingers were strong and slender. She could feel the warmth of his leg beside hers, the press of his shoulder and arm. It was strange, she thought, what an incongruous-looking pair they were. Yet it felt right. It felt as if there was nowhere else she wanted to be ... She pulled her thoughts together. Daniel might become a friend, that was all, and to him she was ... What was she? A bit of female company to while away a Sunday afternoon with? Perhaps someone he could educate with his political views?

She had thought they might find conversation difficult, but instead it flowed easily. Surrounded by other passengers, they talked softly. Before they had got off the tram Daniel asked about her family and she told him, with a frankness that took her by surprise, about her parents and brothers and about her mother's horror at the idea of her coming to teach in Birmingham. Daniel laughed at her descriptions.

'She doesn't want you mixing with the riff-raff then, is it?'

'Mummy's never been anywhere very much all her life. She was born in Hereford, hardly left there until they moved to Worcester, when she married Daddy. She never even seems to *want* to go anywhere.'

Daniel watched her face. 'But you do?'

'Oh yes. I mean, I've never been anywhere much, either. Not even to London or anything. I'd like to go *everywhere*!'

Daniel smiled at her fervour.

'You seem to have been to so many more places than me,' she said. 'Wales, and here and . . .'

'London,' Daniel added. The tram slammed to a halt suddenly, making them all lurch to one side. Gwen was thrown against Daniel for a second.

'Steady!' he grasped her forearm for a moment, then released it.

'You've been to London?' She was talking quickly to cover how much his touch affected her. 'Of course – you were at the college there!'

Daniel nodded. 'I was – a few years back, for a while. Last time I went was on foot. Two years ago. Marched from the valleys. You've heard of the Hunger Marches, surely you have?'

He looked at her quizzically. While her ignorance of political matters had seemed at first to aggravate him, now he seemed to find her other-worldliness amusing.

'I have heard of them!' she protested. 'And you were on them?'

'On that one, I was.'

'So you were all marching because . . .' She dredged her memory. 'Because there was no work?'

'No work for some. And the Unemployment Bill – Slave Bill we call it – that the government saw fit to pass to starve and bully the miners who've already had their jobs stolen from them by fascist bosses and blacklegs. But it brought the people together.' His voice began to rise with excitement. 'They're turning to the party now. They can see that the only way to victory is for the working class to unite, to overthrow the tyrannies of capitalism and fascism!'

A pale, middle-aged man turned his head and stared at Daniel in disgust. 'Why don't you shurrup, you silly

211

bugger? Carrying on as if you're on a bleeding soap-box.'

For a split second Gwen thought Daniel was going to get up and punch the man, but instead he lowered his head, hands clenched into fists. She could feel the tension in him, his whole being seemed to throb with feeling beside her.

'They're all blind,' he said, through his teeth. 'Been duped, all of them. But they'll see. One day they'll all see.'

By the time the tram reached the terminus at Rednal, the sun was out again and the grass sparkled with raindrops. They climbed down and Daniel turned, with sudden gallantry, which took her by surprise, and took her hand. But then he said, 'Right – let's go!' Seeming released, he set off at such a pace that Gwen had to run after him.

'I can't keep up, not this fast!' she panted.

'Sorry.' He was relaxed again now and gave an easy grin, slowing his stride.

They climbed to the spot where they could look across the vista of the surrounding counties.

'Home's over there somewhere.' Gwen pointed.

'And mine's over there . . .' He turned further west.

'Is Wales still home then?'

'Oh yes. It is really. Even though Ma's here. She wanted to be away and I don't blame her. Not after everything she was put through there. But my heart's in the valleys. That's where my people are.'

As they began to walk the paths, between trees and bracken awakening from its winter brown, she asked Daniel to tell her about his home, hoping it would shed some light on him and on his mother's past. She was intrigued by Theresa Fernandez, by the gentle, almost passive exterior, which seemed to conceal something steely underneath that she was at pains not to show.

He described Aberglyn, the narrow, sloping streets following the contours of the valley, the houses shoulder to shoulder and the colours of the hills behind as the seasons passed and as he spoke she could see what he was describing, how in childhood he woke often to the sound of men's boots clumping along the morning streets when it was still dark, all moving quietly to the pit train, which took them to the colliery at the head of the valley, and how he knew that soon it would be his life also, like his father's.

'Except it hasn't turned out like that.' It was sunny again now, and they were walking along a shining sward of green. Gwen unbuttoned her cardigan.

'But your father was Spanish – he didn't grow up in the valleys.'

'No – he started off in the steelworks. 1907 they were brought over – he was twenty. Came over on a ship to Cardiff and then they sent them to Dowlais . . .'

Gwen frowned. 'But why did they come from Spain?'

'Dowlais Iron Company owned one of the Spanish iron ore companies from some way back. So –' his tone became hard – 'true capitalists, they thought they could bring cheap Spanish labour into Wales and undercut wage rates, and that Spanish workers would toe the line . . . Our da worked there for a time. The heat in there – phew! It was terrible! So bad their clothes were smouldering. Had to throw buckets of water over each other. He left after a bit and went to Aberglyn down the pit, became a collier. That's where he met Ma.'

213

They walked, staring at their feet, the worn path edged with sodden grass. To Gwen's surprise, Daniel chuckled suddenly.

'They made a street in Dowlais for the Spaniards – Alphonso Street. Da said it gave them the shock of their lives – a quiet Welsh town and suddenly there's him and the others with their garlic, playing music on a Sunday and being Catholics with their strange ways and that. I s'pose they didn't know what'd hit them to begin with! Course, there were Italians in the towns too – same with them really. Our da played the accordion – it was the one thing he brought over with him.'

'Can you play it?'

'No, I never got the hang of it. Our Paul's the one – he can squeeze some tunes out of it when he puts his mind to it. He's got the touch with it, and Ma likes to hear it.'

'So . . .' she asked hesitantly, 'your father died young, didn't he?' Theresa had told her this, but she wanted to hear Daniel's account of what had happened.

'Dead at forty-three. Heart gave out. He was a strong man, you could see that to look at him. But he was working every spare moment for the federation, the movement, the action committees. Some weeks he hardly slept, barely ate. Ma was forever keeping on, but he wouldn't listen. "What choice is there?" he'd say. "Our energy and determination is the only thing we have left." Everyone came to him – knocked on the door with all their troubles. It was the big strike, did it, made him see what the bosses were capable of. Changed him. He was never the same after . . .'

Gwen was only dimly aware, as they walked on, of heavy grey clouds covering the sky again and in a few moments the rain started to come down, slanting across the side of the hill.

'Oh, here we go!' Daniel said, starting to run towards the trees. 'Come on – let's get under here!'

She ran after him and they huddled together under the branches as the rain poured down. Daniel arranged his jacket over their heads and Gwen felt it rest on her hair, scratchy against her ear. She peered out from under it at the tippling rain. Her left side was pressed close against Daniel.

'It goes hot and cold so quickly!' She shivered, buttoning her cardigan again. She would have liked to put her coat on as well, but it was too difficult to move.

'Come on, I'll keep you warm.' Almost with a sense of panic she felt his arm round her, pulling her closer. Once again it was as if every hair on her body was standing on end, her heart thudding, while she tried to show nothing, to be light and careless about this closeness.

'That better?' Daniel said.

She could feel his gaze on her and did not dare turn her head to look into his eyes.

'Yes, thank you,' she murmured.

The rain fell more and more heavily, so that for a few moments they could barely see the other side of the path. Its force exhilarated her, making her want to run and jump, but Daniel's arm burned into her back so she hardly dared to move.

He moved his arm further down until it was curved round her waist and then, as the rain gradually let up and the sky lightened, they were left with the sound of the dripping trees and the sun came out. They both knew they had to move. For a second Gwen turned and their eyes met. His gaze was deep and serious. Emotions twisted in her and she looked quickly away again. Daniel released her and removed the sodden coat from their heads, tossed what water he could off it then laid it over his arm. Shaken, Gwen followed him back to the path, her shoes shiny with water. The silence between them was so electric that she had to do something to dispel it. She knew what she had seen in Daniel's eyes, and wondered if her own had spoken in the same way. The strength of it was frightening. She had to keep it at bay.

'Your family are so different from mine,' she said brightly. 'Will you tell me about growing up there, about the politics and everything. And why it was all so hard for your mother? You know me – proper old ignoramus.'

Daniel was silent for a moment.

'Ma doesn't like to think about any of it,' he said at last. 'She's put it away, in the past. She prays – offers it up. The Church comes first for her always.'

'What about you?'

He looked ahead along the path.

'Oh, I think about it, all right.'

Nineteen

They walked on, along the paths of the Lickey Hills, paying no attention to where they were going or the other Sunday afternoon walkers and kissing couples they passed on the way. The heavy clouds stayed away for a time and, bright sunlight brought out the vivid spring greens of the grass and trees. But Gwen paid attention to nothing but Daniel's face, heard nothing except his deep lilting voice. Though she had never seen him in action, addressing political meetings, she realized as she listened that he must be good at what he did, that his fluency and passion would convince people and carry them with him.

'It was the big strike, the General Strike – that's what set me off. You couldn't do anything else, see, once you'd lived through all that. That's what it did for our da as well. Course, there were other strikes before – plenty. The year before, over in the west at Ammanford – there was all sorts of trouble there. It wasn't the same over our way, on the east side, but there were all the politicos – Bolshies, some would say. Opinions were divided. But we weren't paying much attention – not then. I left school, started down the pit soon as I got to fourteen – 1925, the year before the strike. I went down with Da and my pal Gomer, who lived along the street. We left school together. Rosa had been born just at the turn of that

217

year.' He paused for a moment and she saw he was smiling.

'Ma stood at the door with her in her arms the day I left for the pit the first time. Dark, it was, light coming out of the house and she was telling us both to hurry, the train'd leave us behind. She used to talk to Da as if he was a child at times.' His face had quickly grown serious again. 'Things were hard enough then for her already, keeping food in all our bellies and that. Thin as a pole, she was.

'So I started off with all the other old butties who'd been working the pit for years, coming up for their tobacco and beer in the evening. Got my lamp, caught the colliers' train: my life was dictated by the pit hooters – I didn't think of any other way. That's what my da did and there was nothing else I could see. You soon pick up the ways of the pit: keep the ventilation doors shut whatever, all the gases down there that could send the place up in a flash – methane, carbon monoxide, black damp. Keep out of the way of the drams – those are the coal trucks. That's what did for my cousin, Billy. Hit by a dram, fifteen years of age. He'll never walk again.' He looked down at his feet. Bread and butter to colliers, all that. And the pit ponies – I knew all their names. You learn fast.

'Then came the strike. Course it was brewing the year before, but the government held the miners off by subsidizing the pits – Red Friday they called it, when Mr Baldwin paid out to the coal owners. I don't s'pose you remember any of this.' His tone was teasing again.

'I was only ten at the time,' she retorted.

'Ten? So you were! Well, they said the pits were losing money. None of us could work fast enough for them so they put some money in for a time, but it had run out by the 26th of May. So the crisis started off again, just as the Communist Party said it would. They were losing markets for the coal, see. The United States were taking markets, that was part of it. So, they said – we'll cut your wages, and you work longer hours. That's how we'll do it. Bleed the workers while the owners milk the profits. Anyone with a grain of sense could see it was downright pillage of the rights of the working man.' He paused as they reached a fork in the path and steered her to the left.

'When the strike started, I didn't realize at first how big it was, what it meant. That all over the country the unions were coming out on strike in solidarity with the miners – railwaymen, dockers, builders – hordes of them, all because they stood together against exploitation and injustice. The working class had unified and raised its voice as one!' Once again, Daniel was becoming heated, his voice rising.

'For those days, the pit was silent. Ghostly, like. But the town streets were full of people, police right up to the isolation hospital, just waiting for any hint of trouble. They'd brought them in from all over – Birmingham, you name it. Everyone was excited, see, on the streets every day reading leaflets, and the *Labour Bulletin*, wanting to know what was going on with the strike all round the country, what Parliament was saying. There were couriers on motorcycles carrying news over the mountains, town to town. The atmosphere was electric. Everyone pulling together, no choice, and the more it went on the more united everyone was. We thought we were going to win against the pit owners. We were all in it together, see, with food and everything – corned beef stew from the soup kitchens every day. The Council of Action met across the road from our house. Da was there nearly every moment, with meetings and speeches and that, and they were making sure the blacklegs couldn't get their coal transported out from the Aberglyn pits, by blocking off the roads. Course, some of them wanted to get going and hound the police out of the town. Why should we have them there? Why should we put up with being victimized for asking for a living wage? Da wanted to stop a fight. "You're playing into the hands of the government if you start on them," he kept saying. "That's what they're waiting for – an excuse to go for us, baton us and shoot us. We've got to keep the peace." They found out that some of the ones calling for riots weren't from the valley at all – they'd been planted to cause trouble. Da was having none of it.'

Gwen was struggling to follow everything he was saying, but she didn't like to interrupt.

'And then . . .' Daniel kicked hard at a clump of grass, shaking his head as if even now he couldn't believe what had happened. 'Next thing is, they're calling us all back to work. Strike's over. The *Labour Party*' – Gwen heard the bitter contempt in his voice – 'and the trade unions sold out on us. Called it off. Ten days, that's all they managed, and then everyone else was back at work. That was the first time . . .' He stopped speaking so abruptly that she looked round and saw he was struggling with his emotions. '. . . I ever saw my da with tears running down his face.' She could hear the thickness in his voice and was moved by it. 'Wasn't the last time that year either. Labour was supposed to be the party of the working man and it sold us down the river in a leaking boat. We miners were left on our own.'

Daniel fell silent for a moment. The sun was still hot

and bright. Gwen wasn't sure whether to speak, to acknowledge his emotion, but she didn't want to interrupt the flow of his thoughts. She could feel the force of the strike, the effect it had had on him at fifteen years to watch his father weep helplessly at the betrayal of everything he cared about.

'It was seven months the strike went on, then, and we were locked out of the pits. There was nothing else, see. The foundry in Aberglyn was closed. It's just a rusting heap, no work for anyone. There was no strike pay: all the Federation funds had been drunk dry. Only thing keeping the soup kitchens going was the subsidy from the Co-op. We used to go to the school and they'd give us stew and a bit of bread. Cocoa, when they could. There was Ma with seven children and another on the way and not a penny for food.'

He smiled, suddenly. 'It wasn't all gloom. There was always singing, choirs and that, and the men got up bands – kazoos, tin whistles, anything they could find – banging on a tin chest for a drum, dressing up and making a show. There was a great spirit in the town, but as the strike went on it bit deep. You could see it all round – the children's clothes. There were plenty without shoes through the cold months. Ma hardly had a stitch to put on Vincent and Dominic and they were poorly and pinched.'

He glanced at her, as if to check she was still listening and their eyes met for a second.

'And there was always trouble with the police. They were vicious bastards – 'scuse me, but they were – tried every trick to make you go over to the scab union in Aberglyn, to work for them. The police round us had been drafted in from the West Country somewhere – in England, I mean. Anyway, a couple of them came

221

round to the house one day with the colliery manager. Da wasn't in at the time and nor was I, but they said to Ma, your husband's known as a good worker (which he was, one of the best). Course, they knew he was one of the best organizers in the town as well. Any group meeting, they'd stamp it out – charge you with unlawful assembly and you'd be straight to the assizes in Swansea or Cardiff. So, they said, we want him at work – he's needed. If he goes back, he'll be given protection. They didn't say much more but they left a florin on the mantelpiece. Well, Da wasn't having that. He sent our Ann to take it back to the manager's office. He knew she was a good one to ask – better to send a girl, he thought, and Ann was full of fire then, even though she was only thirteen. Made her who she is, that strike did.

'Anyway, that was that for a day or two, then two policemen started standing outside our house. They'd follow Ma home if she'd been out and that. Well, my da asked what they were doing and he was told to shut up. But we knew all right. They were trying to make it look as if they were protecting us – turn everyone against us. It made it look as if Da was up to something, as if he was a blackleg.

'"You get away from my door," Da said to them. "I've never worked for a scab union and I'm not going to start now." They went for us then – pushed us in through the door, right in front of Ma and the others, out the back, and they gave us both a beating. Broke Da's nose. He was a strong man but they were about twice the size of him. Both of us were all blood by the time they left. They went for him another time too, when he'd gone out digging a seam out on the mountain. The valley's full of coal, but only the owners think

222

they have the right to dig it up! Sometimes we'd be that desperate we'd be picking cokes out of the ash paths as they were laying them. Anyway, they caught him and beat him about the face.'

Daniel laughed suddenly. 'Didn't get him when he went up and got that sheep off the mountain, though. Best feast we had all year that was! Kiddies on the farms round about, see, they were better off. The miners had almost nothing. We were under the Poor Law. Ma was in a terrible state come the autumn. Starvation levels we were at. Bread and taters and not much of them. The baby came weeks early and it was born dead. She hardly had the strength to birth it.'

He stopped for a moment.

'How awful,' Gwen said gently. It was as if she could feel his pain inside her.

'Da made a little box to bury him. We thought Ma was going to die. There was nothing to her. She was ill for weeks after. Pernicious anaemia, the doctor told her. You'd never think it to look at her now. She was skin and bone. Frightened you to look at her.' He paused. Gwen looked up at him, his set, serious expression. He glanced at her.

'We were all trapped like animals. Nothing we could do, that was how it felt. She's strong, though, Ma. Stronger than she knows. Father O'Connor used to come to the house and see her. She's never forgotten his kindness to her. She pulled through.

'The strike went on to the close of the year. All through, and after, Da still wanted to believe in the Labour movement, the Labour Party. Couldn't let go of the idea that Parliament was where the power lay, that that was where change would come from. We had a branch of the NUWM in Aberglyn and he gave it

223

everything he had. But I was learning other things then, see. I used to walk over to Tredegar – there's a library there full of political books. Best for miles. There were talks and discussions and I joined the Socialist League – me and Gomer set up a branch in Aberglyn, in a room behind the chapel. We had a big poster of Lenin in front of a red flag. That was the first time I began to read Marx.'

'And you joined the Communist Party?'

'Not straight away. But yes – when I became sure that the only way was the revolution. And Da joined soon after. He was . . .' His voice thickened again. 'He was so proud when I got into the college, down London. And then, while I was there, he died. Ma was left with no breadwinner in the family. Ann was work-ing in the bakery up the road and did what she could. I came home and tried to go down the pit but there was hardly any work to be had. Ma was in a bad state. Lucy was born after Da passed on and she was sickly, what with her gammy leg and being small. The fits didn't start till later, but she was a sickly baby and Ma was poorly herself after. That's when Auntie Annie said we had to come to Birmingham.'

'But your mother had so many young children! How on earth did you all manage?'

'Annie and Pat were good to us, but they had their own troubles. There was only Ann and I who were old enough to work. Our Mary was a year off leaving school. Ann got a job first – in a shop. But then they hit us with the means test. You got your twenty-six weeks unemployment benefit and then they transferred you to Public Assistance. They come nosing round to see if you've anything in the house to sell, or if anyone's working, because then they say you don't need assistance and take it away! They'd be asking questions of the neighbours, expecting people to spy on one another, the lot! Ma had a struggle on her hands, even though there was more work over here. In the end, best thing was for Ann to go and live with Auntie Annie and I went back home. Pat had a job and they weren't claiming assistance so Ann was working, giving Ma the money. And me, later – even after she was married she put money my way where she could. Ann was always totally committed to the party and the cause. She's solid gold, my sister. And I was up and down to the valleys, keeping up the politics, working if I could . . .'

'Things seem a bit better now?' Gwen ventured to suggest.

Daniel nodded. 'Oh yes. Annie and Pat helped us get the shop, and Mary and Paul went out to work. Vincent'll be out looking for a job soon. Never feel I do enough for her myself, though.'

They were silent for a moment, walking a spongy path cut through a patch of woodland area.

'She worries about you. What all the politics will lead to.'

'I know.' There was wretchedness in his tone. 'I wouldn't upset her for anything, but I can't do anything else. It's my life.'

'I think it's . . . it's amazing what you do,' Gwen said fervently. She could barely find words for her thoughts, she was so full of emotion after what she had heard. 'It's brave and important and standing up for what you believe in!'

Daniel stopped suddenly. 'Not many people see it that way – that the world's got to change. There's got to be a revolution, to do away with the order of things as they are. Can you imagine living on, knowing things were going to stay as they are, with the tide of fascism sweeping towards us, a world where the jackboot rules, and the honest workers are trampled on?'

'No!' In her mind's eye, Gwen saw a faceless line of soldiers tramping across the country, stamping on everything in their path. 'No I can't!'

Daniel turned fully towards her, his eyes still fixed on hers. 'God, you are a captivating woman, d'you know that?'

Her body felt weightless, fluttery under his gaze, and deeper inside she felt a taut longing, a sense that she could not bear it if he did not touch her.

'And you . . .' She tried to say something but could not finish.

He turned away and walked on along the path. Gwen took a deep breath, watching him in front of her, the wet jacket over his arm. A moment later he stopped. A little branching way led off under the trees, away from the main path.

'Come on in here.' He pushed through the wet grass and weeds, and she could never have not followed him, the white shirt, his striding legs. The warnings in her head were silenced, and it was as if she was tied to him, body and soul, could simply not be anywhere else.

They were moving between young, spindly trees. The green woodland was lovely, their footsteps silenced by the sodden ground. A few yards on Daniel stopped between the trees and turning, dropped his jacket to the ground. Gwen did the same. Once more their eyes met and in a second they were clutching each other in an embrace such as Gwen had never experienced before. The strength of Daniel's arms drew her to him, his hands moving on her back, hard body against hers, not holding back in the gentlemanly way that Edwin held her, but urgently, unabashedly wanting her pressed close.

'I can't keep my mind off you.' He ran his hands down her sides, over her curving hips. 'You're such a beauty – God you're lovely, you are!'

His voice, his touch melted her. 'Daniel,' was all she could manage to say. 'Daniel, Daniel . . .'

She was lost to him, helpless with feeling as his face moved slowly closer to hers and she felt his lips exploring hers.

Twenty

Joey lay in a fever for four days. That was what they told him later. It was all a confusion of sounds, the blood banging in his ears, boots crossing the floor, clattering and coughing. At times he was aware of other people, and voices, a woman's voice in particular which he thought was his mother's, though she was talking in a strange way.

'Ah, will you look at him now, Christie? He's as thin as a sparrow.' A cool hand touched his head and someone lifted him and dribbled water between his dry lips.

'There y'are, darlin',' the voice said. 'Come on, now – drink a bit of this, will ye?' And he could remember trying to swallow and the feel of water running coolly down his throat and chin. He was half certain he remembered being held and rocked, but he knew that must have been a dream. In a blissful part of his dream he knew the arms around him were those of his teacher Miss Purdy, and he saw her pretty face smiling down at him.

Dots of light wavered in the darkness. Sometimes the room seemed a fraction less dark, and a quiet stillness fell around him. The first time he could open his eyes properly and focus it was evening and dark outside, but he could make out an elfin face looking down at him, with a pointed chin and straggly black hair hanging loose over her shoulders. Seeing him look up at her, the young woman smiled. A tooth was missing at the side of her mouth.

'Well, so you're looking at me! Back in the land of the living now, are ye?'

'Is the little fella coming round?' A light appeared in the gloom, a candle held by a dark-haired man with kind, dancing eyes. There was an orange glow of firelight coming from one side of the room. 'Well, here's our little Lazarus – you'll surely be wanting a hot drop of tea now then.' The man moved away again.

Joey tried to sit up, but his body wouldn't obey him. He felt himself to be all bones.

'Don't go thinking you can get up and dance a jig now.' The woman laid her hand soothingly on his. The sound of terrible coughing came from nearby and Joey sensed there were several people in the room. He felt bewildered, but somehow safe and reassured.

'What's your name, sweetheart?' the woman asked. Her face was so pale and thin.

Joey opened his mouth. He could barely remember how to speak. His throat felt closed up, but he noticed that it no longer hurt.

'Joey,' he rasped.

'Joey? You're a Joseph, are ye? Did you get yourself lost, coming in here?' The man was back again now, behind the woman, holding a jam jar of milky tea. He squatted down and Joey felt his strong arms go round him to hoist him up into a sitting position.

'There you go now – nice and sweet. It won't scald you – I put a drop of cold in.'

The tea was delicious: strong and syrupy with sugar and seemed to stroke its way down into his stomach, warming him inside. He drank, then stopped, closing

229

his eyes for a rest. He was so weak that everything felt hazy and distant.

'He's had enough, Christie,' the woman said. 'Don't go forcing him.'

'No!' Joey's eyes snapped open and he clasped his hands round the warm glass, pulling it to his lips.

'Sure, he's like a little suckling lamb!' the man chuckled. 'Go on there now, little fella – you drink as much as you want!'

At last he was satisfied and Christie gently laid him back down. It was only then Joey noticed that he was no longer lying on the bare boards, but on a mattress. He felt warm and comfortable and suddenly happy.

Christie moved away, but the woman stayed at his side.

'Where's your mammy, Joey?' she asked softly.

Once again, he shook his head.

'Is she gone to Jesus?'

Joey wasn't sure about this. He just stared at her.

'Did your mammy pass away?'

She could see by his eyes that this was so.

'Poor little lamb,' she crooned. 'And what about your daddy? Won't he be looking for ye?' When she asked whether his daddy had passed away too, he shook his head.

'D'you have a home to go to, Joey? No? Oh, poor little darlin'!'

He found himself lifted and cradled against her soft breasts, then she rocked him gently.

'You're all skin and bone, so you are.'

Joey heard the door open then and the sound of boots. Another face appeared, but all he could see in the gloom was a squashed-looking hat and a huge black beard.

'All right there, John?' the woman asked.

The man made shy little nodding movements with his head.

'Is he getting better?' He had a high voice which seemed to come through his nose.

'He'll be grand.' A sudden sly look came to her face and she whispered, 'Did you get it for me?'

The man nodded.

'Thank Christ.'

He pulled something from under his coat and a furious cry came from Christie across the room.

'Oh, God Almighty, John. How could you bring it to her?' He stood up and rushed over to them. 'No, Siobhan – for God's sake don't start!'

But she had lain Joey down in a trice and scrambled to her feet, snatching the bottle from John's hand. She took a long swig, shuddering as the liquid went through her, then stopped and wiped her mouth. Christie was at her, trying to pull the bottle from her hand. In a moment, he succeeded.

'Don't let Micky drink all the rest!' Siobhan shrieked. 'He always takes more than his fecking share. I want it – I need it, for the love of God I do!'

Her tone was aggressive, out of control, and Joey felt a chill go through him. Now she really did sound like his mother. He curled up on his side and put his hands over his ears. He couldn't block out the voices, though. Siobhan slid down beside him again and when she lifted him into her arms, the smell on her breath was strong and familiar. It stank of danger. He turned his head to one side, screwing his eyes tight shut. He had the strength for nothing else.

'I want more!' she demanded.

'For God's sake, Shiv!' Christie's gentle voice was hoarse.

231

'Give it to me!'

'John – will you leave her?' There was scuffling the other side of the room. 'You know what it'll do to her!'

'Just a little bit,' John said. 'Let her have a bit. She wants it.'

In a moment John was back with the bottle and she drank again. The smell wafted over Joey. It made him want to cry and shout. He pushed the feeling down inside him.

'That's Christie over there.' She nodded her head, though Joey wasn't looking at Christie, couldn't see what he was doing. 'He's my brother – my *little* brother, though you'd not know it the way he bosses me. And there's John, who'd do anything I ask, wouldn't you, John darlin'? Like a child he is ... And then there's Micky over there. You'll hear him coughing. He's none too good, is Micky. Are you hungry, darlin'?'

Joey felt as if he was floating, couldn't move. He did not want food. He felt sick now, instead of happy. He could smell the liquor and the woman's body close to him.

'Joey – little Joey ...' Siobhan was stroking his head, rocking. 'You make me forget, little Joey, my baby,' she whispered.

She began to sing then, a sweet, lilting tune that he had never heard before and he closed his eyes to shut her out. A few moments later the singing stopped and her body began to jerk next to him.

'I was going to have a baby of my own, Joey. He died, my little baby ... They killed him inside me and I'm going to go to hell, saints preserve me.' Deep,

232

terrible sobs came from her and she was leaning over and clutching him close.

'"The Angel of the lord declared to Mary..." Oh, John, give me a little drop more for pity's sake!' She drank again in long, greedy gulps. '"...And she conceived of the Holy Spirit ... Hail Mary, full of grace, blessed art thou among women..." Oh, Lord God!' Her hair fell over Joey, blocking out the firelight and her tears fell on his face. Her crying sounded very loud to him and he swelled inside with bad feelings. He wanted desperately to push her away, to run and run from these people but he hadn't the strength.

'Come on, Siobhan – come away now.' Christie's voice was gentle. 'Put the lad down – let him sleep.'

Joey was replaced abruptly on the mattress and he saw Christie trying to calm his sister. She was distraught, crying and fighting him as he struggled to keep hold of her wrists.

'Let me go! Just feck off and stop bossing me, Christie. You're not our daddy! I'm going – I can bring in the money as well – that's what I'm good for, isn't it? You know I am! Sister Assumpta always said I'd go straight to hell to sup with the devil ... I'm already in hell, so what difference will it make? Go on, tell me that, oh so perfect Father Christie Cody...'

'For God's sake, Shiv, just keep quiet!' Christie sounded distraught. 'D'you want us thrown out of here? Don't be like this. It kills me when you're like this.'

'For God's sake, Shiv!' She mimicked him in a spiteful tone. 'Tell you what – I'll do it with John. I'll do the one thing I'm good for, eh Christie? John loves me, don't you, darlin' ... No, don't you come taking

233

his side! You're on my side.' Her voice rose to a screech as John attempted to come to Christie's aid.

'What's all the feckin' racket . . .' Micky's confused voice protested from across the room, but then lapsed into coughing and incoherent mumbling.

Siobhan pulled away from her brother and Joey heard her go out of the room.

'Siobhan!' John's nasal voice called.

'It's no good – you'll not stop her.' Christie spoke softly, and his tone was despairing. 'Not when she's like that.'

Hands still over his ears, Joey drifted gratefully into sleep.

Over the following days as Joey recovered his strength, he began to make sense of where he was. There was never full daylight inside because all the windows were boarded up and only fragments of light crept in between the boards. The room seemed very big and he wondered if he was in a school, as he'd never seen such a large room anywhere else. Houses, so far as he knew, were tiny and cramped, though apart from the size this one felt familiar: boarded windows, the walls reduced to bare, crumbling plaster, bare, rotten floorboards and the stink of damp and smoke.

'Whose house're we in?' he asked Christie, that first morning when he was truly conscious.

'It's no one's.' Christie turned to him from the fire, into which he was poking sticks. 'We're just borrowing it for a little while – like birds of the air looking for a place to rest. And we want to keep it that way.'

Joey experimented with moving his body. He wanted to get off the prickly mattress. It felt as if he had been lying on it for years. His body felt weak and shaky, but he managed to get to his hands and knees.

'You ready to get up now?' Christie was beside him in the gloom, lifting him over to the fire. 'Come on over here.' Joey found he was sitting on the man's coat. It made him think of Mr Simmons's coat which had been stolen from him. There was a pan of water heating over the flames. Christie squatted beside him. Something about him felt safe.

'You're looking grand now this morning! I'm just making a hot drop of tea. It's Sunday today – did you know that?'

Joey enjoyed sitting looking into the flames. He didn't feel like running away any more, now it was quiet and he was by the fire. His days spent sleeping in cold parks and wandering the streets alone already felt a long way in the past. He peered round the room. The sound of snoring aroused his memory of arriving. It was coming from a big, dark shape lying over to his left.

'That's Micky.' Christie saw him looking. Joey could just make out a bearded face with thick, frightening-looking features. The other man wasn't there and he wondered where the woman called Siobhan had gone, but a moment later saw that she too was asleep across the room. He remembered her crying and dread gripped him for a moment. But she was quiet now.

He watched Christie as he tipped tea leaves into the pan of hot water and stirred them in with a sliver of wood. The man was thin and didn't look very strong. His clothes were black, his hair was dark and curly and he hadn't shaved for days, but his beard was nothing like as bushy as John's or Micky's. Joey noticed that he was hugging himself, shivering as if cold. He thought the man had sad eyes.

'Here now.' Christie handed him tea and a piece of bread torn from a loaf. His face was kind and gentle and Joey felt soothed by his company. 'You get that down you.'

Twenty-One

'Millie – you're looking ever so well!'

Gwen found Millie waiting for her as she came out through the school gate. Millie smiled bravely. It was a day of showers and she was sheltering under an umbrella.

'You're not looking so bad yourself. In fact –' she peered at Gwen – 'you look like a cat that's got the cream! What's come over you?'

Gwen laughed. 'I don't know – must be the spring weather!' How could she possibly say what was making her glow from the inside with love and happiness and excitement? *Daniel*, she thought, hugging the very sound of his name inside herself. *My beautiful Daniel!* He was busy this afternoon, she knew that, or she might have been rather less pleased to see Millie waiting for her.

'Got time for a cuppa?' Millie asked.

'Yes, of course. Come on – let's get away from here. Agnes Monk'll be out in a minute.'

'Oh Lord – I can't say I'm longing to see her!' Millie grimaced.

They went to a little place along Wellington Street and ordered tea and currant buns. Gwen examined Millie as she took off her mac to sit down. She was wearing a green skirt and neat cream blouse with frills on the collar and cuffs.

'You really do look better,' Gwen said, trying to be encouraging. Millie's freckly skin had some of its bloom back and she looked a little healthier, though tired and strained. As Gwen spoke Millie's eyes immediately filled with tears.

'Sorry.' She wiped them with her hanky. 'Keeps happening. I don't know what's come over me.'

'Is everything all right?' Gwen eyed her anxiously.

'As it'll ever be,' Millie said gloomily.

'The wedding's still on and everything?'

Millie rallied. 'Look – sorry. I'm being such an old grouch. Yes, of course it's still on. That's what I've come to tell you about – to invite you. It's going to be the second Saturday in May and I'd love you to come.'

'Oh, how lovely!' Gwen realized as she spoke that she sounded just a little over-enthusiastic, as if she was humouring Millie. 'I mean – how do you feel about it?'

Millie shrugged. 'What choice do I have?' She lowered her voice, leaning across the table. 'I don't exactly want to bring a bastard child into the world, do I?'

Gwen was appalled by the bitterness she saw in her friend's face.

'I just have to be grateful that Lance is prepared to stick by me and do the right thing.' Millie sat back and fiddled with the spoon on her saucer. 'We'll have enough money and the baby'll have a proper family. I'm lucky really when you think what happens to some people. My mother's been ever so kind and reasonable, and stuck by me. I won't be thrown on the streets. What more could I want?'

'Oh, Millie.' Gwen sat back, looking at her. She could scarcely think what to say to be of comfort. 'It'll be all right. You *do* love Lance, don't you? You must've done to . . . to . . .' She had been going to say *to get into this situation*, but she couldn't finish. Immediately the thought of Edwin came to her. Wasn't she supposed to love him? And look how she was behaving! But somehow Edwin and her feelings for Daniel felt like two completely different worlds. Edwin was her fiancé, of course he was! But as for love – heaven knew, she hadn't known what love was until she met Daniel.

As she spoke to Millie, trying to cheer her up, she was all the time guiltily aware of her hands in her lap under the table. With her right hand she kept feeling the third finger of her left. In the chest of drawers in her room at Ariadne's house was a little dark blue box, and in its silky interior nestled her engagement ring with its tiny sapphires. She had slipped it off the morning she went out with Daniel. It had been in the drawer ever since, and her finger felt bare and strange – and guilty.

'The other thing I was going to ask you ...' Millie hesitated. 'Mum thought we'd live with her, at first anyway. But Lance is dead set against it. Says we need our privacy and all that. He's already found us a flat to rent – just the upstairs rooms of a house in Handsworth. The thing is, it's still quite a lot of rent, what with me not working, and then there'll be the baby. So we thought if there were three of us to share, it would all be easier. I just wondered if you'd think of having the spare room. You seem pretty fed up where you are now.'

'Oh, Millie, that'd be perfect! I keep thinking I ought to look for somewhere else, but I've been so idle about it. I'm sure that woman's going to poison me in the end if I stay there – entirely by accident, but even so. And that Mr Purvis creeping about all the time with

239

his flaming trumpet . . .' She had given Millie a toned-down version of what went on in the Soho Road house. 'Are you sure you can stand having another person around? Married bliss and all that?'

Millie looked earnestly at her. 'Gwen, I think if I don't have other company apart from Lance, I shall go right off my rocker.'

'Come round to ours and see us, any day,' Daniel had said as they parted at the tram stop that Sunday.

She felt dazed, and as if she was dreaming after an afternoon in his arms, with his kisses. They had stood in the woods, wrapped round one another. Daniel was not full of gentlemanly reserve in his embraces, unlike Edwin. He pulled her tightly to him, his tongue feeling its way gently, then more urgently between her lips until both of them were alight with desire, kissing each other's face, neck, lips, breaking away for a few minutes to walk, before they were drawn together again like magnets. By the end of the afternoon her cheeks were tingling after the chafe of his skin against hers, his dark stubble prickling her, and the feel of his strong body was imprinted on her as if she knew him through and through, had somehow always known him. It was a wrench to separate and to say goodbye. But his invitation to come to the house, to see more of him and his family, was compensation.

'Won't your mother mind me dropping by?'

'No, course not.' The serious look he gave her further affected her. 'With the shop there're always people coming in anyway. And she likes you. Lucy talks about you and Ma's liked talking to you when you came. She said you were . . .' He glanced at the sky as if for inspiration. 'What was it now?'

'Stop teasing me.' She poked him and he jumped.

'I'm not! I think she said you were very sympathetic.' He chuckled. 'Oh – and very frightening.'

'Frightening?'

'No, she didn't really say that! But come round.' His face grew serious and he laid his hands on her shoulders. 'Or I'll have to come to the school every day and show all Miss Purdy's class what I feel about their teacher.'

'Don't you dare! Of course I'll come. As long as it's all right.'

'Oh, it's all right.' He held her close and kissed her forehead, just close to the line of her little waves of hair. 'My lovely Gwen.'

That first week, she had left it for a couple of days before visiting, forcing herself to wait, to be measured in her behaviour, even though there was nothing measured in her feelings. Her emotions were in turmoil. Even in two days she had convinced herself that the walk on the hills was, if not a dream – she remembered it too vividly for that – an aberration, and that when she saw Daniel again everything would be different and the love and closeness would all be lost. He had been doing nothing but play with her. These thoughts almost made her afraid to go again because she could not bear to face the loss of him, the expression in his eyes when he looked down at her.

On the third day, when she knew she could stay away no longer, he was waiting for her. She caught a glimpse of him outside the gate as she came out of the school and her heart leapt with excitement. She hurried towards him, attempting to look poised and calm in front of the gaggles of children all trying to push through the gate at once, but a delighted smile broke over her face in spite of herself.

'Hello, Miss Purdy.' Even the sound of his voice brought her up in goose pimples. He was smiling, speaking with teasing formality.

'Good afternoon, Mr Fernandez.' They were surrounded by children. 'Have you come to collect Lucy?'

'That's right. I don't s'pose she'll be first out, though.'

The Canal Street children dispersed quickly, leaving them standing alone. Gwen saw Lucy emerge from the girls' entrance with Alice Wilson beside her.

'I thought you were coming to see us?' Daniel said.

'I am – of course. In fact I was going to come today.' The children were moving closer. 'D'you see this little girl, with Lucy? This is Alice. The poor child can hardly see a thing.'

Daniel looked at Alice's bedraggled figure. Her plaits were roughly tied and her clothes looked unkempt and messy. Nowadays she looked worse than some of the other children in the school. She didn't look like the Alice who had arrived in January.

The girls parted and Lucy walked home with her brother and teacher.

'Miss Purdy's agreed to come and have a cup of tea,' Daniel said.

'Have we got anything to eat?' Lucy asked eagerly.

'Oh, I expect we can find something.'

Theresa was talking and laughing with a woman in the shop as they walked through, but she broke off and said cheerily, 'Afternoon, Miss Purdy!'

On the table in the back, beside the brown teapot

and cups, was a plate of homemade tarts. There was also a jam jar with a little bunch of pink tulips in it.

As Daniel and Lucy were making tea, the bell in the shop rang as the customer went out and Theresa came through to the back, a smile on her face.

'That Mrs Harvey's a character. Always gives me a good laugh, she does.' She sat down at the table. 'Help yourself to a jam tart, won't you?' Gwen, who was hungry, obeyed eagerly. 'I hope those children have been little angels today?'

'Well, yours has!' Gwen laughed. Lucy blushed, carrying a bowl of sugar lumps to the table. 'She's as bright as a button. And you've been helping Alice, haven't you? She can't see what's on the blackboard, you see.'

'She can't see *anything*, hardly at all,' Lucy said.

'I wrote to her mother weeks ago, suggesting she get the girl's eyes tested,' Gwen said indignantly. 'She doesn't seem to have done a thing about it.'

'Can't afford it, most likely,' Daniel said.

'But she's one of the best-dressed children in the school. Well, she *was*.' There was something about Alice that really perplexed Gwen. 'I'm not sure what else to do.'

She finished her jam tart. 'That was *so* nice. My landlady's cooking is very peculiar. I hate to think what she'd manage to do to jam tarts.'

Theresa chuckled. 'Have another one then, my love. I've made plenty.'

'No, it was delicious, but I won't. I'm sure they'll soon go with all your family – let the children have them.'

They chatted on about the schools the other Fernandez children attended and Vincent's first job. At fourteen he had just left school and acquired a job with a coffin maker.

'He has to paint RIP on the side of each one!' Daniel said.

'Always was good at drawing.' Theresa smiled.

Gwen felt relaxed and comfortable sitting in the simple room with Daniel and his mother. Lucy eventually grew bored and after her siblings had come home and polished off the rest of the tarts, she went outside with them. Theresa and Daniel took turns to go into the shop and serve people, and in between they talked about things in the news – Herr Hitler was moving troops back into the Rhineland, and there was talk that the Italians had used mustard gas in Abyssinia – but they avoided discussing politics. Gwen had the impression, with Theresa Fernandez, of a woman who was keenly intelligent and interested in the world around her, but who simply wanted an end to politics taking over her home. She wanted some peace and Daniel, at least for the moment, appeared to respect that. The only mention Theresa made of his activities was to ask if he was going out that night.

'For a bit,' Daniel said. 'I'm going chalking up for the meeting on Sunday.' He looked at Gwen's puzzled face. 'Haven't you seen the signs? We chalk them up all over – for the meetings and that.'

'I haven't noticed,' she admitted.

'Obviously not doing a good enough job then, are we?'

When the shop bell rang again, Theresa got up to go into the shop.

'Do you think . . .' Gwen asked quickly, knowing it was time she went home. Alice was still playing on her mind. 'I'm concerned about that girl, Alice. Would it be completely out of place for me to go and see her mother? Perhaps she never even had my letter? It's just that I think Alice is a clever child and she's being badly held back.'

'I think you're very kind to think of it,' Theresa said carefully from the doorway.

'But wouldn't you think it a bit peculiar if one of your children's teachers arrived on your doorstep?'

Daniel chuckled. 'Oh yes – we would!'

Gwen blushed. 'I don't mean – I mean it was different, the night I brought Lucy home. There was no one else.'

'And we were very grateful,' Theresa said. 'Don't take any notice of him. You do what you think's best, Miss Purdy. It's only a rare person would think of it.'

'Thank you ever so much for the tea, Mrs Fernandez.' Gwen got up. 'I think I will go and see them.'

'Can't do any harm, can it?' Theresa said and disappeared into the shop.

'I'd better be off as well.' Daniel stood up. Suddenly she was acutely aware of him, his lean back moving under the white shirt, his hands, the soft edge of his hairline at the back of his neck. As he came towards her, she felt alive in every nerve. He drew her into his arms.

'I've been waiting for this,' he said. She sank against him with relief, as if she had come home, and felt his hand warm on the back of her neck. For a long, taut moment they held apart as if waiting, holding each other's gaze.

'Daniel,' she whispered. 'God, Daniel.'

Then her lips were silenced by his.

Twenty-Two

It was a warm spring morning. Smoke from factory chimneys hung high and still in the air. Gwen had ventured out into the sunshine without a coat, in a pretty floral frock with a soft, swinging skirt, her bag over her arm. That morning, after she had dressed, she leaned down to the mirror, saw her face smile radiantly back. *I look so happy!* she thought. *Have I ever looked like this before?* She startled people in the street with her smile. She could think of nothing but Daniel and his loving eyes, and when she might see him again, so that she was full of bubbling excitement and wanted to dance along the road, skipping and whooping like a child. Yet, in a strange way, it seemed to her she had never felt so grown up. She was away from home, deciding things for herself!

One thing she had decided was that she would get out of the claustrophobic atmosphere of the house in Soho Road and lodge with Millie and Lance. Not that she'd told Ariadne of her plans yet. She didn't think she would be very pleased.

Gwen waited at the tram stop. When she was out on the streets a part of her mind was always on the lookout for Joey Phillips. After the day when she thought she caught a glimpse of him looking into the playground, there had been no sign of him. What happened to children like Joey? she wondered as the

246

tram drew to a stop. She flinched as a shower of sparks fell hissing from the wires above. It was as if Joey had melted away into the streets.

The first lesson was arithmetic and they were starting to learn long division. Though there were a few children like Lucy Fernandez who were very sharp and picked up things straight away, a lot of them were struggling. Gwen watched as the class copied the sums down from the blackboard. Jack Ellis's head was bent, his hand clutching his pen far too tightly. He snapped a nib off almost every week and dug holes in the paper. Gwen sighed. Jack was ever so dense. It would be a long time before he got the hang of this.

She walked along between the desks, noticing that even now some of the children cringed as she passed, used to being cuffed and whacked for getting a sum wrong.

'No, Ron.' She leaned over Ron Parks, whose tongue was out, almost touching his nose in the effort to concentrate. There was a slug of snot on his upper lip and around him hung an aura of grime and sweet stickiness. 'You have to carry that one down. Yes, down there. Then how many times does twelve go into one hundred and fifty?'

Ron's brow furrowed, then his face lit up with inspiration. 'Seven?'

Gwen walked back to the front. 'Let me hear you all say the twelve times table!' she commanded. The children obeyed, droningly. She went through the sum on the blackboard.

'If twelve twelves are one hundred and forty four, how many do we carry over?'

Joan Billings timidly raised her hand. 'Six?'

247

'Very good. Now try the next bit.'

She went to the desk where Lucy sat beside Alice Wilson.

'Have you got the sums copied down all right, Alice?'

'Yes, Miss.' Alice squinted up at her. Her face was forever screwed up with the effort to see and it made her otherwise sweet face look tense and sly.

'And did you do the sums by yourself?'

'Yes, Miss.'

Gwen looked at Alice's page of numbers. The girl had understood and worked it all out straight away. But if she hadn't had Lucy to help her she would have looked dimwitted and slow.

At breaktime Gwen went into the staffroom, determined to have a word with Lily Drysdale. As soon as she walked in, however, she could sense a strange atmosphere. To her surprise, Mr Lowry was sitting drinking a cup of tea. Usually he hardly ever mingled with his staff, but instead kept himself aloof up in his office. The problem was obvious. Mr Lowry was sitting beside the new teacher, Charlotte Rowley. Across the other side of the room sat Agnes Monk, whose entire body, not just her face, seemed to consist of one gigantic glower.

'I'm delighted to hear you play the piano as well,' Mr Lowry was saying.

Miss Rowley, dark-eyed and inscrutable, stared back with cold politeness and Gwen saw her lean further away from him, drawing her skirt closer round her primly set knees. This only seemed to provoke Mr Lowry to try harder.

'Do you play any other instruments?' Gwen heard

him say as she walked past with her cup of tea. Miss Monk was reading her book, her face and neck an angry red. On the noticeboard above her head was pinned a sheet of paper headed 'Empire Day Pageant'.

Lily Drysdale was sitting to one side of the room, knitting what appeared to be baby clothes. The delicate rows of white stitches looked incongruous in her big hands. Gwen saw that her fingernails were stained with green.

'Hello, dear,' she said as Gwen sat beside her. She gave a wry smile suddenly and leaned in closer, whispering, 'Trying to keep away from the love triangle as well, are you?'

Gwen was so startled she didn't know what to say.

'Er, yes!' She blushed too easily, as ever. 'But I came to ask you something too.'

Lily laid her knitting down on her lap. 'For my niece's baby,' she said with a smile.

'Oh how lovely.' Gwen felt faint surprise that Lily had family and infant relatives like anyone else.

'What is it, dear?'

Gwen poured out her worries about Alice Wilson and how her eyesight was holding her back. 'I just can't understand why her mother doesn't do something about her,' she finished indignantly.

'You have to remember, they're probably living on very slender means,' Lily pointed out. 'I find that paying a call is often the thing.'

'D'you think I should?'

'Best thing. Would you like me to come with you?'

Though she was grateful for the offer, Gwen felt instinctively that she should do this by herself. Two teachers turning up at Alice's house would surely feel far more alarming than one. She thanked Lily, and said she would try and go that afternoon.

'T'ra then – see you tomorrow,' Lucy said, limping to her front door in Alma Street.

'T'ra,' Alice echoed.

Lucy turned on the step and Alice could just make out through the blur that she was smiling before she disappeared through the front door. Alice felt a pang go through her. How she'd have loved Lucy to invite her in! She liked Lucy's mother with her kind blue eyes. She was always in the shop, and the house usually smelt of cakes cooking. There was something comforting about Mrs Fernandez and Alice liked all the hub-bub of the family, with Lucy's brothers coming in and out. She thought Rosa was the loveliest person she'd ever met – after Miss Purdy, of course. And sometimes Dominic would give her a ride in the old wheelbarrow up and down the pavement, until she screamed at him to stop. The combination of Dominic's crazy speed and the fact she couldn't see made the rides thrilling and petrifying at the same time.

She always walked home with Lucy, although it took her a little out of her way, because it put off going home for a bit longer. She dawdled now along Alma Street and crossed Wellington Road, squinting hard. She was always afraid of something coming at her that she couldn't see and knocking her down. Bicycles were the worst because you couldn't hear them. When she turned into Franklin Street the rag-and-bone man was calling out from somewhere along the road. She was so busy peering to try and see him with his cart and his supply of goldfish that she didn't notice the boy swinging on a rope tied to the lamp post near her house. One minute she was walking along and the next a body came flying at her and knocked straight into her from the front. Alice fell over backwards, jarring her back and scraping her elbow hard on the kerb.

'You blind or summat?' the boy jeered, skidding to a halt. 'Why don't you watch where you're going?'

Alice got up carefully, rubbing her back. She didn't want to show him how much it hurt, but she couldn't stop the tears running down her face. She hurried to her house, wiping her eyes. As she went to open the door, she noticed the state of her sleeve. Round the elbow her blouse was all muck and blood.

'Oh no, don't let it be torn as well!' she muttered. Frantic, she struggled to see, pulling her elbow up as near to her face as she could. It looked as if the sleeve was intact. She hurried down the entry. Maybe if she sneaked in quietly, she could get it washed without her mother finding out.

She was already used to the scrubby little yard behind the house and the wall with the loose bricks at the top looking ready to topple off. Her mother still couldn't accept that they lived in such a place, instead of their lovely house with the garden and the tubs of flowers outside the front door. No one else in the family knew they lived here, not even her grandma. Mummy said she would die of the shame of it if anyone came and saw . . .

The back door squeaked open. Alice cringed, but no sound came from inside. If she could just get her blouse washed so that Mummy didn't see how dirty it was, she wouldn't get angry and cry.

There was no sign of her mother downstairs. Sometimes when Alice came home she was sitting in the

251

back room. This meant today was one of her bad days and she was in bed. Normally that would be a bad sign, but at least it meant she wouldn't see the blouse.

Alice hurried into the scullery and took out the wash pail, managing not to clank it against the basin. While it was filling with water she hurriedly undid the buttons, wincing as she peeled the sleeve from her arm. The pain made her eyes water. She shoved the blouse down into the pail. Standing in her little vest she examined her skinny arm and saw a blur of red. The arm stung, but it was nothing serious. Reminding herself to hurry, she seized the lump of wash soap and scrubbed at the sleeve, bringing it up close so she could see what she was doing. To her enormous relief, with each scrub and dunk in the water the blood washed pinker and lighter till it had almost disappeared. She scrubbed at the dirt. It would show a bit, but maybe not enough to cause trouble. Just as she was trying to wring the blouse out over the sink, she heard her mother's slow tread on the stairs. Quickly! She fled outside in her vest and pegged the blouse, still dripping, on the line.

As she came in again, her mother came down into the back room. At least she was dressed, Alice noticed, in her black skirt and blouse, which always looked nice against her blonde colouring. But she had no stockings on, she was standing in bare feet on the lino and she hadn't combed her hair. Alice couldn't see her face properly, but her voice was dull and expressionless in a way that Alice had come to dread more than her anger.

'What're you doing, Alice?'

'I . . . I got my blouse a bit dirty. But it's all right. I washed it.'

252

Her mother sank down on the chair, almost as if she hadn't heard.

'Put the kettle on for a cup of tea, will you?'

Alice ran to fill the kettle, feeling her chest unknot a little. Mummy didn't mind. She hadn't even seemed to notice! She peered out at her mother. Poor Mummy on that awful old horsehair chair with the stuffing hanging out! There was a rickety table and chairs and, apart from the two beds, nothing else. Every stick of their lovely furniture had been taken with the other house. Before, there had been armchairs covered with a pretty pale green material and shiny tables with vases of flowers and rugs on the floor. Alice felt tears rise in her eyes again and her throat hurt. She didn't often think about before, about where Daddy was or what had happened to Mummy because she was too busy trying to survive from day to day, but every so often it all welled up and spilled over and she found herself crying as if she'd never stop. But not now, she told herself, digging her nails into her palms. She must be quiet and not make Mummy upset.

When she'd poured the tea, she found her mother lying back in the chair, arms folded tightly across her, as if she was cold, and her eyes closed. She sat like this a lot now. Alice leaned closer, wondering if she was asleep. Her mother had lovely thick pale hair which had been cut in a fashionable pageboy, though it had grown long and straggly now. She had been so pretty, with her sweet, feminine face and laughing blue eyes, when her friends came round to drink tea in the afternoons. And Daddy's parties – Alice always associated them with her mother's perfume, which had smelt of flowers. All she smelt of now was cheap soap. She'd had a pink silk dress which fitted her slim figure beautifully and brushed the carpet as she walked. Alice had seen her hurl it, screaming and crying, onto a pile of things to be sold, before they left the house.

'I won't be needing this any more!' she cried. 'Since I shan't have any life any more!' Then there'd been a great, agonized scream, 'You bastard! You rotten, deceiving bastard!'

'Mummy—'

Alice didn't want to touch her.

The blue eyes opened, with dull, vacant expression.

'I made your tea.'

'Oh. Thank you.' She hauled herself up in the chair as if she had no energy, and took the cup.

'Why're you in your vest?'

'I washed my blouse.'

'Oh.'

Alice stood by the chair. She was always on tenterhooks with Mummy now, never sure of her mood. Alice was hungry. Should she ask if she should go along to the shops? Was there anything for tea? Mummy didn't leave the house. Not ever. She'd have to put her one other blouse on to go out.

Her mother drank half the tea, then sat back with the cup balanced in her lap. She closed her eyes. Alice didn't know what to do. But then she heard a sound, someone knocking on the front door!

'Go and get rid of them, Alice.' Louise Wilson gave a bitter little laugh. 'We aren't buying anything at the door.'

Alice crept through to the front and went to the window to see who was knocking. Screwing up her eyes, she saw a woman on the doorstep. Her heart gave a jolt before starting to pound madly. It was Miss

Purdy! She could see the blurred blue of her dress. What on earth was Miss Purdy doing here? And whatever was she going to do?

Paralysed, Alice stood very still, praying Miss Purdy couldn't see her and that she'd just think no one was in and go away. Part of her longed to ask Miss Purdy in, to say to her: please help me, just help me, I don't know what to do. But she just couldn't open the door. Mummy would have a fit! Not knowing what else to do, Alice tiptoed away to the back room again.

'Who was it?' her mother asked, indifferently.

'No one,' Alice was saying, when the knocking came again.

'Oh, for goodness sake, go and tell them we don't want anything.'

Alice's body seemed to turn to water. She couldn't argue with Mummy. Full of dread, she went and opened the door.

'Hello, Alice!' She could make out Miss Purdy's lovely smile. 'I've just come to have a word with your mother. May I come in, please?'

Alice had only opened the door wide enough to poke her head round. She squirmed. How could she lie to Miss Purdy and refuse to let her in? Helplessly she stood aside.

'She's in the back,' she whispered.

Alice saw her mother look round as they walked in. At the sight of a stranger in the house she sat bolt upright.

'Who's this?' she demanded sharply.

'Mummy,' Alice pleaded. 'This is Miss Purdy, my teacher.'

'It's very nice to meet you,' Miss Purdy said, with her hand held out. Mrs Wilson automatically responded, and for a second Alice thought it might be all right after all. 'I'm sorry to disturb you. Only I'm a bit worried about Alice. I wrote to you a little while ago about her eyes . . .'

But Alice saw her mother withdraw, fold her arms across her body and lower her head.

'Get out of my house,' she hissed. To Alice's horror she started to rock back and forth. 'Just go away. I never asked you to come here. I don't want anyone here. Leave us alone!'

Miss Purdy turned to Alice, utterly bewildered, but she couldn't look up. She was so mortified she just stared at the floor, tears welling.

'I'm very sorry,' Miss Purdy said wretchedly. 'I didn't mean to . . . to offend you in any way. I'd better go.'

'Yes – go!' Alice's mother screamed suddenly, then broke into sobs.

Alice followed Miss Purdy to the door, her throat closed with emotion.

'I'm sorry, Alice. I didn't want to make things more difficult,' Miss Purdy said, on the step. She looked upset. They could hear Mrs Wilson sobbing in the back room. 'I'll see you at school tomorrow.'

Alice couldn't say anything. Through her tears, she saw the blurred figure of her beloved teacher turn away and walk off along Franklin Street. She got further and further along until she was a small, blue blob, and her disappearing felt like the most desolate thing Alice had ever seen. She couldn't bear to be alone with all this any more. Desperate feelings swelled in her until she could no longer stand it. Her throat unlocked.

'Miss Purdy!' She shouted along the street at the top of her voice. 'Miss Purdy! Don't go – please!'

Twenty-Three

The little girl's cry pierced through Gwen.

Fighting back tears of shock at Mrs Wilson's violent dismissal of her, she turned to see Alice's forlorn figure by the lamp outside her house. Alice's desperate call was the loudest sound she had ever heard from this timid child.

Whatever was wrong with her mother? Gwen had been horrified by the glimpse she had had of the Wilsons' house. The front room was completely bare, not a stick of furniture in it, and the back room hardly better. In its way, it felt even more dismal than the crumbling squalor of Joey Phillips's house because Mrs Wilson was so obviously genteel. Gwen hesitated, unable to think what to do. It would be easiest to run away – Mrs Wilson had made it very clear she didn't want anyone. But the least she could do was to try and comfort Alice.

Seeing her teacher approaching her again, the little girl lowered her head and cried heartbrokenly. It was only then that Gwen noticed that the child was dressed only in a vest with her skirt. Gwen did the only thing she could think of and took the fragile child in her arms, stroking her head.

'It's all right, Alice,' she said softly. The intensity of the child's grief made her want to cry as well, but she fought back her own tears. 'It's all right, dear. It's all

257

right.' The words came instinctively. She held the child and let her cry.

'Is your mummy often upset?' she asked when Alice was a little calmer. She felt Alice nod.

Gwen had no idea what to do next. She could hardly go back into the house when Mrs Wilson had ordered her out so angrily. She was frightened of the way the woman had looked, the hysterical sound of her voice and of her own role as an interfering busybody. She felt completely out of her depth. But how else could she help Alice? The poor child had to live with this day after day, quite apart from not being able to see properly. Surely there was something that could be done.

'Come along, Alice.' She sounded a great deal more decisive than she felt. 'Perhaps I should come in again and see if I can have a word with your mother.'

Alice didn't protest, though Gwen couldn't help wishing she would.

In the house Gwen and Alice could hear weeping. They tiptoed into the room. Mrs Wilson was sitting hunched in the chair, rocking back and forth. The fury seemed to have left her and she appeared smaller, girlish and completely bereft. It was only then that Gwen noticed that although Alice's mother was quite nicely dressed she was not wearing anything on her feet.

Mrs Wilson looked up, her cheeks wet with tears. It was a sweet, blue-eyed face. Gwen realized that she was not a great deal older than herself, barely thirty.

'Oh *no*!' she wailed, her face crumpling again. 'Why can't you just go away and leave me alone? I just want everyone to leave me alone!'

Her voice was light and well spoken, at odds with

the poor, bleak surroundings. Gwen couldn't make any sense of it.

'I'm sorry,' she began, 'only Alice was so upset, and . . . well, you're obviously so unhappy too and I wondered if there was anything I can do to help you?'

'No!' Alice's mother began crying afresh then. 'Just go away! Leave me!'

Gwen could see that despite all her protests, the woman desperately needed someone's comfort. Finding all the courage she could, she went and knelt by the chair.

'Please don't worry. I only want to help – you and Alice. She's such a good girl, and you seem so terribly sad . . .'

These words of kindness made Mrs Wilson cry all the harder. She put her hands in her lap, kneading them in dreadful agitation.

'Oh!' she burst out eventually, between her sobs. 'Oh, I can't bear it any more. I can't go on struggling on alone like this!'

Gwen dared to reach and take one of her hands and the woman quietened a little and looked into her face, as if trying to decide whether she was worthy of trust. Gwen could see how much Alice resembled her, with her pale hair and eyes.

'It's all right.' Again, it was the only thing Gwen could think of to say.

'You won't tell anyone?'

'Of course not.'

'Alice, dear – I'd like to talk to your teacher. Would you go upstairs for a little while, please?'

Alice obeyed. Her face was blotchy from crying, but Gwen could see she was relieved. They paused, listening to her tread on the stairs. Gwen found herself wondering if they had any furniture up there.

'She's a dear little thing,' she said to break the silence.

'Yes,' Mrs Wilson said miserably. 'Poor Alice.' Her tears fell again and she gripped Gwen's hand. 'Can I trust you? I don't know who I can trust any more. I don't know who I am or what I'm about!'

'It's all right, really it is. I just want to help.' For some reason Gwen added, 'I'm not from round here myself.'

Mrs Wilson's pale eyes searched her face.

'Is it just you and Alice who live here?' Gwen asked.

'Yes. We never had any more children. A blessing as it's turned out. I can hardly manage with Alice.' She seemed to come to herself for a moment. 'I should make you a cup of tea . . .'

'No, please don't bother. I'm quite all right.' Gwen imagined that Alice's father must have died, or deserted her, for her to be left alone like this. The poor woman was obviously finding it very hard to cope with her reduced circumstances. She decided it might be easier to be direct.

'What is it that's troubling you, Mrs Wilson?'

While Gwen stayed kneeling on the floor at her feet, Mrs Wilson's story came pouring out. Until a few months before, she and her husband and Alice had lived a very comfortable life in a respectable part of Solihull. Her husband, Bernard, was a partner in a thriving engineering business in Birmingham. He was almost a decade older than her and Louise Wilson – she told Gwen her name – had married young, had Alice, and settled into being the pretty, sheltered wife

260

of a prosperous businessman. She attended the business functions, ladies' nights at the masonic lodge of which he was a member, always pretty and admired on his arm. Alice went to a good private school, where she had nice little friends. Louise had servants, but she liked to make things to decorate the house, curtain pelmets and flower arrangements. Her home was her pride: her project to make it a pretty, orderly haven for her friends to visit and her busy husband to come home to. She felt he was proud of her and that she was a success as a wife. As she spoke, the tears dried on her cheeks and despite her unkempt hair, Gwen could see glimpses of the pretty, contented person she had been.

'I've asked myself over and over again how I could not have seen . . . whether I could have done something to stop it. I feel almost sorry for Bernard and I wonder if it was my fault.' She turned to Gwen for a moment with an agonized expression on her face. 'That's what he said, you see – that he did it for me. Because he wanted to be a good husband . . . But that's wrong. It's so wrong and stupid . . . Couldn't he *see* that?' Tears rolled down her cheeks again.

'It was the end of the summer – a horrible wet day. Bernard came home in the afternoon. He never did that normally, so I thought he was ill. He was in the most dreadful state. I'd never seen him like it before. He was as white as a sheet but he wouldn't say anything. In fact he was dreadfully rude to me. And then the police came. Alice was at one of her little friends' houses, thank heavens. She didn't see them taking him away . . . Stupid, *stupid* . . .' The words were spat out and she clenched her fists. 'That's what makes me so angry – that he thought I couldn't be strong. That all that

261

mattered to me was ... was *fripperies*! And he didn't think enough of me as his wife to tell me what was going on!'

'What did he do?' Gwen asked gently.

'He was siphoning off money from the firm. Embezzlement. I didn't even know the word before. All our nice home, our things, were riding on him stealing. Of course the firm wasn't doing nearly as well as he wanted me to believe but he couldn't admit it. Times are hard for everyone, but Bernard always wanted to be the exception who held the biggest parties, drove the best motor car, smoked good cigars, was generous to people. But –' her voice rose higher with emotion – 'it was all appearance and show to make him the big noise in front of everyone. He didn't care about me or about Alice – he just had to show off all the time. And look where it's got him!'

Gwen had seldom heard anyone speak with such bitterness. Louise Wilson looked hard into her face.

'So you see – here I am. As it turns out, I'm only a stone's throw from Bernard, in there behind the prison walls. The bailiffs took everything we owned, except for a little money I had from my father's will in an account of my own. They didn't find that. I took Alice and came here – I hardly knew what I was doing. I just knew I didn't want anyone to know where I was – my mother, my sister, our friends. No one knows we're here. I didn't go to court with Bernard. I thought: *Damn* Bernard, for what he's done to us. I've never been to see him . . .' She crumpled for a moment, unable to speak.

'I should have gone, I know, but I can't face it. Alice has no idea where he is. I suppose she just thinks he ran off and left us. I don't want her to know her own

262

father was a liar and a cheat. A fraud. I was going to do it without him – show him I didn't need him. But the truth is . . .' Louise Wilson began sobbing then, her body shaking, and Gwen held her hands tightly, not sure what else to do. For a time the woman was unable to speak.

'What a terrible time you've had,' Gwen said.

'I can't . . .' Louise Wilson gulped, trying to speak. 'I . . . I never go out. I'm frightened. I don't know how to live any more, and poor Alice has to go and do all the shopping and . . . I'm so useless. We've almost no money left now and I just don't know what I'm going to do!' She broke down completely then. 'We're going to starve if I don't pull myself together! It's bad enough that Alice has to live here in poverty with all these rough children. She looks like a . . . a *slum* child now – she's even starting to talk like one! Look at how we live – I can't even take care of her properly! I don't know how to and I've no one to turn to. I'm so alone and sometimes I feel as if I'm losing my wits!'

'Oh dear!' Gwen said, helplessly. While she was sorry for Mrs Wilson, upset by her distress and the sight of this miserable, spartan house, she also felt stung by her dismissal of all the other children in this snobbish way. Dismissing Lucy Fernandez as nothing but a 'slum child', if you please! But she kept these thoughts to herself. After all, wasn't that just how she used to think when she had first arrived? 'I'm so sorry, Mrs Wilson. Is there anything I can do to help?'

Louise Wilson shook her head. 'I don't see what anyone can do. What's going to become of us both?'

'Well,' Gwen said hesitantly, 'I suppose you'll have to go out and find some work.'

The woman looked at her in horror. 'Work – what,

round here? I'd have to go out and mix with all sorts of people and what work is there round here? In some filthy, dreadful factory with goodness knows who!'

'Well – or a shop, perhaps? Surely that's better than the pair of you starving?'

Gwen began to feel a little irritated. She thought about Theresa Fernandez and all she had been through. Theresa had certainly worked in factories when she came to Birmingham and it hadn't been what she was used to either.

Mrs Wilson stared dismally ahead of her. 'Bernard always used to say, "My wife will never need to work, you can be quite sure of that."' She gave a bitter laugh. 'And now look at me.'

'But I suppose . . .' Gwen felt out of order giving advice to a woman older than herself, but it was common sense surely, wasn't it? '. . . that really is the only thing you can do, isn't it?'

Twenty-Four

'So I offered to buy Alice some spectacles myself,' Gwen said. 'After all, the woman doesn't seem to have two pennies to rub together, and poor Alice can barely see a hand's width in front of her!'

She and Daniel were walking arm in arm in Lightwoods Park. They reached the bandstand and turned to sit perched on the edge of it. It was a Saturday, grey and muggy, but Gwen couldn't have cared less what the weather was like.

'Well, I should say that was a very kind thing to do.' He looked into her eyes. She felt his arm move round her back and she leaned nearer to him. As ever, being anywhere near to Daniel filled her with excitement, and a sense of being fully alive. And she was close to Daniel rather often now when he was at home. Sometimes he disappeared for days at a time – to Wales or to meetings in London – and she never knew when he would be back. When he was away she felt abandoned, but when he was here, he pursued her with an eagerness that made her breathless. It was as if she could not see round him. He blocked out the sight of anything else, of Edwin or her life before. A letter had arrived from Edwin that morning and she had seen his neat, careful writing on the envelope with a surge of guilt. But her feelings for Daniel were something with which she could not argue.

As they walked across the park, Daniel had been

telling her about the meeting he had been to the night before, in a hall in Smethwick. He was excited. There had been much talk about Spain and how the revolutionaries were standing up to the landowners and the Church.

'They're turning the farms into collectives like in Russia. The revolution is starting to take hold there and we'll bring it about here – I know it!' Feeling coursed through him like a ripple of muscle and he gripped her arm more tightly. Suddenly, though, he turned abruptly, looking across the park.

'What's the matter?'

'Just checking. You never know if someone's following you.'

Gwen burst out laughing. '*Following* you! Why on earth would they want to do that?'

Daniel whipped round, angrily. 'You don't understand. We're seen as enemies, party members. Enemies of the state. They want to keep an eye on what we're doing.'

She stared back at him. Was he exaggerating? It seemed both awesome and frightening. If Communism was so good, why were they worried about it?

'You should come to the meetings, Gwen *fach*.' His anger was soon gone. 'Come and join the revolution and make it happen. We need everyone – not just the poor and oppressed. We're all workers and we all need to join the struggle.' He looked deeply into her eyes. 'Come with me. Come and join us.'

At that moment Gwen felt she would go with him anywhere, but she felt very inadequate. 'The trouble is, I don't know anything about politics.'

Daniel's dark eyes seemed to drill through her. 'But you know about justice and about right. It's deep in you – I've seen it. You believe that the poor should have a say in their own lives, don't you? That they should be able to take control of the work they do instead of leaving it in the hands of capitalist owners who rake off all the profits?'.

She nodded. Yes, this sounded reasonable and right and true. She tried not to hear Edwin's voice in her head telling her not to tangle with this. Edwin did not believe that women needed to involve themselves in any sort of politics, which he saw as messy and fundamentally vulgar – let alone this sort of politics.

Daniel led her to the bandstand then, and they sat leaning close together.

'I suppose I should come,' she said. 'I've never heard you speak to a meeting.'

'Oh, I don't do all that much speaking. There are plenty of others with things to say. And a lot to organize. Getting the word out, communicating with the workers – there's always so much to do and we always need more people to help. But everyone who works for the party considers it an honour to further the revolution.'

Gwen immediately felt humbled that she was privileged to be asked to join something so momentous. It was a feeling she often had with Daniel when he talked about Russia and Spain, about Rosa Luxemburg organizing the party in Germany and being shot, about revolutionaries all over Europe who were drawn together by the class struggle for justice and equality. She felt for the first time in her life as if she were being asked to be part of something important. And what she had seen in Birmingham, poverty and squalor among working people such as she had never known about before, had brought the injustices right before her eyes

267

and into her heart. She wasn't sure how any of this fitted together or what should be done about it: she just knew it was wrong. But Daniel seemed to know and she wanted to learn from him. She wanted to be with him every possible moment.

'I will come with you,' she told him. 'I want to understand.'

His arms squeezed her tightly. 'My lovely Gwen. My comrade.'

At that moment a black, springy dog bounded across the park towards them and sniffed round their knees. It was so full of life, it made them both laugh.

'Go on, boy – off you go!' Daniel said stroking its head. The dog took off again. It made Gwen think of Edwin's father's dog. A terrible stab of guilt went through her, with the thought: *How can I marry Edwin after this*?

Daniel stroked her back and she felt him looking at her. She knew that as soon as she looked into his dark, challenging eyes, she could only surrender to him, the effect he had on her was so overwhelming. She gazed across the park from under the brim of her hat.

'Gwen.' His deep voice twisted right through her. 'Look at me, girl.'

Turning her head, she looked into his eyes and for a moment they sat quite still, caught in each other's gaze.

He stroked her cheek. 'You're so lovely.'

Once again, they were reaching for each other, and she held him close. There was nowhere else she wanted to be. She had never told Daniel that she was engaged to be married. Her ring, with its tiny sapphires, was still tucked into its little silk-lined box.

*

Alice Wilson came and stood shyly by Gwen's desk. She was wearing the spectacles Gwen had collected for her the day before.

'I can see leaves!' she reported with a huge smile. 'And . . .' She looked wonderingly round the class-room. '. . . everything on the blackboard, and faces and . . . and *ants* outside!'

Gwen laughed, delighted.

'This is from my mother,' Alice said, suddenly sober. She produced a piece of folded paper from her pocket.

'Thank you, Alice. You go to your seat now,' Gwen said.

'Dear Miss Purdy,' the note read in a neat hand. 'I am very grateful for the help you have given to Alice in getting her spectacles. It was very kind of you. Sincerely, Louise Wilson.'

Gwen frowned at the stiff little note. She felt very sorry for Mrs Wilson. She seemed trapped as much by her pride as her sudden poverty.

Alice had been eager as anything in class ever since she could see. And they had offered her a place dancing in the May celebrations, but she said she didn't want to. On a cool but bright day the children celebrated the crowning of the May Queen, a sweet-faced little girl in Form Five who was the envy of most of the other girls. Some of them danced round the Maypole in white dresses. Noticing Alice watching the dance with Lucy Fernandez beside her, Gwen saw that this was obvi-ously why she had refused to join in. If Lucy couldn't dance, obviously Alice wasn't going to either.

Millie's wedding was to be the second weekend in May, and Gwen knew she would have to give notice to

Ariadne that she would be leaving Soho Road. This was not nearly as straightforward as she had hoped. She tackled Ariadne one evening after the three of them had downed an unusual version of Lancashire hotpot, topped with slices of turnip instead of potatoes. Being undercooked, they had the consistency of a damp cardboard carton.

'Could I have a word with you, Mrs Black?' They were standing in the dark hall. Harold Purvis passed them and went up the stairs, belching gently to himself.

'Ariadne, *please*. Is it something of a private nature?' She drew Gwen into the front parlour, which was cold and full of dark, heavy furniture. Ariadne stood waiting with a pained expression as if preparing for bad news. Her lips were painted a hard, dark red.

'I'm afraid I shall be needing to move on,' Gwen said, wondering why she felt so frightened about this encounter. After all, she had every right to move to different lodgings if she wanted to. It was just that Ariadne always seemed to take everything so personally. 'I shall be moving out at the end of the month.'

'Oh dear!' Ariadne's face became such a mask of dismay that Gwen immediately felt horribly guilty. 'Oh no! How very upsetting!' Ariadne clasped her hand over her heart. 'And there was I thinking my little abode here was a satisfactory lodging for a respectable young woman – and things seemed, just for once, to have settled into a harmonious situation. We've all been so happy here, you and I and Mr Purvis, haven't we?'

'Er – yes, haven't we!' Gwen agreed fervently. 'Only it's to do with a friend of mine.' She explained about Millie and her need for a lodger and how it seemed the only thing to do. Ariadne seemed a little appeased.

'Well, as long as it's nothing I've done to offend

you. Nothing you've found lacking here ... My George would have been so disappointed in me if he thought I hadn't provided adequately ...'

'No, not in the least! Staying here has been ...' No words seemed adequate. 'Well – it's been a home from home.'

This seemed to satisfy Ariadne, and all was well. However, the next day she announced to Harold Purvis at the breakfast table that Gwen was leaving. Harold took the news silently, though Gwen felt him eyeing her aggressively across the table. That evening Ariadne did not eat with them. She carried in the food – rissoles and blancmange – in silence, with a tragic face, and sat in an easy chair by the fire as they ate, shrouded in clouds of cigarette smoke. Harold was smirking in a way which made Gwen long to kick him, and the silence was too heavy to break.

'Thank you, Ariadne,' Gwen said as they left the table after this painful meal.

Ariadne did not even turn her head.

'What on earth is the matter with her?' Gwen demanded of Harold on the upstairs landing. She knew it was something to do with him from his snide, smug expression.

Harold stood with his hands pushed in his pockets. 'Told her I'll be moving on.'

'You as well! *Why?*'

Harold leaned closer and Gwen flinched. 'D'you think I want *that*?' His mouth contorted with disgust. 'Old bag of bones pawing at me all the time. When it's you I really want ...' He reached out to her and Gwen stepped backwards.

'Please don't touch me, Mr Purvis. You know I don't like it.'

Harold smirked. 'You might if you gave it a chance.'

Ignoring him, she went back downstairs, to find Ariadne still hunched by the fire. She looked up at Gwen with tragic eyes, which immediately filled with tears.

'I gather Mr Purvis is leaving too,' Gwen said gently. She pulled up a chair from the table to sit beside her.

Ariadne nodded, her lips trembling. She had forgotten to put any more lipstick on and her lips were dull and puckered.

'It's cruel,' she sobbed. 'Him going and leaving me like this. And you – you don't need him. I *love* him. I thought he was mine – my Harold! I thought he cared for me and would stay with me. And now he's going away, casting me off like an old piece of clothing!'

'Oh dear, I am sorry.' Gwen couldn't think what else to say. She suddenly felt great sympathy for Ariadne. She looked so pathetic, poor thing. And fancy imagining that that slimy worm Harold Purvis could truly have feelings for her!

Ariadne was looking at her with bitter reproach. 'You didn't have to take him. You don't feel for him the way I do. I've got no one else and you'll have lots of young men interested in you. It's not fair, it really isn't.'

Gwen stared at her, appalled. 'But it's nothing to do with me, Ariadne! I didn't ask him to leave! I'm not the least interested in Harold Purvis, I can assure you.'

'But I've seen the way he looks at you, dear. And why wouldn't he – you're such a sweet young thing. But it's torture for me! I've never seen him look at me like that ... But sometimes I thought he cared for me. I really thought he did!' Tears rolled down her cheeks. 'I'm so lost and alone. I'll have to have another houseful of strangers!'

'I'm ever so sorry, Ariadne.' Gwen was full of pity for the scrawny, overdressed woman beside her. 'But all I can say is that Harold means nothing to me at all. He really and truly doesn't.'

Ariadne looked up desperately at her. 'Do you have to go and leave me as well?'

'I've promised.' She reached over and touched Ariadne's bony hand with its long, painted nails. 'I'm helping a friend – she's having a baby. But it's not far away. I'll come back and see you.'

'Will you?' Ariadne suddenly clasped Gwen's hand, managing a watery smile. 'Oh you are a sweet girl! None of my lodgers has ever said that before!'

Twenty-Five

'If I wasn't having Lance's baby,' Millie said a week before her wedding, 'I think I would have got over him fairly quickly, really.' Sighing, she looked into the distance and added, 'Well – I'll have to see it through. I've only got myself to blame.'

The ceremony was held in their local parish in Edgbaston. Millie's mother, Mrs Dawson, greeted Gwen with a tense smile as she went into the church. She was a kind woman who had stood by her daughter, despite her embarrassment over Millie's condition, though she had drawn the line at 'any fuss' over the actual wedding.

'She just wants to rush it through,' Millie said. 'I feel as if I'm being *smuggled* into marriage.'

The vicar had kindly suggested that as there were to be fewer than a dozen people present, they hold the ceremony in the Lady Chapel, where Gwen sat two rows behind Millie's mother and sister. She had worn her favourite summer dress, a pretty frock covered in sprigs of sweetpeas, in mauve, pink and white. She sat looking at the back of Lance's head as he waited on the other side of the aisle, and pictured Millie arriving outside. She wondered how she was feeling. In a moment there came a small flurry at the back of the church and there was the bride.

Millie had no father or brothers, so she was escorted

along the aisle on the arm of a family friend, a middle-aged man with a black moustache, who was smiling broadly. Gwen warmed to him for trying to add some joy to an occasion which everyone else seemed to regard as one of gloomy necessity. Millie looked very pretty in a cream dress with a softly gathered skirt which hung just below the knee and disguised any hint of pregnancy, and she was carrying a small bouquet of yellow roses and white carnations. She was well made up, and smiled when everyone turned to look at her, catching Gwen's eye as she passed. Gwen felt a pang, watching her. She could see the strain Millie was under, despite the brave expression. She was delivered to Lance, who was now standing and watching her solemnly. He was a tall, gangling man, an academic sort who, Gwen observed to herself, could not even manage to look smart on his wedding day. He had a long face, with a sagging expression, and his clothes, though not actually crumpled, looked somehow limp. Did he want this wedding any more than Millie?

The thought that Millie was now stuck with the droopy, if kindly, Lance for life seemed dismal. And, Gwen thought, as the two of them both quietly pronounced their vows, in less than three months it was going to be her turn. She would have to make the same vows and become Mrs Edwin Shackleton. That was the reality. Edwin was her fiancé and he was kind and reliable. And where, in fact, was Daniel this week? Once again he had gone off without warning. She tried to pretend she wasn't hurt and angry, but the feelings welled up all the same. When he came back, of course, he would be all over her, but sometimes she felt she was being picked up and put down. No: whatever she felt for Daniel Fernandez, she should be facing the fact that he could have no part in her future.

Within days, however, he was back and she went to her first party meeting with him in a murkily lit room in the centre of town.

'What's it going to be about tonight?' she asked on the way.

'Oh, it's not a speaker or anything like that tonight. More of a business meeting. But it'll give you an idea – it's the centre of all the activity, where we get things done.'

The party offices were over a left-wing bookshop. The room was thick with cigarette smoke, though there were fewer than a dozen people round the table, and on first impressions Gwen thought them disappointing. The great majority were men, though she saw three women, all of them dressed in the most workaday clothes and two looked particularly dowdy. The third had a head of thick, black curly hair which could have looked very pretty but was scraped severely back into a bun, and she had thick eyebrows and strong, intense features. A certain intensity marked the atmosphere in the room. Gwen immediately felt as if her pretty frock and hair ribbon and the smile that she directed at them marked her out as trivial and she shrank back inside herself, wondering what she was doing there.

Daniel's manner was confident, though she felt suddenly as if he was very distant from her.

'This is Gwen Purdy,' he told them. 'She'll likely join the party. She's here to listen in, see how we do things.'

There were nods and looks of approval in her direction and she immediately felt proud to be with Daniel. The man closest to her stood up, holding a cap in his hand and offered her a chair.

'Welcome, comrade,' he said solemnly.

Gwen sat, feeling the intense, unsmiling gaze of the black-haired woman on her from across the table. On the wall to the woman's left she saw a banner on which a muscular man was waving a huge red flag.

Once the meeting began, Gwen struggled to concentrate. There was a good deal of talk about the practical details of printing leaflets and recruiting members.

One of the younger men spoke despondently. 'It's such an uphill struggle. Everyone seems to live with their head stuck in the sand. They can't see that it's getting closer. The fascist tide is sweeping over Europe and all they can think about is the next pint, the next pay packet . . .'

'That's for those who get any pay,' an older man retorted scathingly. 'You don't know what it's like to have a clutch of screaming kiddies with empty bellies, that's your trouble. No wonder the masses can't think for themselves when they're drugged with hunger and want. After the revolution, no one will go hungry. They will be awake!'

A debate ensued about tactics. One minute they were talking about a United Front and a Popular Front and about Italy and the National Government's appeasement of Mussolini. Then the discussion moved on, bitter in tone, to the Labour Party and the ILP and during this Gwen began to feel sleepy and wished there was a clock in the room. The trouble was that the problems of fascism and what was happening in Europe all seemed too big and far away for her or anyone like her to be able to do anything about them, and other things like which parties would let the CP be affiliated with them seemed tedious and nothing to do with reality. With a sinking heart she realized she really wasn't made to be involved with politics. All she really wanted was for the meeting to end so that she and Daniel could be alone. She sat pressing the soft cotton of her skirt into sharp creases and trying to stifle her yawns. It was only when Daniel spoke beside her that she jerked to attention again.

'Comrades, once again we're getting ourselves bogged down in discussions which send us round and round like rats in a trap. That's what they want, our oppressors. They feed on our divisions, on our lack of clarity.'

He spoke quietly, but with such conviction and authority that immediately Gwen saw everyone was listening.

'We must keep in mind our strategy. We know that for many years now – I've seen it over and over again in the Welsh valleys – we've been divided, we're broken into splinters and fought a little battle here, a strike there. That suits them. They can defeat us when we are divided and we divide so easily with our preoccupation with the details, with our squabbles over purity and ideology! We must be practical, comrades! The threat of fascism is real and it is growing, and it is a capitalist threat. Unless we keep our eyes on our strategy of unity, we shall be defeated.'

There was a pause and Gwen glanced at him, to see him looking challengingly round the room. He was sitting bolt upright, hands on his thighs, arms straight, tensed, his eyes alight. It was as if he spoke as the conscience of the meeting and she loved him so much in that moment, which, if she tried to see it through his eyes, transformed a tired-looking collection of working people into the visionary agents of revolution. They waited for him to finish.

'But if we are united in right, if we are disciplined and work as a united force of justice for the oppressed, nothing will be able to stop us!'

'Comrade Fernandez is right.' The dark-haired woman said fervently. She had a powerful, well-spoken voice. 'When we bicker and get diverted into arguments we are behaving like amateurs, like a group of small-minded bourgeois shopkeepers! We are betraying the true spirit of the revolution!'

As she spoke she was looking across at Daniel. Gwen saw him nod in approval. She felt herself wither inside again. What on earth was she doing here? She knew nothing about any of this. She wasn't really part of Daniel's world. He needed someone who shared the same passion and could debate with him, walk side by side with him into the revolution that they so believed in! She felt close to tears as the meeting ended.

As soon as they stood up a number of people came to greet her and she had to compose herself to talk and smile. They seemed so glad that she was there and she knew it was because they wanted to recruit her to the party, but it still felt like an honour to be welcomed and treated in this way. The dark-haired woman had come to them straight away. She wore a long, straight dress in dark blue corduroy, a crimson scarf at the neck and flat brown shoes. The overall effect was at once severe and bohemian and she looked striking.

'So – Gwen, isn't it? Are you going to join the party?'

Though she felt flustered, Gwen looked back coolly at her. She wasn't going to bark because this woman commanded it!

'I'll consider it,' she said. 'This is my first meeting, after all.'

'I'm Esther Lane.' She held out her hand and shook Gwen's with masculine vigour. 'I'm from the BCPL but I've joined the party as well.'

'Pleased to meet you,' Gwen said, which provoked an ironic smile on Esther's face which Gwen took to mean that she had just said something bourgeois or in some other way considered not quite the thing in Communist circles. She had no idea what the BCPL was but she wasn't going to let Esther know that.

After that, the woman spoke only to Daniel. Watching her, Gwen tried to place her age, and guessed that she must be in her late twenties, perhaps older than Daniel. Whatever the case, she knew she was not imagining the woman's attraction to him. She was talking about a leaflet they were about to produce and seemed determined to delay him, actually holding onto his arm as they talked. In fact a number of people were keen to talk to him afterwards, and in the end Gwen went and sat down by the table again to wait, trying to put aside a desolate feeling of being ignored. She told herself not to be so childish. This was Daniel's work, after all.

At last his comrades seemed prepared to leave him alone and he came over to her, his smile cheering her immediately.

'Sorry to make you wait like that,' he said. 'There's always so much to be done . . .' He reached for her. 'Come on now, lovely.'

Gwen felt Esther Lane's eyes on her as she and Daniel left the room and she couldn't help feeling triumphant. Esther might be very clever when it came to politics, but it was her Daniel chose to be with.

'Well, what did you think?' he asked eagerly as they set out along the street.

She was happy now, able to be full of enthusiasm.

'It was ever so interesting. But I've got so much to learn!'

'Oh, you'll learn, my girl.' He flung his arm round her shoulder and she revelled in his closeness. 'It's not difficult – not the basic principles, least. What Marx and Lenin and Engels – all of them – were teaching us was justice and common sense. What we have to do is put it into practice – bring it about!'

As they walked home, Gwen asked him what the BCPL was. Daniel told her that the Birmingham Council for Peace and Liberty were a group who were against fascism. Then he set off to explain at length about the discussion the meeting had had about the Labour Party, that it had not wanted Communists in its ranks after the CP was formed in 1920.

'What we're asking for is a Popular Front of all the groups opposed to fascism, but to do that we have to unite all the socialist parties. The Labour Party still won't have us.' His voice was bitter. 'They're not worthy of the name socialist! They've no vision – they've betrayed the working man right down the line!'

He talked on and on and she started to feel glum. Was he going to talk like this all the way home? She was interested, it was true, but she didn't want to hear about politics, politics all the time. Couldn't he give a little bit of time just to her? Suddenly, though, he broke off.

'Here's a good patch!' Taking a piece of chalk from his pocket, he began to write on a smooth piece of wall next to them. He wrote the time and place of their next meeting and stood back to look. 'There – another brick in the wall!'

'That woman at the meeting,' Gwen said as he flung his arm round her shoulders again. 'Esther . . .'

'Oh yes – our Esther.' There was amusement in his voice.

'She seems – interesting.'

'She's all right. Very academic. She's from the university.' He chuckled. 'Quite formidable, isn't she? The sort who won't stop until she gets what she wants. The revolution needs people like her, full of passion.'

She wants Daniel, Gwen thought, going cold inside. Did he know? Did he want her in return? She was horrified by her jealousy, by the sense that she wanted to know about every encounter, every word that had been spoken between them ever. She told herself not to be so ridiculous. Daniel sounded quite offhand about Esther and he'd known her for some time. If he was interested in her, surely he'd had his chance?

She said nothing more, and a moment later Daniel stopped. 'Oh, I forgot! I've got something for you.'

He released her for a moment to pull a little book out of his jacket pocket.

Gwen took it, but could seen nothing in the dark street.

'What is it?'

'*Ten Days that Shook the World.* It's all about Leningrad in 1917, when the Bolsheviks seized power. The man who wrote it was there! Now – you read that and you'll touch the heart of the revolution! I promise you will. You can keep it.'

'Oh, thank you – I will!' She was delighted with the

book, more because he had given her a gift than because of its contents. She felt him watching her as she turned it over in her hands and she looked up at him. He held out his arms and drew her to him.

She wrapped her arms round him with a sense of relief. 'I've been longing to do this all evening.'

Twenty-Six

'Come on now – eat up, little sparrow!'

Siobhan sat beside Joey on the mattress, as he spooned sweet porridge into his mouth. He could feed himself now, but it was one of her good mornings. There were days when she wasn't well after drinking and lay on the floor until the afternoon. Sometimes she got sick and would retch over the old tin can, then ask him to bring her water from the broken pipe in the kitchen. But at the beginning, when he was still too weak to move, she or Christie sat and fed him and every day he grew stronger.

Every day, except on Sundays, Christie was gone by the time Joey woke. He went out, and waited to be picked up at dawn to work on the building sites, coming back like a ghost, sagging with exhaustion and coated in brickdust and plaster. However early he got up, he almost always built a fire and made a pot of porridge. Siobhan told Joey that they had taught Christie regular habits when he was in the seminary in Ireland. Joey didn't know what a seminary was, but Christie made the best porridge over that fire in the grate that Joey'd ever had.

John was out all day too, 'bringing in the taters' as Siobhan put it. Joey didn't know where John went, but there never seemed to be a day when he didn't come back without some money or food, at least, and sometimes the bottles for Siobhan that got Christie angry. Joey dreaded John bringing the bottles too because they made Siobhan bad and she cried and moaned and then often just ran off, out of the house and sometimes Christie tried to go after her. He couldn't stop her, and he'd come back in and sit by the fire so silently, so far away he might not have been there at all. Sometimes, long after he'd settled to sleep, he heard Siobhan come stumbling back in and Christie always seemed to be awake. Joey wondered if Christie ever slept. He hated it when they were both like that and tried to shut his mind to Siobhan's broken weeping. Worst of all, to Christie's. He made himself think about other things. Often he thought about Miss Purdy, remembering how she had put her arms round him and how she smelled lovely, of flowers.

Micky hardly ever moved from his position in the corner.

'He's not a well man,' Siobhan told him as they sat together in the dusky light of the room that morning. Things felt safe for now. Siobhan was sober, and kind. 'He won't be long for this world by the sound of him.' Micky's cough bubbled up from him and he had to fight for each wheezing breath.

Joey scraped the last bits of porridge from the old pan. The bottom of it was black and knobbly with 'mend-its', bits screwed in to block off holes, and they had one bent metal spoon between them.

'There ye go.' Siobhan took the pan from him and snuggled up closer, putting her arm round him, cradling her to him. It was comforting and warm, but the soft feel of her body filled him with dread. He wanted Siobhan in the same way he longed for his mother, and she was like Mom had been, pretty and sweet with her

285

blue eyes and thin, pointed face and – all his instincts screamed – dangerous. With her would come something terrible. He pushed her away and scrambled to his feet.

'You're a peculiar child if you'll not have a cuddle!' Siobhan leaned over on her elbow and held out her other arm to him, looking up through her long black hair. He could tell he had roused some emotion in her, something which crouched curled up inside. 'Ah, come on – come and be with your Auntie Shiv!' Her voice was wheedling now, and Joey felt panic rise inside him.

'No!' He felt his face harden into a scowl.

'Sure, you're the hard man, aren't ye?' she said, and her voice had a savage edge to it. 'Well, please yourself, though you'd think you'd have some gratitude, you little slum rat. Christie and me – we're from a good family, I'll have you know. You needn't go thinking you're anything so special, you little bastard!' She shouted as he let himself into the hall.

Over those days of recovery he came to discover more about the house. The four of them inhabited the front room, which was boarded up except for the loose plank Christie slid back and forth at the side so they could see better. There was barely any light in the hall and all the floor tiles were loose and clinked underfoot. Joey was still learning to find his way round, avoiding the holes where the tiles had come away altogether. The back room was full of rubble where the floor above had collapsed, and if you stepped just inside there was a place where you could look up through the jagged wreckage and see the sky. Beyond was a dark kitchen and scullery from which came the sound of running water. The tap had been wrenched off the water pipe, leaving a trickle of water running constantly

286

into the stone sink. Something scuttled away into the darkness as he approached. The door to the front room had to be kept shut always – it was Christie's strict rule.

'There's two or three things you've got to remember if you're staying here with us,' Christie had told him once he was well enough to listen. They were squatting by the grate and Joey stared intently into Christie's gaunt face. He had immediate respect for Christie and felt safe with him.

'We don't want anyone knowing we're here, right? So you never, *ever* go out the front. There's a way out the back, I'll show you. We never keep the fire going when it's light outside – even in the cold. We don't want anyone seeing the smoke and getting suspicious. So no building up the fire when I'm gone out. Whatever we earn we share – that's another rule. Micky can't work but that doesn't mean we leave him to starve. And –' he pointed emphatically – 'you keep that door shut at all times. Got that, little fella? This place is like a barnyard there's that many rats. You'll hear them running under the boards. But this room's the one place in not bad repair. I've blocked off a couple of holes in the floor and we're sound enough. We don't want to be inviting them in to share our dinner, now, all right?'

Joey nodded solemnly, and Christie's usually woebegone expression lit with a rare grin.

'C'mere.' He held out a thin arm. Once again Joey was struck by how hard and sore his hands looked. Christie put an arm loosely round him and looked into his face. In a whisper, he said, 'And the other thing is ... Siobhan, my sister...' Joey saw a look of pain cross Christie's face. 'She's not always very well.

You've seen she's not always herself. That's all. That's why we're in England, see. We came to . . . help her.'

Christie's face looked very sad as he spoke. Joey nodded. He couldn't think of anything to say, but deep in himself he knew things about the kind of not very well that affected women like Siobhan, like his mom.

He pushed open the back door, screwing up his eyes in the bright morning. A bird was singing close by. He pushed his hair back. It was longer than he'd ever known it before, hanging over his eyes. He stepped out onto the narrow area behind the house, which was paved with broken blue bricks. The rest of the garden was a chaos of brambles. Using the three fruit trees in the garden as a scaffold, the brambles had grown, spread, interwoven to a height about the same as Joey's so that the whole garden was taken over by them. Except in one part.

'This is how you get out.' Christie had taken him outside to show him. 'I cut a way through – with John, and Micky when he wasn't so bad. Through here, look!'

The men had cut a tunnel through the bramble forest. Christie bent right over to lead him through. Joey only had to bend his knees a bit to follow Christie's dark back between the green walls of hacked brambles, treading down some scrawny nettles trying to grow in the gloom. Christie stopped and cut back more bramble suckers which were trying to advance again.

'They're determined fellows these,' Joey heard him say. 'Come on, watch yourself now – we're nearly there.'

They followed the path down the length of the garden.

'Now – this is our gate,' Christie said, squatting

288

down by the hedge. He was talking in a low voice. 'We've not had any problem. The road out there's quite quiet, but you have to look carefully before you step out. You don't want to run into the Guard.'

Joey frowned.

'Your police fellows. Sure, you're a solemn little man!' Christie tweaked Joey's ear playfully. He leaned forwards, parting a place in the hedge and looked cautiously about. He stepped outside and Joey joined him. Christie was still looking warily up and down the street. There were houses further along, but down this end they faced the back ends of gardens and a warehouse and it was quiet. Joey found that he felt tired and shaky, just after walking that short distance. Looking up at Christie, he thought he looked smaller out here, and defenceless.

'When you're coming back, the place to go in is just after that drain.' He pointed. 'You'll soon find it – can't go wrong. But you don't need to be going out and about yet, do you now? Unless you've somewhere to go back to. Have you, Joey? Is there someone waiting for you at home?'

The question made Joey's chest ache. He shook his head fiercely.

Christie reached out and ruffled his hair. 'You can go with John, in a day or two, if you've nowhere else to go. He can always use a bit of help.'

Standing alone in the garden now, Joey looked at the green tunnel through the brambles. He'd been restless since he felt better, and fed up with staying inside. He thought of just going. He could do what he liked, after all! But he wasn't sure he'd be able to find his way back yet if he left. He sat down, cross-legged and poked at the bricks idly with a dry twig. He didn't want to go back inside. He didn't want evening to come either.

At night they sat round the fire. It was John who brought in the food. Christie seemed to trust him with the money he earned. John knew the place well, all the ins and outs. They cooked up stews in the one pan – always potatoes, boiled in the skins, and anything else John could get, flavoured with Bovril. Sometimes meat, and bread to mop it all up. Christie was so famished sometimes he could barely wait till it was cooked. They took turns with the spoon, out of the pan.

No one talked much. They were all too tired. Joey learned odd scraps about the adults around him as they talked to one another. He didn't understand much of it. He picked up that Christie had been in training to be a priest in Ireland. That he'd run away because of Siobhan. Something bad had happened. Joey didn't know what. He could feel Christie's intense protectiveness towards his sister, though. Once or twice he wondered what had happened to Lena. Did they take her away to the home? And Kenny and Polly? But he pushed those thoughts away.

Micky didn't talk now. Christie tried to feed him but he coughed and spat it out. Joey had been afraid of Micky, with his big, whiskery face. He wasn't like a real person to Joey at first, lying there, the coughing, the stink of him, which hit you every time you stepped in the room, but more like some kind of animal, or monster. But once or twice Micky had sat up in the evening and Joey saw he was a real man, heavy and weary and very sick. Once or twice Micky's bloodshot gaze had swivelled towards him and in his thick, rasping voice, said, 'Who's this little fella then?'

The next time, Micky glowered at him and roared, 'Get out o' here you little bastard!' Another evening, while still lying down, he said in a bewildered tone, 'So, you're all grown up then are ye now, Seamus?'

'He doesn't know you,' Siobhan whispered to him. 'He's muddled in his head. Don't go taking any notice. And our John – he's simple in the head too, but he'll do ye no harm.'

From things John said, Joey knew he had grown up somewhere across town. John had an odd, wooden-sounding voice, so different from the fluid rise and fall Joey heard in Christie's and Siobhan's voices. He seemed to speak all on one note and to keep on talking whether or not his mouth was crammed full of potato. He kept complaining about 'the camp'.

'Don't let them ever put you in one of them camps,' he warned Christie, as he did most evenings.

'I won't, John,' Christie said, rubbing his face wearily. 'I've heard you.' Sometimes Christie's mood seemed very low.

'Whatever they say, you're better off on the dole . . . Take you off to the depths of fucking Wales . . . Sorry for my language . . .' He nodded round at them. 'Sorry, Siobhan – didn't mean it.' He was devoted to Siobhan. Often he sat just staring at her while she slept.

'Ah, you're all right there, John.' She took her turn spooning food out of the pan. Her hair fell forward either side of her face and she shook her head to get it out of the way. Joey thought it was strange the way John was always saying sorry to Siobhan when her language was even worse than his.

291

'Wales. Brechfa...' John spat the word out with loathing. 'Christ, what a hellhole. Nothing there – not even a fucking pub for miles. Slavery, that's what it is. Dawn till dusk they had us slaving with a pick and fucking shovel. And for what? I'll have 'em for it one day – you'll see. Last time I take anything off of anyone. I'm never going back down that Labour Exchange. I'm my own man from now on – no dole, no fucking nothing off of none of 'em...'

After a certain point every evening, Christie would say, 'Joey – get to sleep now.'

And as if Christie was his father, Joey, usually tired by then, would settle on the floor and close his eyes while the adult voices murmured on around him and their shadows moved on the walls.

One night Joey woke to the sound of the front door shuddering open and low voices. There was only the barest glow from the fire and he could hear Micky's laboured breathing across the room. Joey lay with his heart pounding. No one came in through the front! They had no way of locking the door but it was so swollen and stiff that it was hard to get open in any case. Whoever had come in was now struggling to shut it again. He heard a bang, followed by a giggle, and whispering outside the door. The tiles in the hall clattered and he heard, 'Ssssh, you're enough to wake the dead so ye are!' in a fierce whisper.

Joey sat up. Inside him a struggle was going on. He should just lie down. He didn't want to know who it was or what was going on. He knew already though, really, that it was Siobhan. She'd been on the booze earlier, had been carrying on, loudly and nastily and

Christie had begged her not to leave the house. 'Don't do it!' he'd pleaded, trying to restrain her. 'Oh God, Siobhan, don't do this to yourself!' Joey knew all right. Like going home. Like Mom. Yet he was drawn up and out of bed and couldn't stop himself, as if he was being pulled by a magnet like the one Miss Purdy showed them at school. He thought no one else was awake.

Barefoot, he felt his way across the room and took the door handle in both hands, hearing the rusty rasp of the catch turning. The door squeaked open. He heard someone stir behind him.

'Siobhan?' Christie's voice was thick with sleep. 'Is that you?'

Without answering, Joey slipped out, closing the door out of habit. It shut with a loud click.

The floor was rough and cold against his feet. He felt his way along the knobbly wallpaper in the hall. Already he could hear sounds he recognized. They drew him, numbed, chill inside, along the hall. He clenched his jaws tightly together in the darkness, barely even feeling the sharp edge of a tile cutting into his foot. They couldn't hear him coming over their own noise. Joey stood at the door of the scullery, forcing himself to listen to the woman's mewling sounds, the man's grunting.

A light appeared behind him. There was a rattle of the tiles. Joey stood holding tightly to the doorframe, aware that someone was beside him, and then the candlelight fell on the pair coupling up against the sink, Siobhan's legs spread each side of the man, her head back against the wall, long hair hanging.

Joey didn't notice Christie moving. He seemed to be upon them in an instant, without a word, banging the candle on the shelf next to the sink, locking his arm round the man's neck and yanking him off. Joey caught a glimpse of a bullish, drunken face.

'What the fuck...?' Three slurred words before Christie punched him with all his force in the face.

'You filthy bastard!' Christie hurled a blow into the great belly. 'You stinking scum – get your hands off my sister!' He delivered another body blow, then another to the head until the man sank with a groan onto his back, flies gaping.

Dazed, Siobhan lowered herself off the edge of the sink.

'Christie ... oh, for the love of God, what've you done?' She was wailing, swaying. Joey could see she was very drunk, her eyelids drooping, voice thick and slurred. 'Why d'you have to come interfering? Why can't you just leave me be?' She sagged to the floor, sobbing. 'He was giving me a baby. They killed my baby, my little baby ...' She folded her arms tight to her and rocked back and forth, weeping in agony. 'Oh God, Christie, why did I let them do it? His little soul's hovering round me, in torment ... I'm a murderer ... and I can never make him rest ... I want his soul to be at rest ... I want to die, Christie ... just let me die ...'

Christie sank to his knees, gathering her into his arms. 'Oh God, Shiv ... Oh Lord Christ, don't do this ...'

Siobhan was crying, but it was the sound of Christie's distraught sobs that drove Joey back, away from them. He flung himself out through the back door, slamming it with every ounce of strength he had in him. The sharp stones on the path bit into his feet as he stormed along, and he didn't care, welcomed the feeling, the hurt. He wanted to do it to himself, for it to hurt more and more. Stamping his feet down, yelping, his body started jerking and he couldn't work out for a moment what was happening to him as his sobs began to release themselves. He limped out through the gate into the street, barely able to see because of the darkness and his tears. He stumbled along the middle of the road with no thought to where he was going or where he would end up. The very air he breathed hurt him. He was lost in it, blind to anything round him.

He didn't know how long the voice had been calling to him. Only when it came close and he heard running feet, did it penetrate through to him.

'Joey, Joey – where're you off to?'

And he was lifted up into Christie's strong arms and held close and tight.

'There now, little fellow ... It's all right now.' Christie's hand stroked his thin back, cradling, soothing him. Joey let out a wail from the depths of himself and for the first time in the years he could remember he cried in someone's arms until he could cry no more.

Twenty-Seven

'Comrades, we know Mosley's thugs are attacking Jews in the East End – attacking innocent working men like ourselves!'

Daniel stood on the platform at the front of the dingy hall, his sleeves rolled up. Behind him was a huge red banner with a black hammer and sickle blazing in the middle.

'We've seen the fascists holding their rallies – even lording it in the Albert Hall! We've seen Oswald Mosley in our own city, in the Bull Ring, spreading his poison to infect the minds of those who know no better ... But we've also seen our people silence their foul fascist rhetoric in Tonypandy last week. What was Mosley's slogan? "Blackshirt Policy Alone Can Save the Coalfields"? And what did our members do? Drowned them out by singing the "Red Flag", that's what!'

There was a brief outbreak of clapping and cheering. As Daniel spoke, he paced back and forth, emphasizing phrases with a clenched fist. His speech was reaching its climax.

'The fascists are capitalists to the core. If anyone knows that, it is the people of my home, the miners of the South Wales valleys! I've seen it, brothers, and I've seen the way we fight it, by the protest of working men. By our dignity and our passion in the struggle!'

Gwen looked round at the people close to her. They were all listening intently. A young man sat along the row from her, his eyes fixed on Daniel, bright with passion.

'Capitalist oppression and despair is bleeding its way across Europe and it is we – us! – you and me, brothers, whose glorious duty it is to stem the tide of this oppression. We've fought against it – we all know that. We've broken up their meetings and rallies. We've stopped them using our halls and meeting places.'

Daniel leaned towards the audience and wagged his finger. 'Oh yes – make no mistake. The capitalists, the police and the fascists are all hand in glove in the valleys, while they destroy our unions and throw anyone who gainsays them in jail to rot! They victimize our workers and slash our wages to starvation levels. But we shall not be beaten! We shall fight it! We shall come together in unity in the struggle. And together, through the strength and solidarity of our party, we'll see a new dawn for our people. We *shall* bring about the revolution!'

Daniel finished with one hand clenched high in the air. The room erupted into clapping and cheering and most of the audience got to their feet. Daniel stood, looking solemn, dignified, nodding in acknowledgement.

Gwen jumped up as well, full of pride. And soon this meeting would be over and she could be alone with him and in his arms! Looking across the hall, she caught sight of Esther Lane standing at the end of the front row and this dented her happiness. Esther was wearing an extraordinary green dress and leading the ovation to Daniel, clapping her hands high in the air. Gwen had noticed that, over the past weeks while she had been going to meetings with Daniel, Esther was almost always there, no matter in what part of the city the meeting was held. Every time she saw Esther she felt a pang of panic, of jealousy. It was so clear that Esther was infatuated with Daniel, and she was such a handsome, stormy-looking woman, strong and passionate like him, and so committed to the party. How could he not be interested in Esther? Daniel always denied it, though, and spoke of Esther with a kind of amused detachment.

'Esther's all right. She's a good party worker – one of the best.' He didn't seem to think of her in any other terms, but Gwen was never comfortable when Esther was around. All she knew was that she wanted to learn to share Daniel's passion, that same commitment to the party. Nothing else now seemed to matter except this life – and Daniel.

Gwen waited patiently, as she always did at these meetings, for Daniel to deal with all the people who wanted to speak to him. She exchanged a few words with people she knew, then sat quietly at the side of the hall with her bag and watched. Though trying not to think about it, she was conscious all the time of where Esther was in the room. The vivid green dress stood out among all the drab clothes of the men as she worked her way over to Daniel. Gwen saw them laughing together.

He may be laughing with you, she thought, *but he's coming home with me.*

She looked down into her lap, at the skirt of her pretty blue frock. *I'm jealous*, she realized. She'd never been jealous before. Never with Edwin. It was a bitter, fearful emotion, which shamed her. She looked up again to see Esther lean forward to say something, then languidly kiss Daniel on the cheek. The sight filled Gwen with outrage. Who did Esther think she was? But Daniel was already trying to move away and, as he did so, his eyes met Gwen's. He raised his eyebrows in acknowledgement that she was waiting.

'I'm going to be off now,' she heard him say. He strode towards her and she got up to meet him . . . 'Sorry about all that. The comrades always have a lot they want to say. Did you meet some of them?'

They went out into the street and Daniel immediately put his arm round her shoulder. At last, they could be close, she thought. But his mind was still very much on the meeting.

'I could feel them tonight – feel the energy,' he said excitedly. 'It's not always like that. We recruited two new members as well.'

'That's marvellous,' Gwen enthused. She had yet to join the party herself, and Daniel was working on her. She knew she would, soon, and wasn't sure exactly why she was hesitating. It was something to do with the shift in her life, stepping over a line away from the past. Joining the party seemed to be a symbol of that.

Daniel talked excitedly as they walked across town in the mild evening. His body felt taut and almost explosive with energy beside her. They were the only ones waiting at the tram stop. Daniel gave his habitual look around to see if he was being followed. Then he turned and took her in his arms, but she was still sore over Esther.

'Why does she kiss you?'

'Esther? Oh,' he said dismissively, 'she's just one of those people who carry on like that. Doesn't mean anything – forget it.' His gaze was burning into her. 'You're so damn lovely.'

299

At the feel of his hands on her back, his lips on hers, desire coursed through her. For these past few weeks she and Daniel had spent so much time together – at meetings and afterwards, talking, kissing in the dark. Every time they met felt more charged and when they were apart she struggled to think about anything except him and being with him again.

They sat close together on the tram out to Handsworth. At the end of May Gwen had moved out of the Soho Road house, parting with a genuinely tearful Ariadne, and had moved into the room she was renting from Millie and Lance in Broughton Road. Daniel stayed on beyond his own stop to see her home. As soon as they'd turned into the road with its big, respectable villas, Daniel stopped her again, kissing her hard and hungrily.

He drew back suddenly, his expression taut. 'God, girl – I want to have you.'

She stared at him, longing and frightened at once.

'I've never ... I was brought up to believe it was wrong ... You know – if you're not married.'

Daniel stroked her back. 'I know. We all were. Church and all that. And bourgeois morality. Anything they could do to control the passions in us.' He looked down at her intensely. 'But we can be as free with our bodies as we can with our minds. Truly free. You needn't ... You know – there needn't be a child from it. I've got something to stop it.'

Gwen felt herself blush all over at the intimacy of what he was saying. She had only the haziest notion of what he was talking about.

'I do love you ...' she faltered.

Daniel ran his hands down her sides, then pressed her close to him so that she could not mistake how much he wanted her. He reached round and pulled the bow undone so her hair fell in waves round her cheeks.

'Don't make me wait any longer.'

She looked up at him. 'How can we? Where can we go?'

'The park? It's not far.'

She thought about the dark park gates, the damp grass. It didn't seem right.

Daniel sensed her hesitation.

'What about your room? You said it was at the back.'

Her heart beat faster. How awful, sneaking a man into Millie and Lance's! But she knew she would – she had to. For all her misgivings she ached to lie with Daniel.

'They'll be in bed by now. Millie's so tired with the pregnancy and Lance is so . . .' She gave a wicked giggle. 'Sort of *limp*. He falls asleep almost as soon as he's had his tea. Least it means they can't argue if he's snoring away on the couch! And Mrs Markham's not bothered with us at all so long as we pay the rent. She's too old to be a dragon landlady.'

Gwen felt in her bag for her key, her hands trembling. She opened the door as quietly as possible. Inside, the hall was lit by one faint bulb. All seemed quiet, but Gwen had to stifle giggles from pent-up nerves, especially as Daniel made exaggeratedly frightened faces at her as they crept up the wide staircase, waiting for each tread to creak like a thunderbolt. Once they'd managed to get safely into Gwen's room at the back, they both erupted into laughter, trying to repress the noise.

'Ssssh – for goodness sake!' she hissed at him as he flung himself down on the bed.

The room was basic, with bare wooden boards and shabby curtains, but half the ceiling sloped where the attic stairs ran up above it and it looked out onto the garden at the back. Gwen thought it had atmosphere, especially now she'd arranged her few belongings in it and her pictures.

'Least you don't have to share it!' Daniel whispered. 'Not like at Ma's – all boys together!'

'Well, not until now, anyway!'

Daniel bounced on the edge of the bed. 'Squeaky bedsprings? No – not bad.'

Gwen's heart beat faster. 'She's a bit deaf, anyway – Mrs Markham.' There was something she didn't like about the way he was testing the bed. It felt calculating and for a moment she wanted to draw back, to say she had made a mistake and ask him to go. It had robbed the moment of intimacy. But he leaned forward and picked up the picture on the table near her bed.

'Amy Johnson?'

'Yes – she's a heroine of mine.'

'Remarkable woman, she is.' Daniel stared seriously at the picture for a moment, then put it back. Gwen was appeased by this, and then Daniel got up and came close to her. They stood looking at one another and his eyes grew serious. He put his hands on her shoulders. She knew she was not going to refuse him. She blushed. 'I've never done this before.'

'I know. That makes me want you even more.'

He kissed her gently, easing her lips apart with his tongue, as if they had all the time in the world and in seconds her doubts had gone. She wrapped her arms round him and he kissed her deeply, his body pressing tightly to hers. He drew back and looked at her again.

'Let's see you, my lovely.' His finger played at the neck of her dress and slowly he unfastened the buttons, peeling back the soft cotton. Her dress fell to her waist, leaving her naked at the top except for her bra. She felt vulnerable, being more naked than him.

'Take it off,' he whispered.

She reached round for the fastening. 'Take your shirt off?'

He pulled it off over his head and flung it on the floor, watching hungrily as she removed her bra and dropped it on the chair beside her. His hands cupped her immediately, fondling her, then he reached down to lick and suck her. With sudden abruptness he took her hand and led her to the bed.

'Get undressed.'

His tone was so urgent that she did not feel offended. He was pulling his clothes off, then pulling her to her feet again, helping her remove the rest of hers, so fast that she did not have time to feel embarrassed or afraid. She was carried along, excited by his need. She reached out to hold him and his muscular arms pulled her close.

'Lie back!' Daniel ordered. She lay on the candlewick bedspread and he kneeled over her. For the first time in her life she saw the strange, alien sight of a naked man, smelt his hungry, sweaty smell, and he was stroking her thighs apart, gently but urgently.

'God, girl, I can feel you want me – let me in. Lift your legs!'

She obeyed, moved by his desire, but with a feeling of somehow having been left behind in what was happening as he pushed into her, groaning as he released himself into her. He lay panting, his head next to hers, and she kissed his cheek tenderly and stroked his thick hair, her arms and legs wrapped round his back, holding him close.

'My girl,' he whispered, looking into her eyes. He kissed her nose playfully. Then she saw the loving contentment in his eyes turn to a look of horror.

'Jesus, Mary and Joseph!' He pushed himself up on his arms.

'Sssh!' she warned him. 'What's the matter?'

'I forgot. Christ, I forgot all about the French letter! I got that carried away!'

A sick feeling jolted into her. It hadn't crossed her mind! After all, she had no experience of this – had barely even been able to visualize it before.

'Does that mean . . . ?' Heavens, why was she so ignorant? What did it mean?

'Not always. It doesn't always mean there's a child. Course not. But there's a chance.' Daniel rolled off her, suddenly far away from the closeness of a moment before. He seemed to decide something, and said almost carelessly, 'Chances are it won't happen. Don't you go worrying, pet.'

He dressed hurriedly and she felt a coldness, as if there was something she had lost. She got up, feeling something trickle wet down her thighs and she had to get a hanky out of her drawer to mop herself with. She put her dressing gown on.

'I'll have to come down and let you out,' she told him.

'Right you are.' He smiled at her, but she thought it was a nervous smile.

'Daniel?'

He was moving towards the door, putting his waistcoat on. He turned. 'What?'

304

She wanted him to be warm to her, to hold her and tell her he loved her, that it would all be all right.

'Was it ... all right?' She felt pathetic, asking like this.

He stepped back to her and quickly kissed her cheek. 'It was marvellous. Night, night.'

He departed along the street with a brief wave. Once she was back in her room, Gwen lay with the light on for a long time, staring up at the cracks in the sloping ceiling. Her body could still feel his touch and between her legs felt damp and sore.

I'm his now, she thought. That was what it meant if you gave your body to somebody, wasn't it? *I've burned my boats. My life now will be with Daniel Fernandez.*

Twenty-Eight

'How do you know when you're first expecting?'

Gwen slipped the question casually into the conversation when she and Millie were washing up the tea things. The cooker and sink were squeezed into a wide part of the corridor between the bigger bedroom at the front and the living room behind it, where Lance was already sprawled on the couch, his eyes closed. Questions about babies didn't seem out of place, with Millie's on the way.

'Oh, well.' Millie held out a wet, soapy pan for Gwen to dry. Gwen saw that her nails were chewed right down to the quicks. 'The first thing was,' she lowered her voice, 'my, you know – monthly visitor – didn't appear. I didn't think much about it because I've never kept track of that very well. Then I started feeling ropy all the time – not just in the mornings. That was when I went to the doctor.'

Gwen made a mental note of all this. She wasn't exactly worried about it. It all seemed too unreal. Even what had happened last night between her and Daniel felt distant, as if she had dreamed it. A letter had come from Edwin that morning and he seemed unreal too. Gwen smiled into Millie's round face. Millie was starting to put on quite a bit of weight. She looked softer round the edges. 'Are you all right?' Gwen asked.

'Not so bad.' Millie's eye wandered towards the

living room, and Lance, and for a moment Gwen thought she was going to say more. Instead she just sighed and turned back to the sink. 'It'll all be different when the baby's here.'

Gwen eyed her, worried. Millie tried terribly hard with Lance, but he was such a lethargic, moody so-and-so and they squabbled often. It certainly would be different when the baby was there but would it be better? Gwen felt a worm of fear twist in her. What if Daniel had – she struggled to think of the term – impregnated her? But she dismissed the idea again. It seemed too ridiculous. And there were plenty of other things to worry about.

The Whitsun holiday, which had occurred a couple of weeks earlier, should have given her the opportunity to go home to Worcester. But the thought of being at home with her mother and Edwin and trying on wedding dresses seemed out of the question now. Whatever was she going to do? She couldn't face the fact that there were decisions to be made, that she could not just go on writing cheerful notes to Edwin pretending everything was as normal. She was supposed to be marrying him in less than three months. She was Daniel's now. She loved him. She had given herself to him. This meant everything so far as she was concerned. Yet she could not quite face the reality that she was going to have to step right out of that secure life, tell Edwin the truth – jilt him, that was the truth of it!

She had written to tell her mother and Edwin that she could not come home because she was moving her lodgings over the holiday, and in order to salve her conscience she had moved to Millie's then. The two holiday days she had spent with Daniel and the Fernandez family. On the Sunday they had gone back out to the Lickey Hills, spending most of the time wrapped blissfully round one another.

A stern letter arrived from her mother:

I can't imagine what you think you're doing not coming home for Whitsun. Your father and I are deeply concerned about your behaviour and your disgraceful treatment of poor Edwin. It's bad enough that you are away at all at this time, without showing any sense of duty. He's your fiancé, for goodness sake! And Mrs Twining is waiting to work on the alterations to your dress. I strongly suggest you come home next weekend and try to make up for it. I'm appalled at the way you're letting everybody down. I can't imagine what you're thinking of.

Gwen didn't go home. How was she ever going to face them? Edwin had done nothing wrong. He was a good man, she knew perfectly well. She had been content to be with him until she found out what it was possible to feel when she met Daniel. Daniel had awoken in her not just passion, but a new sense of herself. That wasn't Edwin's fault and she knew how much she was going to hurt him. She couldn't bring herself to write to him, though, even to apologize. From this distance the situation still all seemed like a dream that might just fade away if she didn't think about it.

'Where're you off to?'

Millie's tone was wistful. It was a warm, humid day and she was on the old couch in the sitting room with her feet up, hair loose, her hands resting on her swollen stomach. She looked hot and tired. The three of them had had some toast for breakfast and Lance had gone out for the day to the Blues match. Gwen felt guilty leaving Millie.

'I'm just going to meet my friend. There're a few things she needs help with.'

Millie frowned. 'You seem to go out such a lot. Who's this friend then?'

Gwen forced a smile. 'Just someone I met. She wants some help printing leaflets – bit of local politics. All rather dull, but never mind.'

'Oh. I didn't know you were interested in that sort of thing.' Millie looked bored by this. 'Why are you dressed like that?'

Gwen had put on her oldest skirt, a very unglamorous, straight navy thing, and a plain black blouse.

'She said we'd get grubby. Anyway' – she picked up her bag – 'have a peaceful afternoon. It'll do you good.'

As soon as Gwen was out of the flat she tore down the stairs, ashamed at her lie to Millie in referring to Daniel as 'she'. Millie had not met Daniel, and as far as she knew Gwen was all set to marry Edwin. It was three weeks since Daniel's secret visit to the flat, but Gwen could not bring herself to confide in her about it all – about her feelings for Daniel. About the party. Daniel seemed like her secret life, yet her real life – the one she hungered for.

There was a yellowed looking-glass in the hall and she paused in front of it. Her hair was pulled back more severely, more carelessly than usual, held by a thick rubber band. She had no ribbons on, no make-up and in the austere clothes and flat shoes she felt serious, more like a proper Communist worker. She had decided now that she was definitely going to join the party, to identify herself with those other passionate, purposeful people who were going to change things for the sake of working people, for the human race. People who got up and did something, instead of just talking about how the world should be a better place! She stared sternly at herself, then, at the thought of Daniel's face if he could see her, an irrepressible smile broke across her face. She let herself out into the street, bouncing with happiness. *I love him!* she sang inside herself. *I love him so much!*

She ran eagerly up the stairs into the offices. Daniel was already there, his dark head bent over the temperamental duplicating machine. He turned and grinned at her.

'Hello – can't come too close like this!' He smiled, holding up his hands, and Gwen saw they were covered in ink. She went to him and kissed him.

'Playing up again, is it?'

'Blasted thing.' Daniel lifted his arm and shoved his hair out of his eyes. 'I've been fighting with it an hour already. Herbert thinks he knows what to do – he'll be back soon.'

Herbert worked as a toolmaker. Gwen was not especially cheered to hear he was coming back. She perched on an old stool and looked out of the back window at the dirty rooftops beyond.

'Isn't anyone else helping?'

Daniel was peering into the machine. 'Esther'll be back soon. She's gone out to buy a couple of things.'

Not anything for lunch though, I'll bet, Gwen thought, deflated by the fact that Esther was going to be there and had arrived long before her. No one in the party seemed to be very practical. They didn't seem to

310

care whether they ate or not. Esther just smoked long, thin cigarettes one after another, and Daniel didn't ever seem to bother about eating. Gwen spent most of her time with the party starving hungry.

'Right – I'm going to give this a go.'

Daniel was just about to try again to get the machine started when Herbert slouched in. He was a sandy-haired man, thin as a greyhound, wearing a seedy black overcoat, even in the heat.

'I shouldn't do that if I was you,' he said gloomily. 'Let me look at it first.'

He gave Gwen the briefest of nods. She wrinkled her nose as he passed her. He didn't smell very nice. The two men busied themselves over the machine. Gwen soon grew bored, so she took out her copy of *Ten Days that Shook the World*. She was almost at the end now, but she'd had to struggle to get to grips with the Bolsheviks and Mensheviks and all the different parties and revolutionary movements. She began a chapter entitled 'The Peasants' Congress'.

It was on November 18th that the snow came. In the morning we woke to window-ledges heaped white, and snowflakes falling so whirling thick that it was impossible to see ten feet ahead . . .

'Well, comrades, how are we doing?'

Esther's booming voice cut jarringly through Gwen's immersion in the Soviet snows.

'I think I know what's up,' Herbert said.

'Oh – hello,' Esther said to Gwen in an offhand way. 'What're you reading?' She bent over to look. She was wearing an extraordinary pair of baggy black trousers and a navy blouse polka-dotted with white

311

tucked into them. Her plump arms protruded out from the short sleeves. 'Ah – *Ten Days*... How sweet! Imagine being able to discover all that afresh again!'

Gwen closed the book and stood up. She was an inch or so taller than Esther Lane. For a moment her eyes met Esther's intense deep blue ones. Esther's stare was provocative and, Gwen thought, rather scornful.

'Well, we all have to begin somewhere,' Esther said, moving away with an amused look. 'I'm sure Daniel's a very good teacher.'

Gwen felt a flush rise in her cheeks, fully aware that Esther had not been referring to revolutionary politics.

Esther joined the men leaning over the machine, deliberately excluding Gwen. Herbert was tugging at something inside the workings.

'There,' he panted. 'If that don't do it, I'm stumped.'

A few minutes later the machine cranked into action and the leaflets came fluttering out. *Bread Not Batons!* it was called. It was about the means test.

'Shall I help pile them?' Gwen asked Daniel eagerly.

'Yes, I can't do a thing till I've been and washed my hands!' Daniel laughed. 'Nor Herbert.'

Glad to have something to do, Gwen arranged the leaflets, which smelt strongly of ink, while the men disappeared outside to the toilet, where there was a tiny handbasin.

Esther rested her cigarette in an ashtray on the desk and carried on with the printing, her dark brows pulled into a frown. After a while, without looking up, she asked, 'So what do you do with your time?'

'I'm a teacher. At Canal Street, Winson Green.'

Gwen saw a hint of surprise on Esther's face. 'I say. That must be a challenge.'

'And what do you do?'

'Oh, I'm doing some research.'

'At the university?'

'Well, I use the library.'

'Gracious,' Gwen said, looking innocently across at Esther. 'However do you support yourself?'

She saw a slight flush rise in Esther's cheeks. 'My father's a lecturer.'

'Oh, I see – *he* supports you?' Gwen felt triumphant. Here was this woman going on about the workers of the world and she was living off her father! 'Well, how very nice! It's so inconvenient having to work for a living.'

'I devote most of my time to the party,' Esther retorted, busying herself with the printing.

The men came back then and for the remainder of the morning they all worked hard. Daniel and Esther discussed a pamphlet that they were working on, but although Daniel sat for some time at the desk with Esther, Gwen knew that his attention kept returning to her. Once he came over to her by the machine and put his arm round her.

'All right, comrade?' He looked deeply into her face. His cheeks were shadowy with stubble.

'Yes, of course.' She smiled, putting her arm round his waist. She felt close to him and as if she belonged, was part of what was going on.

By about two-thirty, Herbert murmured something about having to 'get back to the Missis' and slunk out.

'Thanks, comrade!' Daniel called after him.

Herbert raised a fist in reply, which, given how puny he was, made Gwen want to giggle.

Her stomach was gurgling with hunger by now.

'Shall I go out and get us something to eat?' she suggested, since obviously no one else was going to.

'That'd be nice,' Daniel said, glancing up from the desk where he was writing furiously.

It was good to be out in the sunshine. Gwen felt odd being in the street, amid shoppers leading small children by the hand and messenger boys on bicycles, the ordinary world where people were not interested in the revolution. She bought three cheese and pickle cobs and three iced buns and hurried back to the office with the paper bags in her arms.

As she pushed open the squeaky office door, the sight that met her made her feel as if she'd been punched. Daniel was still sitting at the desk and Esther Lane was standing behind his chair, leaning over him, arms wrapped round his neck. Seeing Gwen at the door she straightened up, unhurriedly, fixing Gwen with a defiant stare. Gwen was too shocked, too hurt to speak. Daniel smiled, apparently oblivious to the shock on Gwen's face.

'Those look a treat. Thanks, Gwen.'

No one, she noticed, offered to pay her for their share. *I suppose I'm the one who's working*, she thought. She couldn't look at Daniel. She was close to tears. Daniel took his food back to the desk and he and Esther continued to work.

'Won't be much longer,' he said, looking over at her. 'Just get this done and we'll go.'

Gwen nodded. The lump in her throat made it impossible to eat.

The hurt sat in her like a stone for the next hour until Daniel pronounced that he'd finished and they could go. They had a brief discussion about which of

314

the party workers had been out chalking up details of the public meeting they were holding on Sunday night.

'Thanks then, Esther,' Daniel said eventually, picking up his jacket. 'Gwen and me'll be off now.'

'All right, Daniel,' Esther said in her smoky voice. She ignored Gwen. 'See you tomorrow night?'

'Right you are.' Daniel took Gwen's arm and they headed out into the balmy afternoon. 'This is nice.' Daniel turned his face up to the light. 'Let's go somewhere different. How about Cannon Hill Park?'

'Daniel.' She couldn't contain herself any longer and pulled at his arm to stop him. 'I don't understand what's going on. Are you in love with Esther?' At last the pent-up tears ran down her cheeks. She felt miserable and stupid.

'Hey, what's the matter?' He pulled her into his arms. They were standing by a shop window in a busy street, but she couldn't have cared less. 'Why're you asking me that? Old Esther – how could you think that?' He pushed her away a fraction to look into her eyes. 'She's got a bit of a thing about me, that's all. Nothing that matters. I think she sees me as a romantic example of the working class – you know, from the valleys and that.'

Gwen looked up at him. 'Romantic – you?' She tried to smile through her tears, then grew solemn again. 'You're not . . . in love with her?'

'No!' Daniel laughed. 'Don't talk daft! She's just one of those Bohemian types – goes draping herself round anyone.' With his thumb he gently wiped her eyes. 'You're my lovely. You know you are – haven't I told you enough times?'

315

She pouted, more playful now. 'No!'

'Well, you are.' He kissed her nose. 'Come on – let's go somewhere where I can really show you.'

They took a tram down the Pershore Road and walked to Cannon Hill Park. For the remainder of the afternoon they strolled across the green spaces with their arms round each other. They bought ice creams from one of the Italian barrows and tasted the sweetness on each other's lips. There were a lot of other people out enjoying the sunshine, but as the sun sank lower and prams were wheeled back towards the big houses of Moseley and children taken home for their tea, the park became quieter. They found a spot near the top of a gentle slope and sat together. Gwen was glowing with warmth and happiness, her fears about Esther Lane pushed aside. It was her Daniel loved – he could hardly help it if Esther had a crush on him.

Daniel moved closer and put his arm round her back. They kissed, then sat close.

'Did you . . .' Daniel spoke suddenly. 'I mean, I wondered if you'd had your . . . your monthly yet?'

'It's all right.' Her cheeks went red. But she was touched that he was thinking of her in this way. 'It started three days ago.' She hadn't realized herself just how much the worry of it had been needling away at the back of her mind until she knew it was all right. She was not going to have a baby! Look what had happened to Millie, after all. But even despite that, she couldn't fully believe it would ever really happen to her. 'You're very well informed, for a man.'

'I was worried, that's all. My stupid fault – not using something to stop it. I don't want to get you into trouble.'

'Well, we won't forget again,' she said, looking into

his eyes. They had not made love since that first time. There had been no opportunity.

Daniel kissed her and she reached round and stroked his cheek.

'I wish we had somewhere we could call our own,' she said. She found herself full of longing just to lie back, to hold him and feel his weight on her and was caught up by surprise at herself. Was this her, feeling like this all the time, behaving in this way? And would they always have to sneak about and hide like this?

With his lips close to her ear, he said, 'If we wait here long enough, everyone'll go home – except for the other lovers!'

'Daniel! We can't – not here!'

'Can't we? Why not?'

She stared at him, her body aching with need.

His eyes narrowed. 'God, I want you.'

'You'll have to wait –' playfully, she touched his nose – 'till the moon comes up.'

Twenty-Nine

Joey started going out in the day with John. People stared at them. John's height, his black clothes and huge matted beard attracted attention. The others in the house – except Micky – washed under the broken pipe at the back, but Joey had never once seen John wash or change. You could always smell him.

'I do a bit of this – bit of that. Anyone who'll give me a bob or two for a job,' John told him. 'If they won't, then fuck 'em. I get this out.' He reached into the pocket of the long, shabby coat and pulled out a mouth organ. 'That can earn you a few pennies if you can make it sing.' Which John could. His favourite tune was 'Waltzing Matilda'.

Some days John took Joey to the Bull Ring and he'd pick up an odd job around the market, carting potatoes, bringing in ice for the fish market. Joey liked the Bull Ring, the bustle and colour, the birds and animals in the Market Hall, the knife grinder showering sparks from his stone. All the smells, especially the rich aroma of cooked meat from the eating places up Spiceal Street could make his mouth run with saliva.

'Why aren't you at school?' the market traders asked sometimes. 'You'll have the wag man after you!'

'He's helping me,' John would say firmly. 'He's my lad.' Joey knew everyone thought he was John's son and he found he liked this. He had a deep, almost

318

adoring, regard for Christie, but John was all right. You never really knew where you were with him, but when he spoke, to Joey's ears he sounded like his dad.

Joey kept a sharp eye out for the School Board man, and was always ready to duck under the nearest stall or run for it. Some days John went house to house, sometimes he was turned away rudely, at others he was invited in to do odd jobs: to chop a pile of logs, distemper the wall of an outhouse, hoe a vegetable patch. Despite the dole queues winding out of the Labour Exchanges – John wouldn't go near them, or any other official body – he almost always found something to do in a day, even if in the end it was to stand in town and squeeze out some tunes. Sometimes they begged clothes off the rich people in Edgbaston and pawned them. And he would send Joey thieving: nipping into shops, even houses, for food.

One day John stole a butcher's delivery bike, which was propped outside a shop in Edgbaston.

'We're just borrowing it,' he said.

Joey liked that day. John got the hang of the bike after a while and towards the end they had a bit of fun on it, whizzing down Rotton Park Road. The metal was hard and uncomfortable under Joey's thighs, but he lodged himself sideways on the crossbar as John wobbled faster and faster along the streets.

Joey clung on, excited, terrified, feeling an odd, bubbly sensation rising in him, a pressure in his chest. He heard noises coming out of his mouth and it took him a while to realize that he was laughing.

One morning Joey woke in the summer dawn, sensing that something had changed. The room was very quiet.

319

He lifted his head. The plank had been slid back from the window and he could see Christie squatting in the corner near Micky, his head bowed.

Joey got up and tiptoed over to him. Siobhan was asleep nearby, curled up on her side with her chin tucked in, her face mostly hidden by her hair. She didn't look peaceful: more as if she was hiding.

Christie looked round at him. 'He's very sick, Joey boy. Our Micky's not got long to go.'

Joey looked down at the bloated body. Micky had not moved for days. Joey saw his belly going up and down, but his breathing was wheezy and shallow. Siobhan had kept saying he was sinking. They'd boiled water and tried to clean him up. He had a terrible smell on him. It hit you when you came in the room.

'Poor old fella,' Christie said.

That evening, when Joey came back in with John, the stench was terrible. Joey could taste it, over the smell of stew and cabbage, like fur in his mouth. He went and crouched at the side of the hearth, hugging his knees, near John, who was stirring the pot. Joey's stomach was twisting with hunger. Siobhan and Christie ignored both of them because they were arguing, though for once this was nothing to do with Siobhan's drinking. She was sober, but distraught.

'Don't you dare go fetching one of them here! We don't want them pushing their noses into our business, knowing we're here! Christie, for heaven's sake he'll go running for the Guard and they'll have us out of here – sweet Jesus, they might even send us home!'

Christie was sitting by the fire, hands over his face. Joey could see that he was coiled like a spring. Christie spoke through his fingers.

'I've got to, Shiv. You know I've got to. It's the only thing left.'

'Don't bring one of them!' She was sobbing. 'They'll see into my blackened soul, sure they will! I can't stand it!'

But Christie was not to be budged. 'God knows he's had little comfort in his life. And he was a right enough old fella.'

Siobhan sprang up suddenly. Joey caught a glimpse of her white thighs before her skirt fell over them again.

'I tell you, Christie O'Brien, you bring a priest to this house and I'm parting company with you – for good. I'll not stop here a moment longer.'

Christie snatched his hands from his face and stood up, so toweringly angry that at that moment he seemed to Joey twice his normal height.

'Have you forgotten I'd still be training to be a priest myself had it not been for you? For your carrying on with Sean Flaherty? Did you forget I ran away from the seminary for you? For *you*, you selfish bitch. Don't you think I mightn't rather be back there now than rotting here in this filth and squalor? You never think of anyone but yourself, do you?'

'You *hated* the seminary!' Her voice rose. 'You never wanted the priesthood and you know it – baptizing brats all your life in some God-forsaken country! Don't you bring that down on my head! It wasn't you wanted to go – you had no will of your own when Mammy was at you all the time. Sure, couldn't one of her sons bring blessings on the family – be a priest and join the missions? Well, Paddy and Donal weren't fit for it, were they? Mine wasn't the only bastard baby on the farm, don't forget!'

'Keep your voice down!' Christie shouted. 'Will you have some respect for a dying man?'

'I'll not stay, I tell ye, Christie. I'll go from you!'

'Will you? Will you now?' Joey had never seen Christie so angry. He was quivering, his face pushed right up close to Siobhan's. It was as if she had twisted at something deep inside him. 'And where will you go, Shiv? On the road? Selling yourself along the way? Or back in the spike bedding down with whores and drunks?'

There was a long silence. The two stood with their eyes burning into each other's in the firelight as if neither could let go. At last Siobhan looked down.

'The *rest* of the whores and drunks, you mean, Christie.' Her voice was low, and filled with an ache of shame. 'For that's what I am and in your heart you know it.'

She sank to the floor, as if all her energy had gone.

'Do what you like,' she said pitifully.

Christie went to the door. Before going out he turned and said quietly, 'He deserves to have the Church at the end.'

John went over to Siobhan.

'I've got some biscuits,' he said sweetly to her. They'd bought broken biscuits in the Bull Ring.

'Have you, John?' There was a deadness to her voice. She stared into the fire. John laid the food they had brought beside her like an offering.

'Did you bring me a drop of anything, darlin'?' Her tone was wheedling now. Joey, crouched at the edge of the hearth, felt himself tighten inside. He hadn't seen John buy anything, but he hated it when she even asked. He didn't know why John did it, making

322

trouble. He might offer to go out again, down to the Outdoor to fetch it for her . . .

'No, Shiv. Sorry,' John said abjectly. 'We didn't make very much today.'

'Never mind.' Her voice was sad, but she patted John's arm. 'You're sweet to me, John, so you are. Come here and give me a kiss.'

John didn't move any closer. He froze, kneeling bent over the bag of potatoes they had bought. Instead, Siobhan had to move, leaning over to kiss his cheek. Then she looked into his face. John looked woodenly back.

'Sure, you're a funny one. D'you not want me, John? D'ye not need a woman?'

John stood up. 'I'm going to get some water.'

The potatoes were boiling over on the fire when they heard footsteps in the hall. Siobhan froze.

'In here, Father,' they heard. 'I'll just get us a light.'

'There's a powerful smell on him, all right,' a voice said.

As the door swung open, Joey saw that Christie was accompanied by a thin, dark-haired man in glasses.

'He was very bad when we woke this morning.' Christie spoke in a low voice, as if not wanting to wake Micky up. 'But he's holding on. Pass us a candle, John.' The priest squatted down by Micky's body. Joey saw him react, just a fraction, to the pungent stench.

The priest took a little bottle from his pocket. He tipped it up, then touched Micky's forehead. He hesitated and reached down for Micky's wrist. Then he looked solemnly up at Christie.

'He's gone.'

323

'Has he?' Christie sounded startled. 'It must have been just in the past few minutes.'

'Well, he's dead, sure enough.' The priest murmured some words which Joey couldn't understand. Christie was standing with his hands clasped. He said, 'Amen', and made the sign of the cross. Joey heard Siobhan say 'Amen' very quietly as well.

The priest stood up and looked round, and Siobhan shrank closer to the wall.

'What is this place? Sure, you're not living here?' His tone was gentle. Joey did not feel afraid of him. 'Have you all nowhere else to go?'

'We haven't,' Christie pleaded. 'We've no other home. When my sister and I came over we were on the road, dossing down in the spikes – we were separated and she was in with all kinds of people ... It's not good for her, Father. We're getting along nicely enough here if we're left alone. Please don't tell anyone we're living here, will you?' Joey almost thought Christie was going to kneel down in front of the man he sounded so desperate.

The priest nodded, seeming to agree. 'Where're you from back home?'

'Tipperary, Father.'

'My grandmother's country. Myself I'm from County Mayo.'

'Are you, Father?' Joey could hear Christie's nervousness in the quick way he spoke, the way he wasn't really listening to what the man was saying. 'I wouldn't have come bothering you if it wasn't for Micky there.'

The priest was silent and seemed to be thinking. After a moment he nodded.

'I can think of a couple of fellas I can get to help move him out of here. They've a handcart – we can keep it quiet. God knows, you'll not be wanting to live with this any longer.'

'Tonight?'

'I'll see what I can do. He's no family that you know of?'

'No, Father. Not over here.'

'Will we move him out of the room? The smell on him's terrible.'

Between them, they lugged Micky's body into the hall. Once the priest had gone, Christie brought a can of water and he and Siobhan scrubbed with a rag at the stain on the floor where Micky had lain.

A couple of hours later, when they'd eaten the thin stew, they heard movements at the back of the house. Everyone tensed. The tiles in the hall clinked and rattled. Christie went to the door.

'Don't trouble – it's only myself.' Joey heard the priest's voice and followed Christie curiously.

Two strapping men were squeezed into the hall by the back door. They touched their caps, saying, 'Evening to you,' and looked round bewildered. 'You can smell the fella, anyway,' one said.

Joey heard the priest say to Christie, 'They won't say anything. We've a handcart out at the front.'

The two men hauled Micky up, taking an arm and leg each.

'God now, he's a weight,' one of them groaned. And they took Micky away. Christie followed them out. Joey went back into the room.

Siobhan seemed to uncurl, as if a great danger had passed. 'God rest him,' she said tenderly. 'That was a hard life he lived.'

325

Thirty

'Lance? The least you could do is answer me – I said d'you want it boiled or poached?'

Millie's complaining voice drifted to Gwen through her bedroom door, mingled with the smell of toast. Gwen heard a brief, languid reply from Lance. She frequently felt an urge to get hold of Lance and give him a good shaking. Compared with Daniel's burning, physical energy, he was like a soggy dishcloth. No wonder Millie was turning into such a nag!

Turning over onto her stomach in the warm bed, Gwen decided to stay there a while longer. It was Saturday. There was no hurry: Daniel was away. At the thought of him she felt a kind of inner lurch, her whole body seeming to long for him, like a deep hunger. Sometimes she could scarcely believe herself: she had given herself to a man without being married! And her life was caught up in politics which she knew it was wisest on the whole to keep quiet about.

And there was Edwin. For a moment the shimmering bubble of joy and excitement in which she existed was ruptured, leaving her with a terrible sense of doubt. Every week brought a more angry and insistent letter from her mother, ordering her to come home. And, of course, many of the things she said were true. Whatever had Edwin done to deserve this? Even his letters had begun to sound a little put out, but Gwen knew Edwin well enough to realize that he would blithely assume everything was all right.

She made herself think about all the happiest times she could remember with Edwin: walks in the Malverns, moments when he had come smiling into her classroom in Worcester, how pleased she had been to see him. She *had* loved him, surely? But then she thought of Daniel and the effect he had on her. With Daniel she was *alive*: with him she flew instead of merely walking. It was as if he set something free in her, and it was inconceivable that she could forget it and go back to what she had been, even though she felt less safe with Daniel, less sure.

'I'll always be back, you dafty, you know that,' he said, with his easy grin, after returning from a trip away without telling her.

She'd reproached him gently. 'It's not very nice of you – just going off without a word. How do I know where you are or when you're coming back?'

There – she was getting just like Millie! She'd seen it even at the time and stopped immediately. A nagging housewife was not what she wanted to be. It would just have been nice to feel as if he considered her feelings, that was all. But she'd told herself she was being trivial and little-woman-ish. *Bourgeois.* There were such big things to consider – the class struggle, the revolution. Where were her feelings in all that?

There was nothing to hurry for so she took a long bath. Their landlady was less of a tartar about hot water than Ariadne had been, but the chance of a hot bath was still rare because of the temperamental nature of the boiler. The pipes groaned loudly as the water ran in. Lying in the bath, she thought guiltily about Ariadne. She'd promised to go and see her and so far she hadn't. In fact, she rather missed Ariadne hovering about when she came into the house, filled with some emotion or other and fussing over her. That's what she'd do today – go and see Ariadne.

'Oh!' Ariadne gave a great cry on opening the door, as if Gwen was a long-lost relative returned from years in the goldfields. She laid her hand on her heart and closed her eyes for a moment. As usual her eyelashes were laden with mascara.

'My dear, how *very* nice to see you. I thought you'd deserted me for ever, like that *dreadful* Mr Purvis.'

She led Gwen along the hall, tottering on her heels, as ever. She was wearing a deep purple frock, with fussy frills round the neck. The house felt chilly after the warm afternoon outside and held its usual dubious cooking smells, but there was a new, sickly aroma mingled with them. Ariadne was clearly aware of it. She paused, holding up one ring-encrusted finger.

'*That,*' she said accusingly, 'is Miss Hines. Simply *douses* herself in it. I hope you're going to have a cup of tea with me? I can't begin to tell you how much you're missed in this house, Gwen dear.'

'That'd be nice,' Gwen said, remembering that tea was the one reasonably safe item in Ariadne's culinary repertoire.

Ariadne settled Gwen in the back room, where she had so often taken meals with Harold Purvis. As usual, there was a newspaper laid open on the table. Gwen eyed it while she waited. A photograph in the middle showed a truck with a tent-like contraption on the back. 'Travelling gas chambers,' the caption said. 'Training for gas attacks.' The report beside it said that the whole of Spain was cut off from telephonic communication, for what were believed to be 'serious political reasons'.

Ariadne carried in tea and arrowroot biscuits and one cream horn on a plate. 'I was going to treat myself, but you must share it with me.'

'Oh no, Ariadne, you have it. The biscuits will do me very well.'

Ariadne beamed at her. 'You always were such a polite girl. Not like *that* one.' She rolled her eyes ceilingwards. 'Proper little piece she is. Calls herself a secretary, but all she is really is a little typist from the pool. And the way she walks! You've never seen anything like it!'

'Does she have a lot of admirers?' Gwen asked, nibbling one of the musty biscuits.

Ariadne gave a fastidious shudder. 'I don't like to think about it. None that are allowed in here, I know that much.'

Gwen thought of herself and Daniel creeping up the stairs past Millie's landlady. She realized Ariadne was looking at her intently.

'Forgive me for saying so, dear, but you don't look quite as . . . well, *feminine* as you did.' She eyed Gwen's old navy skirt and unadorned hair. 'I don't like to pry, but is everything all right? Your fiancé? And your wedding plans?'

'Yes thanks, Ariadne.' Gwen smiled, but a blush seeped into her cheeks. She had been on the point of talking about Daniel. He was so much a part of her life now that it seemed normal to her. But of course she couldn't! Ariadne still thought she was engaged to Edwin. And, she remembered with another jolt, *Edwin* still thought of her as engaged to Edwin as well.

'I'm doing very well,' she said hurriedly. 'I'm enjoying my job, and I've grown ever so fond of some of the children. Coming here has really made me realize how much I like being a teacher. Anyway,' she added, 'what happened to Mr Purvis in the end? Do you hear from him?'

Ariadne's lips tightened into a hard line and she sat straighter in her chair, on her dignity.

'No, I do not hear from Mr Harold Purvis. And I'm not party to any information about his whereabouts. In fact, Mr Purvis is a subject I'd rather not talk about at all, if you don't mind.'

'Of course not,' Gwen said quickly. She wasn't exactly bursting to talk about him either.

Instead, Ariadne was far more interested in talking about June Hines, the 'little number' upstairs, towards whom she seemed to harbour almost unlimited resentment.

'If I could find someone else, she'd be out on her ear, I can tell you,' Ariadne declared, teasing a fluffy dot of cream from her upper lip. 'She stinks like a polecat! But I haven't even found anyone else to fill the *other* room since that fly-by-night Miss Polensky took off.' She sighed. 'George would be *mortified* if he knew how I was having to get by these days.'

Gwen never got to the bottom of what it was that irked Ariadne so much about Miss Hines, but she left to pleas that she come back and rent a room with her again.

'I'd welcome you with open arms, dear, if you'd consider it.'

'Well, that's very nice of you,' Gwen said as they parted. 'I'm all right where I am at the moment. I'll bear it in mind, though.'

Ariadne waved from the step and Gwen felt a little sad turning away from the house. Perhaps she should move back. Mr Purvis was gone, at least. But would her digestive system stand it? And, anyway, for the moment she was trying to be a good friend to Millie and not spend every single night at party meetings. But her heart sank at the thought of another evening in with Millie and Lance and the wireless.

Oh, Daniel, she thought crossly. *Why aren't you here?*

He was back the next day, full of fervour for the Welsh NUWM protests about the unemployment regulations.

Gwen caught up with him on Sunday afternoon. When she reached the Fernandez's house, everyone was at home, him included.

'Hello there!' Daniel didn't touch her, not in front of his mother and siblings, but his eyes glowed at the sight of her and Gwen felt her spirits rise and swoop with happiness. He had caught the sun and looked even darker and more handsome.

'Sit down and have a cup of tea, Miss Purdy,' Theresa said comfortably. 'We've not seen you in a while. Oh, by the way, I called on Alice's mother, Mrs Wilson. A couple of times I went. I can't say I felt welcome. She's very closed in on herself, isn't she? Very miserable.'

'Thank you ever so much,' Gwen said. 'I'm sure she appreciates it really.'

'Poor soul.' Theresa carried the big teapot to the table. 'Daniel – sit, for the love of God. You're like a dog with fleas today.'

'I can't sit, Mam!' Daniel laughed. 'I'm too worked

331

up!' Gwen could feel the fire coming from him. His whole body was electric with energy.

Lucy sat by the table smiling, overjoyed to have her brother back and her beloved teacher there too.

'Have you been back home?' Gwen smiled, already infected by his huge enthusiasm.

Daniel nodded. 'Came back last night. I managed to hitch a lift on a truck full of sheep. Bound for slaughter all of them, and I'm sure they knew it – they didn't half make a racket all the way, I can tell you!' He compromised on his mother's request by turning a chair round and straddling it, back to front, arms resting on the rail and rocking it to and fro.

'Daniel, stop that – you'll break it! You're like a great big baby!'

'So, what's the news?' Gwen said.

'Unity's coming.' Daniel spoke urgently. 'You can almost smell it in the valleys. Down there they've got leadership – and real comradeship. You can feel people rising to it as every week goes by. My God, the state of things there!' His voice rose. 'Auntie Shân said they've knocked eight shillings off Billy's disability payment now, what with Uncle Anthony on the dole. They've hardly a farthing between them for food.' He sucked his breath in, hand clenched. 'If it wasn't for us being able to help them ... Jesus, it makes you want to ...' The fist hovered over the back of the chair.

'It's a wicked, cruel system,' Theresa agreed quietly. 'But blaspheming won't bring it to an end – nor you getting arrested.' She sipped her tea. 'Nor you breaking up our chairs, Daniel *bach*.'

Daniel unclenched his fist and his gaze burned into Gwen.

'Next weekend's the big demonstration – at Tony-

332

pandy. The party is calling on workers from all over the valleys to come together in full strength, show them what we think of the means test! Come with me? Come and see it happen?'

His excitement poured into her. She could feel herself glowing, and beamed back at him. 'In a sheep wagon?'

Daniel's slow grin met hers. 'I was thinking more of a train.'

Throughout that week news gradually trickled out from Spain. There had been coordinated uprisings by the right and the landowning classes against the recently elected left-wing Popular Front government. Franco's garrisons in Morocco joined in the insurrection and Franco himself led the troops who took over Las Palmas.

The party meetings that week were in a ferment with the news. Spain was under threat of fascists overthrowing the government! The republican groupings were struggling to defend a people's government of justice and democracy against the tyranny of military force and capitalist aggression! The party had to respond! What instructions would come from the headquarters in King Street, in London? They must act immediately, get on to the streets and outside factory gates, to raise support and funds for the republican fighters.

Gwen went with Daniel to every meeting that week. The news, as it came in, was at once exhilarating and terrible. Germany, Italy, the Blackshirts at home and now Spain: the urgency to act in the face of fascism was infectious, heady, but at the same time the threat of it seemed to move closer, like an evil cloud.

333

Another cloud was Esther Lane. The party was working ever closer now with the Birmingham Council for Peace and Liberty. Esther was involved in the council as well, and there she was at every meeting, her face set tightly in concentration as she listened to speakers in halls all round the city as they tried to rally support. And she was close to Daniel at every opportunity, and always, Gwen felt, ready to belittle her. Daniel laughed when she complained, said she was imagining it. He always talked about 'old Esther' as if she was somehow amusing and not to be taken seriously, in her outlandish clothing and with her posh, hooting voice. She wasn't Daniel's type – even Gwen could see that – but she could see what was in Esther's eyes when Esther looked at Daniel and it frightened her.

On Wednesday night Daniel came back to the house with her after the evening's meeting, both of them sneaking in again like thieves, both full of a taut, frantic energy. The second they were inside the room, their hands were under each other's clothing, Daniel pushing the door shut with his foot.

'God, girl.' Daniel pulled his shirt off, then hers, in a fever of impatience.

They made love fast, hungrily, fighting the temptation to forget any worries about babies, longing just to surrender to it, naked and complete. The rubbery smell of the French letter was so horrible, the delay such an intrusion, but Daniel insisted, hurrying to put it on.

'We've got to – don't need any complications, now, do we?' His eyes narrowed with desire and he lay back. 'Come down on me. I want to feel you over me.'

She lay crouched, cuddled close round him, for a

long time after, with him still inside her, their skin slicked together in the muggy night. Gwen nuzzled her nose into his neck, felt his hands hot on her back.

'I don't ever want to be anywhere except with you,' she whispered.

She felt him give a low laugh of pleasure and the pressure of his lips on her cheek.

'That's my girl, my beauty.'

A moment later, he said, 'It's going to happen this weekend. They won't let us down. I can feel it.'

She looked into his dark eyes, stroked his cheek. 'Never off duty you, are you?'

And he laughed again, eyes crinkling at the corners.

Letting him go, to creep out into the night, she felt as though they were being torn apart.

Thirty-One

They didn't go to Wales by train after all. Gwen had
been looking forward to a long ride in a secluded
railway carriage alone with Daniel, but Esther Lane
and two other party workers were to come as well, and
Esther announced that they would motor down in her
father's Daimler. Dr Lane, it appeared, was also a
member of the BCPL.

They gathered outside the party offices at five thirty.
Five of them were going: Gwen, Daniel, Esther, Herbert – the thin, red-headed man – and a young, softly
spoken social worker with a neat little moustache,
called Ernest, whom Gwen recognized from some of
the meetings. He wore grey flannel trousers and a red
kerchief tucked into the neck of his shirt.

'Good, I'm glad you haven't overdone the luggage,'
Esther remarked, eyeing the small holdall Gwen had
brought with her. 'It's going to be close quarters as it
is.'

Gwen felt immediately patronized and as if she
didn't in some way measure up, as she always did in
Esther's presence.

Well, at least I'm not colour-blind, she thought
pettishly. Esther was wearing her baggy black slacks
and an equally voluminous short-sleeved blouse in a
sickly shade of turquoise. Her hair was taken up in a
bandanna of glaring pea green covered in yellow polka

dots. Gwen had also dressed casually, in navy cotton slacks and a blue and white striped shirt. She had a sweater flung over one shoulder for when the evening cooled.

'Get in – do!' Esther stood by the open door beside the driver's seat. 'Daniel, why don't you join me in the front so we can talk tactics?'

It was almost a command. Gwen felt herself stiffen with resentment at Esther's proprietory manner towards Daniel. Who did she think she was?

'No, let Ernest sit up front,' Daniel said easily. 'Gwen and I'll squeeze up with Herbert.'

Esther, having taken it for granted that Daniel would do as she asked, had been about to climb into her seat. She stopped, and frowned across the roof of the car. 'I really do think it would be better if Ernest sat behind. I need you here with me.'

But Daniel was already in the car, seating himself in the middle, Herbert to his right. Gwen got in after him.

Daniel gave Gwen a wink. She grinned back at him and under her navy sweater, which she laid on her lap, they linked hands. They began the journey with a great shuddering lurch, which made them grin all the more. Gwen could just see the side view of Esther's face, scowling with concentration under the green and yellow bandanna and a lock of escaped black hair.

'Sorry – don't drive her very often!' she called.

They left Birmingham as the sun sank low in the sky, passed through Kidderminster and turned towards Hereford. The fields were bright with corn and warm air blew in through the windows. In the bronze light and the warm, muggy air Gwen began to feel drowsy and leaned her head on Daniel's shoulder.

At dusk they stopped south of Hereford and shared

337

the food they'd brought. Esther handed round potted-meat sandwiches, and they went to a pub and had a half of warm ale before pressing on. Revived by the food and the cool of the evening, Esther led them in singing the 'Internationale', the 'Red Flag' and 'England Arise' several times through. She had a strident, though tuneful voice. Ernest had a reedy tenor, though Herbert came out with a surprisingly strong baritone. Gwen enjoyed singing with Daniel, hearing their voices mingle.

'This was written during the uprising – the Paris Commune,' Daniel told her, between verses of the 'Internationale'. 'In 1871.'

Pale moths batted into the windscreen and the only light came from the beams of the headlamps. Later the road became more twisty and they were going up and down. Daniel leaned forwards to give Esther directions.

'Just a mile or two and we've reached Aberglyn. It's in the next valley.'

He directed her to a narrow side street. All they could see were little windows, some with lights behind them, in a row of tiny cottages.

'I say.' For once, Esther sounded unsure of herself. 'Are you sure this is going to be all right, Daniel? I mean there is rather a gang of us.'

'They're expecting us. We'll manage – just for a night.'

As they climbed out of the car, a dog barked shrilly at the front of a neighbouring house. The cottage door opened, and framed in the soft light Gwen saw a stocky man. In a deep, melodious voice, he called, 'That you, Daniel *bach*?'

'Hello, Uncle! Hope we're not too late for you?'

'You've come a long way, boy.' Gwen saw his eyes linger on the elegant lines of the Daimler.

'This is my uncle, Anthony Sullivan.' Gwen knew that he was Theresa Fernandez's elder brother.

Esther stepped forward, hand outstretched. 'Esther Lane. So pleased to meet you. This is *awfully* good of you.'

The man took her hand and nodded. 'You a party worker?'

'Oh yes!' Esther said. 'Very much so. And Daniel's such an inspiration to us all!' She introduced Ernest and Herbert, who both shook his hand.

'Uncle Anthony, this is Gwen,' Daniel said, ushering her forward.

Again, the man gave a nod, and Gwen thought he smiled faintly at her.

'Anthony? Are they here then? Bring them in!' Daniel's Auntie Shân appeared in the doorway, a shawl round her shoulders.

'I don't know why he's keeping you out on the step. Come in, come in!' Her speech ended in coughing and she was doubled up by it for a moment.

'You still not well, Auntie?'

'Can't shake it off. Been like it since the end of the winter.' Gwen saw that the woman's face was worn by worry and sickness. She couldn't have been more than fifty, but she was gaunt and stooped as if older than her years. 'How's your mother, Daniel?'

'She's well. Sent you over a few things.' He had brought a bundle from the car. Gwen saw his aunt's eyes fix on it for a moment, lighting up hopefully.

Gwen heard Daniel lower his voice and ask, 'How's Billy?'

'Oh, you know.' His aunt's tone was flat. 'Going along. Come and see him. He's been in a lather waiting for you.'

They all piled in, seeming to fill the place right up. In one of the two threadbare old chairs facing the empty grate, Gwen saw a young man with brown hair and a thin, shadowy face. At the sight of Daniel, a grin broke across it. 'Danny boy!'

'Billy!' Daniel rumpled the young man's hair playfully. 'You're a sight for sore eyes.' He looked round. 'Brought some of my comrades to visit. This is Gwen . . .'

Gwen said hello and shook Billy's clammy hand.

'Nice to meet you,' he said shyly. She felt desperate for him. He was her age, Daniel had told her, and had been felled by an accident down the pit when he was fifteen. He'd got in the way of a loaded dram, the trucks pulling coal through the pits, and was paralysed from the waist down. His two brothers and sister had left home for London to find work, but Billy had no choice but to stay at home. He was a Communist, but he couldn't even move out of his chair without assistance, let alone get to meetings.

'Nice to meet you, comrade,' Herbert was saying. Gwen heard Esther and Ernest greet him as well. She looked around her.

The small front room bore all the signs of poverty. The floorboards were bare and scrubbed, there was a wooden chair as well two old armchairs and a china jug and a candlestick set on the mantelpiece, along with a few other knick-knacks. On such a balmy night there was no call for a fire in the grate, but it would have cheered the room. She caught sight of a china po

340

pushed under Billy's seat – somehow that was the saddest sight of all.

'Anthony, go and get that stool from out back!' Shân said. 'Now, you ladies come and sit down.'

Gwen and Esther were united, for once, in protesting that they couldn't possibly sit and deprive the woman of the house of a chair. Gwen was allotted a stool to sit on, and Esther the wooden chair. Herbert and Ernest settled on the floor on each side of the hearth.

Shân reluctantly took the softer chair, pulling her shawl round her thin shoulders. She managed a rueful smile, and Gwen saw that beneath the veil of tiredness and care her heart-shaped face was rather pretty.

'There's hardly a crumb I've in the house to feed you on,' she said ashamedly. 'We've put the kettle on, that's all.'

'Here, Auntie.' Daniel presented her with the bundle. 'Ma put this together for you.'

'*Duw!* Oh, my, what a lot! My lap can't hold it all!' She was so eager, almost like a child, and laid the bundle, tied in part of an old sheet, on the floor and unknotted the ends. 'Oh, God bless Theresa – she always did have a heart of gold. What'd we do without her? Oh, Billy, look at this now!'

Gwen felt a lump come into her throat at the woman's excitement in the face of the simple things in the bundle. Theresa had included a loaf of bread, a few ounces of butter, some tea, a jar of jam, a large knuckle of ham, some soft buns she'd baked, a cake and a bag of carrots. There were also oddments like a bar of washing soap and a little bundle of candles held together with a rubber band.

341

'Well, we've buns to have with our tea now!' she cried, delighted.

They all tried to protest that the buns were meant for the family, but Shân wouldn't hear of it.

'I haven't even got enough cups to go round!' she laughed, getting up to make the tea. 'Mrs Evans next door has lent us a couple!'

Daniel's Uncle Anthony perched on the arm of Billy's chair and immediately the talk turned to politics. At first the Birmingham group sat listening, riveted. Here they were in South Wales, in the heartland of the party – the place Daniel described to them as the beacon of hope, where there was strong leadership and growing unity! They wanted to hear all about it, to drink it in. Gwen was filled with pride and excitement.

The talk turned first to the latest unemployment regulations, in force for eighteen months now, which were the focus of the next day's protest in Tonypandy. The government's Unemployment Assistance Board had introduced national rates of benefit which in many cases were lower than the previous ones. They heard stories of distress from all over the valleys.

Billy's face lit up with passion. 'I've lost my legs, my livelihood and now I'm sat rotting here, and there's no use I am except to cause my family hunger and worry. It's all wrong. No, Mam –' he flung her arm off as she tried to protest at his harshness – 'that's the truth and you know it. It isn't your fault or mine – it's capitalism does it. Capitalist oppression!'

Gwen realized that Billy did not often allow himself to voice these thoughts. He looked heated, overexcited by all the company and she felt deep sorrow for him. She saw the impact of his words on his mother as well, in the way she clenched her jaw, tightening her lips.

'We need another march like in '34,' Anthony said. He was a dignified man, whose deep, powerful voice held a quiet authority. 'Action – that's the thing. Unified action. We can't sit back and let them starve our people into submission like trapped animals.'

Like Daniel's father, Arturo, Anthony had first been employed at the steel works at Dowlais. The two of them had met there and later moved to work down the pit at Aberglyn. Anthony had been out of work now for over a year and had become a member both of the NUWM and the party.

'Our poverty is what brings us together.' Gwen heard Billy's passionate voice across the room. 'God, I wish I could come to Tonypandy with you tomorrow, Daniel, and hear Lewis Jones. Be there with everyone!'

'I wish we could get you there too, Billy boy.' Daniel frowned, as if he was thinking of a way in which it could be managed. 'Are you coming, Uncle Anthony?'

'We could certainly fit another one in the car, couldn't we?' Esther spoke up.

Anthony Sullivan nodded in a dignified way, as if to say, car or no car he'd get there somehow.

It grew later and later as they moved on to talk about the uprising in Spain, and the limited news reaching them from there, for the need for the party to mobilize in favour of the government, and Gwen, who had heard a lot of this before, found her eyelids beginning to droop. After a time, Shân noticed.

'It's exhausted your pretty friend here is, Daniel!' she reproached him. 'You all talking her to pieces. Let's be getting some sleep now. Boys, you can sleep down with Billy. There's a bed up at the back, if you girls don't mind sharing.'

343

Gwen's eyes met Esther's. She knew they were both thinking the same thing: *I don't want to share with you!* But neither of them would have dreamt of protesting.

'That would be perfectly all right,' Gwen said, getting to her feet. Esther did the same. She seemed humbled by Shân Sullivan and was quieter than usual. Daniel was sitting beside Billy, catching up on news of old pals. Gwen went to him and gave him a peck on the cheek.

'Night then. Goodnight, Billy.'

'Sleep tight.' Daniel smiled up at her.

'Night!' Billy said. As she went to the door, Gwen heard him say to Daniel, 'She's lovely, isn't she?'

'Watch the third step.' Shân turned, holding a candlestick, to warn Gwen and Esther, as they followed carrying the few things they'd brought for the night. The third tread of the bare staircase creaked ominously.

'It's not much, I'm afraid,' Shân said, showing them the tiny back room. Between its whitewashed walls was a three-quarter sized bed, a small chest of drawers and a chair. There wasn't room for anything else.

'It's *perfect*,' Esther said, just a little too enthusiastically.

'Thank you for putting us all up,' Gwen said quietly. She felt a kinship with Shân, could sense all the burden of her life. 'We're an invasion.'

'Oh no – it's nice to have some life about the place. Our young ones slept in here once – all in a row.' Her wan expression lit with a smile for a moment. 'But it's grown up and gone they are now. Except Billy, of course.'

'God, it's so *tragic*,' Esther said once Shân had gone,

wishing them goodnight. 'What life will he ever have now?'

'Umm, I know.' Gwen pulled her nightdress out of her bag. Esther grated on her so much that she felt her usual urge to disagree with her on principle, but there was nothing she could say to contradict her. Billy's situation *was* tragic.

Gwen felt deeply uncomfortable at such close quarters with Esther, whose personality seemed to take up the whole room. Added to that, she gave off a ripe, musky smell. She stripped off with no sign of inhibition, pulling her blouse over her head to reveal dark tufts of hair under her arms and heavy breasts encased in a stout bra, which she then proceeded to unfasten as well. Gwen turned away, though not without wondering, in spite of herself, whether Daniel would find the sight of Esther attractive. She slipped her own pale blue nightdress on and went to get into bed, seeing Esther in a voluminous white garment. Esther unwrapped her hair from the bandanna and brushed it out. It hung on her shoulders, thick and slightly frizzy. Gwen hadn't thought to brush her hair. She was too anxious to lie down and sleep. Neither of them spoke.

At last, Esther climbed in beside her and lumped about, getting comfortable.

'Blow the candle out, do,' she said, as the chest of drawers was on Gwen's side of the bed.

Gwen closed her eyes in the darkness. After a moment she heard Esther's deep voice.

'You're really in love with our Daniel, aren't you?'

Gwen hesitated, wondering whether to pretend to be asleep. What was Esther's tone? Curious? Mocking?

Our Daniel. After a few seconds, she said matter of factly, 'Yes, I am.'

'Ah. Well, you wouldn't be the first.' This time the voice held a knowing sense of regret. 'Poor old you, darling.'

Thirty-Two

Gwen woke to the sound of a train chugging slowly in the distance. There was a high squeal from the engine, releasing steam. The pit train, she thought. Otherwise the house was quiet.

Opening her eyes, she saw daylight on either side of the thin curtain. Beside her, Esther's curvaceous shape lay turned away, and she could hear her breathing heavily. She didn't like lying so close to Esther. That comment she had made last night came stinging back. Gwen had lain awake, furious. The cheek of the woman! What the hell did Esther think she knew about Daniel?

Pleased to be awake before Esther, to get away from her, she slipped off the lumpy mattress, dressed quietly in the gloom and crept down the stairs, wincing as they creaked. But she was not the first up. Shân was already moving about in the kitchen at the back, and Daniel was just rousing himself. Round him the others slept, Billy on his mattress, the others on blankets on the floor beside him. Daniel sat up and waved in greeting.

'Did you sleep?'

'Yes thanks,' she whispered.

He got up and came to her, taking her in his arms. His cheek felt rough against hers and he was warm and soft, somehow, from sleep.

'Big day today.'

'Yes.' She smiled.

They greeted Shân, who was once again wrapped in her shawl though the morning was mild.

'I'll brew us a cup of tea,' she said.

'Just thought I'd take Gwen out for a minute, along the road,' Daniel said. 'Show her the valley.'

'Oh you must show her, Daniel *bach*.' Gwen saw Daniel's aunt looking at her with a new curiosity. 'There's beautiful it is up there for those with the strength to walk. The tea'll still be here when you get back.'

'Here – come and see.' Daniel took her arm and they went out into the sunny morning.

There was no view at first, except for the worn, grey cottages opposite. They were in a little sloping street, and Dr Lane's Daimler looked absurdly large and out of place parked at the kerb.

'Come and have a look this way,' Daniel said, following the upward slope of the road.

The cottages clung along the contour of the incline. They were a poor, unkempt line of dwellings and the sufferings of their occupants seemed to be etched into their facades. The street was quiet except for a woman scrubbing at her step and a man with a stooped, wiry body, walking with a stick, who peered up from under his cap at them.

'Daniel Fernandez? Is that you?' His tone was commanding, and, Gwen thought, not especially friendly.

'Yes, it's me, Hywel.' Daniel sounded tense.

The man squinted at him. 'What're you back here for, mun? Making trouble again, is it?' He shook the stick. 'They ought to round up the whole bloody lot of you and send you to Russia!' He started off up the road again with renewed energy, but Daniel swivelled

348

on one foot and called after him, 'The Labour Movement's dead, Hywel – all over the world. They've given
in to capitalism and fascism! When're you going to face
reality?'

The man turned, banging his stick on the ground.
'We could have kept our men working! Now there's
nothing in the valleys but empty bellies and empty
Bolshevik principles to go with them. No one gains
any fat from principles!'

'What – keep them working by joining the bosses'
Federation, and the blacklegs? That's slavery, Hywel,
and you know it. The slavery of ownership and capital.
The workers are making the revolution – here today,
whether they're in work or not. They'll show their
strength in Tonypandy . . .' Gwen could hear a particular desperation in Daniel's voice as he tried to impress
his views on the old man. His fists were clenched, body
tensed with emotion. She could see that this was a
division which went back a long way and went deep.
'There *will* be a new dawn, Hywel, if you'd only put
your faith in it.'

'The only place I put my faith is in almighty God,
Daniel, and there was a time when you did the same.
You've betrayed yourself by putting it anywhere else.
Now don't speak to me any more . . .' He waved Daniel
away with violent exasperation and continued on down
the road.

'God didn't stop them throwing my ma into gaol,
did he?'

Gwen was shocked to the core. *Theresa* in gaol?
Whatever was Daniel talking about?

The old man strode furiously along the road. Gwen
waited behind Daniel and saw he was quivering with
emotion. After a moment, he shook his head and let

out a sharp sigh, turning to her. 'Hywel Jones and my da were in the Labour Party together. He never forgave Da for becoming a Communist.' He gave Gwen a look, revealing a vulnerability which touched her. 'Why can't he see? Why can't they all see?'

She had no answer for him. She wanted to ask about Theresa, what had happened. Why had he never said anything before?

'Daniel?' But he shook his head and turned away. This was not the right moment. Silently she reached for his hand and they walked on.

They were evidently near the edge of the little town, soon the houses ended and from the road they could see right across the valley. They stopped for a moment and Gwen became aware of the wind in the grass.

'It's lovely, Daniel.' She was slightly breathless from the walk.

'It is.' He nodded, smiling. He seemed to be calmer again. 'Your cheeks have gone pink!'

The valley lay spread out in front of them, a deep summer green dotted with little cottages. Further away, far down to their left, she saw the dark, protruding shapes of the pit, and heaped beyond, black, ugly mounds of slag. In front of them, where they stood, beyond the green swathe of the valley, rose the flank of the mountain on the other side. The breeze blew across, strong and fresh, and there were flowers in the grass at her feet. Further down the bank she saw a shining thread of water and realized there must be a spring running down to the valley.

Daniel went to put his arms round her from behind, but instantly the stance reminded her of Edwin.

'Don't.' She spoke abruptly and to soften it turned round to him. 'I can't see you if you stand behind me.'

They stood side by side and put their arms round one another, breathing in the fresh, clear air.

'Was that the pit you worked in?'

Daniel nodded. 'And my da. And Uncle Anthony and Billy.' He gave a deep sigh. 'Not many of the old butties left working it now, what with them splitting them all up and scab labour, and foreigners being brought in.'

He pointed out things to her, the railway threading along and the stream in the valley.

'Over the mountain there, there's one of the steel works – all deserted. At night-time it used to send up a great glow. It's just a heap of rust now, poking up into the sky.'

They stood in silence for a moment, and then she said, 'Love, why did your mother go to prison?' The emotion behind his outburst had affected her strongly. 'You never said before.'

'No.' Daniel evidently didn't want to expand on it. 'I know.' After more silence, in the sound of the wind, he turned to her.

'We're going to do it today.' There was a catch in his voice. 'Another step towards the revolution for our people. Aren't we?'

He looked searchingly at her, an appeal in his eyes, and she saw that he was still feeling the old man's anger. She looked back and squeezed his waist, wanting to believe that it was true. Russia, the Bolsheviks and collectivization, the idea that things could change so radically still felt distant and unreal. She wondered if he realized how faint her belief was. She wanted to believe it for him because it moved him so much. Because of Auntie Shân, and because it was his life, and now hers too.

351

'It will be a great day.' She took his hand. 'Come down here.'

She made him follow her down the bank to the trickle of spring water, bubbling out from under a thatch of grass, and she lifted handfuls and washed her face.

'Oh, it's cold! It's lovely!' she laughed, and Daniel doused his face too. He took her in his arms then, and they kissed, hungrily, faces still wet.

'I wish we could stay up here,' she said longingly.

'We'll come back here again,' Daniel said. 'Just you and me.' They walked back to the house, the wind blowing the water dry on their cheeks.

'Auntie, we'll be bringing Uncle Anthony back later!' Daniel told Shân fondly as she fussed about what they were going to eat. 'It's not a week we're going for. We've got to go back tonight.'

'Are you not staying a while with us, Daniel?' Gwen saw Billy looking disappointed too.

'No, Auntie. But we'll come back soon, really we will.'

Billy sat drinking in every word excitedly as they breakfasted on bread and tea. Gwen could see how hard he was trying not to show the bitterness he felt at having to be left behind. In a quiet moment she went to Shân in the tiny kitchen. She found her standing pensively by the stove as the kettle reboiled, her shawl pulled close round her shoulders.

'Mrs Sullivan?' The woman turned, smiling, her grey eyes full of kindness.

Speaking softly, Gwen said, 'I was wondering about Billy. I know how much he'd like to be going with us today. If I was to stay behind, he could have my place in the motorcar. I just don't know if there's a way he could manage at the other end. If they could carry him or something?'

Shân Sullivan's face softened, then shaded with further sadness. Slowly she shook her head.

'It's a kind heart you have, Gwen *fach*. But our Billy can't go anywhere for very long. We've the wheelchair out the back, but you couldn't be taking that. And Billy can't even do his business without a helping hand, see. He'd soil himself and he'd hate that more than anything.'

Gwen blushed, feeling stupid. 'Sorry. Only I thought I'd ask. I would have stayed, if . . .'

Shân touched her hand. 'There's the way it is. There are things that even God can't do anything about.'

Gwen sat on Daniel's lap for the journey, the two of them squeezed in beside Ernest and Herbert, while Uncle Anthony sat in the front with Esther, who had replaced yesterday's green and yellow bandanna with a bright scarlet one. He sat very upright, obviously ill at ease in this unaccustomed luxury. They set off towards Tonypandy, and decided to leave the car outside the town so they could join the others walking in for the demonstration.

As they drew near, they started to see people moving along from quite some distance away along the mountain roads.

'Let's stop here!' Daniel cried as they passed a group of people carrying a red banner between them, struggling with it as it bellied out in front in the wind. 'It's all wrong driving when other comrades are on foot!'

'Quite right.' Uncle Anthony sounded relieved at the suggestion.

They were on a hill, looking over the town with its closely packed, slanting rows of houses. As they got out to join the general camaraderie of the walk into Tony-pandy, Gwen began to realize the scale of what was happening. More and more people appeared, from cottages and villages over the mountains, increasing the thick column of people and banners. Herbert and Daniel struck up a conversation on the way with a group of men from the next town carrying an NUWM banner, which read, 'STOP STARVATION IN BRITAIN'. Gwen saw the poor state they were in, their clothes limp with wear and faces gaunt with malnourishment.

One told them about his wife's death. 'They said it was the tuberculosis,' he said, his eyes filling, 'but it all just wore her down. She half-starved herself for the rest of us. Wore herself into her grave, my Myfanwy did, and the little one followed soon after.'

They were all convinced there would be thousands at the demonstration. The only sour note was a woman on the edge of the town, on her step in her bonnet.

'You should all be kneeling before God on this Sabbath day,' she called shrilly. 'Not bowing to the idols of Bolshevism!'

Infuriated, Daniel shouted back at her, 'Does your God want children to starve then?' Scowling, he faced the front again. 'This is politics, not religion. Why can't they see that?'

Light clouds moved across the sun so that every few minutes they were bathed in its warmth. The mountains around them were so close that Gwen almost felt she could touch them. As they moved into Tonypandy, the streets were packed with people, flags and banners rippling around them in the breeze, and there were ragged outbreaks of singing among the crowd. Gwen felt her spirits rise and bubble into euphoria as they turned into De Winton Fields, the site of the demonstration, to the strains of

Then raise the scarlet standard high,
Within its shade we'll live and die . . .

She saw Daniel looking round at the hordes of people and red banners coming from all directions, his face breaking into a wondering smile.

Though cowards flinch and traitors sneer,
We'll keep the red flag flying here!

'Look at them all! That's unity for you, Gwen *fach*! At last the message is getting through. Look at us – there's thousand upon thousand here. We're far stronger than they could ever know!'

'I say.' Esther moved closer. She and Ernest were carrying a BCPL banner between them. Ernest looked quite radiant. Esther took hold of Daniel's arm. 'Let's see if we can get close to where the speakers are going to be.'

Gwen felt herself tense up angrily. Why was Esther grabbing Daniel like that, as if she owned him? Her odd remark from last night about Daniel came back to her. *Poor you!* Gwen seethed. Had Esther been warning her off?

Herbert, his thin, foxy face the most animated Gwen had ever seen it, was nodding enthusiastically. 'We want to make sure we hear Lewis Jones,' he said. His real hero was the NUWM leader Wally Hannington, but he was addressing the big demonstration in London that day. But Lewis Jones, a miner, had been elected as a county councillor in Glamorgan for the Communist Party – one of the only two Communist councillors.

They inched their way through the growing throng of people towards the speakers' platform. The morning seemed to pass quickly as De Winton Fields filled with more people than Gwen had ever seen together on one place before. Round them, people were singing and cheering. In front of her a banner read, 'BREAD NOT BATONS'.

At last, when the space was filled with demonstrators and police patrolling at the edges of the crowd, figures began to appear on the platform and a great cheer went up. A man came to the edge of the platform.

'Comrades!' he shouted. 'Why are we here? We are here to defeat the means test! The iniquitous regulations of the UAB!' Great rippling cheers and clapping followed each phrase, and it was some time before he could move on to the next. 'As we gather here, our comrades in London are marching on Trafalgar Square with the same demands . . .'

The first speaker was a local MP, then, after he'd finished, the strong, distinctive figure of Lewis Jones appeared on the platform. Gwen strained her ears trying to catch every word.

'Comrades!' he roared across the crowd, and they roared back in response. 'Can we, from this vast demonstration, call for five hundred men and women who will march on London and take the fight to the Labour Members of Parliament, both inside and outside the House, against these cuts?'

Lewis Jones was met by a vast swell of sound. He held up his hand until at last the shouting died down around the park.

'We can light the flame,' he cried, 'that will consume these iniquitous regulations, and with them the National Government which gave them birth!'

He was met by a huge, full-throated cry of enthusiasm which went on and on. Daniel was yelling and Esther and the others and Gwen heard herself shouting as she'd never shouted before from somewhere deep inside her, and she felt a power rise in her, as if something was unlocking, being untethered and she might lift off and fly free over all the heads in the park.

They were all exhausted during the long drive back to Birmingham, and Gwen had to give Esther credit for her stamina in keeping going. Ernest offered to take over more than once, but she replied breezily, 'I'm really quite all right, thank you. I'll let you know if I need you.'

Gwen slept for almost the entire journey, leaning alternately against the window and Daniel's shoulder, exhausted by all the newness and excitement and fresh valley air. She woke when Daniel gently shook her arm.

'Esther's going to drop us off,' he said. 'We're nearly there.'

It was dark outside. Daniel gave directions to Millie and Lance's place and soon Gwen was kissing Daniel goodbye and slipping into the dark hall. She switched on the light and looked at the clock. Nearly eleven o'clock. No doubt Millie and Lance would already have turned in. Could she make a cup of tea without disturbing them, she wondered?

The upstairs landing light was on, and when she crept upstairs, she saw that the light was also on in the little sitting room. Bother, she thought. Did that mean

Lance was still up, sitting reading the paper? She was so tired, and she'd hoped to be able just to go to bed without facing anyone else. If he was up, though, it would be better to go and speak to him and get it over with. She put her head round the door, ready to say something brief. Her heart hammered with shock. Sitting in the chair by the reading lamp was Edwin.

There was a silence as he sat looking up at her. At last he got to his feet.

'So – you've come back.'

Thirty-Three

Seconds passed. Edwin didn't move towards her.

Gwen looked at him, trying to adjust to the situation. She could still feel Daniel's goodnight kiss on her lips. Thank heavens he hadn't come up here with her tonight! Edwin's face was in shadow, but she could feel his gaze on her like a physical force.

'I suppose they know you're here?' She jerked her head towards Millie and Lance's room.

'Of course. I've been here half the day. They were charming to me. Even provided me with bedding, as you see.' He indicated the rolled-up eiderdown on a chair. 'Not that they seemed to know where you were either.'

His voice was clipped. She could feel the anger in him waiting to be released and she knew he was expecting her to tell him where she'd been.

'I'm sorry – if I'd known you were coming . . .' she said, taking a step back. 'Look – I'll put the water on. Would you like some tea?' She hurried out of the room, trying to gather her thoughts as she filled the kettle and put it to heat on the two-ring stove. She felt cruel and sinful, yet also certain somewhere inside herself. She pulled her shoulders back and went into the room, closed the door and leaned against it, feeling utterly weary at what was to come. But they had to pass through this, somehow.

359

'Gwen, for God's sake! How can you be like this? I don't recognize you!' Edwin moved closer. His pale hair was falling over his forehead and there was a terrible, strained expression on his face. To her horror she realized he was close to tears and that she had done this to him. He gave a shrug in which she could see great hurt.

'I've been patient, haven't I? But you never come home, you barely tell me anything of substance in your letters. My mother keeps asking for you, yours keeps making excuses for you! What the hell's going on? Don't you see that makes me feel a proper fool?' His anger subsided for a moment. 'Darling, we're getting married in a month's time and you're never there. I know you'd never be deliberately cruel, but you don't seem interested – in me or in our wedding. I feel as if you're . . . you're lost to me.' This last sentence was said with desperation.

Gwen found it impossible to speak. If she told him, she had to make it real: Daniel, all that had happened, how she couldn't possibly go back to her old life. Now she knew starkly, seeing poor Edwin, that she couldn't marry him. Everything had changed. Yet putting it into words would be momentous. She stared back at him, at the open collar of his shirt, his pink neck, unable to look him in the eye.

'Where have you been?' He spoke quietly, but she could hear the swell of emotion underlying the question.

'To Wales. With some friends.' She pushed herself away from the door, picking a white thread off her sleeve.

'So you can go to Wales for a day, but you can't

360

manage Worcester?' He was barely able to contain his hurt and anger now.

'We went for a special reason.'

'Well, *what* reason?'

'A demonstration – against the UAB and the means test.' She looked into his eyes for a moment. 'It's breaking people, Edwin – it's persecuting the poor, the people who are already barely able to live. It's bad enough here, but in the Welsh valleys . . .' Her voice rose with excitement for a moment before she remembered that they had to be quiet. 'You should have seen all the people there – thousands and thousands all together! There was another demonstration in London as well.'

Edwin took another step towards her. Every line of his body was tensed.

'What are you getting involved with, Gwen? You're keeping secrets from me: you're like someone else! For God's sake, tell me what's going on!' He looked as if he was going to lay his hands on her shoulders, but he held back, clenching them at his sides. At last he began to lose his hold on his emotions. 'Tell me, Gwen. You're miles away from me. I don't know you any more and I don't know what's happened.'

She opened her mouth, then closed it again. It felt impossible to make the stride, in words, across her changed feelings. She barely knew herself either, she felt as if she'd left herself behind.

'You're not . . . a Communist, are you?'

'I am, yes.' She had to seize the moment, to carry this through. Holding herself strong inside, she said, 'Edwin, I'm so very sorry. This is awful. You're a kind, good man and you don't deserve this. But I can't go on

361

pretending. I can't marry you next month. I should have told you before and I ... I couldn't.'

She saw him start to crumple, but then he held firm. He turned away from her and moved across the room until he could go no further. He stood with his knees pressed against the little coffee table.

'Truth at last, then. May I ask why?'

'I ... I love someone else. Edwin, I'm sorry.' She knew she was hurting someone who didn't deserve it. She wanted to go to him, to offer comfort, but how would that help?

There was a long silence.

'And when exactly did you think you might get round to telling me, had I not come here?'

'I don't know.' Her weeping, suddenly, took her by surprise. 'I kept putting it off ... It affects so many people. After term finishes on Tuesday, I was going to come home ...' She knew she would have had to, but she had not even faced that yet. 'I'll have to tell Mummy ...'

'And how long have you been *pretending*, as you put it?'

'Don't, Edwin—' She went closer to him, wiping her eyes.

'Don't what?' He turned to her, his face taut with hurt and anger. 'Don't ask for the truth? Don't expect to be treated with a bit of straightforward decency when my fiancée's run off with some blasted Communist agitator! D'you think I like being deceived and made a complete fool of?'

He picked up Lance's glass ashtray from the table and hurled it against the wall behind her. It smashed in halves on impact and clattered to the floorboards. There was nothing else on the table but the day's newspaper, so he threw that as well and it fluttered into a scattered mess. He stared round the room in contempt.

'Look at yourself! You don't belong here with these people. With all this political stuff. God, Gwen, that's what I loved about you when I saw you – when I walked into that schoolroom! You were so sweet and fresh, so unspoilt. I'd never seen anyone quite like you. You're so beautiful, and you belong there – with me – not here. Can't you see that? It's as if someone's put a spell on you!' He sank into a chair.

'I did belong there – but I don't any more.' She spoke gently. 'I feel terrible about this, Edwin. I haven't been able to face it because of how much it would hurt you ... But even when I was there, I felt...' She shrugged. Felt what? Stifled? Hemmed in? It was hardly fair to tell him that. 'I've changed. I needed to branch out. To grow into myself.'

Edwin looked up at her as she spoke. Seeing her determination, he put his head in his hands and let out a long groan.

'Was I holding you back? Can't you come home, grown and changed, and still let me love you?'

She had to hold herself very strongly against his expression as he looked up at her. His boyish face was full of hurt and longing.

'Oh, Edwin—' She knelt beside him. 'I can't. Because of Daniel.'

Steam was pouring out of the kettle. She made tea for them both, but found there was no milk. She could hear Edwin's defeated weeping in the other room. He was sitting back in the chair as she came in, and

363

took the black, sweet tea she handed him, wiping his face. Gwen moved the eiderdown and sat opposite him.

'Why are you here today? It's Sunday.'

'Bernard gave me the day off. Said he was fed up with me mooning about and I should go and get myself sorted out.'

Gwen tensed. The reality of what she was going to have to face at home, everyone knowing, was awful to think about.

'Did you tell him then?'

'Not exactly, though it was pretty obvious. You haven't been near the place for weeks, have you? He's no fool.'

Gwen looked down into her cup. She thought about telling her mother. After a long silence, in which Millie's clock ticked, Edwin said very sadly, 'Don't you think you could come home and, well, give it a try? I mean, if you got away from here. Couldn't we recapture something?'

'Oh, Edwin.' Her eyes filled with tears again. Why was Edwin so decent? It might have been easier if he'd stormed and raged more, made demands on her. 'No. I really don't think we can. Well, I can't, anyway.'

'Tell me something.' Edwin spoke in a hard, distant way, looking into the empty grate. 'When you told me you loved *me* – were you ... pretending? Lying?'

'*No*. Of course not. I just ... I mean I do love you, Edwin. And I care very much about what happens to you. I'm thoroughly ashamed of myself for causing you so much pain and trouble. But things change. *I've* changed. Because I've found that you can ...' She was groping for the words. 'You can expand and discover that you can love more deeply than you ever realized.'

Edwin nodded. 'I see,' he said bleakly.

He left early to catch a train the next morning. Lance was up getting ready for school as well, so they said their goodbyes down in the hall.

'You will have to come home and face up to it all.' Edwin was distant now and on his dignity, not allowing the sadness of the evening before.

'I know.' They stood just inside the front door. 'Edwin, I'm so sorry.'

'Yes,' he said bitterly. 'So am I. You really haven't behaved very well, Gwen.'

'No.' There was nothing else to say.

He leaned down and gave her a quick, impersonal peck on the cheek, and then he was gone. She stood on the step in the mild, wet morning, watching him walk away, his strong, steady walk, the light hair. Every line of him gave off reliability. She knew how good he was, yet even now in her guilt and sorrow for him there was something about the sight of him that made her feel earthbound and restricted. She couldn't go back.

'You be happy,' she whispered after him. Tears ran down her cheeks. 'Someone else'll make you happier than me.' A moment later he turned the corner and was out of sight.

'Settle down now for the afternoon register, please!'

Gwen watched fondly as Form Four settled, wriggling in their chairs, or turned from chattering to face the front. After the emotions of the night before she felt a sudden lightness, a relief that it was over at last. She had done wrong, she had hurt Edwin terribly, and she would have to face the wrath of her parents. But she was free! She didn't have to go home, she was earning her own living, and she could be with Daniel, her beautiful Daniel. Ron Parks's cheek was still bulging with something, even though the dinner hour was over. Gwen looked sternly at him.

'Ron? You're not eating sweets are you?'

'No, Miss Purdy.'

The boy hurriedly swallowed whatever was in his mouth. The whatever-it-was was rather large and Ron gulped. Gwen was reminded of a snake swallowing an egg. She tutted.

'Do you need a drink of water?'

'No, Miss Purdy,' Ron gasped, eyes goggling.

'All right. Well, don't come in here with your mouth full again. You'll choke.'

She opened the register.

'Donald Andrews?'

'Yes, Miss Purdy.'

'Joan Billings?'

'Yes, Miss – Purdy,' Joan said absentmindedly. The thought flashed through Gwen's mind that she would never, now, be Mrs Shackleton.

'Lucy Fernandez?' Mrs Fernandez? Would she be that instead?

'Yes, Miss Purdy.'

Tomorrow they'd be handing out a few prizes for achievement to some of the children. Lucy was outstandingly the top child in Form Four. No one took the rise out of her or called her 'cripple' any more. She could run rings round most of the others in class.

Gwen passed the place in the register where Joey Phillips's name was crossed out. She could still see his ghostly little face looking at her from the empty space where he used to sit. The memory came to her of the half-seen figure pressed against the railings of the playground that spring day. Had that been Joey? What on earth could have happened to him?

When she had reached the last name she put the register away.

'Now, all of you, I've got something to tell you.' Her heart beat faster. 'When I came to teach you this year, I thought it was only going to be for a little while. But things have changed. I went to see Mr Lowry this morning and it has been decided that next year, when you come back into Form Five, I shall be your form teacher again.'

She heard a little gasp from Lucy Fernandez and saw the child's face light up with delight.

Thirty-Four

'Joey – come on. Let's get back.'

John's high, wooden-sounding voice came to him over the barrows, all packing up for the night in the Bull Ring, which they were passing through on their way back. Joey dived under one of the stalls, seeing the murky orange of half a dropped carrot no one else had spotted and crunched into its earthy sweetness. There was still a long walk ahead and his belly was gurgling with hunger.

'You again!' the stall owner called after him with mock annoyance. 'You'll put me out of business you will, young nipper!' He watched Joey scurry after John. 'Poor little bleeder,' he remarked.

The Bull Ring was full of late-afternoon activity on this mild summer evening. There was a whiff of ale coming from the pubs in Digbeth, and the faint aroma of meat cooking on the breeze with the smells of rotting fruit and vegetables, cauliflower stalks and crushed apples trampled underfoot. Someone was singing loudly as he shut up shop for the night, shop awnings were being put away and someone was playing a slow, idle tune on the accordion by Nelson's statue. A newspaper seller was shouting about Spain. The working day was over and most of the men were heading off to the pub. They were passing one man when Joey saw a little head pop out of his breast pocket and tiny, bright eyes fixed on him. Joey jumped, startled.

John chuckled. 'That's old Ted with his ferret – he's the rat catcher at the station.'

Fascinated, Joey turned and watched the man go by, and almost collided with a market trader.

'Oi – watch where you're going, will yer!'

Ignoring him, Joey took another bite of the carrot, staring into its orange core.

'We've had a good day today,' John said. They'd spent the day filling boxes with metal brackets at the back of a warehouse. The gaffer had turned a blind eye and let Joey stay and work as well. Now they were well set up with a bag of taters, cabbage and scrag end. 'We'll stop for a drink.'

They went to a pub in Digbeth that Joey remembered going to once before, called the Royal George. John went in while Joey sat on the step outside with a glass of lemonade. It tasted delicious. He listened to the rumble of male conversation inside, amid the wafting smells of beer and cigarette smoke. He still had the little stalk of the carrot in his hand and he threw it under the wheels of a tram as it came up the sloping street. Now and then someone passed him, going in or out. One or two men spoke to him, but the rest ignored him. Sitting down now, he noticed the soreness of his feet. His socks were in tatters and what was left of them had almost grown to be part of his feet. The boots, which had been so big, now almost fitted. He looked down at his grimy legs, bare between his short trousers and the boots. It felt strange seeing them. His body was something he took no notice of normally. His hands came into focus, bony, gnarled, with long nails, dirt scraped under them, cupped round the glass, which although scratched and murky, felt like a jewel in his hands. He held it up to the light and saw blurry shapes through it. Slowly he sipped the lemonade, making it last.

The voices inside grew louder: men shouting, drunken and quarrelsome. At first he took no notice. In a few seconds something in the sound started to vibrate inside him. He began to shake. He didn't know what was happening. The voices came closer, two men brawling in the pub doorway. They were coming out and they passed him, dark trousers and boots. One of them shouted a final oath and stormed off along the road. The other stood swaying, calling after him, slurred and loud. The voice sank into Joey. He looked up at the beaten-looking man standing with his legs braced apart to steady himself, at his pale, pinched, familiar face.

Joey managed to get to his feet. His legs felt rubbery. He stood looking up at the man, whose cheeks were covered in stubble, his eyes glassy with drink.

'Dad?'

Joey didn't need to ask. He knew who it was, that hunched back which had moved away from them all along the entry that cold morning.

'Dad, it's me. Joseph.' He had to struggle almost to remember his name. It felt a long time since he had been Joseph Phillips. 'It's Joey.'

The man's gaze swivelled towards him. At the blankness in his father's eyes, Joey felt something give way inside him.

'Dad!' He grabbed the man's arm, pulling at it in a frenzy. 'Dad, it's Joey! You're my dad – and Lena and Kenny and Pol's! Dad – *Dad*!' Sobs choked out of him. 'There's no one else, Dad – I dunno where they've all gone!'

Wally Phillips jerked his arm violently, sending Joey tripping and stumbling backwards. He landed on the hard step and jarred his back.

'Get off of me, yer little bugger! What're you playing at? Go on – gerroff!'

And Wally staggered off up Digbeth, cursing and shouting.

Joey watched him go, his back disappearing again.

And then he couldn't see. Trying to look out through his tears was like looking through the blur of the murky pub glass.

Summer Holidays

Thirty-Five

Gwen didn't see the *Daily Worker* until Wednesday, the first day of the summer holidays. She read Monday's edition in the party offices, sitting near Daniel as he banged away on a typewriter, scowling with concentration. The room was abuzz with activity. The nationalist uprisings against the republican government in Spain had galvanized the party into action in a way none of them had seen before. New members were joining at an unprecedented rate.

'ANSWER TO THREAT ON SPAIN' read the banner headline. 'THOUSANDS CHEER POLLITT'S CALL TO ACTION.'

Most of the news was about the London demonstrations. Harry Pollitt, General Secretary of the Communist Party, had been speaking in Trafalgar Square.

'You not only have to reckon with the people of Spain,' he had told the huge crowd, thundering a challenge to the fascists and militarists. 'You have to reckon with the people of every land where democracy is in existence. Behind the Spanish people stand millions of men and women of all political parties who are not going to stand idly by, while your gang of parasites, moral perverts and murderers get away with it.'

Gwen read the report about the march on Tonypandy, swelling with pride. They had been part of this great movement, making things happen!

'Sixty thousand of us, it says here!' she exclaimed to Daniel.

He looked round at her, his face intense. 'That's just the beginning. Our time's come. We've got to carry it through now.'

She could never have foreseen how totally their lives were about to be taken over by the party. What had begun as a nationalist uprising in Spain quickly turned into a civil war, and the Communist Party seemed to be the movement responding most promptly and vocally for the republican cause.

Gwen spent almost all her time now with Daniel and the other party workers. Daniel was in constant demand as a speaker.

In the early days of the war in Spain, it looked as if cooperation between the Communist Party, the Labour Party and the Birmingham Council for Peace and Liberty would be possible. 'About time they saw sense,' Daniel said. 'We can't afford divisions now.'

Of course they all had to work together to fight the evil of fascism! There were to be joint meetings and rallies all round the city, public addresses in parks and halls and at factory gates in support of the workers' organizations in republican Spain.

The party offices were in a constant fever of activity: organizing meetings, printing leaflets, organizing speakers and 'chalkers' to announce them. Now the holidays were here, Gwen was free to throw herself into the work, caught up in the emotional intensity of it all. A national committee was formed, the Spanish Medical Aid Committee, especially to support the republic.

All of them were caught up in a cause bigger and more important than their own needs and lives. Gwen found herself feeling ashamed of her petty jealousies about Esther Lane. She didn't much like Esther whose bossy ways grated on her, but she could see her genuine commitment to the cause. And Daniel was far too busy to be paying Esther any attention. The truth was, he was almost too busy to pay any to Gwen either, but she swallowed down her periodic feelings of rejection and neglect. They were working for the party, for the revolution, compared with which individual feelings were as nothing.

One morning when Gwen arrived, the offices were already very busy. Esther was talking on the telephone in a loud voice to someone from a church group supporting Spanish aid, party workers were moving busily to and fro and a collection of cartons was piled just inside the door.

'What are these?' she asked Daniel, who was poring over a paper on a desk with Jim Crump, one of the main party officials.

'Pamphlets. From King Street,' Daniel said, without looking up. 'Can you get some of them out? We're going to the works along Bradford Street today – we'll start with them there. We've asked them to send more for the sixteenth.'

King Street was the party's national HQ. Gwen reached into the top box and pulled out a handful of red pamphlets. They were titled simply, *Spain*. The party was planning a special demonstration in the Bull Ring.

By the late afternoon that day she went out with Daniel and some of the others to Bradford Street in time for the end of the factories' afternoon's shifts, carrying bundles of the *Daily Worker* and the *Spain* pamphlet. Daniel had his big canvas bag slung over his shoulder. Gwen walked beside him, though he felt remote, caught up in his work. And Herbert began needling him again about the Catholic Church and its role in Spain. How could he be a Catholic when the Church was officially backing the nationalist cause?

'Don't start,' she heard Daniel say tersely. He was frowning and she could hear the tension in his voice.

The Fernandez household was full of anguish over this. Theresa read the Catholic paper, the *Universe*, which was full of reports about Catholic neighbours killing one another, churches being burnt, nuns and priests being dragged out and shot by republicans, the very people whom Daniel was ardently supporting and she frequently said so. Gwen knew that Daniel, like many Catholics on the left, was torn in two by the dilemma and she was tempted to tell Herbert to shut up and leave Daniel alone.

They reached Bradford Street just before the factory bulls began to go off at the end of a shift. When the men streamed out of the works they were waiting with their pamphlets and papers. Sometimes a sympathetic factory worker would take a copy of the *Daily Worker* and leave it in the factory toilet, so others could get a look at it. Gwen handed the *Spain* leaflet into dirty, workworn hands. Some men appeared interested, but others said, 'No, ta,' with tired indifference, while others called them 'bloody reds' or walked straight past, ignoring them.

'There's a meeting in the Bull Ring – every Sunday evening,' Daniel kept telling them. 'Come and join us, comrades. Unite the workers. Together we are strong!'

By the evening, Gwen was off with Daniel on the

speaking trail. Some evenings he did several, one after the other, and they had to have a car to get the speakers from one place to the next. Tonight there were only two meetings: Saltley followed by Alum Rock, and for once Esther needed to be elsewhere. Gwen sat in two drab halls, her stomach rumbling with hunger, while Daniel spelled out to his audience with apparently tireless passion the iniquities of the National Government and the means test, the betrayal of the working class by the Labour Movement, the plight of the Welsh mining towns and the Spanish republican causes of justice, collectivization and the power of workers' movements. In the car on the way back he was still full of life.

'I could see it in some of their faces tonight,' he said, on fire with his own oratory. 'They were hearing me. Really hearing. It's no good, see, thinking you can just go out and feed people propaganda. It's like Comrade Lenin said – the people have to have the political experience *for themselves*. They have to be *reborn* politically. They have to feel it in their *blood*.'

Gwen listened, leaning against his chest, tired and hungry. She could feel when he took a breath, the strong muscles of his chest. She leaned round and looked up at him.

'Do we have enough money for fish and chips? I'm ravenous.'

Daniel laughed, though she could sense his impatience with her. He wanted response, debate. 'You don't leave the ground for long, do you?'

'Well.' She was determined not to rise to this. 'An army marches on its stomach – that's what they say. Anyway, aren't you hungry too?'

'Come to think of it, yes.'

She looked solemnly up at him. She was longing to spend some time with him. Although they were so much in each other's company, they were seldom ever alone these days. She put her lips right up to his ear.

'Are you coming back to Millie's?'

Both of them knew what she meant. That they would sneak up the dark stairs, make love in the dip of the old bed. That she would hold him close, longing for a day when he would not have to get up and creep out again, to the dark streets, but that day had not come, nor could she see that it was going to. She would have to be content with being left to sleep alone.

'D'you want me to?'

'I wouldn't have asked otherwise, would I?' She kissed the tip of his nose.

'You're a very forward woman.'

They were both whispering, trying not to laugh and attract the attention of the party worker who was driving them. She *was* forward, she thought. Sometimes she felt like someone different altogether. Who was the person who had lived in Worcester and had been going to marry Edwin Shackleton? Did she miss her? No – scarcely ever. In those moments she was perfectly happy because Daniel had come back to her again, to be close, and that was all that mattered.

Daniel squeezed her. 'I'm coming with you all right.'

Going back to Millie's now felt like retreating into a different and increasingly irrelevant life, and the more caught up she became with the party the more glad Gwen was to stay out, even though it made her feel guilty.

Millie was seven months pregnant and was feeling huge and ungainly. Now the heat of the summer was here she was suffering with swollen ankles. The doctor had told her to rest and keep her feet up as much as possible, so she was no longer able to escape to her mother's as often as she had done. Her face was puffy and her hair hung limp and straggly so that she looked quite altered. She was always complaining about her hair, of which she had been rather proud until now.

'Why don't you go and get it trimmed?' Gwen had asked the day before, trying to be patient as she bustled about, just in from the party offices. There they were, she and Daniel, involved in making the revolution happen and all Millie could think about was her hair. 'It'd make you feel better.'

'Oh, it all feels too much effort.' Millie was sprawled along the couch, sipping a cup of tea. 'And Lance will keep on about me spending money. You know what he's like. There's some tea in the pot if you want it.' Reproachfully, she said, 'Where've you been again? You're never in. I thought now school had broken up you'd keep me company more.'

'Oh, I will – I'll try.' Gwen took her tea and sat on the chair opposite.

'You're always with Daniel, I suppose?'

Gwen felt her face light up at the mention of his name.

'Mostly, yes.' She managed not to make a face at the tea, which was lukewarm and bitter.

Millie sighed and looked at her. 'I don't understand you. I thought that Edwin chap of yours seemed very nice.' After Edwin's arrival and Millie and Lance having to look after him, Gwen had had to explain what was going on.

381

'He *is* nice. I just don't feel for him the way I do for Daniel.'

Millie almost glared at her. 'You're really *in love*, aren't you?'

'Yes.' Gwen was aglow.

'What does that feel like?' Millie pushed herself up a little on the cushions. Her ankles were mottled and puffy. 'What does being "in love" really feel like?'

All Gwen could feel was a deep stirring inside her. How could you ever put that into words?

'I'm not sure I can tell you. I just know I am.'

Millie sighed, putting her cup and saucer on the table. 'Better you don't tell me, anyway,' she said grumpily. 'I'd better not know what I'm missing. I'm not going to have the chance to find out now, am I?'

On 16 August there was a Communist Party weekend for Spain in Birmingham with a rally in the Bull Ring. Gwen stood out in the sun selling the *Spain* leaflets, looking over the sea of heads at the CP and BCPL banners and straining to hear the speakers as they railed against the neutral stance Baldwin's government had taken on Spain. Between them they sold five hundred pamphlets in the centre alone, and there were other meetings scattered round the city.

As Gwen patrolled Spiceal Street that afternoon with her leaflets, a figure came towards her from the crowd whom she suddenly recognized. Small and urgent looking and dressed in a baggy cream frock patterned with huge blue roses.

'Hello, dear.'

'Oh!' Gwen was startled. It was so strange to see another of the school staff in a different place. Though with Lily Drysdale it seemed less strange. 'Hello, Miss Drysdale...' Her mind raced. Lily Drysdale was here at the rally. Had she just come as an interested bystander or could it be that she too was a party member?

'I'm a supporter of the BCPL,' Lily Drysdale announced. Lily's dress had short sleeves and with her soft, rounded arms protruding from them, she looked rather attractive. 'Are you a Communist? A member, I mean?'

Gwen blushed. 'Yes, I am,' she said defiantly.

Lily nodded. 'Well, I can understand it. But if I were you, dear, I'd keep very quiet about it when you're at school. Mr Lowry doesn't hold with that sort of thing. You don't want him finding out.' She squeezed Gwen's arm for a second. 'See you about the place.'

As she walked away, Gwen saw a tall, bearded man join her, at her side. Gwen watched, fascinated. Was that Lily Drysdale's secret lover, whom Millie had told her about? No wonder Lily knew when to keep quiet!

'Letter for you.'

Millie slipped the envelope under Gwen's bedroom door with a slight grunt. It was the following Tuesday and Gwen was getting ready to go out again. The writing was familiar but it took her a moment to recognize, with a horrible jolt, that it was her father's hand.

The reality that she was supposed to have been marrying Edwin this coming Saturday flooded in on her. She had behaved so badly, not going home to face things, to sort it out! When Edwin had left here, the pain of her answer to him written on his face, she had known he would be the one to tell her parents. How shameful that she had left him to face it for her! She sat down on the bed, her heart thudding, telling herself she was lucky to get away with just a letter. Her parents might have arrived on the doorstep to remonstrate with her. At the same time, the fact that they hadn't taken the trouble to was hurtful. She was the one in the wrong and should have gone home. Yet they didn't care enough to come and find her.

She stared at the envelope. Perhaps she'd delay opening it until tonight. But then the dread of it would hang over her all day. Shakily she got up and found her paper knife to slit it open. The letter did not even cover a whole side of the paper:

Gwendoline

Just her name. He couldn't even bring himself to write 'Dear'. He wrote in deep blue ink, with his precise, pharmacist's handwriting.

Your mother and I have waited for you to come
home and explain yourself, the least you could
manage in the circumstances. Instead, it was left up
to poor Edwin, who has been treated atrociously.
You have behaved in a deceitful, cowardly and
selfish manner, bringing shame and acute
embarrassment to your mother. Have you even
given a thought to all our friends and to all the
preparations which were in train? I would never
have expected anything like this from my own child.
A complete disgrace.

It's no good coming back now, thinking you can
make amends. Your mother and I feel that we have
washed our hands of you. She can't bring herself to

384

communicate. Since you seem to want to live an independent life you'd better consider that you have left home. Don't think you can just come running back when it suits you.

Your Father

Thirty-Six

'Ah, come on – dance with me!'

John was squatting by the grate, trying to rouse a fire to cook on for when Christie came home. The doors were all open and the summer breeze blew along the hall from the garden. They lit the fire even in daylight now, risking it. The evenings stayed light too long to wait that late for food.

Siobhan was worrying at his shoulder, trying to force him.

'What's with you, John? ... John, John, John...' she chanted in a sing-song voice. 'Will you not come and have a dance with your little Shiv? You're a funny kind of a fella, John...' She jigged around him like a sprite, dark hair lifting and falling, then prodded him again.

John kept his head down, blowing on the smoking sticks in the grate. Joey was crouched beside him, wrapped in a filthy old curtain that had been left in the house. Underneath, he was naked as a babe, except for his boots. He could feel the heaviness of the curtain's dusty fabric against his back. Inside him was a tight, swelling sensation. *Why* did John bring the stuff for her? *Why* the bottles? *Why* make her be like that? Her voice was sweet now, cajoling, but he knew it wouldn't last, that her mood could turn in a split second. Joey sat with the edges of the curtain gripped tightly in his fists.

Siobhan snatched her hand away from John's shoulder.

'You're not natural!' Her tone was hard, and edged with spite now. 'You're not a real man, are you, John? What's the matter with you – you're a girly, John Cliff, that's what you are!'

Joey got up and ran over the loose tiles out into the garden. He didn't like the feel of being naked. The curtain wafted round him, puffing little breezes against his skin. It made him remember the Christmas play at school, the kings adorned in old curtains. That was before Miss Purdy came, Christmas was. He knew she hadn't been there then. This curtain, under the dust and filth, was a deep red with gold swirling patterns across it.

Earlier Siobhan had been tender with him, and motherly, as she could be sometimes, though that frightened him too because sooner or later her mood would change and you could never tell when. The deep, frightening hunger to be held welled up in him. It had been different when Miss Purdy held him. But Siobhan was dangerous.

'You're a filthy urchin, sure you are,' she said when he and John came back that evening. She had seemed quite well, cheerful even and with sudden energy. 'We're going to wash those clothes of yours, what's left of them, God love you. Will you look at those shorts – there's no arse left on them! John, can we not get hold of something else for the child to wear? These rags are almost dropping from him!'

'S'pose so,' John said in his wooden tones.

'Come on now, fella, get them off – you can give yourself a scrub then cover yourself with this.'

Joey looked down at his little pile of clothes when

he had removed them. They were nothing more than a pile of rags. He gave himself a quick wash with the cold water, feeling strange with the air on his skin.

Siobhan kept going on at him. 'Come on, now – get some soap round that neck. Will you look at the filth on you!' She was strange and overexcited. He didn't like it and escaped as soon as he could, wrapping himself in the curtain while he was still wet. Siobhan pummelled at the clothes in the old sink at the back with a sudden burst of energy. She had wrung them out and now the clothes were laid across the bushes and brambles outside. The vest was worn so thin you could see through it and there were holes all over it. The clothes weren't yet dry, but he put them on anyway and felt safer.

The air was warm and balmy. Now that summer had come and the leaves were all out, the house was completely secluded at the back. They had all relaxed about the worry of being discovered. The house next door was empty and in bad repair and no one further along seemed to want to know. In the spring there had been pink and white blossom on the two apple trees and now they were covered in tiny, unripe fruits. Joey had given himself belly ache by gnawing at them long before they were ripe. He had had to stay in that day, curled up with cramps.

Sitting on the back step, he shivered in the wet clothes. His boots were dry and bleached, the leather moulded to his feet. At least they fitted now. The feet had gone from his socks, just rotted away, so now he wore the boots with nothing inside. He pulled them off, enjoying the feel of air on his feet, and wiggled his toes. His feet were filthy and callused, with rough, discoloured patches. He stared at them indifferently for a time. Then he realized he could hear Siobhan's voice inside, high and aggressive.

Things had got worse since Micky died and that priest came. That's how Joey remembered it. Before, there had been more times when she was peaceful, motherly to him. Those were the worst times. When she wanted to cuddle him and sing him songs like a baby which made him ache inside so that he had to push her away. He saw her as wearing a mask that would split open at any second to show her other face: crazy and frightening. At least when she was drunk and screaming like a witch he knew he was seeing the real thing: there could be nothing worse hidden underneath to leap out and hurt him.

Since that night she had been forever on at John for drink, begging and wheedling. Joey never understood why John bought it for her. It was almost as if he wanted to cause devilment. He bought cheap, harsh liquor, which was all he could afford, and night after night now she drank and sobbed and picked fights. Finally she would slump to the ground and sleep. But sometimes she just went out, slamming the door so that the house shook and returning long after Joey was asleep. She was never awake when he and John left in the morning. And she had money after those nights, which she gave to John for 'another drop' for the next night.

Hearing her again now, Joey got up, carrying his boots, and moved away into the shelter of the tunnel through the brambles, where there was no shouting and the light was green.

Christie stood with his head under the water pipe, washing the plaster dust from his face and hair. His

389

trousers and boots were white with it. He stepped back and flung his head back, showering Joey with water.

'Oh – sorry little fella – didn't see you standing there!'

Christie tried to sound chirpy, but Joey could hear the flat exhaustion in his voice.

'All right, are you?' He pushed back his hair with his hands, trying to flatten it. Water dripped from his chin and rivulets ran down from his hair.

Joey nodded.

'Cat still got that tongue?' Christie's rough fingers chucked his chin.

Joey nodded again. Couldn't seem to find words.

'There's taters over the fire. Come on, now.'

Joey followed him. Things felt safer when Christie was there.

But not for long. Siobhan was swaying in the middle of the room, the bottle in her hand.

'He won't talk to me. He won't dance with me.' She looked down and after some time, managed to take a step forwards. 'He's . . .' She had to take time to think. 'He's a bastard . . . A freak . . . He won't listen to me. Won't take any notice of me . . .'

'Siobhan, for the love of God . . .' Christie's tone was despairing. He seemed past being able to summon anger with her. 'Sit down and we'll get some food into you . . .' He pulled the bottle from her hand, despite her struggle. She was too drunk and weak to be able to fight back and Christie flung it against the far wall. It smashed and Siobhan started to cry.

'You bastard, Christie, taking away my one bit of comfort in this world. I hate you . . . I do . . . you bastard *priest* of a brother!' The word priest held all the contempt she could muster.

390

She gasped all this out between sobs as Christie seized her arm and pulled her over to the mattress. Joey could sense a new intensity in Christie's mood. Joey stood stock still in the corner by the door. In his head he went back outside to the quiet green peace among the brambles and trees.

'No!' Siobhan shrieked and yanked away from him. 'Don't boss me! I hate you, Christie!'

'Sit down, I'm telling ye!'

In search of shelter from the shouting, Joey sank down in the dark corner, arms round his knees, rocking back and forth, his back slamming against the wall. *Not Christie . . . not Christie . . .* Christie was the one who didn't shout or drink, who was safe . . . He squeezed his eyes closed. *Make it stop . . . make it stop . . .*

Christie pushed his sister down roughly onto the the mattress.

'Why d'you bring it to her?' He turned on John, completely beyond control. 'How many times have I told you? A thousand times I've told you not to bring it to her!'

John stared dumbly at the pan of potatoes over the fire. This time it was Christie who went and shook him violently by the shoulders. 'What is it you're wanting, John, eh? The ruination of us? Can you not see it's like feeding poison to her – that she can't help herself . . .'

'She asks me for it,' John said without looking up. 'She wants it. So I give it to her.'

'You don't give me anything else, though, do you, you freak show?' Siobhan's harsh shriek rang across the room.

'For the love of God!' Christie was still shaking him. 'Can't you see what it's doing to her?'

Peering through his fingers, Joey thought Christie

391

was going to throttle John. 'What is it – are you stupid? You're an idiot, John . . .'

John got to his feet, hurling Christie away from him. He was taller than Christie and, roused to anger, he looked fearsome with his great curling beard. He stood with his legs apart, arms working. In his strange nasal voice, he yelled, 'I'm not an idiot! I'm not . . . Don't call me that!'

'Yes, you fecking well are for giving strong liquor to my sister – just look at the condition of her!'

'Don't call me that! Don't call me that!' John was howling, over and over, springing up on the balls of his feet as he did so, like a crazed jack-in-the-box.

'I'm going from here.' Siobhan dragged herself to her feet and started to make for the door.

'No, you're not – come back here . . .' Christie flung himself over to the door and stood backed up against it.

'Are you going to stand there all night to stop me?' she mocked. She could not stand without swaying.

'You'll not leave this room . . .'

It went quiet for a moment. John stopped shouting. Christie was panting and he and Siobhan stood close, their eyes blazing into each other's.

'There's you, Father Christie,' she goaded him. 'Always the hero, weren't you? Mammy's favourite – the priest, the family saviour . . . Couldn't save me though, could you, Christie boy? Couldn't stop me spoiling myself.'

'Shiv – for God's sake . . .' His anger was gone. He sounded close to weeping.

'I'm going to hell anyway, Christie. It's too late. My sin cries out to heaven for vengeance . . . and yours . . . you helped me and you know it . . .'

'You didn't leave me any choice.' It was barely more than a whisper.

'Move, brother. You'll not be able to stop me.' She seized the door handle and pulled on it impotently. 'Are you going to stand there all night? Just get out of my way, Christie!' It was a harsh shriek. 'You can't save me.'

He did not move immediately, but at last, caught in her burning gaze, released his weight from the door. In a moment, Siobhan was gone.

Christie came and sat by the hearth. He put his face in his hands. When he heard the sobs, Joey crept closer and sat beside him.

Joey sat up, hearing Christie move about, striking matches for the fire. Daylight forced into the room through crevices in the wood. No one was lying on Siobhan's mattress. Joey rubbed his eyes, got up and put his boots on. He had an urgent need to relieve himself so he went out to the garden and pee'd in the bushes. He looked back at the dark bricks of the house. The hour was very early, the sky hazy, and the garden was quiet except for pigeons somewhere in the trees and one on the roof, cooing and puttering. Joey liked the sounds it made. He could see its plump shape perched on the ridge beside the chimney stack.

Inside, John was still asleep. He hadn't taken his hat off to lie down but now it lay displaced by his head. Christie was blowing on smoking twigs.

'Where's . . .?' Joey began to ask.

'How the hell do I know?' Christie snapped.

Joey slunk away and sat in the corner. Normally, when he spoke harshly, Christie would come to him after, in a kinder mood and make peace. But not today. He brewed tea in silence and woke John. He handed Joey a jar of tea and a lump of bread.

'Where's Siobhan?' John said. He stared vacantly at the empty mattress.

'Not back. I don't know. There's nothing I can do just now.' Christie chewed in silence for a moment. 'I expect she's found a spot to sleep it off. She'll be right by tonight.' But his tone was desperate.

Joey spent the day with John shovelling coal for a firm at one of the wharves, and when they got back to the house, black from head to foot, Joey expected Siobhan to be there scolding him about coming home in a state when she had washed his clothes. In an odd way he was almost glad of the thought. It had seemed strange and empty without her there this morning. He noticed that John did not spend any of their earnings at the Outdoor this time, getting drink for her.

When they arrived home, the room was empty. John stood in the doorway as if he couldn't take it in.

'Where's Siobhan?' he kept saying. 'She's not here. Where's she gone?'

Joey thought if John said it again he would explode. How did he know where Siobhan was? Silently he went into the garden and began looking for sticks for the fire to add to the assortment of bits they'd picked up on the way home. He tried not to think about Siobhan. He shut her out of his mind.

But Christie's face, when he got back, cut through him. His gaze sweeping the room, his expression when he saw she was not there.

'Not been back?'

Their silent looks gave the answer. Without another word, Christie left again.

It was hours before he came back and he was alone and so weary he could barely move. John handed him the pan of food and he sank down by the remains of the fire.

'I've walked the streets for hours. I tried the pubs, the priest. Where would she go?' His voice cracked and he put the pan down. 'Oh God, where is she? Is she doing this just to anger me? I can't think she'd do that. She can't manage on her own. She's like a child ... She needs me with her...' Once more he put his face in his hands.

Three days passed. A week. Each night they came home full of hope that she would be there, but each time the room was empty and there was no sign of her. Christie stopped looking for work and spent the days searching.

'I'm not calling the Guard,' he said. 'We don't want them coming here. If anyone can find her, I can.'

In the evenings he told them where he'd been, the streets, parks, pubs, churches. Then one day Christie did not come home either. They kept his food warm in the pan until late at night while they waited.

In the end, John said, 'He ain't coming, is he? We'll eat the rest of this.'

Between them they shovelled down the potatoes and stringy bits of meat.

Thinking of Christie, Joey could barely swallow the food. But then he thought, he should've come back at the right time if he wanted it. Too bad.

Thirty-Seven

The summer weeks were flying past. They lived and breathed the party, the meetings, the debates at the factory gates and in the parks, flags and banners flapping over the scuffed summer grass. Every day in the offices they pored over the newspapers for news about the Spanish campaigns: the nationalists' bloody push on Madrid, the waves of reprisals in the republican zone against the Catholic Church. Gwen watched Daniel as each fresh piece of news arrived. He showed no reaction, especially to his non-Catholic comrades, but she knew the situation hurt him deeply.

Gwen worried about him: the way he constantly drove himself. His face was thin, and sometimes he looked glazed from lack of sleep. She knew his mother was worried about him too. Gwen had grown very fond of Theresa Fernandez, and sometimes popped in to see her even if Daniel was not there. Theresa didn't often talk about her feelings, but one afternoon when Gwen paid her a visit, she said, 'See if you can slow our Daniel down a bit, will you, Gwen? He won't listen to me, course, but he's hardly been in his own bed these last few days. He's starting to look like a ghost.' Since the holidays had begun, she had dropped the formality of calling Gwen 'Miss Purdy', even in front of Lucy and the others.

Gwen avoided her eyes. Theresa was so upright

in her morals, Gwen knew it would never occur to her that the main reason Daniel had been away from his own bed so much in the past week was that he had been in hers. Millie and Lance had gone away for a few days to Gwen's great relief. They had started arguing more openly lately, as Millie got more heavy and uncomfortable and less tolerant about everything, especially her husband. Gwen and Daniel had been able to snatch a few hours together in the flat without anyone else about, before Daniel crept out in the small hours back to his own bed at home.

'He's so like his father,' Theresa sighed over her teacup. She looked tired and strained herself. 'On and on – driving themselves. They just can't seem to stop. I'd thought coming to Birmingham would end all that, but . . .' She shrugged. 'I can see it coming out in Dominic too. Heaven help us when he gets older.'

'Daniel says he wants to go back and see your brother and his wife,' Gwen said hesitantly.

'Our Anthony and Shân? Oh yes!' Theresa's eyes lit up. 'You see if you can persuade him, Gwen! Get him to take a rest for a bit. Knowing our Daniel, though, he'll go down there and be running up and down to Tredegar and along the valleys to every meeting he can get to! I don't know . . .' She looked forlorn. 'I'm proud of him, God love him, I really am. I know he's right and he's trying to do the best for all our people. I just don't want to lose him – have him go the way Arturo did.' She looked up at Gwen as if a light had just dawned.

'Tell you what – perhaps you could go with him? You could try and tie him down a bit!'

Gwen smiled at Theresa's obliviousness to the fact that accompanying Daniel was exactly what she already had in mind.

'Just for a couple of days,' she pleaded with him. 'You can spare a little while away – Esther and the others can take up the slack and you did promise your Auntie Shân . . .'

They were on their way back from a meeting in Small Heath Park, where voices had boomed through megaphones over the ragged crowd, while the ducks glided past on the pond behind. Daniel had not been speaking today: they had both been busy selling pamphlets and the *Daily Worker*. Gwen's few remaining pamphlets were in the bag slung over her shoulder. The two of them caught a tram into town. It was a great relief to sit down; her feet felt sore from standing in the heat all afternoon.

'There's just so much to get done here,' Daniel said, staring ahead of him. He was in one of his distant moods again, somewhere she felt she could not reach him, and he looked very tired.

Gently she touched his back. 'Your mother really wants you to go. We could take all sorts of things over for them – books for Billy as well.' As she spoke, Daniel gave a great exhausted yawn.

'See!' She kept a teasing tone in her voice. 'You're tired out all the time. You'll be no good use to the revolution if you collapse in a heap, will you?'

He came to himself suddenly, was with her again, and took her hand. She was filled with happiness.

'All right. Are you coming too?' He asked so carelessly that she was hurt. She had taken for granted that they would go together. Didn't they do almost every-thing together now?

'D'you want me to?' she asked uncertainly.

'Yes.' He squeezed her hand and forced a smile to his exhausted face. 'Course I do.'

The local train pulled into Tredegar late on the follow-ing Thursday afternoon, and they caught the branch line to Aberglyn. It was a warm, muggy afternoon, and they had both slept for much of the journey. But the air grew a little fresher as they toiled up the hill, along the narrow streets to Anthony and Shân Sullivan's house, Gwen carrying the bag with their clothes in and Daniel his mother's bundle. Smells of cooking came to them on the breeze.

They stopped for a moment, panting, and looking back down the street. Two barefoot, ragged children were tearing down the hill away from them, after a runaway hoop, a small black and white dog barking excitedly at their heels. A couple of people had greeted Daniel on the way up. Everyone here, Gwen thought, looked so worn and weary. So ill fed. The children playing outside had pinched faces.

'You did tell her I was coming with you, didn't you?' it occurred to Gwen to ask.

'I sent a telegram. All I said was, "Coming Thursday p.m. Bringing friend."'

'Honestly! You could have put my name!' She felt genuinely aggrieved. Fancy him sending a telegram about a 'friend' as if she were just anybody.

As they approached the houses higher up, they saw that Billy was sitting outside the front door. He soon spotted them and waved madly with both arms.

'Mam!' they heard him call into the house. 'Our Daniel's here!'

When Shân Sullivan stepped outside, Gwen was momentarily shocked by the sight of her. Her shawl had hidden the true extent of her emaciation the last time they met. Now she came to the door in an old pale pink frock with an apron over the top and Gwen saw the frightening thinness of her arms and neck, from which her faded hair was taken up into a loose bun at the back. But her tired face was full of pleasure at the sight of them.

'Daniel!' She came out through the gate towards them. 'Oh and it's you, Gwen *fach*!' She sounded startled. 'Oh, Daniel, you silly. Why didn't you say it was young Gwen coming with you? I thought you were coming with another of those boys from the party.' She kissed Gwen, a quick peck. Close up, Gwen realized she was probably no thinner than she had been the last time. Her wristbones were very prominent, her hands bony and raw from hard work.

'Billy's been waiting for you all afternoon! Come on, I'll make us a cup of tea. Oh, it's a treat to see you both!'

But as Shân turned towards the house, Gwen wondered if she imagined the momentary combination of worry and puzzlement in the other woman's eyes as they fixed on her.

'Daniel!' Billy was pushing up on the arms of the chair in his excitement.

'All right, Billy!' Daniel cuffed him again in his friendly way. 'Got something for you here. Pass us the bag, Gwen.'

He squatted down by Billy's chair. From the bag he pulled out a book and handed it to his cousin.

'There, that should keep you busy for a bit.'

Billy turned it over, stroking the red-bound cover. *'World Politics, 1918–36,'* he read in awed tones. 'Rajani Palme Dutt. *Thanks*, Daniel.'

'Gwen's idea,' Daniel admitted. 'It's from this new thing, the Left Book Club.'

Billy shot Gwen a radiant look.

'Don't eat it all at once!' Daniel stood up again and ruffled Billy's hair. Gwen wondered if Billy minded being treated as if he were a child, but he grinned, seeming to enjoy it.

'I'll go and give Auntie a hand.'

Daniel went inside. Not liking to desert Billy, Gwen stayed out, enjoying the warm evening.

'How're you keeping?' she asked shyly, squatting down so that she wasn't towering over him.

'I'm all right.' He spoke guardedly, still fondling the book. Abruptly he looked round and words seemed to burst out of him. 'I say I'm all right. What else can I say when my mam's having to do everything for me like a baby?' He looked down, blushing. 'Don't know how long I can stand it, that's all.'

'Oh, Billy, I'm sorry.' She was surprised by this immediate outburst and somehow honoured by it, as if he had to say it to someone while he had the chance, with Shân out of earshot. 'Not much help to say that, is it?'

He shook his head. 'No. Not really. But at least I could say it to you. Don't know why.' He couldn't meet her eyes but the words kept pouring out. 'I try and keep a diary, see. I'm not much of a writer but it's someone to talk to. I'd've liked more schooling.' He gave a harsh laugh. 'Not much hope of that round here.'

401

'You like reading.'

'Oh yes. I like Dickens. He's a good long read – *Hard Times*, that's my favourite. And *David Copper-field* ... And Jack London...' Billy seemed to get excited easily, with the least bit of stimulation and encouragement. 'I read *People of the Abyss*. It was the best book I've ever read. It's a proper demolition of capitalism. Everyone should read it – everyone should be made to, to understand! Have you read it?'

Gwen was just admitting that, no, she hadn't, although she'd heard Daniel talk about it, when he and Shân appeared with a cup of tea in each hand. Shân handed Gwen her tea and perched on the doorstep, patting the narrow space beside her.

'Come and sit here, Gwen. There's enough space beside my old bones.'

Gwen obeyed, and they were so close together they touched at the hips and shoulders.

'Billy was telling me about the books he likes.'

'Oh, he's a reader, all right,' Shân agreed.

Daniel was squatting beside Billy now, near the gate. The two women watched them for a moment in silence, the dark heads close together, Billy apparently asking urgent questions about Daniel's work. Gwen glanced at Shân Sullivan and saw her watching them. For a moment her eyes clouded with pain. Billy looked so like Daniel in some ways that seeing him must be a walking reminder of all that Billy might have been.

'He wanted to go to the Labour College, like Daniel did.' Shân spoke very softly. 'Full of dreams, he was, right from a boy.' She sighed, hands clasping her cup as if for warmth, although it was not cold. 'D'you know, Gwen, if I could do it for him by giving up my own life, I would.'

'I'm sure he wouldn't want that.'

'No. But that's the truth. There's no life here for any of us the way things are. Survival level – that's how we live. Nothing but taters, one day to the next the winter through. Will there be enough for the next meal? How to save enough for anything to wear. Shoes!' She gave a grim laugh. 'When do we ever think we'll be able to afford shoes? Can't even afford the blacking for them!'

'Theresa's put some in for you, I think.'

'She's all kindness. And she sends us a bit when she can. That's more than many ever get. But that's not the point. The truth is, people here are wrung out with it. You go looking for a woman in this town who'll tell you she ever has a night she can sleep without worrying and you'll not find one. They've betrayed the miners' families – all of them. Bosses, government, unions – the lot. We've reached the end of the line. You know, I was never much one for politics. I never joined the party. Not till now. Even when Anthony became a Communist I still thought they were trouble, dividing up our people, dividing our *family*, then, was how it felt. I thought there must be another way. But if there is, I'd like to know what it is.'

Gwen was moved by the gentle woman's bitterness. 'Have you joined?'

'A fortnight back.'

Gwen could feel a smile tugging at her lips. 'Does Daniel know?'

'Not yet. I'll tell him inside.'

There was a pause. They drank their tea and heard

403

the murmur of the two men's voices. Then, gently, Shân said, 'When you came last time, with the others, I didn't know you and Daniel were ... well, if you were courting.'

'Oh yes,' Gwen said. 'We are.' In her own voice she heard the effusion of all the love she felt for Daniel.

Shân was examining her closely. There was a strange closure in her expression suddenly that Gwen could not read, and Shân looked away. 'Well, that's nice.'

Gwen was hurt. Did that mean Daniel's aunt didn't like her? Didn't think her suitable for Daniel? It wasn't to do with being a party member. How could it be? The woman had just admitted to joining the party herself. She couldn't bear to talk about something else without clearing the air.

'Is there something wrong?' she asked.

'No, Gwen *fach* ... What on earth makes you think that?' She stood up. 'And look you – here am I sitting about when that chicken needs the oven straight away!' She swayed, leaning against the door for support.

'Are you all right?' Gwen leapt up to help steady Shân, alarmed by her sudden pallor.

'What's up, Auntie?' Daniel ran to her as well.

'I'm quite all right.' Shân laughed it off, bending over for a moment. 'I just stood up too quick, that's all.'

Thirty-Eight

Shân did seem to be all right, and for the next couple
of hours the smell of roasting chicken filled the little
house. All the time, Daniel's aunt made conversation,
obviously trying to keep things pleasant and cheerful,
asking Gwen about her home and the school. Gwen
found herself pouring out the story of little Joey Phillips, and as she told Shân what had happened and how
he had gone missing, she found herself fighting back
tears.

'Oh, the poor little lamb.' Shân stopped slicing the
carrots and looked intently at her. 'What a thing. It's
really touched your heart, hasn't it?'

'Yes, I suppose it has.' Gwen was surprised by her
own emotion. She tried not to think about Joey normally, knowing there was nothing she could do about
it.

Shân's eyes clouded. 'There's a harsh, cruel world
we're living in, and no mistake. And you've a kind
heart, Gwen, I can see that.'

By the time the meal was ready it felt like a cele-
bration. When Anthony came home Daniel went out
with his uncle to fetch a jug of ale and the five of them
sat round the scrubbed table enjoying the chicken,
potatoes and carrots, and a few beans which Gwen had
help Shân pick from the tiny garden at the back.

'This is a real feast!' Shân said. Her pale cheeks had

405

some colour in them from the hot kitchen and she seemed more relaxed and younger suddenly.

'Let's raise a toast to our Theresa!' Anthony said, lifting his cup. He smiled across the table at Gwen. She had always assumed that Daniel was in every way like Arturo, his father, but now she'd met Anthony with his deep, rumbling voice and laughing eyes, she could see how much Daniel resembled him as well.

Shân wanted to hear all about the Fernandez family and Daniel told her all the news of his brothers and sisters.

'They think Dom should try for the grammar school,' he said.

'And will he?' Anthony looked up from his plate.

'I think he should. More education he can get the better. We'd have to pay for uniform and all that.'

'He always was a bright one,' Shân said. Gwen saw that she looked better for a good meal. 'And Rosa too – will she try? The others never wanted to, did they, Daniel – not after you!'

'Well, times were hard.'

There was a silence, in which Gwen again realized that there were so many things she didn't know about Daniel's family.

'What about little Lucy?' Shân asked. 'How's she getting on, now?'

'You'd better ask her teacher!' Daniel looked at Gwen.

'Oh, I was forgetting!' Shân laughed, a bubbling, full-hearted sound. Gwen saw Anthony look at her. She wondered when he had last heard her laugh like that.

'Lucy's a lovely child,' Gwen said. 'And she's easily

the cleverest in my class. If she has the chance to go to the grammar school, I'm sure she'd get a place.'

'Well now, who'd have thought?' Shân looked wonderingly at her. 'I suppose we all thought – you know, what with her leg, and the turns she had and that . . . And she must be all grown up now. Oh, I'd so love to see them all.' Shân had not set eyes on most of the family since they left Wales four years earlier. 'Is she . . . is her leg . . . ?'

'She's still wearing a caliper,' Daniel said. 'They think maybe she'll be able to walk without when she's older.'

Shân's eyes clouded. 'And the fits?'

'Still every so often,' Gwen said. 'Although I'd have said a bit less often than before?' She looked at Daniel, who nodded.

'She's full of beans. Mad about school – and her teacher.' His smile warmed Gwen across the table. 'Miss Purdy has done wonders for her.'

'Well, you were always the shining star in school I remember, Daniel,' Shân said.

Gwen looked at Billy. 'I bet you were too.'

'Oh, he was clever enough,' Anthony said brusquely. Billy flushed, and Gwen could tell this counted as high praise.

After that, the men could hold back no longer from talking politics. Billy asked Daniel about his work in Birmingham, and they were soon on to the NUWM in Wales. The government had brought in new unemployment regulations the previous month.

'Now we're two bob worse off that we were before,' Anthony said. He sat with his elbows on the table, rubbing his big, strong hands together. He spoke quietly, his voice deep, controlled, but the anger in it was unmistakable. 'There's got to be this next march. Something's got to be done to make them listen.'

'All the government does is bring out reports to tell us we're starving,' Billy said. ' "A Distressed Area." Not as if we need a report to tell us that, is it?'

'The party's behind another march,' Daniel said.

'It's got to be more than just the party. We need a national march – the Labour Movement, the workers. If it's just the party, they'll dismiss us as a bunch of reds. All in, full unity – that's what we need.'

In the shadow of the men's powerful voices, Gwen said quietly to Shân, 'You look so thin and tired. How are you managing?'

She saw tears rise in the woman's eyes, but Shân quickly wiped them away.

'It's all right – I'm just a silly. I get so tired all the time. There's no end to it, see.' She tried to smile, bravely. 'Every day if I go out all I see is working men standing on corners or going to meetings, when they should have a livelihood and all the while the pit's full of scab labour. And the women . . .' Against her will, her eyes filled again and she shook her head. 'I've seen some terrible things . . . The state of the place, of people . . . Sometimes –' she looked at Gwen and her face was hard suddenly – 'I just loathe all of it. Politics, all the talking and meetings and speeches. All the struggling. I want to be a family – normal, like, without it all . . . Selfish, there's what I am, I s'pose . . .'

'No, you're not selfish,' Gwen said. 'I think Theresa felt the same, didn't she?'

'Oh well, Theresa. After all that happened to her. I'm surprised she's not . . .' Shân cut off abruptly. 'Still – let's not dig it all up again.'

Gwen helped her as they cleared the plates away and made a cup of tea.

'Here, Billy – I can teach you the "Internationale" in Spanish,' Daniel was saying as they filled the teapot.

Shân's eyes met Gwen's over the cups and she gave her an uncertain smile, as if unsure whether to speak. Behind them, under Daniel's instruction, the men all burst into singing, '*Arriba, parias de la tierra...*' and Shân said, very quietly, 'You know how much politics means to Daniel, don't you?'

'Yes,' Gwen said, puzzled. 'He lives and breathes it – I'm used to that, if that's what you mean.'

'How long have you know him?'

'A few months. I only came to Birmingham this year.'

Shân nodded. Gwen felt herself tense inside. What was Daniel's aunt trying to say to her? At the same time, she felt she didn't want to know. She was about to turn away when Shân caught her wrist.

'All I'll say to you is this. Daniel's a good boy – I've known him all his life and you'll never find a more loving son to his mother...'

The men's voices rose for the chorus: '*Agrupémonos todos, en la lucha final. El género humano...*'

'It's just – I've never known Daniel put anything, *anything* before his politics. Not anything. Just remember that, Gwen *fach*.'

Billy was waving his cup as they sang, '*Es la internacional!*'

Gwen understood that this gentle woman was warning her, in the way Esther had tried to warn her too. But of what? She sat at the table with them all and Daniel didn't appear to notice her at all, even though

409

she tried to smile at him. She felt cold inside and full of doubt.

Gwen slept in the little upstairs room again, but alone this time. Without Esther's voluptuous form beside her, she enjoyed lying across the three-quarter sized bed, between threadbare cotton sheets, looking round at the room in the light from the candle on the chest of drawers. To her left was a chair on which lay her blue frock and underclothing from the day, and to the right was the window, open a crack, through which came the occasional sounds of the night: a dog barking in the distance, a low murmur of male voices on the path outside.

She would have liked to stay downstairs and be part of the debate, but Shân had grown sleepy and when she suggested showing Gwen up to her room, it was hard to refuse. And it felt right to leave the men to talk. Anthony's voice was a steady rumble through the floorboards, Billy's chipped in, ardent and excited at times, and she could hear Daniel talking passionately, voice rising and falling. *The voice of the man I love*, she thought. He was there, doing the thing most dear to him. Sadly, she wondered whether the next day he would just go off with his uncle to meeting after meeting, or whether he would save any time for her. She didn't mind the thought of being left with Daniel's aunt: she was growing to like her very much and had a high regard for her. But Daniel had promised . . . 'We'll go up on the mountain when we go back there.' But she was learning with Daniel never to take anything for granted.

What had Shân meant by her warning? And Esther?

Leaning over to the chest of drawers, she blew the candle out and lay longing for Daniel, needing his reassurance. She felt miserable and alone. *It's like being in love with the Scarlet Pimpernel,* she thought. Would she ever be able to be sure of him? With a sigh she turned on her side and hugged herself, falling asleep in the muffled sound of his voice.

'So – are you ready for a walk?'

He was waiting for her when she came down the next day into a golden morning, beams of sunlight pouring through the little windows of the kitchen, motes of dust swimming in the light. Shân was at the stove, stirring a pan of porridge. Daniel stood, loose-limbed by the kitchen table, face dark with stubble, a teacup in his hand. Gwen had dressed in her slacks and a comfortable short-sleeved blouse, in the hope that he would honour his promise to walk out with her. She felt her spirits soar.

'Of course – I'd love to!'

It was a relief to be out of the house. Billy said goodbye to them without displaying any resentment.

'He's so brave, isn't he?' Gwen said as they set off up the hill.

Daniel nodded. 'Could have happened to any of us. I don't think I'd have managed it at all. It appals me to think of not being able to get about, stuck in with his ma all day ... And given a pittance for it – for a life ruined.' She touched his hand, moved by the bitterness in his voice, and he squeezed her fingers for a moment.

'I've never seen the town properly,' Gwen said as they left it behind and headed up to the mountain.

'Well, it's no size. Town hall, chapels, churches and

411

a few shops trying to scrape a living. They have a job surviving when there's no wages for anyone.'

They left the road and climbed the path. Daniel obviously knew the way intimately and she followed his assured stride up and up, as the path became steep and rocky. They stopped for a breather and looked down over the town, a tight scattering of buildings strung along the valley, towards the pithead, the railway passing through like a steel spine, and the enclosing hills around in varying shades of green and grey. The slow-moving clouds passed as shadows over the valley.

'It's so beautiful,' Gwen said. They were both breathing heavily. 'Did you come up here a lot?'

'Oh yes.' Daniel shielded his eyes from the sun. 'With my pals – and Ann sometimes.' He pointed ahead. 'There's a seam over the other side. We came up here, she and I, when the big strike was on – we'd dig out as much as we could carry and bundle it up in a sack for home. Ann was always strong. We never got caught – it was illegal, see. The pit owners thought they owned that as well.' His voice was harsh and he seemed on edge, full of raw emotion. But at last he reached out and put his arm round her shoulders and kissed her, and they walked on further, still climbing.

When they reached the top of the rise the scenery opened out ahead of them, the peaks and shoulders of the hills all bathed in sunshine. It was one of the most beautiful places Gwen had ever seen.

'Daniel.' She had been wanting to ask him since the last time they were here but the right moment had never come. She could not forget the emotion in his voice when he had shouted after Hywel Jones that morning. 'You said that your mother was sent to prison?'

Looking up, she saw Daniel's jaw clench. He reached into his pocket for a cigarette and lit one.

'What on earth happened? Why her?'

'Oh, it was all a mistake,' Daniel said furiously. 'Whyever would our ma go to prison? They treated her like . . . like dirt.'

For a moment they walked in silence. She could feel the hot sun like a pressure on her face.

'It was after our da died. Only a month or so. There was all sorts of trouble. Up until then there'd only been a handful of scab labour here in Aberglyn. But then it started. There are rules in the pit, see, always have been – about seniority, who works where. A pecking order, if you like. The management wouldn't keep to it. This was in the spring of thirty-two. There was a protest and they locked them all out again. I wasn't here then, not just as it started. I was at the college, see. Anyway, they started to bring in scab workers from round the valleys. Course they were starving, needed work like anyone else. You couldn't blame them in a way.'

He paused to take a drag on the cigarette. 'Most days there was a crowd out early, protesting behind the scabs when they came to the pit, shouting and that. This particular morning Lucy was ill with a fever. She wasn't even two years old. Ma had been up half the night with her and she . . . well, she should've got someone else to get the doctor – Mary or Paul. But she wasn't thinking straight. She was in such a state, I s'pose. Da'd died and she didn't have the money to call the doctor out. I suppose she panicked and thought if

413

she went to him ... It was only just getting light and she went out with Lucy wrapped in a shawl. Course the streets were filling up and she got caught up in it. The police were waiting and there was a baton charge – all hell let loose. Ma was just at the edge of it, she said, but this policeman grabbed hold of her – arrested her and another woman who was nothing to do with it.

'Ann and Mary were at home and they didn't know what had happened for a time. It was the neighbours who saved us. The Prisoners' Aid Society tried to take Lucy away from Ma – said she wasn't a fit parent. They wouldn't listen, she said. She tried to tell them her husband had died and all of it, but no one heard a word. She was issued a summons for unlawful assembly and they sent her to prison for two months in Cardiff ...

'Ann sent me a telegram and I came straight home. Everyone had banded together and offered to pay our rent. And they threatened to go and wreck the pit if Lucy was taken away. Mary and Ann got her back off the Prisoners' Aid people and we all managed the best we could. There were enough of us old enough to manage. But we were all worried sick about Ma. She wasn't considered a political prisoner, so they put her in the reception part, dishing out the rags of clothes they had. But she was in a state over Da. She'd lost him so sudden like, no warning. And she was worried about all of us. Pining really, she was, as well as torn apart with the injustice of why they put her there. And then she fell sick. She was so bad they had to release her to go to the hospital in Cardiff. We thought she was going to die in there. Ann went down once and managed to get in to see her. She was so delirious she didn't know who Ann was ...'

Daniel stopped talking abruptly and Gwen looked round at him, shocked to see he was fighting back tears. He ground his cigarette stub fiercely under his heel.

'The worst thing was not being able to do anything. We were stuck. And the way people helped . . . There was a lady along the road, a Mrs Morgan. Her husband was dying then. Miner's lung. Coughing and gasping all day long. She'd never been one to have much to do with us – chapel lady, and us being Catholics. But she came along every day after she heard, to see if we were managing, giving us a loaf she'd baked, or a pan of broth. And her hands were twisted and hurt her all the time. But she was like an angel to us, Mrs Morgan was. She died the next year after him, God rest them both.'

He couldn't hold back his tears then, as if a well of tension was waiting to be released, even though he was embarrassed by his emotion. It did not last long, but she held him until he was quieter, her forehead pressed into his shoulder as she stroked his back.

'My love,' she said, as he quietened. 'Dear one – you're so tender-hearted.'

'I just want things to be right.' He looked out over her shoulder, reaching up to wipe his cheeks again. 'For everyone. For our people not to suffer so much . . .'

Thirty-Nine

They were back in Aberglyn by the late afternoon, the grey walls of the town bathed in mellow sunlight. There were some people about and one or two greeted Daniel. They passed the Bethel chapel and a few poor-looking shops with very little to be seen inside them. Then they saw a queue of people waiting outside a door, and across the road a man sat at a small table talking to a couple of others.

'Labour Exchange.' Daniel nodded at the queue. 'It's pay day. There'll've been a queue right along the road earlier on.' He then nodded at the man at the table. 'Uncle Anthony was there this morning.'

The NUWM offices were straight across the road from the Labour Exchange and Gwen knew that their officials gave advice to the unemployed workers collecting dole, or being refused it.

'He doesn't get paid for doing it, does he?' Gwen asked, watching one of the men standing in front of the table, talking emphatically to the NUWM official seated behind it.

'No, no,' Daniel said. 'People pay in a contribution every week . . .'

The official suddenly caught sight of him and waved. 'Hello there, Daniel!'

Daniel waved back. 'Hello, Mr Gallacher!'

'Coming to the meeting tonight with your uncle, are you?'

'I'll be there!' Daniel said.

Everyone was looking at them by now and one or two more called out greetings. They walked along to the main square, then round by the back roads towards Shân and Anthony's house. They walked side by side, but without touching. Gwen was conscious of feeling watched all the time. This was a small community and anyone different attracted interest.

Shân was at the stove cooking when they got back. She smiled wearily. Billy had not had a good day, she confided quietly to them both. He had not been feeling too well, his stomach upset. He was having a lie down when they came in and he looked up, unsmiling and said a curt hello. But Gwen couldn't help feeling also that their presence was upsetting for Billy. When would he ever be able to walk out over the mountain with a girl? Or work or give his energy properly to the party? It wrung her heart to see him lying there with all his young energy frustrated, such a cruel sight after the day she and Daniel had spent.

Anthony was sitting by the back door on a stool, leaning forward with his elbows on his knees, intent on his copy of the *Daily Worker*. He looked up long enough to nod at them and say, 'Coming tonight, boyo?'

Daniel, downing a long drink of water, nodded.

Gwen waited to be asked as well, but it became clear that this was considered men's work. She felt hurt and indignant for a moment. Wasn't she a comrade as well and a member of the party? She didn't seem to be considered worth asking to the meeting and she would have liked to see the NUWM in action.

I'm not going to beg, though, she thought proudly.

And anyway – I'll stay in with Shân and Billy, poor things.

Everyone seemed tired at the tea table and they ate mostly in silence. The evening had grown close and muggy, as if a storm was gathering. Billy seemed to liven up a little with food and company. As soon as they'd finished the stew, which seemed to consist mainly of potatoes plus additions from Theresa's parcel, Anthony stood up and picked up his cap from the sill.

'Best be off, Daniel.'

'See you later.' Daniel got up and Gwen struggled once more not to feel affronted by her exclusion.

She helped Shân clear up the dishes and afterwards they sat by the hearth with Billy, playing dominoes and drinking tea. It seemed to cheer him up and Gwen realized that he enjoyed her company. He was especially animated when she asked him about his reading and he showed her his copies of his favourites: Dickens, Jack London and Elizabeth Gaskell's *Mary Barton*.

'I wish we had a proper library here like in Tredegar,' he said wistfully. 'It's not often I get hold of a new book and I like it better than reading the papers, see. You get into the story and it carries you along . . .'

'I'll see if I can send you some,' Gwen said, 'when we get back home.'

'Oh, would you?' Billy lit up.

'Don't go giving Gwen trouble now, Billy,' Shân said, but Gwen could see she was delighted.

'Would you write me a letter now and then? Only I get ever so bored and fed up sitting here. I'd like to hear from you.'

He asked so sweetly that Gwen could only say yes. She liked him, as well as feeling so sorry for what had happened to him.

'Will you write back?' she asked. 'If it's not too much trouble?'

'*Trouble!*' He beamed. 'It'd be . . . *magnificent!*'

The evening passed companionably, though Gwen sensed at times that Shân seemed distant, as if she had something on her mind. She felt like asking if everything was all right, but as things were so obviously difficult all the time it seemed a foolish question and presumptuous of her to ask it, so she kept quiet.

'Well,' Shân said at last, yawning and stretching. She had put her shawl on now the evening was a little cooler. 'We'd better get you to bed, Billy.'

'Let me help.' Gwen stood up.

'All I need is a hand to the bed,' Billy said hastily. 'I can do the rest for myself, ta.'

Between them, the two women helped Billy manoeuvre over to the bed from his chair, his arms over their shoulders. Gwen felt the strength of them, the potential power in his upper body, and it made more poignant the dragging uselessness of his legs. With dignity he removed his arms, not wanting to be helped a moment longer than was necessary. There was a light sheen of perspiration on his face and she saw that the exertion of getting to bed had cost him more effort than she'd realized.

'Goodnight then,' he said, smiling.

'Those men won't be back for a while yet.' Shân stood with her at the bottom of the stairs, arms folded, looking very tired. 'You know what they're like. Might as well get some rest.'

'Goodnight.' Gwen felt she would like to kiss the woman's cheek, but Shân was not a demonstrative person and Gwen wasn't sure it would be welcome.

She was turning to go up the stairs when Shân, in a

lowered voice, called her back. Gwen went to her. In the dim light she saw a tight, anxious expression in the woman's eyes. Her arms were clenched tight across her chest. She seemed to be deciding whether to speak.

'Gwen . . .' She paused again, seeming to struggle for the right words. 'Has Daniel . . . has he told you anything much about himself?'

Gwen thought about that morning on the mountain, his tears. She had never felt closer to anyone than she had to Daniel that day.

'Yes!' She knew she sounded defensive, and she felt it. Of course she knew Daniel! They had shared so much, and he had told her some of the most painful memories of his life. Why did everyone feel they had to interfere?

'Why?' Gwen was polite, but she knew there was still a challenge in her voice. 'Is there something I should be told?'

Shân shook her head slowly. 'No, it's all right, Gwen *fach*.' She spoke in a conciliatory way. 'Don't you worry. I was only wondering. You know what boys can be like – never open their mouths to tell you a thing. You go up and get a good night's sleep.'

As she undressed upstairs, Gwen realized it had begun to rain. There was a low growl of thunder somewhere in the distance. The men would get wet walking home from the meeting, she thought. She felt glum. She would have liked to see Daniel before going to bed. But she comforted herself with the thought of spending more time with him tomorrow.

There was a bowl and pitcher of water in the room

this time, so she washed her face in the candlelight before she got into bed. All the fresh air and activity of the day had tired her and she felt drowsy already. Blowing the candle out she settled down, falling asleep almost instantly.

The next thing she heard was a great crash of sound. Her heart was beating fast, startled at being woken so abruptly. She got out of bed, moved the curtain aside and opened the window, feeling cool air on her face. There was nothing to see, the only sound the hard, steady fall of rain. Moments later there was a flash of white and the street was lit up for a second. Then came another wrench of thunder, then hard rainfall. She heard running feet and men's voices. Even at that distance she could recognize the timbre of Daniel's voice. He and his uncle were hurrying back from the meeting. She heard them reach the house and go inside. Immediately she wanted to go and see Daniel, have a goodnight cuddle. If she waited, maybe she could catch him on his own.

She pulled her cardigan on and stood by the window, enjoying the sounds of the storm. Before long she heard Anthony's lumbering tread on the stairs and the bedroom door across from hers open and close. Gwen dared herself to go down. The house was so small – surely they'd hear every sound she made!

Barefoot she went to the door, opening it as quietly as she could manage and crept down the stairs, wincing at every tiny creak. She stopped halfway down and listened. Something wasn't right. She could hear Shân's voice down there. Billy was asleep in the front, but Shân must be with Daniel in the kitchen. Gwen cursed under her breath. Curious though, she paused.

421

She heard Daniel say, 'What good will it do? That's the thing, Auntie. What's past is past.' He sounded angry and defensive.

'It's stayed past because I've kept quiet for you,' Shân said. 'And God knows there've been times it's weighed heavily on my conscience. There's ashamed of you I am sometimes – and of myself.'

'There's nothing for you to be ashamed of,' Daniel said.

'But plenty for you to be.' This sharp retort was followed by a silence. Then she said, 'This Gwen girl is very sweet and good-hearted. If you're serious about her, you can't keep her in the dark for ever you know, Daniel. Things come back to haunt you . . .' The rest of what she said was drowned out by a crash of thunder from outside. Gwen clenched her fists, desperately trying to hear.

'Don't go on, Auntie.' Daniel sounded weary, as if they'd had the conversation a number of times before. 'Digging it up. The damage is done – there's nothing more I can do about it now!'

'Nothing more! Daniel, for goodness sake!' Her voice rose. 'Sometimes I wonder if you've got a heart in your body, truly I do. The party isn't everything – there's a life to be led as well . . .'

'Oh, don't start on me again, woman . . . I'm going to bed.' Gwen saw a shadow move on the floor and she fled up the stairs and into her room. Holding the door open a crack she listened and a moment later heard Shân coming upstairs. Gwen slipped quietly into the lumpy feather bed.

She was wide awake now and wretched. She wanted to go down and have it out with Daniel. She felt

422

suddenly as if she didn't know him at all: he was like a stranger. And after this morning, when they had seemed so close, it was a cold, desolate feeling.

Gwen slept later than she intended the next morning. It was Saturday, and she and Daniel were to travel back that afternoon, so she had wanted to make the most of the day. But it had taken her so long to get to sleep the night before that she did not wake until almost nine. When she went downstairs, Shân was kneeling sweeping dust from the hearth and Billy, already washed and in his chair, lit up at the sight of Gwen. But this was little compensation for Shân telling her that Daniel and Anthony had already gone out.

'Where's he gone?' Gwen asked, trying not to let her disappointment show too much. But she felt tired and close to tears. She needed to see Daniel, for him to hold her again and prove to her he was not the complete stranger he had seemed the night before.

'They've gone off to meet more of the party members at the movement's offices over in Tredegar. They're full up with the idea of this march . . .'

'Tredegar?' Gwen's spirits sank even further. Daniel hadn't thought to invite her to go, and now he wasn't even in Aberglyn!

Shân turned, hands resting on her knees.

'This is the life if you marry the party,' she said gently.

'Yes, I know,' Gwen said bleakly. But she thought, *I don't want to marry the party. I want Daniel . . .* She longed to ask Shân what she had been talking to Daniel about. What was he hiding from her? In another way though, she also did not want to know. Trying not to show how low she felt, she asked, 'D'you know when they're coming back?'

'There's no knowing with them, once they get on to party business. But Daniel said something about catching an afternoon train.' Shân got stiffly to her feet. 'Come on, Gwen *fach*. You know what I think of it all. But let's make a cup of tea, and you can spend the day with me and Billy. It's not much to make up for it, though, I know.'

Gwen gave a watery smile, trying to swallow down the lump in her throat. 'I'd love to spend the day with you both.'

By the time Daniel and his uncle came back that afternoon there was only just time to make it to the valley train. Gwen said fond goodbyes to Shân and Billy, with renewed promises to write to Billy. But as she and Daniel set off she felt tense inside with pent-up hurt and anger.

'Plans are coming on,' he said, full of excitement, as they walked down the hill. The day was dull, cooled by the previous night's rain. 'They're thinking about making it October. Nothing's getting any better here, whatever the out-of-work figures say!'

Gwen nodded, silent.

Daniel continued talking animatedly. His complete obliviousness to her misery made her feel even worse, and once more she found herself on the verge of tears, but she forced them away. How could she ask Daniel anything about what she had heard last night when she wasn't supposed to have been there to hear it? But how could Daniel just go off for the day like that without

her, and not think now to apologize or ask her anything about her day?

Daniel was still distant, but full of talk. *And I'm just
a willing audience for it all*, she thought bitterly. By
the time they changed trains, she was so tense with
hurt she was ready to explode.

They settled into a carriage in which there was only
one other person: an old man, asleep by the window.
As the train moved off, Daniel turned to her and went
to put his arm round her.

'Don't!' she said, affronted. How could he start that,
acting as if they were close when it felt as if he had
never been further from her?

'What's the matter?'

'What's the *matter?*' The conversation was con-
ducted in a venomous hiss so as not to rouse the old
man. 'What d'you mean what's the matter? You're so
caught up in yourself and so oblivious to anything else
going on around you, you can't even see, can you?'

Gwen got to her feet. This time she couldn't push
the hurt away, pretend she didn't mind.

'What . . .?' Daniel began.

'Oh, don't ask me "what" again! I just can't stand it.
And I can't stand sitting with you for the rest of this
journey, either.'

'Gwen – for heaven's sake!' He got up to stop her,
but she pushed him forcibly aside and went to the
compartment door.

'Just leave me alone!'

She found another compartment, empty except for a
man reading a newspaper. She sat by the window and
silently let the tears roll down her cheeks.

Forty

There was a playful breeze tickling his right cheek, and a sudden press of sun rays against his eyelids. He opened his eyes, rolled onto his back on the prickly straw bed and looked up into the high barn. He could hear the dogs, and a moment later a wet nose edged with black and white hair nudged at his face, the tongue licking him.

'Molly! Ugh – gerroff!'

He sat up, clinging to her. The dog's eyes seemed to smile into his. She was a shaggy, rumbustious, farm dog and, of all the good things here on Elm Tree Farm, to Joey she was the best.

'Time to get up, you lot!' Mr Belcher had swung open the barn door and dusty rays streamed in. Joey could see the man's round face beneath the brim of his hat, pink in the warmth. 'Come on – shake a leg!' They had been on the farm for a week and so far he had said that every morning, nothing more, nothing less.

Joey was stroking Molly, her hot, panting breath on his face, as the men woke around him. He kept touching the soft bit of black fur between her ears. Stroking that velvety spot made him feel nice. Next to him John sat up blearily, straw caught in his beard. Frank always woke very fast, was on his feet and moving within a couple of seconds, body a lean silhouette in the doorway as he went out to relieve himself. Steven lay curled up, as if he hadn't heard anything. He'd shouted out in his sleep again in the night.

Mr Belcher disappeared and a moment later they heard him whistle Molly, who obeyed instantly, pulling away from Joey.

'Molly . . .' he whispered after her hurrying form. He wrapped his arms round his knees.

All that week they had been picking potatoes, gathering them in sacks in the long, sloping field beyond the farmhouse, hands burrowing in the dry soil to uncover the dusty potatoes, the smaller ones pale, like buried eggs. They worked on their knees, sacks under them, to save their backs. Once they'd worked for an hour and a half or so, they gathered with the other farm workers in the yard – only in the house if it was wet – and Mrs Belcher handed out plates of food. The first time Joey saw what they were to have for breakfast, the other men laughed at him.

'His eyes're going to pop out of his head!' one of them teased. 'You never seen food before, then?'

'Don't look like he has to me – 'e's thin as a stick . . .'

Joey was too busy tucking into the porridge to respond. It was thick and creamy and topped with a spoonful of treacle and he felt it sliding down into his stomach, warm and utterly comforting. He licked every last bit off the big spoon and stared at his face in it, stretched into a funny shape. As if the porridge wasn't momentous enough, the next thing to appear was a great platter of curling bacon rashers, which they ate on hunks of bread, and white, thick-rimmed cups of tea into which he could put as much sugar as he liked. Joey ate until he thought he would burst. Later his stomach went crampy and he had to go and be sick at the edge of the field. After a couple more hours' work,

427

one of the men brought round a basket of bread and cheese and more tea, then later every day there was dinner and tea, pies or roast meats with lashings of gravy and mashed potato and vegetables and big, filling puddings with jam or raisins or treacle and custard. Joey had never known there was this much food in the world, that it could taste like this! He was getting used to eating better food and at every meal he bolted down as much as he could possibly manage.

Mrs Belcher was a blunt, comforting person, with muddy-coloured plaits coiled round her head. Joey never saw her without a huge apron on, either white or made out of colourful flowery cotton.

'Why's this little 'un on the road with you, then?' she asked John on the first day. Joey and John had limped along the rutted track to the farmhouse and asked for food and water. She looked doubtfully at John with his filthy black clothes and wild beard, but then her gaze fastened on him. Joey saw a horrified expression in her eyes.

'He's with me,' was all John would say in his wooden way.

'Is he your boy then?'

'He comes with me.'

'Dear God – he's all skin and bone.' Joey saw her make a face when she came closer to John, though Joey could see she didn't mean to. Joey was used to John's stink. 'Are you hungry, boy?'

Slowly, Joey nodded. When was he ever not hungry?

'You'd better come on with me then.'

She had sat them down at a long wooden table in the kitchen, where there was a large range and lots of huge pots and a kettle bigger than Joey had ever seen. She fed them tea and bread and butter. On the table in front of them was a dish of brown eggs. She didn't ask any more questions. They needed help bringing the potatoes in, she said. And there was haymaking to do. They could sleep in the barn with the other men who were helping out.

'Wait there, before you go out.' She disappeared upstairs and appeared with clothes for Joey.

'These were my son's – don't fit him no more. They'll be too big on you, but you can't go round dressed like that! Give me them rags of yours and we'll put 'em on the fire. Here – you'll need a bit of twine to keep them trousers up.'

In the barn, Joey changed into the trousers. They were made of brown corduroy, well worn so that they were almost bald from thigh to knee, and were capaciously too large. Even tying them round the waist was not adequate – two or three Joeys could have fitted into them. John managed to rig them up by using the thick twine crossed over Joey's shoulders so that the trousers reached halfway up his chest, and turning the bottoms up. There was a blue-and-white checked shirt that reached below his knees and he rolled the sleeves up almost to the shoulder. The clothes felt heavy and awkward after the threadbare remnants he had been wearing and when he started work in the trousers he kept having to adjust the string on his shoulders. The farm workers started to call him Coco the Clown.

Later that day they'd met the two other migrant workers who had been taken on for the time being. Frank was a tall, lean, ginger-headed man who, Joey noticed, talked like Christie and had two fingers missing from his left hand, the little finger and the one next to it. All that remained were stumps with no nail and the flesh was stretched and shiny. Joey kept looking at

429

them when they all sat at table together. When Frank used the rest of the fingers on that hand they looked like hooks. He had a scar on the side of his face next to his left eye. He joked with Joey, called him the 'little fella' like Christie had done. Sometimes he picked Joey up and spun him in the air. He was stringy thin, had prominent cheekbones and vivid blue eyes and Joey didn't feel safe with him. His eyes were hard, whereas Christie's had been soft and kind.

Steven was older, balding, with large, deep brown eyes. Frank called him 'the toff' as he had a soft, well-spoken voice. He was gentle and nervous and had bad dreams, crying out, screaming in the night. The first time it happened, a high, unearthly shriek out of the pitch black, it woke Joey and left him trembling with fear. Then Frank's voice came, blearily, 'Give it a rest now, Steven. It's all right, pal.'

Other things shrieked at night: owls, and rats which pattered and rustled through the straw. Joey lay on the soft stalky bed, stomach distended with Mrs Belcher's food, his back aching, limbs twitching with exhaustion after a day of hard work and sunshine. His face and arms, at first a raw pink, were turning brown. Occasionally at night the men walked three miles to the nearest pub, but usually they were too tired and sat outside the barn smoking. Joey would hear the rise and fall of their voices. Sometimes he heard them talking about life on the road, comparing spikes – the dirt-cheap doss houses – and characters they'd run into. John barely said anything and was always the first to come in. Joey knew, though nothing was said, that he didn't like Frank. He called him, 'that Frank'. Frank

430

was always talking about Ireland and about guns and fighting, and he had a short temper which could whip out in a flash. Sometimes, as he drifted into sleep, Frank's voice would get muddled in his head with Christie's and Joey would have an ache in him to know why Christie had left them and where he had gone, and Siobhan too. And then he wouldn't think about it any more. Nor about his mother, nor Miss Purdy. He tried not to see their faces. In the daytime he didn't think about them.

He and John had left a few days after Christie failed to come back.

'I'm not staying here no more,' John said. 'We're going to get out on the road when I find some boots.' The next day he bought some in a pawn shop, and a hairy brown wool coat for Joey, which was too big and hung round his shins. They bundled a few things into the old red curtain: the pan, knife and spoon, the remaining candle stubs, matches and what little they had in terms of food and clothing. John carried the curtain over one shoulder, the contents clanking as he went along. Joey slung the coat round his neck, hanging forward over his shoulders.

They walked out of Birmingham along the Warwick Road.

That first day was very hot. They passed through Greet and Acock's Green, the glare of the sun in their eyes. The soles of Joey's feet began to burn on the hot road and each step hurt. The coat felt like a great weight and made his neck hot and prickly. In Acock's Green they stopped at a vicarage and asked for water. The woman gave it to them in jam jars and made meat-paste sandwiches. She told them to sit in the shade of the church. With the sandwiches were two pieces of fruit cake, and they ate them and lay dozing in the heat until a man came past and yelled at them to clear off. Later they got down onto the towpath along the cut, watching the boats go up and down, and moving out of the way of horses. It felt cooler there by the water. They sat for a while by a bridge and Joey took his boots off and dangled his feet in the filthy water. John didn't take his boots off. Joey wondered why not. He had never once seen John change his clothes. He barely ever even took his hat off. His beard was so tangled it looked as if it had melted into one big mass. They never said much to each other, just plodded on all day, Joey following behind John's black-clad figure. That night they slept in a park, the next tucked under a hedge in a field. It rained on the second night and the drops gradually trickled through the canopy of leaves, though the curtain and the coat, which Joey wrapped round him, helped keep some of it off. They woke the next morning and rolled out from under the hedge, looking out across a pasture of thistles and dock leaves dotted with black and white cows, all shrouded in a fine mist, which burned off as the day grew hotter. There were brambles woven into the hedge, but the fruits were still green and hard. Joey tugged one off its shoot. It was tough and gritty, and made his face twist at the bitterness, so he spat it out. The grass smelt so nice when you lay close to it that he tried eating that, nibbling at the young, green shoots.

'That ent no good,' John remarked. 'Only animals can eat that. You'll make yourself bad.'

After a lot of effort John lit a fire at the edge of the field and eventually they had a pan of black tea. They had spent almost a week on the road, wandering, begging from village rectories and farmhouses, sleeping

432

in barns and hedgerows, when they walked up the track to Elm Tree Farm.

The potato crop was picked and they were put to haymaking. To save the horses from the hottest time of day, Mr Belcher began mowing soon after four in the morning. The others went out with him, still heavy with sleep, into the grey, uncertain light and the smell of night and dewy grass. A shred of moon still glowed in the sky. Joey was given a rake to gather in the long, damp grass, which dried in piles as the sun rose and the heat grew. The air was moist from the dew, then warm as a steam bath. In that early part of the day they worked in silence. All the men were quiet except Frank, who after breakfast would often whistle or hum lively, jigging tunes to himself. Joey liked the songs, his mind followed the thread of them, but for some reason they seemed to enrage John, who Joey sometimes heard mumbling that Frank should 'fuckin' shut up' or 'shut his cake hole . . . bloody Irish carry on . . .' Joey didn't understand what made John like this about Frank. You never knew with John. He had liked Christie.

The sun beat down on them as the days grew hotter. Mr Belcher stood the horse and cart in the shade of the one tree in the field for as long as possible. Frank and Steven flung forkfuls of hay up onto the cart and the mound grew higher and higher.

'You can get up there now.' Mr Belcher picked Joey up and almost threw him onto the pile, passing him a pitchfork. 'Get it spread out. We've a lot more to get on there yet.'

Joey stood, legs splayed, on the top of the cart. Molly was allowed to lie panting in the shade underneath. Part of the time Joey was busy with his fork while the others pitched up bundles of hay. As they went off to get more, he had time to stand and look around from the whispering green shade of the tree. The next field was full of waving heads of oats, which Mr Belcher said would be the next job. Beyond it, way down at the bottom edge of the farm, was the railway and every so often they heard the LMS trains chugging in the distance, puffing out clouds of steam to the blue sky, the sound building, then receding. Every time a train came by, Joey felt a thrilling sensation. He stood wanting to wave and shout. There were moments when everything seemed right, a perfection in the puffing of the train, the warm ease of his body fed with the morning bread and cheese, the smells of cut grass and horse, the animal nibbling at the grass and giving out loud breaths away to his left. There was Molly with her lovely soft head lying near him, only leaving the shade of the tree when she spotted a rabbit across the field and tore off after it. It was too quick for her and she returned with her tongue lolling to one side. He thought nothing could be better, ever.

There came a couple of days of rain, so heavy that they had to wait before anything else could be harvested and the Belchers found them odd jobs to do round the farm. Joey was put to cleaning the stiff, filthy harnesses in the barn. Afterwards it grew very hot again. They had a day's haymaking left. But the day was interrupted.

The heat built up. Even though they were gathering hay right from the top end of the field, Mr Belcher wouldn't move the horse. Frank cursed about this.

'The animals get treated better than us here ... Treats her like a queen and us like scum ...'

'No, he doesn't – you know he doesn't.' Steven reasoned with him. 'He's a very fair employer, Frank – you know he is.'

Joey liked Steven. He was gentle and kind. Steven had once worked in a bank. Joey didn't know why he was on the road now. He wondered if he ever screamed and shook when he was in the bank.

After a dinner of bread and meat pies, they rested for a while in the shade. Soon after they had picked up their rakes and pitchforks again, they heard a train coming up from the south. Joey watched it from the top of the cart. There was a heat haze across the pale oatfield and the train, dark and metallic, seemed the one thing with any definition in the landscape. Its steam was a cloud of white and the sound began to decrease. Then Joey saw something. Something which shouldn't have been there: flecks of coloured light. He narrowed his eyes. The light was leaping up, orange, dangerous.

'Fire! Down the oatfield. Get down there!'

At Mr Belcher's cry, everyone was running. Joey slid down from the stack, not knowing what to do but run. It seemed such a long way across the field. He was with Frank, John and Steven and Molly came with them too, her tail a flag amid the oat stems. Mr Belcher had disappeared, shouting that he was going to get some sacks. The four of them saw the fire take hold of a seam of the crop, licking hungrily at it.

'Thank heavens there's no wind,' Steven panted. 'Must have caught from a spark from the train.'

They had nothing but rakes and forks to beat at the fire. Molly circled, barking shrilly.

'Make a break round it!' Frank was shouting. They were all beating down the stalks around the fire, trying to keep it from advancing any further. John beat at the flames with his pitchfork. Joey copied him. It frightened him hearing the crackling fire, feeling the heat of it on his face if he went too close.

'Help us make a break!' Frank yelled at him. 'It's no good doing that, you stupid fucker – get over here!'

Joey could see Frank was right, but John just ignored him and turned his back, thrashing away with his pitchfork, mumbling angrily to himself.

'Come and help us over here!' Steven insisted, but John ignored him as well. The others saw he wouldn't listen and left him. Joey joined them, beating down the crop in a semi-circle round the flames.

It seemed an age until both Mr and Mrs Belcher came running, staggering under the weight of rolled-up sacks. Joey saw the sacks were dripping water. They threw the sacks over the edge of the fire, stamping it out, then moving on, eating into it until it got smaller and smaller. Joey saw quite soon that they were going to beat it.

'What if we hadn't been there and seen?' Steven said as the last flames were stamped out.

'We'd've lost the crop,' Mr Belcher said. Both he and his wife wore sober expressions. Mrs Belcher wiped her puce face on the end of her apron. 'We try and plant away from the edge but it only takes a stray spark like that...' He looked round. 'You saved it, though. You're good blokes – thanks.'

''Cept for that feckin' idiot over there.' Frank nodded at John, who was standing, fully clothed as ever, in the heat. 'What's the matter with you, eh? Got a screw loose or something?' He tapped his head. Something had got into Frank. He seemed wound up and tremulous, his body tense with the need to goad John.

'Don't, Frank,' Steven said. 'It's over. It doesn't matter.'

'No, it doesn't matter,' Frank shouted. 'Except the man's an idiot – just look at him!'

Joey jumped as John launched himself abruptly from beside him and threw himself on Frank, punching him in the head.

'I'm not stupid!' he screamed. 'Don't call me an idiot!'

Of the two, John was the bigger and he caught Frank off balance, knocking him to the ground. But Frank was full of crazed, wiry strength and in a few seconds he hurled himself out from under John and over on top of him, snarling into his face, his teeth bared.

'Think you can push Frank Monaghan around do you? You stinking, shite-thick English bastard . . .'

Joey felt himself shrink with dread. He backed away as Frank began to punch John and Steven and the Belchers went to pull him off. Joey turned, hearing the blows and ran up the field away, away to the tree and its shade. He lay curled under the hay cart, eyes screwed shut.

Forty-One

Gwen spent the days after coming back from Wales feeling truly miserable. For part of the journey from Aberglyn she had sat in a separate carriage from Daniel, utterly hurt, weeping tears of anger and frustration. When next they changed trains, Daniel found her on the platform.

'Well, thanks for coming to find me!' she erupted at him.

'I just *have* come to find you,' he said, exasperated.

'I mean back there – on the train.' She was trying to keep from crying, but barely succeeding. There were people milling about on all sides of them. She pulled her hanky from her sleeve and blew her nose, feeling pathetic.

'But you told me to leave you alone!'

'I didn't mean *actually* leave me *alone* for the whole journey, I meant ... Oh, never mind. Forget I said anything.'

'Hey.' He went to put his arm round her waist. 'Come on – I don't know what I'm s'posed to have done, but I didn't mean to upset you.'

'That's the trouble though!' She flared up again. 'You've no idea, have you? You ask me to come with you to Aberglyn and then you spend nearly all your time off at meetings and ... I know it's important but you could just show a bit more consideration.'

438

Daniel sighed, pulling her closer. He looked dog tired and she began to relent a little.

'Sorry,' he said. 'Only – it's what I do down there, see. Habit really. And it's important.'

And aren't I important at all? she wanted to say, but she gave a stiff nod, swallowing her tears. *Why do I always have to come second?*

'We need to get to the other platform.' Daniel took her hand and she allowed herself to be led.

She hoped it would be better now, that they would sit close, talk again. And they did sit holding hands, but it was hard to begin. She didn't find the courage to mention the conversation she had overheard the night before. And very soon after the train left Hereford, Daniel's eyes closed and he slept until they arrived. By the time they had got on the last train, Gwen herself felt low, and sleepy and past talking about anything. They parted in Birmingham with a quick hug and kiss in the dark street outside Millie's and Lance's flat.

'See you tomorrow,' Daniel said wearily.

'Umm.' He saw her into the house and she stood at the door watching as he walked off along the street. A deep sense of melancholy came over her. She felt so close to him sometimes, as if they inhabited the same skin, yet there he was, a stranger heading off into the night without turning round.

I just need a good night's sleep, she thought. *I'm feeling tired and gloomy.*

She crept up the dimly lit staircase. At least Millie and Lance would be in bed by now and she wouldn't have to contend with them.

But she was wrong. As soon as she opened the door to the flat she heard Millie's angry voice raised shrilly in the sitting room.

'... but you don't – you never do anything except go to work and come back. It's bad enough now, but how are we going to get by once the baby comes?'

'Oh, do stop going on, darling ...' Lance sounded plaintive and at the end of his tether. He evidently slammed something down on the table. 'Let's just go to bed – I can't keep this up.'

'No – that's just like you. Run away, go to sleep – anything to avoid me ...'

Millie was crying. 'I feel as if I live on my own all the time! Gwen's never here and you have no time for me.'

'I do have time for you. But you're tired all the time – and so am I ...'

'Well, it's not much of a life, is it? We haven't even been married a year and all you do is ignore me already ...'

Their bickering voices went on and on. Gwen slipped quietly into her room, wishing the door would muffle the sound of their quarrelling completely. She was so tired she barely had the energy to get undressed before falling into bed, where she lay listening to Millie and Lance moving about, sniping at each other in an exhausted way before finally closing their own bedroom door behind them. She'd always felt sorry for Millie, but she didn't half go on. No wonder Lance got irritated. And he was such a drip! What on earth had Millie seen in him in the first place? Gwen lay there, fed up with the pair of them, resolving that she would never, ever get into a situation like that. But then her spirits sank even further. Hadn't she and Daniel sounded the same today? He had hurt her so badly by being blind to how she was feeling and she still felt sore about it. She thought of his parting words, 'See you tomorrow.'

No, you won't actually, she thought, as her eyes began to close. *Don't you take me for granted like that.*

The party was working towards another big demonstration in the Bull Ring with the the BCPL the following Saturday, in support of republican Spain. Gwen knew Daniel would be totally taken up with it and that all hands were needed, but she woke the next day even more sure she couldn't face going in. School would start again in a couple of weeks and she wanted a bit of time to herself. And – the thought that she kept trying to push away from her – that same Saturday she had been supposed to be getting married to Edwin.

In defiant mood she lazed around in bed with a cup of tea, then pottered about, doing her washing and catching up with odd jobs. Later in the afternoon she sat in the wicker chair in her room trying to read, but it was impossible to concentrate on the book. She found thoughts about her family and Edwin crowding into her mind. If the wedding had gone ahead, how would it have been? All out in the garden at the Shackletons' house, where they had planned their reception, tables with food, the children running up and down to see the pony in the paddock and her in that dress Mrs Twining had been making. She could hardly bear to think about Edwin and, more even than Edwin himself, his parents, whom she felt so guilty about. She knew Mr Shackleton had had a genuinely soft spot for her and she thought of him caring for Edwina so gently and unselfishly. What must they

441

think of her? What kind of person was she, the way she had behaved? And she had cut herself off from her family completely now. The thought of this was both sad and frightening, yet when she thought about how it would feel to go home, to be back in her parents' house, with Edwin again, she felt the old sense of claustrophobia – panic even – wash over her.

Leaning over, she picked up the framed photograph of Amy Johnson, her handsome, inscrutable face looking out from under the goggles on her forehead. *How do you find freedom to fly in this world?* she wondered sadly. *Is it ever possible to do it without hurting someone else?* She thought, painfully, about Daniel. Here she was, trying to take off and fly and she had immediately got herself tangled, tied to him.

Impatient with herself, needing relief from her feelings, she put the picture away and went out, catching a tram into Birmingham. She went looking for books for Billy and, after a long time of musing along the shelves, found a translation of Victor Hugo's *Les Misérables*. It looked the sort of novel Billy would like and it would certainly keep him busy for a long time. Sitting in the sun near St Philip's Cathedral she wrote him a note to go with it, saying that she hoped he had not already read it.

Two more days passed and it became almost a matter of principle to stay away from the party offices. Gwen felt guilty, knowing how busy they would be, but she wanted Daniel to come and find her, to show he cared about her as well as politics and the party. She knew it was childish, but her feelings were hurt. She sat talking idly with Millie on those warm afternoons, listening to all her woes, the windows open to the street, the sound of voices and passing traffic floating up to them. They drank homemade lemonade and made toffee in a pan, as it was the one thing Millie 'just had to have!' and ate it until their jaws ached. Millie seemed to want to do nothing except eat and sleep, although the baby was not due for a few weeks yet. She always left her hair loose now and wore a succession of billowy cotton dresses.

By the third day there was no sign of Daniel coming to find her. *I could be ill*, she thought self-pityingly, *and he wouldn't know*. She felt restless, unable to settle, and longing to see him. Was he missing her? she wondered. Probably not – he would be too busy. In the end she decided she was punishing no one except herself.

If I want to see him, I should just go and do it, she thought. *I'm being ridiculous!*

Instead of going to the offices, she did the next best thing and walked to Alma Street. The school, when she passed it, was all locked up, silent in the sunshine. There was something sad, Gwen thought, about a school without any children. There were plenty of them about, though, out in the streets, playing.

Round the corner she found Lucy Fernandez sitting on the shop's front step watching Rosa and her brothers throwing a small rubber ball to one another back and forth across the street.

'It's Miss Purdy,' Gwen heard Rosa say as she approached. 'Daniel's not here, is he?'

Gwen was struck once more by how beautiful the girl was. Lucy was smiling shyly up at her.

'Hello, are you having a nice break?' Gwen said.

'Yes, thanks.' Lucy had on a skimpy, pale pink

frock, and sat with her good leg bent, the calipered leg stuck out awkwardly in front. She leaned aside to let Gwen into the shop.

'Hello there, Gwen!' Theresa called from behind the counter. Gwen felt cheered immediately. She was calling out a reply when she realized someone else was standing at the back of the shop. It took her a few moments to realize who it was.

'Afternoon, Miss Purdy,' the woman said. It was her soft, well-spoken voice that made Gwen realize.

'Oh – Mrs Wilson! Good afternoon.'

Alice's mother was wearing a pretty floral dress in pinks and greens and her hair had grown since the last time they met and was tied back. Unlike the last time, her face was calm.

'Mrs Wilson's just popped in to tell me the good news,' Theresa said.

'Oh, what's that?' Gwen asked.

'Well.' Louise Wilson blushed. She seemed unable to meet Gwen's eye. 'Just that I've got myself a little job.' She was going to be serving in a stationer's, she told Gwen. 'It's not much, but it's a start.'

'Well, I'm very pleased for you,' Gwen said carefully.

'Alice can come round here after school, see,' Theresa said. 'Lucy's pleased as anything.'

Gwen repeated her congratulations and looked gratefully at Theresa Fernandez.

'Daniel's not here, I'm afraid,' Theresa said. 'Course, you can stay if you want . . .'

'No, thanks, I'd better be getting along.'

Gwen smiled and parted from them. Her smile faded once she was along the street. She had to go to the party offices or she was never going to see Daniel!

Once more she went into town. As she did so her mood changed. Of course Daniel was busy! How could she be so self-centred? And she was supposed to be helping collect food and medicines for Spanish Aid, not sitting in Millie's flat feeling sorry for herself! Ashamed, she shook off her mood of gloom and resentment. She had to put other things before her own feelings. They were working for a cause and Daniel was very committed, very adult, about it. She strode along, full of new energy.

She was waiting to cross the street when she saw Esther Lane come out of the offices. *Good*, Gwen thought, *at least she's not going to be there.* But then she saw Daniel coming out after Esther. She didn't know why, but she shrank back, not wanting them to see her. In any case, they were not looking her way. Esther turned her head and said something to Daniel and Gwen saw him laugh. As they walked away, Gwen's saw Esther lazily put her arm round Daniel's waist. With equal casualness, he laid an arm across her shoulders. Then he reached down and kissed her in an easy, familiar way on the lips.

Forty-Two

It was like being punched. The breath seemed to have left her body. All she could do was stand at the kerb watching as Daniel and Esther went off along the road, wrapped round each other, talking away nineteen to the dozen, until they disappeared into the distance. Still she could not move, almost unable to believe she wasn't caught in a nightmare and would wake up.

'How could you?' She found her lips moving. 'How *could* you?'

When she managed to move away she almost collided with several people. It was as if no one else existed. In a dream she caught the tram back to Handsworth, but the thought of going home and facing Millie or sitting alone in her room seemed unbearable. Instead she wandered the streets until she found herself outside Ariadne's house. Unable to think what else to do, she knocked on the door.

It opened with a waft of cheap perfume and there was Ariadne, clad in a floaty frock, navy blue and covered in tiny white polka dots. Her hair was newly dyed and caught up in a loose chignon. Even in the state she was in, Gwen couldn't help noticing how hard and lined Ariadne's face looked in the bright light, all powdered and with her eyebrows pencilled in. But she beamed at the sight of Gwen, seeming quite overcome.

'Gwendolen, come in! Ooh, I'm so pleased to see

you. And I've just made tea! Fancy you coming to see me again!'

'I did say I would,' Gwen murmured. She felt quite disorientated. Ariadne immediately started complaining about 'that strumpet' Miss Hines and her perfume.

'I've told her about it,' Ariadne said, with a censorious sniff, leading Gwen into the back room. ' "I don't appreciate these odours," I said, but she gave me that look of hers.' The tea gushed out of the spout, narrowly making it into the cups. 'Have a cake, dear?'

'No thank you,' Gwen said. 'I'm sorry – I'm just not hungry.' It would have been a good time to eat since the Eccles cakes were obviously shop bought, but she felt too queasy with distress even to attempt it.

Ariadne sat herself down, smoothing her skirt under her in her affected way and proceeded to complain for some time about the indignities visited upon her by her lodgers. A travelling salesman called Mr Mealing had stayed for a couple of weeks with promises to be stable and long-term, and then upped and gone.

'You can't rely on people today – they've no staying power.' She bit resentfully into an Eccles cake and looked across at Gwen, who was cradling the cup between her hands, trying to warm them.

'You're not cold, are you? On a day like this? Perhaps you're sickening . . .' She looked more closely. 'You really look rather peaky, dear. Are you sure you're all right?'

Gwen had no idea it was going to happen. Afterwards she realized it was the look of real motherly concern in Ariadne's eyes that had done it, but suddenly she was sobbing, so hard that the tea started slopping out of her cup onto her skirt.

'Dear, oh dear!' Ariadne leapt up and took the cup

447

from Gwen's shaking hands. 'My dear girl, whatever is the matter?'

Gwen shook her head, unable to speak. All she could feel was pain ... *Daniel, Daniel* ... In her mind was fixed the sight of him with Esther, so comfortable and familiar as if they had walked that way, intimately entwined, many times before. And she could hear Esther's words, spoken in her superior tone when they were in Aberglyn, '*poor old you*...' The sense of hurt and humiliation was so great, she couldn't speak. She was beyond even embarrassment about having broken down in front of Ariadne.

Ariadne pulled her chair up close. Eventually, taking courage, she laid her arm round Gwen's shoulders. Even in the state she was in, Gwen was touched by the timidity of the gesture. She could smell Ariadne's perfume. It was quite pleasant, she realized, not like that smell in the hall.

'You can tell me,' Ariadne said, after letting Gwen have a cry. 'I know what it's like to be unhappy, dear, believe me. Has someone been playing with your heart?'

Gwen fished out her hanky and blew her nose, more tears coming as she did so.

'I've been such a fool and it hurts so much ...'

She spilled it all out then, desperate to talk to someone, all about meeting Daniel, and Edwin and the wedding and the fact that her parents never wanted her home again and, most terrible of all, what had happened this morning.

'She's been chasing after him for ages. I've seen her. I've tried so hard not to be jealous, but every time we do anything, *any* meeting we go to, *she's* always there, making up to him, taking his attention ... And she's so

448

bossy, and she's older than he is,' she finished petulantly. 'Why would he want to go off with her when he's told me he loved me so many times? I can't understand him...' Once more she dissolved into tears. She realized Ariadne was lightly stroking her back.

'Poor child,' she said. 'Oh, what a thing. But that's men for you, dear. I've spent my life trying to get over men. You give them everything, pour your heart out to them and they run off and leave you, and you think: one day I'll find the one who's different, who'll be true...' The melancholy in Ariadne's voice cut through to Gwen and she wiped her eyes and turned to look at her.

'But you found your George, didn't you?' Both their eyes went to the photograph of George in its frame on the mantelpiece, with his moustache and military stance. 'He was different, wasn't he?'

There was a silence. Ariadne looked down into her lap. 'No,' she confessed miserably. 'He wasn't. Not in the end.'

Gwen stared at her, unable to make sense of this. Ariadne looked up, and Gwen could see the sad, defeated look in her eyes.

'I tell everyone I'm a widow, but it's not true. He left me – just like the others.'

'Oh, Ariadne!'

Ariadne withdrew her arm and looked down into her lap. 'You get over some of them. Most of them – but I've never got over him. Took the heart out of me, he did. Don't let this one do it to you. Look at you – your pretty face is all blotches! You're too young for all that.'

It's too late, Gwen thought, tears welling in her eyes

449

again. *He already has.* But she didn't say anything to Ariadne, just leaned over and gently touched her hand. Ariadne looked up at her, nodding gently, shame and hurt in her eyes.

'Your room's empty, dear, since Mr Mealing went,' she appealed. 'I do wish you'd come back and take it.'

Gwen thought of Millie and Lance's flat, the constant bickering and life with them at close quarters.

'Just give me time to give them notice,' she said.

Millie was not at all happy.

'But I thought you were going to stay and help me when the baby comes,' she complained. 'It's going to be ever so lonely, and I shan't know what to do!'

'I'm sorry, Mill – I've promised to go now. I'll come and see you whenever I can. It's not as if I've the faintest idea how to manage babies, you know.'

'Lance will be so cross – we need the rent, you see.'

But Gwen was determined. Now she knew she would be leaving in a couple of weeks, the realization came as a great relief, even though Lance was short and snappy with her. She was in far too much distress herself to care what Lance thought about anything.

Thursday and Friday she spent in a terrible state. She kept bursting into tears and lying on her bed, face pressed to the candlewick bedspread. She was so desperate, she thought sometimes she should go and find him, have it out with him. But her pride wouldn't let her. Nothing would have dragged her into the party offices. On Friday evening she was sure he would come to her, that he would want her there with him at the demonstration the next day. She waited all evening in a

450

state of almost unbearable tension, thinking every sound was a knock on the door, but he did not come.

Saturday was the day of the demonstration. She decided that the only way to get through it was to try and keep busy, so she went out, buying food on the way, to Handsworth Park. In the afternoon a band was playing on the bandstand and she sat nearby amid the crowds sprawled on the grass, listening to marching tunes as they rolled across the sunlit grass, trying not to think about what was happening in the Bull Ring, the speeches, party members selling the *Daily Worker* and the BCPL banners. She should have been there with her bag of leaflets, one of the party's workforce.

Damn them – damn all of it, she thought savagely, hugging her knees and peering out from under the brim of her straw hat. They didn't care about other people – not really. All they cared about were abstract ideas, and slotting real people into them. Was that what she was for Daniel – an idea? A comrade so long as she thought as he thought, and joined the party and did as she was told? What if she had feelings and ideas of her own? Every time she thought about Daniel it was with a terrible lurch of pain inside. It was as if he had sucked her right in, body and soul, and then casually spat her out again.

That night she lay soaking in the bath. She had a good cry. When she got out her body was pink all over, her head felt muzzy and she had reached a point of numbness where she had thought about Daniel and dwelt on her feelings so much that she couldn't any more. Barefoot and in her nightdress she went into her room and sat numbly on the bed. She didn't know how long she had been sitting there when there was a rap on her door.

'Gwen?' Millie sounded impatient. 'It's Daniel.'

She didn't have time to move. She had been in such a daze she hadn't heard the knock on the outside door of the flat.

His face, coming round the door, looked very dark. He obviously hadn't shaved for several days and his skin had tanned well in the sun. His white shirt hung outside his trousers and he looked generally dishevelled, but full of energy. He beamed at her in a way which indicated so clearly that he had absolutely no idea of her feelings, that she froze even further and just sat, staring at him.

Daniel closed the door quickly behind him. 'You missed a big day today! It went really well – crowds of 'em! Where've you been all week? We've been rushed off our feet!'

He sat on the bed beside her. 'Off to bed already? You been poorly?'

'No.' She kept her voice even and controlled. 'I just didn't come in. I had other things to do. Didn't you notice I wasn't there before today?'

'Yes – course. Only we've been non-stop all week before the big day today. I've barely been home, slept or anything! I fell asleep on the floor in the office once or twice. And today was big – crowds there. We got rid of hundreds of leaflets!' He talked on excitedly about the demonstration, the speeches and how it had all been. Gwen sat growing more and more tense with pent-up hurt and anger, yet she was already beginning to feel ashamed. She was being so trivial and womanish, being wrapped up in her own feelings when Daniel was

452

spending himself every hour of the day for the party. If it had just been that it wouldn't have seemed so bad. But there was Esther . . .

'So –' he stopped at last – 'where've you been then?'

'Do you really care?' She stood up and walked away from him as he reached out to put his arm round her. 'Daniel.' For a moment she stared at him, feeling her cheeks burning red and a wave of tears barely held back. 'Don't come here and pretend to me.' He was looking up at her from under his curling fringe, frowning. She could see the dark rings of exhaustion under his eyes. She had trouble getting the words out. If she said what she had to say, it would change everything. But it had to be said. 'I saw you. On Wednesday. With Esther.' Tears rolled down her cheeks. Her throat felt as if it was about to close up.

Daniel was looking completely baffled.

'Oh, don't act as if you don't even know what I'm talking about! You and Esther came out of the offices together just as I was about to cross the road, and you were . . . you . . .' She began to lose control of herself. 'You put your arm round her and you kissed her on the lips. I saw you, so don't say you didn't! And then you both went along the road, all over each other . . .' She really began to weep now. 'And . . . why did you say you loved me, when all the time . . .' She put her hands over her face. 'I can't bear it!'

Daniel was beside her at once.

'Come here.' He pulled her into his arms and for a moment she tried to resist, but then she sank against him exhausted. She felt him press his cheek against the side of her head. 'What've you got yourself all upset for?' he said soothingly. 'Have you been fretting about this all week, silly?' She nodded against his chest, feeling his shirt button against her cheek. 'What, and worrying about old Esther? Gwen – you know what she's like – she's forever on at me. She's a strange one and I feel sorry for her, that's all.'

Gwen pulled back and glared at him. 'But you don't have to kiss her on the lips just because you feel a bit sorry for her!'

Daniel shrugged, comically. 'It doesn't mean anything – it's just easy come, easy go – we're comrades, that's all.'

'Oh, I see – is that it! So that's how it is with me as well, is it?'

'*No!*' His eyes held an intense expression which moved her. 'You know it's not, by now, don't you? God, Gwen, how much more do I need to show you?'

'You could have come and found me – this week,' she said bitterly. 'How am I supposed to know whether you care for me or not? Everything we do is when *you* want it or need it! I've been in such a state, and what do you care?'

He looked chastened. 'I just didn't have a minute . . . There's all the talk about the march at home and Spain, the demonstration . . . It's just been non-stop . . .' He looked deeply into her eyes. 'I'm sorry I've made you unhappy. But for heaven's sake don't let Esther be anything to worry about.' He laughed at the ridiculousness of it. 'I love *you*, girl. Like no one else. That's all.'

She leaned back into him with a sigh. She felt exhausted, foolish, wrung out. His hands were stroking her back.

'Oh, Daniel – you'll be the death of me.'

'Sorry. I'm sorry.' He put his face close to hers.

She could hear that he meant it. They stood close, absorbing each other's presence.

'You're lovely and warm,' he said.

'I had a bath.'

He moved one hand and cupped it round her breast. She could feel the heat of his hand through the thin nightdress. They stood like that for a moment, looking at each other, then he took her hand and led her to the bed, making love to her with a taut urgency which moved her. They lay holding each other in silence for a long time. Then Daniel lifted his head and looked down into her eyes, again without speaking, and she stared back in a moment of pure concentration.

'I never want to hurt you,' he whispered.

'You're hopeless.' Tears welled in her eyes again. Daniel gently wiped them from the side of her face with his thumb. He stroked her neck.

'Don't be so afraid. I love you.'

She held him tight to her. 'Not Esther?' It humiliated her asking this, but she had to know.

Daniel smiled. 'No. Not Esther. Absolutely not old Esther.'

'Stay with me tonight, Daniel, will you?'

He leaned down and kissed her nose. 'Course I will. You'll have to move over.'

She put the light out and they lay holding each other, talking very quietly for a long time. Daniel poured out his feelings about the work he was doing.

'Sometimes I feel I'm running round, but I never manage to be in the right place at the right time,' he said with a sigh. 'There's so much to get done, to make the revolution happen, and never enough people who've understood, who've caught the fire...'

Gwen felt a pang of guilt. She was working with him because she loved him, but had she caught the fire? Had she really?

'I'll be back at school in a couple of weeks,' she told him. 'I'm afraid I shan't have as much time.'

'No – what you're doing, educating the children . . . Sometimes that looks like a far more worthwhile thing to do – not like me . . . Sometimes I just wonder . . .'

'What're you talking about?' She lifted her head off the pillow in alarm. Never had she heard him express such self-doubt before. 'You're doing all the things you believe are right, aren't you? I thought you were pleased with how it's going?'

'I am.' She heard him let out a long sigh beside her. 'I s'pose I'm just worn out this week. But sometimes I think . . .' He faltered.

She stroked his chest. 'What?'

'That I'm not much of a person when you come down to it.'

'Oh, Daniel – you are! You're the best person I've ever met!'

'No – there are things you don't know about me, Gwen. Things I'm not very proud of.'

A twist of fear went through her at the sad tone of his voice. She remembered Shân's words downstairs that night in the house at Aberglyn. What was it Daniel was hiding? It sounded as if he had been in trouble at some time – with the police?

'What things?'she asked faintly.

'Oh, just – you know. We've all said and done things we're not proud of.' His voice was brisker now. He evidently wasn't going to tell her, and how much did she really want to know? 'It's nothing really. I'm just overtired and gloomy tonight.' He kissed her neck. 'Turn over, my lovely. I want to lie behind you.'

Pressed together, bodies fitting close, they slept.

Autumn Term

1936

Forty-Three

'Donald Andrews? Joan Billings?'
  'Yes, Miss!'
  'Ernie Davis?'
  'Yes, Miss!'
The register held few surprises. A boy had left to be
replaced by a new girl, but otherwise Gwen found she
was facing the same set of faces as last year. Now,
though, they had a new classroom upstairs, at the front
of the school overlooking the playground. Opposite
Gwen on the wall was a large picture of a cross-section
through a flower. She kept seeing the word 'stamen'
when she looked up.
  'Lucy Fernandez?'
  'Yes, Miss.'
Gwen was about to let out the fond smile which she
would naturally have given Lucy had she been at her
home, but she curbed it. She knew the children must
have realized she was walking out with Daniel, but
none of them had the impudence to say anything to
her about it. She didn't want to be a teacher who had
favourites.
  She went on, past Ron Parks, who, she noted, had at
last lost his two black front teeth, and Alice Wilson
peering eagerly through her specs. She closed the
register.
  'Milk monitors...' she said, thinking aloud. She

459

looked round at the class. 'But first – I hope you all had a nice summer? You look bigger!' The summer months had made last year's Form Four sprout up to a size fitting for Form Fives.

'Anyway – it's very nice to see you all again. I hope you're going to work very well for me this year?'

There were a few scattered replies of 'Yes, miss.' Lucy was watching her every move. What a sweet face she had, Gwen thought. She looked so like Daniel it was almost unnerving having her in the class. She found she too was glad to be back.

The staffroom was its usual drab self and things were much as ever, except that Mr Lowry was no longer spending time there during the teabreaks, and last term's new teacher, Charlotte Rowley, often did not come in either. Miss Pringle announced that she had seen her going into Mr Lowry's office at the beginning of break in the first week of term, at which Miss Monk said nothing but swelled visibly with inner emotion. Gwen wasn't interested in whether Charlotte Rowley was in the staffroom or not. She thought she was a chilly woman anyway.

Lily Drysdale was in her corner of the room rummaging through a canvas bag which appeared to contain a collection of socks.

'Hello,' she said distractedly, giving Gwen a knowing look, which Gwen took to mean, 'I know you're a Communist, dear, but don't worry I won't tell anybody,' though it might not, of course, have meant anything of the sort. But having been mainly with party members all the summer, Gwen was conscious of coming back into a quite different environnment, where Daniel's passionate views might not have met with much sympathy.

'Are those for the children or for Spain?' Gwen asked.

Lily smiled, faintly. 'Oh, for the children. Though I do think as a staff we might think about gathering a few things together for the Spanish people.'

Mr Gaffney was nodding in his vague way, but Miss Monk looked up from her chair and said aggressively, 'Ah, but *which* Spanish people?'

'Well, which would you suggest?' Lily Drysdale asked.

'Oh.' Miss Monk sniffed. 'I have no views on the subject.'

'Perhaps it's time you had then,' Lily replied sharply.

Gwen grinned, her back to Miss Monk. Only Lily Drysdale could get away with treating Miss Monk like that. She perched on the table beside Lily, who told her more about her church's work in collecting medicines for Spain. There was talk of an ambulance going from Birmingham.

'Cup of tea?' Lily said after a while, about to move away.

'Yes – I'd love one. But I wanted to ask you – have you heard anything more about that boy – Joey Phillips?'

Lily bit her lower lip and shook her head. 'No. Poor little scrap. That was a very sad case.'

Gwen had moved out of Millie and Lance's flat at the beginning of September. Ariadne welcomed her back with enthusiasm, a newly repainted room and a meal which was almost edible and which they ate alone because, Ariadne said, 'that young trollop' upstairs had announced she wasn't eating any more meals in the house because – and here Ariadne almost pulsated with affrontery – the food was only fit for the pig bin!

'Oh dear, what an awful thing to say,' Gwen said, trying to suppress the powerful sense of fellow-feeling she suddenly developed with the hip-wiggling Miss Hines.

'No gratitude or consideration,' Ariadne said. But she gave a genuine smile at Gwen across the singular stew they were eating. 'But it's lovely to have *you* back. Like having a daughter come home, almost, dear!'

Gwen was startled at this, but also touched. Never could she have imagined anyone less like her own mother, but she knew Ariadne was genuinely pleased to see her.

'Thank you for making my room look so nice,' she said. Ariadne had had it painted a pretty shade of green, and had hung new curtains at the window.

'Well, it was getting so shabby. I thought it would brighten life up for you.'

Gwen hadn't been quite sure whether Ariadne was pleased or disappointed when she told her that Daniel had turned out not to have betrayed her after all and that they were as close as ever. Ariadne didn't say much, but gave her a look as if to say, 'You just wait.' But she had said she was glad Gwen was happy and indicated that a blind eye would be turned to Daniel visiting the house.

Those early weeks of the Michaelmas term were very happy ones for Gwen. She was busy at school and spent spare time when she could in the evenings and at the weekend working for the party, which was also a way of seeing Daniel. He barely ever stopped, but in

462

the snatched times they did have together things felt good between them.

One night in late September they were walking, arms wrapped round each other, through the smoky evening. There was a nip in the air.

'They're closing the parks early now,' Daniel was complaining. 'Means we can't stay on late of a weekend. We're having to have meetings on street corners, village greens and all that. Bit of a pity.'

'Never mind – it's going well.' Gwen squeezed his arm. 'Think how many copies of the *Worker* we've sold already this month!'

'Any chance of smuggling a few into the school?' Daniel asked, teasing.

'Oh, I don't think so. There's a couple would be sympathetic – to some of the others it'd be a proper red rag to a bull!'

Daniel shook his head, as if unable to understand anyone who was not a Communist.

'I had another letter from Billy today,' Gwen said. 'He's already read *Les Misérables* and was pleased to get the other books I sent. He writes a good letter.' Despite his confined life, Billy wrote fluently and Gwen had found herself laughing at some of the descriptions of life in Aberglyn perceived from Billy's wheelchair.

'He's a gifted lad,' Daniel said wistfully.

'Perhaps he should be writing stories himself?'

'Well – you suggest it. It'd come better from a woman.'

'Why?' Gwen laughed.

'Well, not very manly, is it?'

'But Billy can't do man's work!'

'You suggest it, anyway.'

'I will!' she said. 'Honestly, I've never heard anything so daft.'

'I must get down there,' Daniel said. 'There's so much energy going on Spain now – we've got to make sure we keep up our solidarity with the miners instead of leaving them to the struggle on their own.'

'Are you going to go? Can I come with you?'

Daniel turned to take her in his arms and kissed the side of her neck.

'Oh, I think I might let you!'

Forty-Four

They were on the road again, between fields where the corn stubble had been burned black and the air smelled of ash. The hedgerows were full of haws and berries and Joey gorged himself from the brambles and damson trees. That day, as they walked, in the red curtain slung over John's shoulder, were stashed orchard apples and pears. But this was food that did not satisfy for long. It made their stomachs gurgle and churn and turned their bowels to water. Every hour pain clenched Joey's innards and he had to hurry into a field or wood. He walked mutinously behind John's black figure. John's hat was always worn at the same angle, his pace never varied, and he seldom spoke.

Joey didn't want to be with John. He wanted to be back at Elm Tree Farm. The morning after the fire in the oatfield and the fight with Frank, John woke him long before dawn, shaking him hard.

'Ow!' Joey yelped. It was pitch dark.

'Shurrup!' He recognized John's whisper in the darkness. 'Get up – we're going.'

'Where?'

'Just going – come *on*, will yer?'

Joey could hear from the faint clanking sound that John had their little bundle of belongings already gathered into the curtain.

'Bring that coat – don't leave it.'

Joey obeyed automatically. He just went where John went and that was that. He felt round for his boots and pulled them on, shook out the coat, hearing rats scuttle away over the straw, and pushed open the barn door.

There were still stars outside, and the moon, high and thin. As they crossed the dark yard, Molly set up a barking and came running out.

'Christ,' John muttered. 'The hound'll wake the lot of them. Shurrup, yer fuckin mutt!'

'Molly!' Joey called softly to her and she came and nuzzled at his outstretched hand. He stroked her head, fingering the soft spot between her ears. Feelings welled up in him. 'Can we take her?'

'Don't be stupid,' John said. 'Another mouth to feed. She won't come anyhow – she wants to stay here. C'm'ere – get moving.'

'Where're we going? I want to stay here.'

John took his arm and dragged him to the farm gate. 'Bloody get moving!'

Joey did not fully realize then that John was leaving for good, that this was the end of their time at Elm Tree Farm. They walked out as they had walked in and kept moving into a grey, mild day. It was only later, when he was exhausted and hungry, that Joey knew it was all over. He had had a glimpse of wonder and now it was snatched away. On the road into Warwick he flung himself at John's back, clinging on and kicking him in the backs of the knees, overcome with sobs.

'I want to go back to the farm! Why've we come here? I'm hungry and I hate you. I don't want to come with you!'

'Get off, you little fucker!' John reached round and wrenched him off, dropping the curtain bundle with a clunk as he did so. He seized Joey's hands. Close up,

466

Joey noticed afresh the matted state of John's beard. His eyes burned into Joey. They were stony grey.

'I hate you!' Joey shouted. 'I want my dinner!' All the other things he longed for stayed locked inside him. He had no words for loss, or for safety, comfort, kindness. For the feel of a soft spot between a dog's ears.

'There won't be dinner there no longer soon ... They'll finish with us and we'll be on the road again. And I ent staying with that mad bloody Irish fucker no longer.' John yanked on Joey's arms as if there was a switch in them that would silence him. 'Just shut it. Right?'

In Warwick John used some of their earnings from the farm to put new soles on their boots. Then they left the town again. John didn't like towns. The boots felt hard and rigid for a time but now they didn't let so much water in when it rained. The summer was waning, sunlight slanting across the fields onto the red-flecked hedgerows, picking out each fading leaf on the trees. In the morning there were drenching mists and the apples began to fall and rot. Every day they walked. They asked for work at another farm soon after leaving Elm Tree Farm, but the woman there was not round and comforting like Mrs Belcher. She looked thin and crabby.

'You can collect the eggs today as my boy's not here. Long as you don't go stealing them.' She had a pointed, suspicious-looking nose. 'Then you can be on your way. I don't want the likes of you hanging around.'

They collected all the eggs they could find, John

slipped four of them into his pockets and the lady gave them half a crown. She looked as if she wanted to search John for stolen eggs, but he was too revolting.

'Go on now,' she shooed them. 'Away from my door. And don't come back.'

The nights were spent in hedges and haystacks again. The hay was new and sweet smelling. Sometimes Joey asked where they were going, but he never received an answer. Then he stopped caring where they were headed. The days passed.

One evening, at dusk, they were close to the railway. They slid down into a siding where John had spotted an old railway carriage left to rust at the end of the track. They were approaching it, boots crunching on the stones by the edge of the sleepers, when a head appeared through the open door. In the gloom, Joey saw a man in a cap looking down at them. They could see the glow of his cigarette.

'Looking for a kip?'

John nodded. The man had a rough, gravelly voice.

'Thought you was trouble for a mo' there. Who'd come out 'ere poking about I don't know, but I thought you was it. Come on up – it ain't bad. Blimey – this is a young nipper you got 'ere. Running away to sea, are you, chum?'

Joey didn't know what to say so he said nothing.

'Is it just you here?' John asked cautiously. John did not trust people.

'Yep – just me, chum. I ain't the first to kip down in 'ere but there ain't no one but myself 'ere now.'

The man was stocky and bandy legged, and rocked from side to side as he walked. His face looked as if he'd had plenty of punches in his time and he had a rough beard. He led them into the first compartment.

The seats that were left by the window were in a terrible state and the rest, nearer the door, had all been ripped out leaving only the metal frame.

'There's places a-plenty to kip down out the wet. I've been 'ere a couple of nights, resting up. I'll be moving on tomorrow or the next day.'

The man told them his name was Bob Barron and he was from Catford.

'That's London to you, chum.' He laughed with a chesty wheeze and slapped John on the back. John sat woodenly. Joey knew the man had made a mistake. He shouldn't have touched John. But Bob didn't seem to notice the hostility of John's reaction.

'If we're careful we can have a little fire this side – no one can see. Got any grub? I've got a bit of bread and a couple of eggs ... There's a farm over there – easy as winking to get in of a night and get a handful of eggs. Nothing to it. Even got water from the butt...'

As Bob and John built the fire, Joey explored the railway carriage. He'd never been on a train before. He forgot his rumbling stomach and sat in the compartment at the far end, where there was a seat on one side, half tilted off the frame. He thought about the noises the trains made as they went across the fields by the farm. He thought about the railway bridge by Ron Parks's house in Winson Green. He saw Ron's face suddenly, his black-toothed grin and the classroom, up close, like a picture. Thinking of that gave him feelings, so he got up and ran down the corridor and jumped out into firelight.

'Where's the fire?' Bob asked, then laughed his wheezing laugh. 'Blimey – look at them.' His gaze took in Joey's enormous trousers. 'Sure they're big enough for yer?' When Joey just stared, he said, 'It was only a joke, chum. Ain't you got big eyes, an' all? Like saucers, they are.'

They ate eggs, bread and potatoes and waited an age for the water to boil for tea. Bob had a billycan, which sat well on the fire. Joey saw John staring at it. Bob drank from a bottle of something and passed it to John. The nights were getting cold and Joey pulled the scratchy brown coat round him. Bob tried asking John questions, but didn't get anywhere until he mentioned that he'd been on the dole and sent to one of the camps to work, which set John off again about the camp in Brechfa, in Wales. Bob was just as scathing about it.

'The Labour Exchange made us sit through some bleeding picture about going there and what a cushy time we was going to have. *On the Way to Work*, it was called. Right bloody laugh. I ended up digging with a load of blokes – the underground. End of the Piccadilly line. Stuck it for a couple of weeks and I threw my pick down and I was off. Bugger that. I thought I'd be better off on the road – and I have been. Reckon it's three years now. Got everything I need, I have. Don't need nobody, me. How long you been on the tramp?'

'Just lately.'

'Been in the spikes?'

John shook his head. 'Not going in them.'

'Some of them're not bad. The Sally Ann – alleluia stew and all – better on me own, though, if I can. Some nights though, I've been in a spike or two.'

Joey knew John had a horror of the hostels, all of which he regarded as workhouses, offering a roof for the night for work in the morning. He remembered John saying to Christie once, 'I ent never going in one of them places. They took me mother in one and she never come out.'

'You want to get kitted up better if you're staying on the road in the winter,' Bob said. 'Need a reefer, mate – that jacket of yours'll let the cold in. Get some bacon fat on your boots – keep 'em supple . . .'

Joey was beginning to shiver as the two men talked on. The moon was rising. It was almost full, and its light poured down so he could see the railway track and the pewter-coloured fields stretching to their left. He went inside and fell asleep in the third compartment. Next thing he knew, John was shaking him awake again.

'Don't make a noise, right? Out of 'ere – now.'

Bob was asleep in the second compartment, snoring gently.

John's whiskery lips came close to Joey's ear. 'Go and get his stuff – that billy of his.'

Joey crept in, stepping round the man's body. But as he bent over to pick up the billycan, Bob Barron leapt up in a second and was on him. Bob didn't say a word, but Joey felt himself caught in two immensely strong arms, one round his neck, pulling tighter so he was soon fighting for breath. He struggled frantically, hearing himself gag as the man's forearm gripped his throat. In those seconds he became aware that John was there in the darkness with them, and there were thudding sounds, blows behind him and a grunt, and at last the arm loosed round his throat. Joey pulled away and heard the man slump down behind him, unconscious from John's blow. They took Bob's things: billycan, matches and the rest of the bread, and put them all in the curtain. A few moments later they were up the bank and away across the fields.

Forty-Five

Summer turned to autumn. Village after village across Spain fell to the nationalists. General Franco was now commander-in-chief of the nationalist forces, and the republicans were having to defend themselves mostly with pitchforks and a few old shotguns and blunder-busses. Neighbour turned against neighbour and groups of civilians were rounded up and shot.

The last evening before Daniel left for the valleys, Gwen had a few snatched hours with him in Ariadne's house. A few days before, on 2 October, there had been a big rally in the Town Hall for Spanish Aid organized by the Communist Party, the BCPL and the Labour Movement. Ellen Wilkinson, the MP for Jarrow, came to speak and there was a torchlight procession through the centre of Birmingham. Gwen marched beside Daniel, following the dancing train of lights through the streets. Esther was, as ever, nearby, but Gwen had got past worrying about her now. She knew Daniel loved her and her alone. He had shown her time after time. What did Esther matter?

'This should do us well!' Daniel's eyes were alight with enthusiasm as he looked at all the people and banners around them in the evening streets. By the end of the rally, to the excitement of the organizers, they had raised £120 for Spain.

Gwen knew Daniel was torn in two, never sure

where best to put his energy – in Birmingham for the Spanish cause, or in Wales. He had waited until after the rally – then he was going to leave for Aberglyn, where she was to join him at the weekend.

That night they were sitting on her bed, against the wall, arms round each other. The news from Spain was grim.

'They're killing people for not going to Mass,' Daniel said. He had one of her hands in his and his grip tightened on it sometimes to emphasize what he was saying. 'And for reading philosophers like Kant and Rousseau – or criticizing Hitler or Mussolini.'

'Well, of course they're going to criticize Hitler and Mussolini!' Gwen said heatedly. 'What do they expect?'

She could see how deeply the situation affected Daniel. Apart from his political views, Daniel had relatives on his father's side in Spain. She held him tightly, thinking that she didn't know anything about Kant or Rousseau or why the nationalists should get so agitated about anyone reading them. A few months ago she would have felt ashamed and inadequate about this and about the level of her own commitment to the revolution. She had begun to sense, though, that there was something about her very ignorance that Daniel needed: she provided him with a way out from the intensity of the struggle, another viewpoint, a refuge perhaps.

Though they had to snatch these times together, it seemed to Gwen that she and Daniel had never been closer. She felt borne up by love, humming with feeling for him, with a sense of passion and completeness which gave her almost endless energy. She was loving her work and one or two of the other teachers commented on how radiant she was looking. On Saturdays she went out with other party members selling the *Spain* leaflets and the *Daily Worker*. Ariadne not only allowed Daniel to be in Gwen's room but seemed to applaud it, and anything else that kept Gwen happy and in her house. Miss Hines had finally left, fed up with Ariadne's cooking and her endless criticism, so for the moment Gwen was the only lodger. Ariadne thought Daniel was 'a beautiful specimen of a man', and seemed to take pleasure in having the lovers in the house. So on their few evenings together they could relish each other's company, talk and make love and lie, warm and tired, in each other's arms.

Gwen only just made it to the station to wave Daniel off when school was over for the day. She tore from the tram stop through a downpour of rain and saw him waiting by the clock, where they had arranged, his jacket wet with rain, canvas bag thrown over one shoulder.

'I thought I'd missed you!' She flung her arms round him, face flushed, panting from running.

'Hello, comrade!' He laughed at her flustered state.

'I want to come with you now!'

He pulled her close and she could feel the beat of his heart. 'Only a few days. Billy'll be waiting to see you too.' He nuzzled her face. 'I think he's got a bit of a crush on you!'

'Poor Billy – he's such a nice boy. Will you come and meet me when I get there?'

'Course I will.' He hugged her. 'I'd better go.'

She saw him off, keeping the image of his face smiling from the window in her mind as she made her way back to Handsworth, thinking: *only four days and we can be together again.* How slowly those four days were going to pass!

Instead of spending her days longing only to be with Daniel, Gwen found that when she got back to school there was an unexpected distraction.

On the Wednesday morning, Ron Parks was late coming into the classroom. He missed the register.

'Ron? He must be poorly.'

Gwen was about to mark him down as absent, when one of the other boys said, 'No – he's here, Miss. I seen him.'

Gwen frowned. It wasn't like Ron to be late. He was still not there by the end of the register, so she left the space blank and began the lesson. They were learning about the life cycle of the butterfly. She was just trying to explain how a butterfly hatches from a chrysalis when Ron came in.

'Where have *you* been?' she was asking rather sharply, when she turned and caught sight of his face. Ron's cheerful, slightly eccentric demeanour had entirely gone and instead she saw a stony expression, as if he was struggling to control some deeply felt emotion. He also looked as if he had been crying.

'Are you all right? Has anything happened?'

'No, Miss Purdy.' His voice was subdued, and mutinous. Gwen stared at him perplexed, and saw him take his seat very gingerly, in the pained way the children did when they had had a thrashing from Mr Lowry, though nothing had happened at assembly. Realizing that the whole class was staring at Ron too and that his face had gone a deep, painful red, she said, 'Eyes to the

475

front all of you – get on with your work.' She would get to the bottom of this later.

When the bell rang for break, she asked Ron to stay behind and he came cautiously up to her desk. Some of the others hung around curiously and Gwen shooed them away and closed the door. When she sat down at her desk, Ron just stood there, staring at the floor, whether in anger or shame she could not decide.

'This isn't like you, Ron.'

There was no reply.

'Will you look at me when I'm speaking to you, please?'

He raised his face to her and she could see his lips were quivering. His second teeth had come through and they made him look different, more serious.

'Why were you late this morning?'

'Because he gave me the cane!' Ron blurted, and Gwen could tell that he felt a terrible injustice had been carried out.

'Who – Mr Lowry?' Seeing him nod, she said, 'But you weren't in assembly?'

'Not in assembly – in his office.'

Gwen was silent for a moment, unsure what to say. As a teacher she should be loyal to the head of the school and not undermine his decisions. But she had great misgivings about Mr Lowry's version of punishment. Of course a lot of the children needed a telling off, maybe a slight taste of the cane if necessary. She had even done it herself, reluctantly, once or twice – a couple of strokes with a ruler on the hand perhaps – but not the sort of hard and humiliating treatment the headmaster meted out in front of the whole school. And what might he be like in the privacy of his office?

'Why did he do that, Ron?'

Again, Ron did not seem able to look her in the eye. He appeared to be really distressed. 'I'm not allowed to say.'

'Who told you that?'

'Mr Lowry.'

'I see.' Feeling she could hardly go against the head's wishes and ask directly, she said, 'Well, I'm sorry Mr Lowry felt he had to do that. Let's just hope that whatever it was for, it won't happen again.'

Ron was silent. Eventually, with obvious resentment, he squeezed out the words, 'Yes, Miss Purdy.'

She let him go, but throughout the day she felt troubled. Ron was obviously in pain and he was just not himself. She wondered if he would come back after the dinner break, but he did, and sat miserably through the afternoon classes.

At the end of the day, when Gwen went into the playground, Mr Lowry was standing just outside the back door of the school talking to Mr Gaffney. As she set out, Gwen caught sight of a small, dumpy woman coming in through the playground gate, hugging round her a big, brown cardigan as if she was cold. It took Gwen a moment to recognize her, but then she saw that it was Mrs Parks. She had only met Ron's mother once when she had bought sweets that day in the shop.

Mrs Parks never usually came to the school to collect her boys. She was not walking especially fast, but there was something determined, steely almost, in her manner. She put down her feet in her old flat shoes as if nothing was going to divert her from her path. Gwen said, 'Good afternoon,' as she passed her, but Mrs Parks didn't even seem to hear. Curious, Gwen turned to watch and could hardly believe her eyes when she saw what happened next. Mrs Parks made unwaveringly for Mr Lowry, brought her fist back and delivered a whacking great punch right into his face. There was a collective cry of surprise from everyone around. She gave him no time to recover before following up with another punch with the other fist, slamming it right into Mr Lowry's nose and knocking his spectacles off. Gwen gasped. The playground went suddenly quiet. Children stood staring.

'That's for what you did to my Ron,' Mrs Parks bawled. 'And don't you ever lay a finger on my boys again, you rotten bully!'

Mr Lowry was clutching at his face. His nose was bleeding. Mr Gaffney bent to pick up his specs and handed them back and Mr Lowry peered down to take them, trying to retain some dignity. He had no time to say anything, as Mrs Parks was already storming back across towards the gate, shouting back over her shoulder, 'You want to pick on someone yer own size next time! Think you can get away with doing anything you like, don't you? Bloody bullies, you teachers – that's what you are!'

And she was gone.

Gwen told Ariadne about the day's upset over a meal of lamb chops. She had started to give her landlady a hand with the cooking. Ariadne was so scatty that keeping an eye on anything was half her problem. Gwen stood guarding the chops under the grill to make sure they emerged a healthy, cooked colour rather than a singed mess.

'That sounds a queer carry-on to me,' Ariadne remarked, peering into the pan of potatoes, which was boiling so frantically that the room was already like a steam bath.

'It might be all right to turn those down now,' Gwen suggested.

'Oh . . . yes.' Ariadne fiddled with the gas stove as if she'd never seen it before, peering longsightedly at the dial. The fringe of her silky shawl hung perilously near the gas flame.

'There's certainly more to it than meets the eye. I'm going to see if I can get Ron to talk to me tomorrow.'

Once again, she called Ron to her at breaktime.

'Ron, I'm very concerned about what happened yesterday, and your mother obviously is too. Did you tell her why Mr Lowry gave you the cane?'

Ron shook his head, lips tightly pressed together.

'Why didn't you tell her?'

'Because . . .' Ron's face filled with emotion and his lips were trembling. 'He said he'd . . . he said I wasn't to say . . .' He wiped his eyes fiercely with his knuckles, smearing his grimy face. Suddenly he burst out, 'And it weren't my fault. I wish I'd never gone and seen what I seen!'

Gwen stared, at a loss.

'*Seen*? What did you see, Ron? Where?'

He gazed at her desperately and she could see he was close to telling her. But something was stopping him.

'I'm not to say.' He looked away, sullenly. 'Or I'll be in trouble.'

'What sort of trouble?' she asked.

'He said . . . he said he'd get me sent away.'

Gwen was horrified. What sort of a man was Mr Lowry to be making such threats to a ten-year-old boy?

'I don't think he can do that,' she tried to reassure him. 'Especially when you haven't done anything wrong.'

479

But she could see the boy was afraid and she didn't want to press him any more.

'Go on – go out to play,' she said. 'And don't fret.'

'What on earth am I to make of that?' she asked Lily Drysdale in the corner of the staffroom, where she hoped no one else could hear. 'The poor boy seems frightened out of his wits!'

Lily sat silently, a cup of tea held halfway to her lips and staring ahead of her almost as if listening to a voice that no one else could hear. Gwen began to wonder if she had heard what she said. Then Lily returned her cup to its saucer.

'Mr Lowry,' she pronounced, 'is almost certainly some kind of pervert. Though I've never managed to work out quite what kind.'

Forty-Six

They were chugging along the last few miles now, into Aberglyn.

It was dark outside the railway carriage. All Gwen could see in the window was her own reflection, her face, wide-eyed and solemn, gazing back at her, her hair tied softly back. She had taken her hat off and was holding it on her lap.

I look older, she thought. She remembered sitting on a train in just this way, pulling into Worcester, knowing that Edwin would be waiting for her under the platform lights. It seemed so long ago, another life in which she had been nothing more than a child. She wondered how Edwin was. Would he be bitter, or be putting experience behind him in his usual, blithely optimistic way? She thought of her parents. Sooner or later she would have to go back, to try and make peace. It was a dreadful thought and she pushed it away, pressing her face to the window to see something of the outside, but apart from occasional dots of light from houses and villages, there was nothing but the night. Sitting back, she closed her eyes for a moment. The air in the carriage smelled of smoke and dusty upholstery.

I'm someone else now. She swelled inside with joy. Daniel's girl. That's what the party members had finally started to call her, seeing them together. Apart from

Esther, of course, who treated Gwen in relation to Daniel with an arch irony. Gwen ignored her. She had also chosen to put out of her mind the conversation she had overheard last time she was in Aberglyn. It couldn't have meant anything much. And everyone did wrong things when they were young – herself for a start! She had jilted Edwin, more or less – she was a disgrace to her family! She and Daniel were both people who lived passionately, she decided, and were having to learn from their mistakes. That was why they were so well suited. They were Communists, revolutionaries: there was more to their lives than petty jealousies.

The train began to lose speed. They were pulling into Aberglyn and he would be there. In a few moments she would be in his arms!

As she stepped out of the carriage onto the darkened station, the train let out a great belch of steam, like a sigh of relief. There were not many people on the platform and she looked around, smiling in anticipation. She could not immediately see him, her eyes looking round hungrily, anticipating the sight of Daniel's beloved body, which she felt she knew as well as her own. But he did not appear. She stood by the little ticket office, keeping her lips turned up, trying not to feel deflated. He'd be here in a moment – he had said he would be. But the minutes passed.

'Gwen?' She turned to see a woman beside her, hair tucked under a little felt hat, and it took a moment to register that it was Shân Sullivan.

'Oh, hello!' After waiting alone, Gwen felt uplifted just seeing anyone she recognized. And she liked Daniel's auntie very much. In the dim lights, Shân looked pale and painfully thin.

'I came to meet you, Gwen *fach*. Daniel was coming, but he and his uncle have gone and got themselves tied up in a compo case . . .'

'A what?'

'Oh, it's over compensation for injury, like with Billy.' Shân sounded weary to her bones. 'There's another lad lost the use of his legs . . .'

'Oh, I see.' Gwen pushed away her feelings of disappointment. Of course a young man being crippled was more important than her. How could she argue with that? And, anyway, it was lovely to see Shân.

They began walking the two miles up from the station. Gwen couldn't help feeling cross with Daniel that his auntie had had to come all this way in her frail state.

'I could have come on my own,' she said. 'No need to drag you out.'

'Oh *duw*, no! There's a terrible thing, leaving you to walk on your own. Billy wanted to come and meet you as well, Gwen, but I hadn't the strength to push him all the way down here and back, so he's sitting stewing at home. He's been like a cat on hot bricks all day. You've been very good to him, girl, sending him the books and that.'

Gwen smiled in the dark street. She heard singing coming out of a little church on one corner. 'Oh, it's just something to keep him occupied. He seems to love reading so much.'

'Proper one for book reading, Billy is. Always has been, but of course since the accident it's meant everything to him.'

Gwen's arm was aching from carrying her case, but she tried not to show her discomfort. She asked after the rest of the family and Shân said Anthony was

483

spending every waking moment at the NUWM offices making arrangements for the march, which was only two weeks away.

Daniel's absence was almost made up for by the radiant look of excitement on Billy's face as they came in through the door. He was in his wheelchair, a piece of blanket over his knees, which he snatched off impatiently as they came in.

'You're here – finally! Took you all evening to walk up the hill, did it!'

'Well, I'm an old lady now, you know that,' Shân retorted, going into the kitchen. 'I've made us a bit to eat – you settle in and talk to Billy, or he'll never forgive me!'

Even while Gwen was taking her coat off, Billy was already launching off enthusiastically about *Les Misérables*, what a fantastic story it was and how on earth had Victor Hugo managed to write such a *lot* and the chase at the end through Paris was so exciting! He said it was the best book he'd ever read and he was going to start at the beginning and read it all over again.

Gwen sat down beside him, laughing at his enthusiasm.

'Well, I'm glad you liked it so much! I'm having to guess what would be best out of what I can find.'

'Well, you found the best book ever written. Have you read it?'

She had to admit she hadn't.

'Oh, well, you read it! I've read lots of adventure stories and that – and Jack London's been one of my favourites, but I've never read anything like that before.'

'And I've never met anyone who loves reading so much.'

484

'Well, it takes you out of yourself, doesn't it? Sitting here all day – you know . . .' He looked crestfallen for a moment, but then smiled. 'Hope you don't mind me writing to you?'

'Mind? Of course I don't mind. It's lovely – and your letters are so nice to read. You've got quite a way with words, Billy.'

Billy looked so pleased when she said this that Gwen wondered whether to say more, to suggest that perhaps he might want to write other things, but she decided to wait. After all, she'd only just got in through the door.

They chatted as Shân heated the food. Gwen told Billy about her class, about how Lucy was getting on, and Billy laughed at some of her stories. She didn't tell him about Ron Parks. By the end of the week she had still not got to the bottom of what had happened to Ron.

'Those men won't be back yet,' Shân said, calling them to the table. 'We'll eat ours, or there's curling up with hunger we'll be before they decide to come home.'

Gwen pushed Billy's chair into the kitchen.

'Daniel's an idiot,' Billy said, as she walked behind the chair. 'I mean, I know the party's vital, and the march and everything – but if I had you here for me the way he has, I wouldn't be at any meeting tonight, I can tell you!'

Gwen felt a lump rise up in her throat for a moment, both for Billy's predicament and for herself. She liked being with Shân and Billy, though. It always felt cosy in the steamy little kitchen. She tried to relax, not to imagine each sound, every footfall, was Daniel and his uncle coming back.

'I hardly see Anthony these days,' Shân said. 'If it's

485

not problems with the dole or compo claims, it's the march ... I know they've got to do it, but I'll still be glad when it's over. Is anyone ever listening in the government? – That's what I want to know.'

'Now they've got the unemployment figures down in England they don't care two hoots about us here,' Billy said. 'You have to show them – *force* them to listen!'

Hearing the passion in his voice, Gwen immediately felt proud of Daniel again and all he was doing. After all, he could have gone to Birmingham and just looked out for himself. Instead, he was putting all his energy into his people and where he came from.

It was after eleven when the men came home at last. Daniel's eyes met hers as they came in and she beamed at him.

'Got here all right?' He came straight over and kissed her cheek. 'Sorry I wasn't at the station.'

'Not to worry.' She smiled, free of resentment now.

Before she went up to bed, Daniel came to speak to her in the little hall. Conscious of the others next door, they held each other close and he whispered into her neck, 'I'm going to have to be at a few meetings tomorrow.'

She had half expected this. 'It's all right.' She knew she had barely managed to sound as if that was true.

Daniel drew back and peered at her in the gloom. 'It's such a busy time. So much to do.'

'I know.' She hugged him tight. 'And they need you.'

'On Sunday we'll have time – we'll go out some- where, start early.'

Her spirits rose. 'Promise?'

He kissed her. 'Course I promise!'

He won her round. He always seemed to be able to.

'Do you think Billy would like it if I took him out today?' Gwen whispered the question to Shân in the kitchen, out of earshot of Billy.

It was a brilliant, autumn morning. Daniel would be off and away. Why shouldn't she and Billy enjoy the day?

Shân looked doubtful for a moment, then smiled. 'Have you got the strength in you, girl? That boyo's heavier than he looks.'

'Of course – I'm sure I could manage, if you think it'd be all right?'

'Oh – he'd love you to, I know he would!' Shân looked wistful. 'He doesn't get out enough. To the odd meeting, or when his father's got the time. He'd be ever so pleased if you took him – for a little while, mind. Don't you go overdoing it.'

After breakfast, and when Gwen had kept tactfully out of the way while Shân saw to Billy's physical needs and helped him dress, they eased his wheelchair out through the door, and Gwen and Billy set out into the golden morning.

'Where would you like to go – up the hill?' She leaned down to talk to him and was suddenly uncomfortably aware of a blush rising in his cheeks. It only then occurred to her how much of an effect her physical presence had on Billy.

I must be careful, she thought, standing up again. She felt ashamed suddenly, realizing that it had never crossed her mind to think of Billy in that way, that he might be interested in her, because he was younger and because – it was an awful admission – he had been maimed, and seemed stripped of his manhood by his injuries. She had assumed somewhere in her mind that he was not whole as a man, that his body was numb, without a man's feelings. Now she was not sure and felt suddenly confused.

She leaned hard against the wheelchair, pushing Billy up the slope she had climbed with Daniel on that summer morning. There were a few crisp, brown leaves on the pavement, crackling underfoot. The air was full of the ripe smells of autumn: leaves and smoke and a hint of decay, sunlight pouring in at a low angle which seemed to make everything glow, the bracken a deep rust colour on the sides of the hills. Gwen pushed the chair on and on determinedly. The road curved round and, branching off it, she saw a steep track to the right. They had left the houses behind and were climbing steeply so that she had to lean all her weight into pushing the chair. The air was chill, but she was soon sweating with exertion.

'Shall we go on up there a little way?' she asked, trying not to let Billy hear how much she was beginning to pant.

'No – it's too much for you!' He sounded anxious and she wondered if he felt safe in her hands.

'I really think I could – just some of the way.'

'You can see a long way from up there,' he said and she could hear the longing in his voice.

'Well, we'll do it!'

Bracing herself, her chest level with the back of the chair, she heaved against it and slowly inched Billy up and up the steep incline. Once her foot slipped on a little stone; she almost lost her balance and let out a cry of alarm.

'What's the matter?' Billy tried to look round.

'Nothing – it's all right.'

After a time, there was a level resting place off the track. To one side was a rock, flattened on top to serve as a seat, and she pushed the chair over to it so that she could sit down beside Billy. They sat in silence for a few moments, each drinking in the great expanse of the green valley, smudged in parts with black, the little town nestled in its palm. The sound of a train whistle rose from the town, made soft by the distance and the gentle wind.

Gwen then became aware of Billy beside her, of the way his grey eyes were looking along the sweep of the valley with deep, almost meditative attention. She had been about to speak, but she sensed she might be interrupting his thought processes. His head was turned slightly away from her. Gradually, he looked back towards her again.

'The hills are so close – they seem to have a personality of their own,' she said.

'They do. They've all got names.' He pointed around the valley, telling her the names of the rusty peaks. Then he breathed in deeply, as if drinking the air. 'I've never lived anywhere but here.'

She nodded, understanding that the elevation of their position gave him a perspective on his home he rarely had, and of sensing the wider world beyond and all he might be missing.

'It's a good place,' she told him.

'It is.' He nodded emphatically, then laughed. 'Though I don't know anywhere else to put against it. Good people here, they are.'

'Daniel's always talking about it.'

'Is he?' He didn't follow this up, but just kept looking. 'I only know about anywhere else from book reading. You can go anywhere in a book, the way you can in a dream.'

'Billy, I've really enjoyed your letters.' She hesitated, and he turned to her with a candid, vulnerable gaze, and she saw, to her discomfort, in that moment the power of his feelings for her. It made her feel sad, flattered and uncomfortable all at once. She looked down in confusion, trying to hold on to what she had been going to say. 'It's just – well, the way you write – you've got a talent, you know. Describing things, bringing them alive. I wondered if you'd thought about writing other things, not just letters.'

'I do.' He was the one blushing now, with shy pleasure. 'Least, I've done a bit – a few stories and that. Don't know why. Something to do, I s'pose. No one'd want to read them.'

'I'd like to.'

There was a pause.

'I've never shown them to anyone – not even Mam.'

'Well, only if you want to . . .'

'Oh, I'd like to know if anyone – well, if they . . . If anyone else can read them and understand about them. D'you know what I mean?'

'I think so.'

'I keep them in a box. Under the bed.'

'Doesn't your mother ask what's in there?'

'Oh yes, but she's not much of a reader. She just calls it my scribbling. She doesn't want to read them.'

Gwen looked out over the valley to the mountain beyond. Clouds were beginning to gather.

'What about Daniel?' she asked. 'You've never thought of showing them to him?'

'No. Daniel's so clever with his book learning. I thought he'd laugh at me.'

'Surely he wouldn't.'

There was a silence, then, in a different tone, casual but solemn, Billy said, 'Daniel's not always straight with everyone, you know.'

A cold feeling gripped her. This warning that kept coming. She found she was angry. 'What d'you mean?' She heard the hostility in her own voice, but why was everyone trying to sow seeds of doubt in her mind about Daniel?

Billy looked into his lap. She could see him trying to decide what to say. 'I just mean I haven't felt like showing him my stories.'

Once she had pushed Billy back to the house, they had a bit of dinner with Shân and afterwards Shân went out to visit a neighbour at Gwen's urging.

'I'm so pleased Billy's got a bit of company,' she whispered to Gwen in the hall before she went.

Once she'd gone, Billy pulled a rough wooden box out from under the bed and showed Gwen some of his stories.

'You've done a lot!' she exclaimed, seeing him pull out a thick collection of dog-eared papers.

'You don't have to read them all.' He was excited. 'Look, take a couple. Will you?'

'Of course. I'd really like to.'

He handed her a sheaf of paper. All the stories were written on small sheets of cheap lined paper which had yellowed, in a tiny copperplate hand, as if he was trying to fit the maximum possible number of words on a page. The top one was called 'King of the Clouds'. As soon as she began reading, Gwen realized the story was about a boy who longed to fly aeroplanes. She looked up, smiling at him.

'I've always wanted to fly an aeroplane. Like Amy Johnson.'

Billy grinned, delighted. 'Proper heroine she is.'

He sat looking through his other papers while Gwen sat by the fire and read, sometimes having to stop and ask him to decipher a word for her. The story was quite simple, about a boy who dreams of flying and becomes a pilot, with his own plane. Something about the way it was written, though, drew her on. There was an intensity in the story which moved her. As she finished it, she kept her eyes lowered while she thought what to say. She could feel Billy watching her and his powerful need to know what she thought. She looked up into his hungry face.

'It's lovely, Billy. You could be a writer.'

And she could see she had said something which meant the world to him.

Forty-Seven

The next morning Gwen went with the family to early Mass in Aberglyn's small Catholic church. Anthony pushed Billy down the hill, well wrapped up as the morning was cold and wet. It all seemed very foreign to Gwen, the women's heads covered with lace or scarves and everything in Latin. When they came out into the narrow, grey street, amid the little knot of people, it was into bright, stormy sunlight which made them screw up their eyes.

'Still want to go walking?' Daniel teased. They had talked about going out after he got back the evening before.

'I've got my coat and hat – and my boots.'

'Welsh rain is wetter than English rain, you know,' Anthony teased.

Gwen laughed. 'I suppose I'll just have to get wet then!'

'You going over the mountain?' Shân asked. Her thin face was framed by a flowery scarf.

'We'll go to Tredegar,' Daniel said. 'It's a good walk.'

'You don't want to go tiring her out – she's got all that way to go back.'

'I don't mind,' Gwen said eagerly. 'I love walking.'

Daniel had, for once, put his greatcoat on and they set off for the head of the valley, then branched off on

493

one of the steep paths over the mountain. To begin with, there was brilliant sunshine, but very soon, in the distance, clouds gathered like thick smoke over the mountains and moved towards them.

'Oh dear,' Gwen panted. 'We're in for it in a minute.'

'No doubt about that.'

Daniel seemed oblivious to the weather. When the rain started to come down, it was as if they were wrapped in water. Gwen laughed, as rivulets poured from her hat and down her neck.

'We're going to be soaked!' she shouted. Her lungs were straining. They were climbing steeply, barely able to see anything beyond a few yards all around.

'Never mind. The sun'll be back soon,' Daniel called to her. Suddenly he stopped and took her in his arms, kissing her fiercely, and the rain fell on her upturned face and ran down her neck. She broke away, gasping for breath and laughing.

'It's gone right inside my clothes – I'm soaked!'

By the time they reached the highest point, the rain was easing off. Gwen felt all-over warm and damp, clothes heavy and chafing, but there was a glory in reaching the top with the sun breaking through and everything wet and gleaming.

'Look now.' Daniel came and put an arm round her shoulders. 'There's Tredegar. Back there.' He pointed down at Aberglyn, from where they had just climbed. 'I was forever walking up and down across here at one time.' He stood, looking for a moment across the Sirhowy Valley. 'First deep pit in Wales was sunk here.'

The two towns below them looked small and defenceless with their straight little rows of houses. She felt a great rush of affection for them, of belonging.

With the sunlight and the mountain breeze on her face, the valleys spread out on either side, she was filled with certainty that she had been brought here for a reason. She saw her life spread in front of her: she would marry Daniel and he would come back to his home where he belonged and she would come to belong too. She would be part of this place, and have Daniel's children, even learn Welsh. It felt so right and meant for her. She turned and held him close.

'I love it here, Daniel. I love you.'

'Love you too, girl.'

She hoped he might say something more, that perhaps his thoughts had been the same as hers, that he might even make some promise for the future, but he was silent, just held her close.

After a time, Daniel said, 'All these valleys – there'll be men coming on the march . . .'

Gwen broke from him, stung, and walked a few paces away. She had imagined his thoughts might be running on similar lines to hers, but, as so often, she was wrong. Daniel was thinking about politics, as usual! *Can't you think about anything else, just for a moment?* she wanted to shout at him. *What about me? Don't you ever think about me and our future?* But then she thought of his tears over his mother and the lockouts, the poor pinched faces of the valleys, and she was ashamed. How selfish she was being again, when Daniel was always thinking about other people.

She went back to him and took his arm. 'They've got to make the government listen,' she said. 'And you *will*, all of you.'

'Everyone should listen.' His voice was low, passionate. 'The whole world.'

She watched his face as he looked out across the

landscape and for a moment she felt afraid for him. Would the world listen to the message of Communism? Were they even listening now?

'Shall we go on?' she said.

It was easier to talk on the way down since they were not so short of breath and the sun stayed with them. Daniel told her how he used to be back and forth over here to the library in Tredegar.

'One of the best socialist libraries anywhere. I was in the Socialist League here before I joined the party. Aneurin Bevan's family are all here – he was elected MP for Ebbw Vale in twenty-nine. Marvellous, it was. Talks on Marxism, philosophers – as good as any university, I'd say. Plato, Hegel, Kant – we had a genius of a man called Oliver Jones, gave us classes. It all started to make sense, fit together – all the injustices, what they'd done to us . . .' He held his hand out to help Gwen down from a rocky step in the path. 'Nothing was ever the same again. It's genius. And yet even here not everyone could see – wanted to appease the colliery owners, keep their jobs at any cost . . .'

'Like Hywel Jones?'

Daniel shook his head. 'Men like Hywel will never change anything,' he said bitterly.

The descent went quickly and soon they were walking through the narrow streets of Tredegar. The streets were quiet, except for a few people sitting outside their houses in the sun who nodded a greeting. The bright warmth stayed and Gwen was filled with a great sense of wellbeing after the exercise. Daniel lit a cigarette and showed her round: the library where he had spent so many hours, the NUWM offices, the square with its tall clock tower, which said that it was almost eleven o'clock. As they walked on, arm in arm, people started to come out of one of the chapels along the street in front of them.

'It's such a shame we don't have longer,' Gwen said. She had to catch a train in the afternoon and it felt like a pressure.

'Quick run up and down the mountain for you again,' Daniel teased, throwing down the butt of his cigarette. 'Good for you, that is.'

'I wish I could stay. It's gone far too quickly!'

'I'm no company. I'll be at meetings all the week, with the committee and that.'

'I know. And there's a class waiting for me.'

They crossed the street so as not to get tangled in the knot of people outside the chapel. Someone called, 'Morning, Daniel mun!'

'Hello, Albert – see you tomorrow!' Daniel raised a hand in reply as they walked on along the street. He exchanged greetings with a few other people, and was just saying, 'He's a good bloke,' about someone he had spoken to, when another voice called him from behind.

'Daniel? Daniel Fernandez?'

The voice was shrill and furiously challenging. They both spun round to see a dark-haired young woman, slim and in a pretty though shabby pink dress. On her hip she carried a little boy.

'So – deigned to come back here again, have you?' she demanded. Gwen could see she was quivering with such emotions that she could barely contain them.

'Couldn't come back when you were needed could you? Not to fulfil your responsibilities? You're a rotten, wicked man, Daniel – making your own son into a bastard. Going off without a hint of care for me – for us . . .'

Gwen was struggling to take in what the young

woman was saying. She could see that her taut demeanor was giving way to tears, however much she didn't want it to. There was obviously a great reservoir of pent-up emotion waiting to be released in her, even though she didn't want to lose her dignity. She didn't seem to care who heard her.

'Megan . . .' Daniel breathed.

'That's right – just stand there, nothing to say!' The woman turned to Gwen in a combination of fury and apparently looking for an ally. 'Are you the latest one, then? Well, all I can say is, I pity you, lovey. Don't believe a word he says – he's a cheat and a liar. Left me to bring up his son all alone without a word, ever. This is Evan, Daniel. He's nearly two years old now, and he's your son, remember?' She went as if to thrust the child into Daniel's arms, but then snatched him back, hugging him protectively to her. 'Not that you care . . .'

'I didn't know—' Daniel started to say. A couple of people had stopped to listen, tutting loudly.

'You didn't *know*? Course you knew! I came to Aberglyn looking for you, but no, you were never there, were you – always off somewhere else with your politics and your superior ways. You make me sick, Daniel. What about my letters? Didn't you get those either? What did you expect – for me to come to Birmingham chasing after you to make you see what you'd left behind? I didn't have any money, remember! Nothing but my drunken da and Auntie Beth. And not *once* – not one answer, or word, not one penny to help . . .' She was weeping now, angry with herself, Gwen could see, but unable to help it.

'You could have written back! What did you say those things to me for, Daniel? That's what I can't forgive you for. Why did you say you loved me and then treat me like that? Always politics, never people, that's you, Daniel. You're a cold, cruel man.'

A great chill went through Gwen. She was stunned, barely able to take in what was happening in front of her: the harsh words which, deep down, when she admitted it to herself, rang so true, the beautiful, brown-eyed boy who was so obviously related to Daniel. She stood paralysed, wishing with every fibre in herself that this was not happening, that she was dreaming.

'I couldn't,' Daniel was saying. His voice was neither apologetic nor defiant, just flat, as if his nature was an inevitability which he could only accept but not defeat. 'I couldn't just come back here and marry you, settle down in the valleys, Megan.'

The woman shook her head, more tears coming. The little boy was beginning to be upset too by his mother's emotion.

'I hate you, Daniel,' she wept. 'I love Evan, but I hate you. You've ruined my life. I was going to get away from here too – you know I was. And now I'll never be anything but the shame of Treherbert with the bastard child. D'you know why I'm here? With Auntie Beth again now she's had yet another baby, that's why. Good old Megan – she'll stay at home and be the skivvy. She'll come and nurse her auntie when no one else'll be bothered. That's why I was here in Tredegar, remember? Looking after auntie. Politics was my only way out. And *you* . . .' She looked up at him, wet cheeked, eyes searching his face as if trying to find hope, to understand. 'I loved you. And now I hate you more than anyone else alive. It's the only way I can get

499

through.' She pulled her son close so that their cheeks were touching. 'That's your father, Evan. Take a good look at him – he's everything a man shouldn't be.'

'I could send you some money,' Daniel said desperately.

'Oho – talk about better late than never! I don't want your money, Daniel.' She almost spat at him. 'It'll be cursed, like everything else that comes from you. I just want you to know what you are – what you've done. I hope you rot for it.'

She turned away then and walked off, quickly, head down to shield herself from the staring bystanders, and in a few moments they saw her, in her pink frock, disappear past the chapel and round the corner.

Forty-Eight

'I can see something's upsetting you, Gwen *fach*. Is it anything you want to tell your Auntie Shân?'

Gwen could barely remember the walk back over the mountain, the having to be polite back with the family in Aberglyn, trying to eat thin stew and potatoes with them round the table. She could see, though, that the fact that she could barely swallow, or meet anyone's eyes for fear of bursting into tears, and the silence between herself and Daniel were not lost on Shân. After dinner, when they had moved from the kitchen to the front room to sit by the fire, and Shân was boiling the kettle for a cup of tea, she put her head round the door. 'There's a little bit of help I'm needing, Gwen. Can you come in here a minute?'

Once she was in the kitchen, Shân closed the door firmly behind them and spoke very softly. 'You haven't been yourself since you came back today.'

Touched by the woman's kindness, Gwen felt her eyes fill with tears again. She had cried on the walk home, trying to get Daniel to talk to her, to explain. All he seemed able to say was that he couldn't help it, hadn't meant to hurt her. But staying in the valleys, marriage and children – it seemed like a living death to him.

'The party, the movement – that's life and hope to me,' he said. 'I was only twenty-three when it

501

happened ... My life had only just begun – I couldn't just be here and be tied down. It was a mistake. It's on my conscience – course it is! And it doesn't mean I don't love *you*, Gwen. I love you more than anyone I've ever met.'

'I bet that's what you told Megan!' She suddenly remembered his great anxiety that she did not fall pregnant. No wonder! Now she saw all too clearly just how familiar a problem that was to him.

'But I didn't love her the way I love *you*,' he said pleadingly.

She was so hurt that she could not think where to begin with Daniel's aunt. In the end she just blurted out, 'Did you know?'

'Know what, lovey?' Shân asked cautiously.

'About Megan? About the child – *Daniel's son?*' Tears ran down her cheeks and she put her hands over her face. The pain of it seemed enough to overwhelm her. She felt Shân's thin arms round her shoulders.

'Oh, my poor girl, oh dear, oh dear, So that's what's happened. Oh Lord, I knew she'd come back to haunt him one day.'

Gwen looked up at her. 'You *did* know?' The hushed conversation that night – of course she had known. 'Why didn't you tell me?'

Shân looked stricken. 'How could I? I'd only met the girl twice. She was staying in Tredegar, going to the League meetings there and that's how they met, but he never brought her back here. I think she was staying with an auntie, a strict young woman from what I hear of her. Megan Hughes is not from a good family – lots of trouble. I never knew Daniel was so involved with her then. Not until later. The family'd just left, see, Theresa and the rest, gone to Birmingham. Daniel wasn't coming back much at first – couldn't afford it. He even walked once, all the way. Come the time Megan knew she was expecting, she came here, trying it on, telling me she was carrying Daniel's baby. I mean, at first I wouldn't believe her. How did I know if she was lying? But she kept on – course, she was upset, see. In the end, I thought, well, Daniel knows the truth of the matter, whatever it is, so I gave her the address in Birmingham. I've asked him about it so many times. He wouldn't see her. Said what's done is done.' She shook her head, looking at the ceiling for a moment, as if in despair.

'She's not from round here, see, she's from the Rhondda. Once she'd gone back there and expecting a child, I suppose she wasn't in a position to keep running off trying to find him. After a time we all thought, let sleeping dogs lie. I don't think she kept on writing – she must have given up, poor girl. So you see –' she looked into Gwen's desperate face – 'that's our Daniel, I'm afraid. God knows I'm ashamed of him for this. I've told and told him he should face up to his responsibilities ... And then he came here with you, and you're lovely, girl, and I could see how he is with you, and what could I do? You're so good for him, Gwen, and how could I just destroy all that for you by bringing her up again? You must believe me – I've never seen Daniel be with anyone the way he is with you.'

Gwen started crying again. It was all impossible, the pain, the enormity of it. Looking up desperately into Shân's worn face, she said, 'But I can't be with someone who would deceive me like this! How could I ever, *ever* trust him again?'

As she was speaking the door opened and the two women realized that Daniel was standing looking at

503

them. His face was filled with shame, and a sadness which wrung Gwen's heart. But in that moment she knew, really knew for sure, with a cold sense of reality. This was how it would always be, that he could hurt her so much then melt her with a look. She would come back again and again to burn herself against him, hoping it was safe, that she could love him and know deep, lasting trust – and that somehow, in one way or another, whether it was with women or politics, he would always let her down. Some women could live with it, but she knew she couldn't.

She drew away from Shân and went to him. She stood looking into his eyes, seeing that he was anguished, and sorry, but it was no good. He had betrayed her too badly this time.

'I'm going home, Daniel. I'm sorry. I love you too much and I can't live with what you might do to me.' She started to walk away. 'I don' t think I want to see you again.'

The train journey home was a blur. It rained much of the way so vision was limited, and along the way, after the extreme emotions of the day, Gwen shut down and sat numb and stunned. Parting with Shân, Anthony and Billy had been terrible. They already felt like family to her, but how could she ever see them again after this?

'Keep writing to me, won't you?' Billy asked, looking in a troubled way at her tear-stained face. And she could only promise that she would.

Shân embraced her silently and Anthony shook her hand and gruffly wished her well.

'I'm sorry, girl,' he said gruffly. 'Don't know what to say.' And this made her cry all over again.

Daniel accompanied her to the station and most of the way they walked through the drizzle in a cold, sad silence.

When they reached the station, Daniel stopped her outside. 'I can't let you go.' His voice was anguished. 'I've made a terrible mistake, I know, but I've learned my lesson. I'd never leave you, Gwen. I love you too much.'

She closed her feelings against this and looked up at him. 'As much as politics – the party? No, Daniel, I don't think you do. I've seen it, all the way along, although I've tried not to. I wanted to believe you could really love me and put me first in the line sometimes, but you can't. And I've seen you playing about with Esther. That was bad enough, but I tried to forgive you. But now this. You've got a *son*, Daniel, and you just walked away! I can't stay with you if I can't trust you. I can't keep giving you my heart and having you tear me to pieces.' She was dry eyed now, with a stony calm.

He looked down at her, and in that second's silence she saw that he knew she was right.

'I do love you.' He reached out to stroke her face but she pulled back.

'Don't, Daniel, please.'

Suddenly she couldn't bear it any more, being near him, even now the pain of being drawn back to him. She said an abrupt goodbye and walked away from him fast. She did not turn back, did not want to see if he left immediately or waited to watch her move out of his life.

She did not tell Ariadne what had happened. The next few days she taught her class in a stunned,

505

automatic way, dressing herself in her role as teacher every morning and going through the motions. Seeing Lucy every morning in front of her brought home just how many connections she had made with Daniel's family, how she had come to love them. Breaking with Daniel was not going to be so simple. She couldn't abandon Lucy and Billy just because of what Daniel had done, could she? And what about the party? How could she bear to do anything connected with that now? She found it hard to pay attention to anything at school. What had happened to Ron Parks, for the moment, escaped her attention. The evenings she spent miserably in her room. Ariadne kept asking if she was sickening for something and Gwen told her she did not feel quite well. Somehow she could not face up to talking about Daniel to anyone yet.

Lying on her bed a couple of evenings after she had come back from Aberglyn, her mood sank very low. Everything she had wanted to do in coming away from home seemed to be cast into doubt. Look at what she had done! She had thrown away everything because of her love for Daniel: marriage to a good, decent man, her own family's approval and welcome, her own happiness and security. Here she was, in a room in a strange household, teaching the children of the poor. What was her life going to be now? More of the same, stretching ahead for ever until she was like Lily Drysdale? Or Agnes Monk? She lay for a long time, staring at the light above her and wondering how it would be if she admitted defeat and begged her parents to take her back. Even begged Edwin to take her back? For a few moments she longed for the familiar, its safety and security, imagined their wedding, as they had planned it at St Mark's, her home in a vicarage, children, Edwin talking over his thoughts and sermons with her, jigsaw puzzles on a table in the parlour to put visitors at their ease.

She sat up suddenly.

'No!' she said out loud, startling herself. Her heart was beating fast. She did not want that, had never really wanted it, but had not seen that there could ever be anything else. Whereas Daniel ... Caught between what she longed for in him, the passion of it, the sense of being so fully alive in his presence and the reality that it was never going to be possible to make a life with him that she could trust, she burst into tears. Hugging her knees, she sat rocking in distress on the bed. She felt torn up, as if Daniel had physically imprinted himself on her and then been ripped away, leaving her utterly bereft.

When she got home the next afternoon, Ariadne said, 'There's a message for you, dear. Came just after you left this morning.' And she handed Gwen a hand-written envelope. The looping script was unfamiliar and she opened it frowning.

Dear Gwen,
    Millie asked me to let you know that the infant has arrived and is a female. She's doing well and is at home. Millie would like some company so do come over.
    Sincerely,
    Lance

With a wan smile she showed it to Ariadne.

'A *female*?' Ariadne exclaimed. 'Well, isn't that just like a man – and not to tell you her name!'

'Perhaps she doesn't have one yet,' Gwen said.

'Or her date of birth, or weight or where she was born!'

'Well, that's Lance for you. He's not very sharp – not at this sort of thing.' She felt slightly cheered by the distraction and was glad all had gone safely for Millie.

'I think I'll go and see them now.' The thought of sitting alone in her room again was depressing. 'I don't have anything to take her.'

'Ah – now, I might be able to help you there,' Ariadne said. And she disappeared upstairs and came back with a soft parcel wrapped in tissue. 'It's a little matinée coat – I made it for my sister's baby, years ago now. She died a few days after she was born, poor little thing, and I've never had the heart to do anything with it.'

When Millie opened the parcel, the garment was a lovely pale pink, and Millie was delighted with it. She was sitting up in bed, the room in a great state of disarray because 'Lance is hopeless', as Millie kept saying. Lance, who appeared exhausted by the experience of becoming a father, was laid out in a chair in the sitting room. The baby was a dear little thing with a film of carroty hair like Millie's, and her name was to be Amy Jane.

'That's pretty,' Gwen said, perching precariously on a chair by the bed, on top of a pile of clothes.

'She's a poppet,' Millie said, looking down at the child in her arms, whose eyes were closed, the bluish lids flickering gently as if she was dreaming.

'How was it, Mill?' Gwen felt shy asking. Millie had been through something which put her beyond, into a new kind of adulthood.

'Pretty grim.' Millie made a face. 'Never mind – it's over now. Never again, though.'

'I bet everyone says that.'

'Maybe. I mean it, though.' She lowered her voice, leaning close to Gwen. 'What am I going to do? He just doesn't want to know.' Tears were rolling down Millie's round cheeks and they fell on Amy's tiny face as Millie looked down. 'She's so lovely – how can he not want anything to do with her?'

'Oh, Mill!' Gwen put her arm round her friend's shoulders. She had a warm, milky smell. 'I'm sure he does really. He's probably a bit shocked by it all. After all, he hasn't had to carry her round inside him all this time. It's early days.'

'But he's barely even been in to look at her! And he treats me as if I'm a terrible nuisance because I need help, and I'm so tired and sore . . .' Millie broke down and really cried now. 'Oh God, why did I marry him, Gwen? I wish I'd never set eyes on him! How am I going to bring up our little girl with him? I feel so hopeless – I just want to go home to Mum's.'

Gwen held her, stroking her back, desperately trying to think of something hopeful to say. Millie and Lance's marriage had been a disaster from the start: it was no good saying everything would all be all right.

'Men often don't get close to their children until they're older,' she said, dredging up something she remembered her mother saying.

'That's what Mum says. Course, she'll come and

help me, but he is her father – he should care about her, shouldn't he?'

Gwen sighed. She thought of Megan Hughes and little Evan. Daniel didn't seem to care a fig for his existence. As far as she could see, men were so different as to be an utter mystery. But it didn't seem helpful to point that out at this moment.

'Well, I think he should. She's beautiful, Millie. You'll just have to be very strong for her and hope he follows on. It's his loss if he doesn't.'

Gwen read about the Hunger March in the newspaper, sitting in her room at Ariadne's. Contingents of marchers were coming from all over the country. Ellen Wilkinson, the MP they had heard speak in the Town Hall, was marching with her constituents from Jarrow. The Welsh marchers, five hundred and four strong, had all assembled in Cathays Park in Cardiff to head east to London. She read the words spoken by the march's leader, Councillor Lewis Jones:

> We are going to London to meet the government
> and the House of Commons, and if they refuse to
> see us we will force ourselves upon the Cabinet and
> if necessary upon the King and we will force this
> pack of gangsters to abolish for ever the means test.
> They are ruining our country.

Gwen sat with the paper on her lap, staring ahead of her. She could see the great crowds of men in her mind, as they had been in Tonypandy: their poor clothes and caps, their Welsh accents, their hunger and the power of their determination. And among them, always, she could see Daniel's face, there with his people, alight with a passion that he could never quite find in anything else, not in her, not in his family, not in anything settled. And she ached with a pain that seemed to fill her whole body.

Forty-Nine

Day after day, they trudged on.

The days were cold now and the nights freezing, iron hard. Along roads and tracks they went, through towns and villages, begging food and sometimes work. Odd jobs came their way, on farms especially. Some people took one look at them and turned them away. But there had been work, along the road. They spent the best part of a week picking apples and pears and sleeping under the trees. They gathered late potatoes, mucked out horses and collected eggs when farms or stables were shorthanded. They helped pull down a rotting barn and burn the wood on a huge pyre. The farmer was kind and brought potatoes to cook buried in the heat. Many others cursed them and turned them away, especially when they left the country and tried begging round the towns. The days passed, hungry, cold, no beginning or end to anything except the daylight, the alternate rising of the sun and moon. Apart from that there was no shape or purpose. They just kept walking.

The night of the first frost they were sleeping in a barn, and in the morning stepped out to find the ground white, the cow-nibbled grass rigid underfoot. Joey walked round and round in circles, feeling the crunch of it under his boots. He had never seen a field covered in frost before. They had had to find him new

512

boots when the soles of the others fell away from the uppers and he could no longer walk. These were old and too big, and inside he had wrapped his feet in rags. That day he remembered the name of the next village because they brewed up tea and walked on between icy hawthorn hedges, ploughed fields on each side, breath white, noses and ears frozen, and he saw a sign saying, ASTON.

Words spilled suddenly from his mouth. 'Aston – that's where my nanna's house was!'

John stopped, turned on the icy road and stared at him.

'This ain't Birmingham.'

Joey looked back silently. John's face looked pointed now, like a fox's.

It grew warmer again after that. Rusty leaves had rotted in drifts and the wind blew them into swirls. Nuts and haws rolled under their boots. There was no work now the summer was over. They passed through somewhere called Faringdon. People steered away from them as they passed. 'Dear me – look at them,' he heard. 'It's a disgrace.' Or 'How terrible.' In the main street Joey caught sight of a strange pair of people walking along: a boy with a head that looked too big for his body, staring eyes, clothes like a clown and a wild giant beside him, all black, bushy beard ... John, that was John, and it was only then that he saw he was looking in a shop window at his own reflection.

John sometimes mumbled to himself, but never looked anyone in the eye. Neither of them had the energy to say anything. They had no proper food, had not had a hot meal for weeks. John coughed a lot. Everything seemed distant, Joey felt, as if he was floating and not part of things. He had felt invisible and seeing himself was a shock.

The weather turned wet. One afternoon, on a stretch of open, chalky downland, they were caught in a downpour with no hope of shelter. The rain slanted down, turning the track to slippery clay which clung thick and heavy to their boots so that it became a struggle to lift their feet. They kept having to stop and try to wipe the caked mud off on the grass. John let out muffled curses. He had been even quieter than usual lately. He coughed, doubled up with it, making a racked, liquid sound. The sky was a thick swathe of cloud, no break in it and they were already soaked through. John put his head down against the wind and Joey walked in his shelter, the legs of his trousers sodden and heavy.

They stopped that day long before they normally would. There was a barn at the foot of a hill and they went into its hay-smelling gloom. Neither of them could stop shivering, their teeth chattering. Their clothes were soaked, and so were the contents of the curtain. Even the matches, which John usually kept safely stowed in the pan, had fallen out and were sodden and useless. Joey was surprised how quietly John took this. They could not build a fire, had no food, but he didn't shout and swear like he often did.

He just said, 'That's it, then,' and sat hugging himself, shaking.

Joey's clothes were so cold and uncomfortable that every move he made caused him miserable discomfort. They had eaten nothing that day. He stared out at the rain falling over the grey clay. When he looked round, John had lurched over sideways and stayed just where he was, fast asleep. In the end the hazy feeling Joey had so often filled his head completely and all he could do was curl on his side and let the darkness fill him completely.

When he woke it was light and seemed to be morning, but he wasn't sure. He could hear rats moving in the barn. He lay for a long time in a dazed state, without the strength to get up, listening to sounds from outside, those big black birds calling in their scraping way from trees in the distance and a smaller bird somewhere nearer. He could not feel his feet. Perhaps he had no feet any more? He tried to wiggle his toes but felt nothing. After a time he thought about moving, about turning his head. Where was John? It was so quiet in here. It took a great effort of will to make himself move, having to think about it, to tell his neck to turn. When he did he saw John had shifted onto his back and was still asleep.

Now I'll move my arm, he thought. *Sit up, sit up . . .* His clothes were still wet. Moving was misery, barely seemed worth the trouble. In the past he might have sobbed but that took too much from him too. He hauled himself up and sat staring, hearing John's wheezy breathing coming to him faintly. John twitched, coughed. Joey pulled himself up and saw their bundle on the floor of the barn. He rifled through it, the pan and knife and spoon, the old rags, hoping there might be a morsel of food in there they had overlooked. Apart from a few crumbs, there was nothing. He looked at John again. In the end he went over and shoved at his arm, trying to wake him. John groaned, but his eyes did not open. Joey shook him but there was no response. He knelt, staring down at the man's face. There was dirt deeply ingrained in his forehead and nose. Joey saw yellow sticky stuff was coming out of the corners of his eyes. Everything else was hair, bushy, black and matted.

'John?' His voice sounded reedy and strange. No reply came.

Joey stood up, steadying himself, feeling light enough to float away, and wandered out of the barn, squinting as the light stabbed into his eyeballs. He set off across the field, but it was so wet that he was soon weighed down by the thick clay and he turned back and moved along the edge where there was a rough strip of weeds. In the distance he could see some farm buildings and he made for those. They were two fields away: another ploughed field, then a meadow for grazing, which was empty of animals. As he moved closer, he could hear cows bellowing in the farmyard, which reeked of manure. He crept closer and saw a wooden shed, which he took to be a henhouse. Keeping to the backs of the buildings, he edged round the farm until he was able to sneak over the iron fence and into the hut. It was, as he thought, full of the feathery warmth of hens, the stink of their muck and their fussy clucking noises. He groped around for eggs, found three and put them carefully in his coat pockets.

When he put his head out of the henhouse, though, he saw a man, walking across the yard in the distance. Joey froze, almost retreated into the henhouse – but he'd be trapped in there! He ran the short distance to the fence.

'Oi! What d'you think you're doing, you thieving little . . .'

Joey could hear that the man was running and he tore away across the field of cowpats, his lungs fit to explode, trying desperately not to lose his boots, grasping the ends of his coat to keep the eggs cradled and safe. He was convinced the man was chasing him and that he could hear shouting, but when he turned, there was no sign of him. By the time Joey got back to the barn he was stumbling, barely able to stand. He flung himself down and took out one of the eggs. Knocking the top off carefully with the knife, he slid the raw egg into his mouth, swallowing its slimy contents in two goes. There was no one coming outside, but he kept peering out just in case.

John was still asleep. He had not moved.

Fifty

People started disappearing from the school. First of all, Alice Wilson was absent for the register for two days in a row. Gwen assumed she was poorly and didn't give it much thought. She was caught up in her grief over Daniel, carrying her heart about inside her like a hard, painful stone. She kept thinking about going to see Theresa Fernandez. Had she known about Megan Hughes as well? Had they all made a proper fool of her?

But soon after, Charlotte Rowley vanished. Rumours started to circulate and days later Agnes Monk also failed to arrive at school. In the staffroom there was talk about nothing else. Mr Lowry did not issue an explanation, but one came, eventually, from an unexpected source. Lily Drysdale, as ever taking her own individual approach to the care of the school's children, had managed to get Ron Parks to talk to her.

'There was something not right about the boy, I could see,' she told Gwen. 'He looked troubled. And, my goodness me, I can see why now.'

What he had told Lily, in an empty classroom after the end of school, was that he had 'seen something he shouldn't have' and that was what had made Mr Lowry so angry. When Lily gently suggested that he might have been beaten unjustly and that it might be a good idea to get it off his chest, Ron looked deeply uncomfortable. He muttered that he had seen Mr Lowry 'doing something' to Miss Rowley in his office at the end of school the day before his beating. Lily felt it would be too delicate to ask what exactly Mr Lowry was 'doing' but Ron volunteered the information that she was 'lying across the desk, on her front' and they were 'fighting'. Ron said her face was 'all queer' and that it looked as if Mr Lowry was about to give her the cane just like he did the children, but he didn't hang about long enough to find out.

'But what were you doing up there?' Lily asked. 'Had he sent for you?'

Ron looked even more shamefaced at this point. He and his pals thought that Mr Lowry was out of his office after school. He often appeared downstairs, standing in the playground as they all left. A couple of Ron's pals had made a bet with him that he couldn't sneak up to Mr Lowry's office, pinch one of the canes off the desk, run down to them with it to prove he'd done it, and replace it without Mr Lowry ever knowing.

'Goodness – that would have taken some guts,' Gwen said admiringly.

'Well, quite,' Lily said. 'Except that he was so sure Mr Lowry wasn't going to be in there that he forgot to knock and find out and just went barging in.'

Gwen put a hand over her mouth, laughing in horror. What on earth had been going on?

'No wonder he's got shot of Charlotte Rowley . . .'

When Miss Monk failed to arrive at school a couple of days later their classes were run by last-minute replacements. It was the talk of the staffroom all week, and at home Ariadne was enthralled by the story.

'That poor Miss Monk,' she said.

'Poor be damned – she's a right old tartar,' Gwen said.

'But she was carrying a flame for him, from what you've said.'

'More fool her.'

'You're becoming very harsh,' Ariadne said.

'Well, the pair of them are just so horrid. I wish he'd leave as well and we could get someone else. It would make all the difference to the atmosphere in the school.'

Once things settled down, Alice Wilson still did not come back.

'Have you seen her?' Gwen asked Lucy.

Lucy Fernandez shook her head. 'Our mom went round to see her mom, but there was no reply when she knocked on the door.'

Gwen knew that she would have to go and see Theresa Fernandez. The pain of anything associated with Daniel was so great that she didn't know if she could bear it. But she knew that one day she was going to have to face her and ask the one question that she dreaded.

She went after school that afternoon.

'Hello, dear!' Theresa greeted her warmly. Gwen could still barely imagine this rounded, lively woman almost dying in a Welsh prison. Had Daniel been telling her the truth about that? Somehow she was full of doubt about everything now. It was achingly hard to be in this house again.

'Come in and have a cup of tea!' Theresa talked as she bustled about the back room, where most of the children were sitting or coming in and out. 'There was something I wanted to talk to you about – you've heard about Alice, I suppose? Mrs Wilson came round to see me today before they left. I don't know how, but her mother tracked her down and she seems pre-pared to take her and Alice in. I think it's up in

Staffordshire somewhere – the family are quite wealthy, I believe. Lucy will miss little Alice, though. She was ever so upset when she heard ... Don't s'pose you've heard from that lad of mine – the march is starting in a few days, isn't it, but he doesn't let me know anything!'

Gwen was completely taken aback. Theresa was treating her as if nothing at all had changed. Only then did it dawn on her that Daniel had been in Wales all this time and hadn't told his mother what had happened. It took her a few moments to cope with this. She felt as if the shape of the world had changed and become full of pain and sadness, yet Theresa had no idea! She kept chatting on about this and that, until Gwen could no longer stand it.

'Please.' She fought the tears she could feel rising. 'Could I have a word with you – on our own?'

Theresa looked startled, hearing the desperation in Gwen's voice.

'All of you,' she called to the children, 'out of here! Miss Purdy and I have something to discuss in private. Rosa, mind the shop, will you?'

The children scuttled out through the shop door.

'What is it, lovey?' Theresa said, and the comfortable tone of her voice suddenly filled Gwen with fury. She had been duped by the whole family! No one had told her the truth and she felt used and hurt and very foolish.

'You didn't think to mention to me –' she stood with her arms tightly folded, speaking in cold, clipped tones – 'that you already have a grandchild living in the valleys. Daniel's son.'

Theresa's face was a blank of bewilderment. She sank down on a chair at the table.

'*What?* What're you saying to me?'

Gwen stared at her. It dawned on her that Theresa's complete bemusement was real.

'So – he hasn't told you! And your sister-in-law hasn't let on either?' She couldn't keep the anger and bitterness out of her voice, even though none of this was Theresa's fault.

'Whatever haven't I been told? Look – come and sit down, love.' Agitated, Theresa pointed at the chair opposite her. 'I don't know what you're talking about – what's this talk about a grandchild? Whatever are you saying to me?'

Gwen stayed standing. 'Daniel has a son called Evan. He's the image of Daniel. His mother is called Megan Hughes and she lives in Treherbert.'

She could almost see Theresa Fernandez reading her lips, such was her need to make sense of what Gwen was saying.

'We came face to face with her – in Tredegar. Daniel's not denying it. He had an affair with her and she has a boy and now . . .' She couldn't hold back her tears any longer. 'And I can't stay with Daniel – not after this. He's betrayed me. I thought he was good and true and he's just lied to me all the way along . . .'

Theresa had been listening, apparently stunned, as if she couldn't make sense of what Gwen was saying, but seeing the girl's distraught state she got up and came closer to her, seeming unsure whether to touch her or not. Instead she stood wringing her hands.

'Are you telling me the truth? Gwen, you don't strike me as a liar but I can't believe what you're saying to me! You mean, my son . . . ?'

Gwen nodded, sobbing. 'He didn't deny any of it. He knew because she wrote to him, but he didn't do anything, didn't go back to her or help her. I feel as if I don't know him at all.'

'Holy Jesus,' Theresa breathed. Gwen could hear how appalled she was. Staunch, Catholic Theresa. She could hardly have learned anything more distressing. 'If this is true ... How could I not have known? He never said a word ...' There was real anger in her voice now. 'I thought he was a good boy – he used to serve at the altar! I brought him up to be good that way ...' She sank back on to the chair again, in shock. 'What's the boy's name again?'

'Evan.'

'A grandson.' Theresa shook her head. 'How old is the child?'

'She said nearly two.'

'And all this time ... For shame. Oh my Lord, for shame ...'

There was a long, pained silence, then Theresa saw how it was for Gwen and said, 'You poor young thing. And Daniel thinks the world of you – you do know that, don't you?'

Gwen shrugged, looking down at the pitted surface of the table. 'Not enough to tell me the truth though.'

She looked up and the two women regarded each other for several moments in silence. Theresa's blue eyes held pity, shame, and an appeal to her.

'Can you forgive him?'

'I've told him it's over,' Gwen said flatly. 'How could I ever trust him again after this?'

Theresa shook her head, her face full of sorrow. She looked as if she was trying to decide whether to speak. Eventually, with difficulty, she said, 'It's the choice we often have, lovey. You forgive them or you lose them.'

'I can forgive him.' Gwen wiped her eyes. 'Least, maybe I will be able to one day. But I can't forget, and I'd never know again if he was telling me the truth about things, would I?' Gwen gave a great sigh and brought her hands up to cover her face.

'I love him so much, Theresa. I can't bear it!'

Fifty-One

The sun and moon rose and sank in the sky. Joey didn't know how many times. He felt hazy in the head, as if he was never completely awake. He stayed with John, waiting for him to surface. There was an old trough flung away at the side of the barn and he drank out of it. The water tasted of metal. He tried to dribble some into John's mouth, but most of it ran down into his beard. Joey ate the eggs. He hadn't the strength to go back to the henhouse to find some more. Most of the time he slept. After dark, rats scuttled and cheeped in the barn and sometimes he felt one brush past him, solid and sleek. At the beginning of the time in the barn, John coughed. Then his breathing rattled. Joey didn't like it and prodded John sometimes to make him stop. John's eyes and lips had white stuff round them. After a day or two he went quiet. At night the rats seemed to have come closer.

Joey woke sometime during a sunny day. It was bright outside and he felt a sudden increase in energy, like a flame drawn by the wind. John lay very still. He was silent now. His face looked different and sunken. When Joey went to prod him he saw the lobes of John's ears were nibbled away and there was blood. Joey didn't think about it any more. He left the barn and walked away without thinking of the curtain or the pan and knife. His clothes were dry by now. There was nothing to think about except putting one foot down, then the next, on and on along the fringe of the field, watching his feet because at first the slanting sunlight seemed too bright to look into and if he raised his eyes everything seemed to whirl and spin around him and the space was too wide, the sky so high and far it made him dizzy. He did not think about food now. There was no food. He had no memory of when he had last eaten. He stumbled on and on across the fields, lurching like a drunk, not looking for anything or heading anywhere.

Fifty-Two

It was drizzly the next day, and cold, and the men marched as briskly as they could, sometimes slapping their arms round themselves to try and keep warm. Some carried banners. At times they broke into song. The 'Internationale' was a good marching song and it helped pass the miles to sing. They sang political songs and songs from the valleys and in some places they earned money by singing. They had walked east, through Bristol and Bath and were now passing through Berkshire on their way to London, sleeping in church halls or workhouses, wherever hospitality was offered to them.

Two young men were marching together, talking, sometimes joining in the rich-voiced singing or discussing the impact the march would have when it reached Hyde Park. The government *had* to listen and abolish the means test.

'Catch you up in a mo', Dai,' the younger of the two said. 'Call of nature . . .'

'Careful now,' the other teased. 'Cold out, today!'

Despite the days of walking, the man vaulted with ease over a five-barred gate into the nearest field. He was dark-haired and lithe and had been toughened up by a collier's life. He disappeared behind the hedge, which glistened with water droplets. Having relieved himself, he straightened his clothes and turned to rejoin the marchers, but something caught his eye a short distance away in the field. It looked like a little heap of discarded clothing. This seemed a rum place to throw away clothes. He narrowed his eyes, peering at them. He thought he made out an arm, stretched out to one side of the bundle and, frowning, he moved closer.

For a few seconds he could not make sense of what he saw. The pinched face was obviously that of a child, though it had the worn, exhausted look of a very old man. There was a twig-like arm, and yet the creature seemed to have been stuffed, clown-like, into a set of clothes far too adult and bulky looking for him.

Leaning down, the man said, 'Hello, there. Can you hear me?'

There was no reply. He pushed gently at the body and assumed the boy was dead. Conscious of the march moving inexorably on ahead of him, he thought, well, nothing for it, and scooped the emaciated little body up into his arms. It was floppy as a rag doll, but not cold and stiff: there was still life in the skeletal frame, just. Poor little beggar looked close to death though! Whatever had become of him? The young man was full of rage suddenly. That was the reality of capitalism, of the country under this betraying government: children were starving to death, not just in the valleys, but all over!

As he began to walk, the child gave a slight moan and his big, prominent eyes flickered open for a second.

'It's all right, little man,' Daniel said. 'I'll take you somewhere safe. D'you know where you are?'

There was silence. What could he do? He'd have to take the child to the nearest house where they would have pity on him. A church perhaps, or a farm?

'Muur . . .' the boy groaned.

Asking for his mother, Daniel thought. God alone knew whether there was anyone for him in this world.

He was almost back to the gate now, and about to shift his stance and put the boy over his shoulder in a fireman's lift to climb over, when he heard something else which riveted him to the spot. No – he was imagining things – he could only have been mistaken.

'What were you trying to say then, lad?' he asked gently.

Quite clearly, just once, the little boy parted his parched lips and with a huge effort, murmured, 'Miss Purdy...'

Fifty-Three

'Gwen, dear, there's a letter for you – *and a telegram!*'

Ariadne was all of a flutter, the envelopes in her hand as Gwen came in from school.

'I hope it's not bad news!'

Ever since she had told Ariadne what had happened with Daniel, her landlady had adopted an even more motherly role towards her.

'Oh, you poor, poor young thing,' she had exclaimed with tragic eyes. 'And you thought he was the One didn't you? I know you did – I could see it in you when you were with him. And he was so polite and *handsome.*'

Gwen took off her hat and shook the rain off it, then hung up her coat, somehow not wanting to know what the news was. It was bound to be from home – her mother or father ill or some other unpleasant problem she would have to face. Wearily she took the envelopes and went into the back room, where it was not so dark. Ariadne followed like her shadow. The handwriting on the letter was Billy's. She smiled faintly. His letters were always bubbling over about something he had read and she found them uplifting. First, she tore open the telegram.

'Oh my dear – what is it?' Ariadne saw Gwen's first reaction, one hand going to her heart.

All she saw at first was the name at the bottom, DANIEL, and the rest took her time to make sense of, her eyes going over and over it:

HAVE FOUND JOEY PHILLIPS STOP IS IN
WALLINGFORD WORKHOUSE STOP VERY
SICK STOP WANTS YOU STOP DANIEL

Gwen looked up at Ariadne, completely bewildered. 'Where on earth is Wallingford?'

It was the middle of the next day when she stepped out onto Wallingford station and asked the way to the workhouse.

'We don't call it the workhouse any more,' one woman she made enquiries of told her severely, then instructed her to follow the Wantage Road.

All morning Gwen had been in a turmoil of emotion. The slightest thing made her tense and over-flowing with tears these days. It had not taken a second's hesitation to decide she would not be in school. Once she discovered that Wallingford was far to the south in Berkshire, though, her confusion increased. For Daniel to be there obviously had some-thing to do with the route of the march, but however had Joey got right down there? And hearing from Daniel again stirred up all the sad and bitter feelings which had not yet even begun to subside in his absence. Sitting on the train, she was full of her old hunger for him, as if his very being was imprinted on her, and yet the thought of him now gave her nothing but pain. Every time she thought of him, she could see the tired, pretty face of Megan Hughes, the hurt in it, and what

531

Daniel had done in leaving her and his son without any apparent regret or care.

She looked out at the damp autumn countryside and let herself think over all the close, happy times she and Daniel had shared together, allowed the sense of hurt and betrayal to overwhelm her for a time, and tears ran unstoppably down her cheeks. She was caught in a painful collision of emotions, longing both to be held in his arms and to punch him hard in the face.

Walking along to the workhouse, she wondered, had Daniel come here himself, carrying the boy? Had he left the march? She had no idea exactly where the route had gone. Or had Daniel handed him to someone else? How on earth had he found him?

The workhouse was a sturdy-looking brick building and she was admitted by an equally sturdy-looking woman whom she took to be the matron. In the hall inside, she explained that she was looking for a little boy, Joseph Phillips.

'I've come to take him back to Birmingham,' she said. 'I'm his teacher.'

'Birmingham?' The woman looked incredulous. Her tone was brisk but not unkind. 'Well, what's he doing down here?'

'I've really no idea. He disappeared from school months ago. We'd have to ask him how he got here.'

'Oh, I don't think he's in a fit state to tell you that at the moment. He's very poorly – I was surprised he lasted the first night after they brung him in.'

'Who brought him?'

She looked surprised by the question. 'A farmer, so far as I know.'

Not Daniel then, by the sound of things.

'I really want to take him back with me today,' Gwen suggested.

'Ooh no!' The woman pursed her lips and kept shaking her head. 'Oh, dear me, no – he's far too ill to be moved. Oh no, I don't think so.'

Gwen sighed. Perhaps the woman was right. How was she going to manage with a sick child all the way back?

'All right. I'll come back and fetch him when he's better. But may I see him? I've come a long way today.'

Well, I suppose that'd be all right. He's in the infirmary. I'll get someone to take you.'

A puny-looking young man was enlisted to lead her to the infirmary, where they walked between two rows of black iron bedsteads amid the sounds of coughing and hawking. From the far end came a terrible sound of groaning. On one bed she saw a tiny, crumpled figure lying like a fallen bird. It took her a moment to recognize the boy. Joey had always been a scrawny child, but now he was obviously extremely mal-nourished. His head looked disproportionately big, the skin tinged blue under his eyes, the rest of his face deathly pale. He lay prone, eyes closed, as if he had not an ounce of strength left to move. As she moved closer and leaned down to look at him, she saw his little hand, ingrained with dirt, the wrist so thin it looked fit to snap at the slightest touch.

'You poor little chap, what's happened to you?' she whispered. Tears filled her eyes once more as she stood looking down at him. The state of him! He was nothing but a bag of bones.

She wiped her eyes and knelt down beside the bed.

'Joey?'

There was no response. She could not see him breathing and, fearful, she hurried to check his pulse. But he was alive: she could feel a regular flickering through the veins. Gently she touched his hand, wrapping her fingers round his curled ones.

'Can you hear me? It's Miss Purdy.'

He seemed to breathe more deeply, like a little sigh.

'I've come to take you home, but they say you're too poorly. But I'll come back for you. All your class mates have missed you, you know – Ron and all the others. They'll be ever so glad to see you.'

She wondered if he could hear a thing she was saying. She looked at him, filled with gloom suddenly. Maybe he was too far gone. It looked as if he wasn't going to make it.

'Joey? It's Miss Purdy.'

And then she felt it. A movement in the wasted little hand, which gripped, at first almost imperceptibly round her finger, then clung on with a force which took her by surprise.

She knew then, with a certainty which filled her with dread, that she couldn't leave him here. He couldn't be abandoned yet again. Not surrounded by all these strangers, dying old men with phlegmy chests. How could he ever really know for sure that she was coming back? She knelt there full of tension, trying to decide what to do.

'Joey, listen to me,' she whispered. 'The matron says you should stay here because you're not very well. But if you want to go today, I'll take you with me. We'll manage it somehow.'

For the first time, his eyelids flickered. He did not speak, but the huge eyes looked at her suddenly with such urgent intensity that she knew the answer. Whatever the matron thought about it, they were going home. She was not leaving without him.

By the time the train pulled into Birmingham it had long been dark. She had argued her case with the matron, who caved in without too much protest, especially when Gwen pressed a ten shilling note into her hand. Joey was dressed in a roughly sewn sort of nightdress of coarse cotton, which was far too long so that it covered his feet, but not nearly warm enough for the October weather outside. Gwen paid the matron more to take the blanket from his bed to wrap him in. She bundled him up carefully and they went in a taxi to Wallingford Station. He was as light as a paper kite in her arms.

On the way back to Birmingham they found themselves near a kind, middle-aged lady, who introduced herself as a nurse, and helped Gwen to feed Joey a little of the milk diluted with water the matron had given her in a jam jar. It was a struggle to get him to take anything because he was barely conscious.

'His system won't be able to take too much at first,' she said. 'When you get home you'd be almost better off using a baby's bottle to begin with. You'll need to go very gradually. Dear me, what an awful thing – and in this country too! Where are you taking him to?'

'Well, I've got lodgings in Handsworth. My landlady was a bit unsure, but she said I can take him back there at least for now. She's not really used to children, you see.'

'He's not going to cause any trouble for a while, the state he's in, is he?'

When they got out at New Street Station, the woman helped Gwen lift Joey into a taxi.

'You can't possibly manage on the tram!' she said. 'Now let me give you a contribution to the fare. I think you're a very kind person indeed.'

She thrust a couple of half crowns into Gwen's pocket and barely waited to be thanked.

When the taxi reached Ariadne's house, she had evidently been waiting on tenterhooks.

'My dear – at last!' she cried as the door opened. Seeing Joey in Gwen's arms, her hands went dramatically to her face. 'Oh, my word! Oh, look at that little mite. The state of him! Don't you think he should be in the hospital? He looks . . . well, he doesn't look as if he'll last the night.'

'I think I should put him to bed,' Gwen suggested.

'Oh yes – of course! I've got the little room up at the back ready . . .'

It was no more than a boxroom, but there was a bed squeezed in which Ariadne had made up for him. Gwen told Ariadne of the help the nurse had given her and her suggestion about the baby bottle.

'I'll get one tomorrow,' Ariadne said. They were both talking softly. She kept staring down at the tiny, frail figure in the bed, seemingly unable to get over the sight of him. 'He's really rather beautiful, isn't he?'

'I'm very sorry, Ariadne. Maybe you're right about the hospital. I was so worked up about just getting him out of the workhouse and back here I hadn't thought how much work it's going to be looking after him . . . It's too much to expect you . . .'

'Oh, don't say that,' Ariadne burst out. She sounded really upset. 'No one ever expects anything of me – that's the trouble! They never have. And what have I ever done with my life, really? I mean I know I wasn't sure about him coming. I've no real knowledge of

536

children – never had the chance. But I'll try – I want to! Poor little lad. It's the least I can do!'

Gwen hesitated, then dared to take Ariadne's hand for a moment. It was knobbly with all her rings, and Gwen gave it a gentle squeeze.

'Thank you,' she said. 'You're so kind.'

Fifty-Four

'Ron – stay behind a moment, please!'

The rest of the class were hurrying out for their first breaktime the next morning.

Ron came over to her desk and Gwen was disturbed to see a hunted expression in his eyes. It made her angry. He had always been such a carefree, sunny sort of boy. Whatever had been going on that afternoon in Mr Lowry's office, and the treatment he received as a result, seemed to have left him in a state of anxiety.

'Shut the door, Doreen!' she called to the last departing child, then smiled reassuringly at Ron. 'It's all right. You haven't done anything wrong.' He looked up at her in a hangdog fashion and she weighed up in her mind whether to say anything. The consequences of the headmaster's behaviour had affected Charlotte Rowley (though Gwen had very little sympathy for her) and Ron – not himself. How typical that was, she thought. She was on dangerous ground, she knew, saying anything against another member of staff to a pupil, but this was a question of justice.

'Look, Ron – all that's happened this term – nothing was your fault. It wasn't fair, and you shouldn't have to keep worrying. Try and put it behind you, eh?'

'Yes, Miss.' He stared at the ground, not seeming cheered by this.

'I've got some news to tell you. Good news.'

He looked up at her.

'I went down south yesterday. That's why I wasn't here.' She could feel her smile broadening. 'And guess who I brought back?'

Ron's brow furrowed.

'He's very poorly at the moment and won't be up to playing out for a long time. But tucked up in bed in the house where I live is your pal Joey.'

Ron looked blank for a moment, then his eyebrows shot up.

'Joey Phillips?'

Gwen nodded, delighted to see a smile spread across Ron's face once more. And some white teeth.

'Is he coming back to school, Miss?'

'Well, I hope so – eventually. He's got a lot of resting to do first, before he's well enough. But in a little while, a few days perhaps, I hope you'll be able to come round and see him.'

Ron was grinning now. 'That's bostin, Miss!'

Ariadne was a devoted, if rather agitated nurse. All Gwen could feel towards her was gratitude. Her life became centred round nursing Joey Phillips back to health. As she said, what else could they have done with the poor little mite? After all the lengths he had gone to to escape the orphanage, they could hardly just pack him back there now.

For the first few days, Joey lay fading in and out of consciousness. They managed to get him to drink a little: water with glucose powder, some diluted milk. He could manage to drink better soon, and open his eyes, and as soon as he had swallowed a few mouthfuls he would slip back into his long sleep again. Despite the doctor's advice just to keep him safe and warm, Gwen was worried, wondering if he should be in hospital, but to her surprise Ariadne took it all calmly.

'Do him good,' she said, tucking the blankets round him. 'Sleep is a great healer. And the doctor said we're doing all that can be done.'

'He reminds me of something in hibernation,' Gwen said. 'Like a hedgehog.'

As the days passed he became able to take more: milk with an egg whisked into it, and some thin soup. He was obviously going to get better. But although he was awake quite a lot, lying looking round the bright pink painted room, he barely ever said a word.

'D'you know,' Ariadne told Gwen, 'when you come into the room, his eyes never leave you, not for a moment.'

Joey was almost all their conversation now. Ariadne had taken to wearing flatter shoes so she could hurry up and downstairs easily, and her porridge making had come on no end. She often sat beside Joey, reading him stray snippets out of the daily papers.

By the end of the second week, Gwen told Ron he could come and visit after school and asked him to tell his mother where they were going.

'Just for a few minutes,' she said. 'He's ever so weak still, you see. He's not saying much. But I'm sure he'd be pleased to see you.'

She thought about asking Lucy if she'd like to come as well. Lucy had had another fit in class earlier in the week and Gwen thought it might be nice for her to feel chosen for something special. She felt awkward about it, though, not sure if Lucy knew of the rift between herself and Daniel, but the child showed no sign of it. The march was over – Gwen had read in the papers about the gathering in Hyde Park, the speeches. Aneurin Bevan had visited the marchers when they were sleeping in Reading cattle market and addressed them there. No one was sure if it was going to make any difference to anything. She didn't know where Daniel was, and was on pins in case he suddenly appeared to meet Lucy. She had said to him that she didn't want to see him, but she could hardly prevent him from living in the same neighbourhood as the school, could she? But the thought of seeing him again was very painful.

'Is Daniel home now?' she asked Lucy casually as they sat on the tram.

Lucy shook her head. She had a white Alice band holding back her long hair.

'He went back with the other marchers. I think he's coming soon.'

Ariadne had bought iced buns and lemonade for Ron and Lucy and laid the table with a lacy cloth. Gwen could see both the children looking round, overwhelmed by the big, cluttered house and Ariadne's fussing attention.

'I'll take them up to Joey before they have anything to eat, shall I?' Gwen said.

They followed her up, Lucy laboriously hauling her calipered leg up each step, and went into Joey's room. He was awake, and stared at them all as they came in. Gwen thought she saw a flicker of something in his eyes, but otherwise he remained expressionless.

Of course, the children found it difficult to know what to say.

Lucy said quietly, 'Hello, Joey. You all right?'

Ron was tugging at something in his pocket. He produced a squashed little brown paper bag.

'Here y'are, pal. Brought yer some rocks.'

He sounded so gruff and grandfatherly as he spoke that Gwen found herself smiling. Ron laid the bag of sweets on Joey's bed. There was a silence.

'I'm Ron,' Ron said. 'From school. D'you remember us?'

Gwen watched Joey's face. He said nothing, but his expression was not blank. She could tell there were thoughts going on.

'Well,' Ron said. 'Sorry you're bad. I hope you're coming back to school soon. Weren't the same after you went.'

There were no words, but Gwen saw something she had not seen before. There was a slight twitching round Joey's lips and, for the first time, a light in his eyes.

'Says here the king's been in Wales,' Ariadne said over tea one night. As usual she had a newspaper open on the table. King Edward had visited South Wales after the Hunger March.

' "Something must be done," he said,' Ariadne read. 'D'you know, it says here that *three-quarters* of the people in Merthyr Tydfil are on poor relief!'

'Yes,' Gwen said. 'Things are in a bad way there.'

Ariadne considered her across the table and said tragically, 'The least thing makes you think of *him*, doesn't it?'

Gwen kept her eyes on her plate of macaroni cheese. They had cooked it together. 'Yes.' It was no good pretending otherwise. She was so hurt that she wanted all thoughts of Daniel just to fade from her mind. Instead, he kept coming back to her. Ariadne was right. Any thought she had of Lucy or Billy made her think of him. And she couldn't forget, longed for things to be otherwise, for her to be able to trust him. But she couldn't and that was the truth of it. And yet she couldn't get past him either, couldn't get over him and feel better.

She swallowed down the lump in her throat. 'I've just got to stop thinking of him, that's all.'

It was getting close to the end of November. The weather was damp and unpleasant, but in spite of that Joey was getting better every day. He was still weak, but he was gaining weight, and once on a good diet, proved extremely resilient. He was soon able to get up and start moving about.

One Saturday afternoon Gwen sat with him up in his room, teaching him to play snakes and ladders. He was very withdrawn and she could still hardly get him to say anything at all. Trying to keep his attention focused on anything was difficult too.

'There –' Gwen pointed at the board – 'you've landed on a ladder. You can move right up there, look.'

Joey peered at it and solemnly moved his counter up the ladder, pressing his finger hard onto it.

'Joey?'

He looked up at her but wouldn't quite meet her eye.

'Can you remember your school? The class – Ron and Lucy and the others?'

Joey nodded.

'Would you like to go back to school one day?'

There was a faint shake of his head.

'No? Well, maybe not yet. You do know you can stay here for as long as you like? Ariadne's very kind and she likes having you here. And so do I.'

She heard a knocking on the front door, and, after a short delay, Ariadne talking to someone.

'It'll be all right, Joey. You don't need to run away again.'

'I'm never going to the orphanage!'

The words seemed to explode out of him. He was suddenly seething with emotion, eyes narrowed in an animal way, so that for a moment she found him almost frightening.

'The orphanage? No, of course we won't put you in an orphanage! Oh, Joey – that's why you ran away in the first place, wasn't it?'

'The man was coming. They took Lena and Kenny and Poll, but they weren't having me!'

To Gwen's irritation she heard Ariadne's tread on the stairs. She was just beginning to get something out of Joey and now they were going to be interrupted.

'Don't worry,' she told him.

'Gwen!' Ariadne hissed, poking her head round the door. 'It's Daniel – *your* Daniel. Downstairs!'

Gwen shot to her feet, in a complete panic.

'Tell him to go. I won't see him – I can't!'

'I can't just tell him to leave, dear. Do calm down! He wants to see Joey – he did rescue him after all.'

'Well, let me get into my room. I can't see him . . . Don't let him up here yet.'

She fled along to the front of the house and shut herself in her room, leaning back against the door. Through the blood pounding in her ears, she heard Ariadne calling from the landing, 'You can come up now, Daniel,' and his feet climbing the stairs. She stood with her arms folded, crushed against her, heart pounding, her breathing shallow. The longing to see him was so overpowering that it was all she could do to stop herself tearing the door open. Yet this collided head on with her dread of him, of the strength of her feelings, which gave him such power over her, a power which he had betrayed and could betray again and again. She closed her eyes, trying to make herself breathe properly, straining her ears to hear what was going on. She caught the deep timbre of his voice coming from Joey's room. He was speaking gently, reassuringly. Pain washed through her. How extraordinary it was that those two had been brought together, both so far from home – that it had been Daniel, of all people, who had found Joey. She still did not know the exact circumstances and she wanted to ask. Not long ago all this would have felt so right, as if it was meant – like her soft spot for Lucy, her rapport with Billy. As if all these things had brought her to Daniel, tied her so closely to him, given her that feeling she had of coming home every time she was with him, as if it had all been set in the stars. And now everything was wrong. There was no trust. It was broken.

She went to sit on the edge of the bed, and watched her hands trembling in her lap as if they belonged to someone else. She could think of nothing, nothing except that he was here, a few paces away from her, and that soon he would leave and the house would be empty of him. And how would it be, his not trying to see her? Seeing or not seeing him – which was the more painful?

Then she heard footsteps and before she could even move the door opened. She jumped. Seeing him again was such a shock, at once so familiar and so strange.

'Gwen – for God's sake . . .'

He sounded distraught, but somehow this enraged her instead of making her pity him.

'What?' She got up off the bed. 'For God's sake *what*? No – don't come any closer!'

Daniel turned and shut the door. 'Why won't you even speak to me?'

'Because . . .' She was having to hold on very tightly to her emotions. 'Because I can't stand it, that's why.'

'Please . . .' He walked a couple of paces closer. 'I know I've done something terrible, so wrong, leaving Megan like that – and the boy. I can't even make amends for that because she won't have me anywhere near . . .'

'You've tried, then?'

'I've been in the valleys. I went to Treherbert, but she wouldn't even let me in the house. But the thing is, Gwen, I was younger then and on fire for what we were doing. I never really loved her – not the way I love you. I've told you. I don't know what else to say . . .'

'She seemed to think you did.' Gwen felt suddenly overwhelmed with weariness. Here they were again, back in the same place, and it would always be like this. 'Look, Daniel – please, just go. I can't do this any more. I need to be by myself.'

Again, he came closer. They were only a yard or so apart, and she had to fight the feeling, the tingling that came over her when he came near. She stepped backwards.

'So are you saying you don't love me? All those months, all those words didn't mean anything. Was it just lies then, all you said, if it just disappears like this, like a puff of smoke?'

'You know it wasn't.' She could feel tears coming and loss of control and she fought them hard. 'I did love you – I do. I think I love you too much. What

546

you do affects me *so much*. I can't live like that, never knowing if I can trust you – with Esther, or with whoever turns up next, or knowing that you had a woman and child all this time and never told me, never seemed to think it mattered!' She began to cry then. 'How could you, Daniel? I poured myself out for you, month after month and you just hurt me so much...' She put her hands over her face.

'I know. Don't you think I know? Look, I'm sorry...' He came close and gently put his arms round her, and she did not resist. 'But I want – I need – to tell you that it matters. That you mean more to me than any woman I've ever met before. I need to know whether you'll give me a chance?'

The feel, the smell of him, were so achingly familiar she longed just to surrender, to press him close to her, for everything to be back where it was and all right. But she was shaking her head. It was not all right. What they had had before had been ruptured.

'I want to know if you're with me.' His voice was very solemn and he drew back and looked into her tearful eyes. 'I'm going away.'

'*What?*' She stared at him. 'Where to?'

'There are volunteers going to Spain. Some have gone already – a few, here and there. The party is starting to get people signing up. They want to get something more organized going, when there are more volunteers.'

'You're going to go – to Spain?' Suddenly she laughed, incredulous, pushing him away from her. 'God, Daniel, you're the end. You come back here, playing with my feelings all over again and then announce that you're disappearing to heaven knows where!'

547

'We can do some good over there—' He was all fired up, she could hear. 'Something direct. Not like here, fighting against this cowardly government and all the apathy on the left! In Spain they're really making the revolution happen. They're up against it, see? It's so clear what's going on when you're fighting the fascist enemy face to face. I'll be leaving within the next week or two, to go to Catalonia.'

Gwen was lost for words.

'That's why I had to see you, my girl . . .'

'I'm not your . . .'

He laid his hand gently over her lips. 'Don't say that now. Think about it. Think of me when I'm fighting in Spain and see whether I matter to you. Because I know you'll be the light I carry in my heart . . .'

'Oh, Daniel, stop,' she said miserably.

'Will you write to me?'

She hesitated, then nodded. 'Are you really going so soon?'

'Within days. You know me – never sit still if I can help it.'

'It doesn't mean . . . It doesn't mean I'm just sitting here waiting for you to come back.'

He looked silently down into her eyes and she fought desperately not to be moved by his expression. She reached up and stroked his cheek.

'Give me a kiss for the leaving?'

His face moved closer to hers and she closed her eyes and kissed him back.

After he had gone she rested on the edge of the bed, lost in thought. Her emotions were completely different now from those of the previous weeks, and she realized to her surprise that she might reach a place of calm. The future held so many challenges. One day she would have to reckon with her family. There were the children in her charge, her life at the school. There was Joey to care for.

And there was Daniel ... She knew now some of the things she didn't want – with him or with anyone. She didn't want her mother's dead respectability, nor did she want to be trapped like Millie, who'd rather run home to her mother than be with her husband. She didn't intend to run slavishly after men like Ariadne had done either. She wanted to make a different way, deciding things for herself because she was learning from hard experience.

Daniel was in her life, and whatever difficulty and pain that involved she did love him. She believed that he also loved her. But he was going away and there was no knowing what it would mean for him. The future, for now, was without him and all she could feel was a delicate balance of the certainty of love and a surrender to not knowing whether she would ever be with him.

When she had sat for some time, a smile came to her lips and she reached across and picked up her picture of Amy Johnson. She looked into Amy's strong face.

'I'm learning to fly too,' she said.

Epilogue

February 1937

'It's from Daniel, isn't it?' Ariadne was full of glee as she handed Gwen the envelope. 'Boys, shoes off and sit by the fire. I don't want your slushy water all over the house! And there are doughnuts in the kitchen.'

Gwen had come home from school with Joey and Ron in tow. Outside, the place was bright with snow. She left the boys to Ariadne, who had been waiting to pounce on them and take charge.

In her room she read the letter, hearing his voice:

Albacete
30.1.1937

Dear Gwen,

It was very nice to get your letter at last. I'm glad Joey is back at school and seeming more himself. I suppose his strange moods are not surprising, what with the time of it he's had. I wonder if he has talked to you any more about what happened and how he came to be all the way down there. Say hello to him for me, won't you? I'm glad Ariadne is 'like a new person' as you said. She must have been lonely and now you've given her a family, of sorts. Where would Joey be without her, eh?

Things are quiet here today so far, so that's why I'm taking the chance to write. Being here has given me so many thoughts, about the revolution and where we're all going. I don't possibly have time to write them all down. One thing that strikes me with great force is that when you hear about 'war' at home it sounds like something more organized and militarily set up than it ever is here. It really is neighbour against neighbour, men, women and even children. No one can escape and I've seen more inhuman treatment of man by man here already than I had ever imagined seeing in a lifetime. Even without extremes, there is so much misery, hunger, orphaned children etc. What we need desperately is more aid coming in to help the Spanish people. So, all of you – keep it coming to us. Your work is not for nothing! Even more than by the misery, I am affected by the courage, determination and self-sacrifice here in the face of Franco and his fascist thugs. The republicans are fighting for all the best things there are – freedom and justice and right. With all our efforts, these are the things we have to attain if barbarism is not to take over the world.

I am feeling especially melancholy though today, as a terrible sad thing has happened. I think I told you in my last letter that I had palled up with an Irish lad, Christie O'Brien? He'd come from England, but he said he'd been training as a priest in Ireland and left the seminary. Wouldn't say why, but he seemed to have had it hard. He was killed by a sniper yesterday – hiding out in the church tower they were. Got him straight through the head. I feel badly as I have no address to let his family know. He didn't talk much about where he came from. I'll miss Christie, though, God rest him. He was a good *compañero*.

I'm going to have to stop, when I feel I've barely

begun, there's so much to describe and there's so much to feel. But this is to let you know how we are so far. Go and see Mam now and then for me, will you? And keep up those letters to Billy – you've done wonders for him.

All I want to say is too much to put down, about how you're in my heart and all the bad I've done I'm ashamed of. But I'm rushing now and it's coming out wrong. I do love you, however hard it is for you to believe me. You're my light. I hope I'll get another letter from you soon, dear Gwen.

Anyway, *Salud!* as they say here.

My love,
Daniel

Author's Note

The 'Federation' and the 'Movement' referred to in the text are the South Wales Miners' Federation and the National Unemployed Workers' Movement respectively.